THE TALES OF DRACO
Rise of the Dragon

THE TALES OF
DRACO

RISE OF THE DRAGON

To David

JORDAN B. JOLLEY

Jordan B. Jolley

LUMINARE PRESS
WWW.LUMINAREPRESS.COM

The Tales of Draco
Rise of the Dragon
©2018 Jordan B. Jolley

Cover Art: Marissa Durfee
Cover Design: Melissa Thomas

Luminare Press
438 Charnelton St., Suite 101
Eugene, OR 97401
www.luminarepress.com

ISBN: 978-1-64388-054-9
LOC: 2018966101

This story is dedicated to all who educated me about great literature.

Special thanks to my mother, my sister, and my high school English teacher.

TABLE OF CONTENTS

Prologue

Many years had passed since the dragon last set foot on the other world. At times he felt homesick, but nothing gave him as much pleasure as his true home. He still remembered the mixture he had once held in his grasp that lifted his spell. Since then, he had had many adventures, among the humans and beyond.

As he sat in his cave with a fire burning in front of him, a young dragon, smaller than he, came and sat next to him. The younger dragon's white body glimmered in the flickering light while the elderly dragon remained unseen in the dark.

"Welcome back, my grandson," the older dragon, whose name was Jacob, greeted the younger. "It seems that life has treated you well, Yselliar."

The young dragon eyed Jacob's shaking aged body, noticing the many scars over his grandfather's black scales.

"I have seen your scars before, grandfather," he said, "but I was never able to ask you, are the stories of your adventures you tell me true?"

Jacob gave a delicate smile, which exposed his sharp yellow teeth. "Indeed. I've had many. Though they were long ago. I remember my adventures well."

"I am confused about your experiences," Yselliar confessed. "I remember you talking about this other place, but I have never seen it myself. I don't know what it looks like. But you do. Do you remember it well? I want to learn."

"I have time to tell you," Jacob said. "Our world is filled with magic and mystery. The other world is like that, but it's a little different. I can show you the life on the other world if you want. Now to start, close your eyes. Use your imagination."

With excitement, the grandson did as he was told. Jacob closed his eyes, too. He was digging deep into his long memory.

Jacob told Yselliar of the strange world. Almost immediately, the little dragon could picture what his grandfather was describing. Some images were good: The celebration of a cultural festival and someone spending time with his family after a day of hard labor. However, some of the images were devastating: wars tearing innocents apart and a hurricane destroying a dam that suddenly released the water to roam free in a town's streets. Yselliar did his best to feel the authenticity.

Jacob explained what he was describing, "People over there are a curious and creative sort of species. Many use the Earth and her resources to construct awe-inspiring wonders. In their early age, they began to form individual civilizations until they grew vast and strong, from the Stone Age to beyond. Occasionally the inhabitants of this place would get along with one another, but most of the time they would fight against each other. Just as it may be here, the line between harmony and bloodshed was a constant blur."

Smoke from the young dragon's nose blew out over the fire as he imagined the construction of the Great Pyramids, the Great Wall of China, and the Roman Colosseum. He saw moments of culture and peace. He saw a tribe cheering with thankfulness. He saw war, too. Some were small while others spanned the entire planet. He saw times of joy: a family at play in their home and two friends attending school. He saw times of grief: a tornado ripping through a neighborhood and the many attacks involving terror. After picturing everything Jacob had described, Yselliar opened his eyes.

"You have experienced all that?" he asked.

"Life is complex there," said Jacob. "Those creatures, specifically humans, do not practice the same magic we do, not even the evil sorcery. Still I have had many interesting experiences on that world that some may consider magic."

Yselliar grew anxious. He bounced up and down. "Tell me all that happened! I want to hear another story of your journeys!"

"Very well, I will," Jacob humbly said. "There is one memory that sometimes comes to the surface. But first, I must show you something. Follow me."

Jacob rose on his quaking legs and limped slowly out of the cave. Yselliar stayed right beside him until they reached the entrance. On the side of a tall rocky mountain, they looked down over the lush, sunny valley below. The woods were a lovely green and a bright blue river slithered down its wide path, on its way to the great waters.

"Take a look at what you see," Jacob told his grandson. "See the beautiful landscape; the river flowing calmly to its destination, the birds flying in the open sky, the elves and dwarves living in harmony with one another in the villages down below, the trees of the forest dancing in the wind, and most especially see the castle with no walls."

Yselliar looked at what Jacob had pointed out. Not far off from the village, there was a giant castle with colorful spires. Its sides shone white in the sun. The castle had no outer wall and no draw-bridge. Its door remained open for anyone to enter.

"I enjoy this very much," said Yselliar.

Jacob turned to him. "This is our peaceful world at its finest. Never has it been better. Now, what do you hear?"

Yselliar took a moment to listen, ears erect. He held his tongue before answering. "I hear the breeze whispering to me. I hear the laughter of the inhabitants of the elfish villages below, and I hear the birds in the air, squawking as they fly."

"Now, you are imaginative," said Jacob. "I want you to think of a place where none of that exists. Find everything you love here and remove it from your mind. Replace the woods with yellow sand. This was my mission: to save a man's life in the heat of the desert, where the air was as hot as my fire."

The ancient dragon told of a vast desert called the Sahara. It was a brutal region, truly a place where not many would want to spend time. Water was scarce, food was nowhere to be found, and there was no way anyone could cross the desolate land without preparation. Jacob remembered how his mouth had been dry and how his feet had sunk into the loose sand. It was the complete opposite of the land where he lived now.

"I was standing in the middle of this desert," Jacob began.

"Who was this man you had to save?" Yselliar asked.

"I'll tell you who."

Jacob continued his story. He explained that someone from his own land had been kidnapped. The man had been captured by a band of ruthless bandits. They held him hostage and were about to execute him.

"I had to sneak across the base in the dark of night so I wouldn't be spotted," Jacob explained.

"You must have been hidden very well," said Yselliar. "You can camouflage in any dark place with your black scales."

"Indeed, they gave me an advantage. But it was still not easy. Any source of light would expose my brown wings. I did my best to prevent detection."

Jacob told of reaching the prisoner's cell and finding him shackled to the wall. The man had been frightened at first, but Jacob said he was a friend. He placed the chain in his mouth and bit down as hard as he could, using the heat of his breath to melt the chain. As they escaped, they were spotted. The bandits tried to use whatever weapons they had on Jacob, but he was able to fight them off. His claws and fire were no match for them. Fighting those bandits was no trouble for a dragon. The man safely returned to his family. He had a wife and two children in a town called Crossett, Arkansas.

Yselliar stood up, entertained by Jacob's story. "Wow! You showed those desert folk a thing or two!"

Jacob suddenly roared and blew a ball of fire over the slopes. "Yselliar, you must know how that world is. It is not an evil realm, but it's very complex. You wouldn't last a week there if unprepared. Much of their technology is used for good, but that was not always the case."

Jacob stopped to take a breath. He found a path and started walking down the slope of the mountain with Yselliar behind him.

"This place of ours wasn't always this bright and happy, either. Do you know the reason why? Do you know what kind of foul creature would spread such darkness here?"

Yselliar silently shook his head.

"Dragons!" Jacob exclaimed. "Dragons like you and me. We are evil beasts. Throughout history, we've been responsible for life at its worst. Many of us robbed and set fire to villages like the ones you saw a moment ago."

Yselliar was shocked. "You mean we would kill innocent dwarves and elves?" he asked.

"Much more than that, my young one."

Yselliar almost cried. "Why would we be so cruel?"

Jacob did not answer his question but continued speaking. "You enjoy this world. No fierce force can destroy it. The most complicated thing is the magic that comes in many different forms."

The two reached the bottom of the mountain and were on their way to the castle. As they passed a village, Yselliar saw the dwarf children playing together with a large rubber ball while a group of young elves nearby were playing music that could sweeten anyone's mood.

"This place is close to perfection," said Yselliar. "I cannot believe the thought would cross the mind of any soul to hurt the lovely inhabitants of this valley."

"I've told you, dragons and other kinds of monsters," answered Jacob. "Just take a good look at me. In fact, take a look at yourself. You have sharp claws, spikes that run down your back, you have two long horns that are as smooth as carved wood, and a mouth full of teeth; teeth that are used for slicing into your helpless victims. How else do you think we prey on the things we eat, not to mention the makings of fire you carry in your lungs too?"

"What is the reason why we have all these features?"

Jacob gave his answer firm and clear, "Because we are cruel. Because we are evil. Because we are dark. Because we are wicked. The qualities of death are all over us. Why? Because we were made to kill the innocent and the meek. We are beasts to be slain. Not long ago, we were not seen as we are today."

Yselliar sat down on the grass. He did not know how one could be as Jacob described. The young dragon had more questions. "If that is the case, then why are we no longer like that? How does this connect with the destructive nature this world and the other face? My mother has told me a little about the time you were there. I cannot even begin to imagine. You have the answers in your adventures. I want to hear it. I want to hear all your adventures. I want to hear about your rise that caused the fall of the evil dragons!"

His grandfather chuckled at the chatter. "Very well, but let me start with a little introduction. This story is about an evil force that plagued this world and the first. This is about me and a long-trusted friend finding our true selves. Not only will you hear my experiences, you will hear about the experiences of others.

"Now let me first inform you about your ancestor long ago, then I will tell you about myself and my friend. We had to eliminate something on the First Earth and find our way back here to our home world. We had to learn about the dragon's destructive image that we carried from a land called Europe, and the good luck and hope we carried from a land called Asia. We had to learn to combine the two depictions to know who we really are and who we should be. Our rise was our enemy's fall. Now... let me tell you about my experience on the First Earth and our quests on this Earth to destroy an evil force."

Yselliar sat still, listening to every word Jacob spoke.

"It all started a long, long time ago, long before you or I were born...

Millennia ago, in the ancient days of Imperial China, dark forces loomed. As evening set its daily routine, the village lay as silent as a midnight cemetery. When darkness overcame the land, a light twinkled on the horizon, followed by more and more glimmering lights. The people of the village locked themselves in their homes, expecting the worst.

Time rolled by, the lights became brighter. The cavalry of the imperial army rode in, loud and strong. Sent in by the emperor, the army was to secure the village to prevent the uprising and rebellions from within it.

The horses of the night thundered in. The soldiers leapt from their backs to invade the people's homes. In one of the houses yet to be secured, an elderly man engraved a message in stone:

> *"The era of the dragon is ending. He who protected us from harm shall visit us one last time. The world shall remain dark for thousands of years until he returns with triumph in the west. These words must be passed down to my children. The last visit from the dragon will give us a sign that will be used to know when the dragon shall rise again. To the one who will inherit this stone many generations to come in the west, the day of the dragon shall come again before the end of your days."*

The old man finished the last of the message as two royal soldiers of the emperor stormed in. The man cowered, seeming to be helpless when a distant roar came from the wilderness.

"The dragon shall come for you on his last day," the old man warned the soldiers.

The soldiers did not know any better. One of them raised his sword as a warning, but the man was right. He had knowledge not many had. The moment the old man finished speaking, the dragon arrived.

He stood on four feet in the doorway, his scales of the color of brass. He glared at the soldier, growling. The soldier did not know what to do. Before he could even think of some way to escape, the dragon spat strange venom over the soldier's eyes. Stunned and yelling, the soldier fell backwards. He had visions of non-worldly images.

The elderly man was free. "You have saved me," he said to his hero.

"My last day has come," stated the dragon in the man's language. "My foes from the west shall rise years after my spirit has departed to a world in the heavens. Do not fear; the day they rise will be the day of my rise. My coming will be foreshadowed with an emblem of my kind. Rain and sun will bless you while I am not present."

The dragon had said enough. He had no time to lose. He took flight into the moonlit sky. The elderly man watched as he vanished into the night, gone on ahead until the day of the return.

The imperial soldiers regrouped outside the village. The old man knew his days on this Earth would soon end. Below the engraved doctrine, he carved an image in the stone. The image of the dragon had its large wings spread out while its feet stood firm and strong, one paw lifted. Its jaws were held open, as if it was about to breath fire. When the image was complete, the man buried the stone in a spot where his son would know where to find it.

WEEKS PASSED. IN THE FOREST OF A DISTANT LAND, THE DRAGON who had just been in the heart of China glided over the cold region. Looking down, the dragon saw a violet glow on the ground. Curious, he had to look. His plan, when he arrived, was to warn the inhabitants of the forest about the coming of his descendants.

The dragon dove to the ground, landing perfectly. His claws dug into the hard dirt as he looked around. At that moment, one of the natives of the forest jumped from his hiding spot, pointing a knife at the dragon's nose.

"My plan worked! Roar in sorrow if you please. You are not winning this one. We have killed dragons before and we may do it again!"

Knowing just what to do, the dragon tripped the hostile stranger with his forepaw. The hunter fell flat on his back. The dragon did not want to harm him, so he let the hunter be.

Remaining on the dirt at the dragon's feet, the hunter wept. "Please do not hurt me! I'm alone in the woods. I was just fooling with a simple kitchen knife. Oh, please don't hurt me. Your kind is nice and peaceful. You would never harm the innocent, would you?"

"You are a Monolegion dwarf of the woods," said the dragon.

The hunter gave him a lost look. "Monolegion?"

"The only Nibelung legion left on this Earth; the Monolegion. Untrustworthy are your characteristics, much unlike the Elsovian dwarves I have known. I've visited this forest one too many times. I am now on a final mission before I will travel back to my homeland. Your people will live in peace for many years until the final ones emerge, then you shall prepare to attack your fellow men. Oh, but remember, that day is also the day of my mighty return! Your kind shall possess an emblem, a moon, before my blood returns. Heed my warning."

The small dwarf continued complaining, "But I didn't commit any crime. I'm innocent. The Monolegions you speak of lie to the north. I have my doubts the sorcerer shall overcome your power. Please do not harm me!"

The dragon's eyes glimmered as he simplified what he was saying, "You will give my message to your people. Tell them that my descendants shall return in my power. This will happen in years to come. That is your message, now move!" His voice became harsh.

The young Nibelung dwarf took off in a flash. The dragon felt a deep sense of satisfaction. His errand in the forest was complete. He still felt uneasy, though, wondering what his descendants would bring to the world. Only time would tell, he knew. Now the time had come for him to leave.

"This world is now in the past," he said to himself. "May the two dragons of the new world bring peace, luck, and knowledge... and defeat the forces of evil."

He watched the young dwarf disappear into the woods, then he spread his mighty wings and took off like a rocket. Flying higher, he knew exactly where to go in order to travel to his home.

He flew for many days before he found the ground of his home. The forest, from a distance, looked similar to the one he had visited previously. He landed on the side of an isolated hill, and approached the entrance to a cave. He entered, coming upon a fire burning inside a rocky ring and some meat roasting on a spit. A figure stood behind the fire. The figure was another dwarf like the young one the dragon had met in the other forest. This time the dwarf gave a friendly wave at the dragon.

"You have returned," the dwarf said. "Your last visit on the other Earth has ended, I see. Welcome back. Have some of this food if you're hungry."

The dragon ripped a piece of meat from the spit with his teeth and swallowed it whole. "I am very disappointed. The last Nibelung tribe on the First Earth will not turn to peace. They are the only legion of their kind there, loyal to the wretched throne. Thus, I gave them the name Monolegion. I only wish their tribe was more like yours. Also, before I forget, I would like to see the wizard."

The dwarf nodded in approval and left. Minutes later, a tall figure in a shimmery blue cloak appeared in front of the dragon. The wizard bowed with respect. "You have returned. Was your visit enjoyable?"

"No," the dragon answered. "It is a difficult fact that I am currently the only dragon who chose to be your ally. My brethren have tried to take my life several times when they found where I was. They have conquered the western lands of Europe. I could only take refuge in the east. Therefore, the land of the east has a different opinion of my species. I'm afraid the west has seen who we truly are."

"I sense that is not the only problem you face," the wizard mused.

"Of course. The only land I could fly to in the west safely was where the only dwarves of the other Earth were located. They are not of our friendly tribe. They are evil. I fear they may cause trouble in the future."

Closing his eyes, the dragon used the power of the wizard to envision the future. Images appeared in the dragon's mind. The wizard explained what he was envisioning; "The people of the west despise your species, believing your kind is unholy. Those in the east look up to you. Now I see the entire Monolegion tribe fleeing up north. They remain there for many years until some start venturing back into other parts of the world. Men have created many clever inventions. Oh, but what is this? The Monolegions are infiltrating the governments of many nations. They are trying to spread the dark kingdom over the world."

The dragon opened his eyes. The wizard comforted him.

"You are saying my brethren will spread their evil ways through the Monolegions," said the dragon. "Unholy is my kind, you say. I must confess that that is very close to the truth. The Monolegions must be stopped, but only at the right time or it will not be successful."

"Calm your worries," the wizard said in a passive tone. "With my abilities, I will cast a spell on you. Your descendants who follow the right path will have light-colored scales and live away from here. They will not be unholy, trust my word. When two are born with the mark of darkness, send them to the other world in human form. They will find out who they are when they are in their nineteenth year. By then, your brethren may send a sorcerer, maybe the Keeper, who will bring wickedness to the people. The two young souls may remove him from the face of their Earth. This is not a prophecy, but a hopeful prediction."

"An educated prediction, I must say. My descendants that are marked will fulfill the promise I have made. I accept the spell. When I retire to my grave, my spirit will be with them until they are ready to be the beacons of hope they truly are. I will be their guide to the end of the Monolegions and maybe a key to end the wretched regime on our own world."

The two made a bonding promise. Before the dragon could take another bite out of the meat, the dwarf rushed back into the cave with tears in his eyes. "Help! He is here. Your brother. He is setting fire to my village." He started to weep. "My family is in danger!"

The dragon stood up and followed his friend. When he exited the cave, he looked down at the nearby village from the slopes. Many buildings were ablaze. The people were running in panic. The dragon's heart sank at the carnage.

"It is my brother. Dragons are such terrible beasts. I regret being one."

"Do not despair," said the wizard. "We must face the truth. The dragons, sorcerers, and others will become powerful. And though your descendants may be few in number, you can win the long war. Our first victory will be in another era. It will start with the two darkscales. They will be good at heart, remember that. Holy will be their purpose."

The brass-scaled dragon sadly watched as his own flesh and blood laughed in the dark sky at the scene of despair he had caused below. The dragon shook his head. "May my young do well," he whispered.

And that was that. Centuries would pass since the dragon's departure of the First Earth.

But when exactly would the prediction come forth? That was a question not even the wizard knew. All they had to do was wait...

All they had to do was wait...

CHAPTER 1

TROUBLE IN THE TROPICS

Indonesia, the land of the tropical jungles. I was surrounded by thick vegetation of many kinds under a hot sun and misty sky. My friend and I had spanned the globe for scientific reasons. We had been collecting blood from a variety of animals across the planet. One might wonder why two friends would be on such a trip, but the reason why I was so far from home went back to my youth. I was born and grew up in the isolation of Oklahoma. I loved to be out on the rolling green hills and under the blue sky. I would have enjoyed having siblings, but I did not mind being an only child. I lived on the open landscape with many different pets to accompany me. It astonished me how every animal had its special gift. They had different behaviors, instincts, and qualities that nature had given them to prepare themselves for life.

This made me wonder if something was possible. What if there was some way to connect all these living things together? I had been pondering how this could be done. For years, I focused on that question. I worked hard in my classes and I had many friends who respected me.

But when the first decade of my life came to a close on a cloudy day, I suddenly found myself alone. On what started out as a normal day, my father was killed during a destructive storm known as a *derecho*. He was protecting me the best he could when a power line blew over and struck him. To this day, I can still see even the trees toppling over in the strong wind. The large birch tree in our backyard uprooted and its branches broke the window to my bedroom. The loud wind rang in my ears. Several days after my father's funeral, my distraught mother lost herself. She was forced to leave me. The sheriff had to drag her into an ambulance, leaving me in sorrow as I watched from the front window of our damaged house. I had no idea where she went.

After that, I lived in several homes until I eventually reached New York City. It was far from my rural, native land. I lived with foster parents for a while. This was no environment for me. Though my foster parents took good care of me, I still felt lost in the new world. There were too many people for comfort. They would stroll along on their own businesses. Not once would they stop and say hello. For someone who lived on a farm, that was unusual.

After my difficult teenage years I managed to get many valuable scholarships. When I graduated, I decided to attend the Atlantic College of Biology. I excelled with a zoology major until I was a graduate student at a relatively young age. I had a dormitory with a friendly roommate. To me, this meant I did not have to live with random foster families anymore. My life started to improve. I met someone who came from the cold plains of Saskatchewan, Canada. He had moved to the city and felt as lost as I did. Like me, he had no parents to take care of him. We discovered our similarities and became very close friends. Our birthdays were even on the same date. With my new friend, I no longer felt like a lost soul with the name of Jacob Draco. Everyone saw Clipper, who went by his family name, and I as two loyal friends. Clipper was just as fascinated with animals as I was. We began attending the same college because of this.

A few years passed and the time was right. We were ready to find out if we could study many living organisms and their genetics in a new way. We traveled to the Arctic, Africa, Europe, Asia, and the Americas for months. Now we were on our last expedition on Komodo Island, a part of Indonesia.

A native guide drove Clipper and me over the dirt roads through thick jungles in an ancient Jeep. One path crossed over the side of a steep slope. Vines and trees wound their way up the slope while thick ferns and bushes grew with freedom below us. We traveled along the trail to find our last animal, a lizard that would be happy to eat us alive: we were after the mighty Komodo dragon. As we ventured to our calculated spot, the guide stopped in the middle of the road and shut off the engine. Clipper and I hopped out of the vehicle and scrambled down the slope to a pit where we saw the lizard below. We watched a Komodo dragon munching on the helpless prey that did not stand a chance.

"Be careful," whispered the guide when he joined us. "If she knows we're here, we are in great danger."

"I remember," I replied.

The guide handed me a tranquilizer gun, giving me the honors to take down the breathtaking creature.

I strongly opposed the offer. "Sir, I already told you. Yes, I know it is only a tranquilizer gun. But I still can't hold a weapon like that. It just doesn't fit well in my hands."

"Oh, that's right," said the guide. "I understand your feelings. In that case, I'll take the shot. The animal won't be harmed."

He aimed and squeezed the trigger. The dart whizzed through the air then rested right in the neck of its target. The dragon roared from the startling puncture and fell into a harmless sleep. Clipper slipped down to the pit, cautious because the lizard's mate that might be in the area. He quickly acquired the blood that contained the DNA we needed. He placed the blood sample inside a vial then scurried back up to me. He took a deep breath away from the sickening stench of the pit. He gave me the vial and I placed it safely in my knapsack.

"After all these months, we finally have the entire set of blood we need," I said with excitement.

"We still have a long way to go," said Clipper. "We have to find the right doses of each sample. We'll then test this experiment in our lab."

The guide put away the gun. "Congratulations anyhow. Now can we go? I don't want to be here when the beast wakes up from her afternoon nap, or if her mate returns."

The three of us climbed back into the old Jeep and were on our way back to the local village. We would then take a charter plane back to Jakarta. We patiently traveled along the bumpy road.

"Well, we may have a long way to go, but we're more than half-way done with our experiment," I said.

Clipper was not quite as enthusiastic. "We may almost be done, but I don't think anything will happen. Genetic matching and the like are not as easy as it seems, especially for us."

"I know," I said, "but it's worth a shot. If it doesn't work, at least we tried."

As we conversed about our experiment, the engine of the Jeep suddenly made a loud bang. It started smoking as if it was on fire.

"Something is wrong with the steering wheel!" the guide yelled as he fought for control. "I can't do anything!"

"Great, just another obstacle we have to go through!" Clipper griped. He seemed a little scared, so was I.

The guide started to slow down so he could stop and address the problem. The vehicle ran over a semi-buried rock in the road. The jolt caused Clipper to fall off and roll out of sight in the trees. Seconds after he disappeared, I jumped out to rescue him. I slipped past the trees and rolled down the steep side of a rocky knoll. It all happened so fast. I landed on the ground, upside down at the bottom of the hill. I slowly righted myself and noticed a campfire burning in the middle of the day, surrounded with strange people. Clipper, who was luckily not injured, pulled me into a nearby bush. I must have been more hurt than him. My back felt sore, nothing more.

"Rebels, I think," Clipper said with uncertainty in his voice.

I glanced back at the men from our hiding spot. "In Indonesia? Does this country even *have* rebels? Do the local villages know about this?"

"I don't know anything about this," said Clipper. "But there they are, clear as day. I'm just saying they're rebels or they're not. They're more than likely something else."

No matter who they were, it was hard to believe what I saw. A flag waved from a pole. It was black with a strange orange symbol in the center. The symbol almost looked like a spider. This was before I knew the dreadful impact that symbol was to have on me.

I could not believe my eyes. How could Indonesia possibly have rebels or some other type of rogue army on an island like this? Some of the soldiers marched by, holding aged revolvers and other odd weapons in their hands. The thing that puzzled me most of all was their physical appearance. They did not look native to the land. They looked like they had come from Europe or North America. Many had big, bushy, and uncombed hair of red, brown, and blond. They reminded me of fictional Vikings with the sharp-pointed horns on their helmets. Not only that, but they seemed shorter than normal. I was possibly a good foot taller than they were, considering I was about six feet in height. They cooked large chunks of meat and vegetables over a fire and drank what I presumed to be ale or beer out of wooden beakers.

"Who are these people?" I murmured.

Clipper did not say anything. We looked beyond the marching line where we saw two prisoners tied up on separate wooden poles in front of a large, enclosed building. The poor men appeared to have been whipped and beaten. In my heart, I knew they had to be saved. I could not sneak away, thinking that these prisoners might be executed or worse. That thought would haunt me for the rest of my life. They might have families waiting for them to return home.

"What are we going to do?" asked Clipper.

"Well, I don't know how to rescue those prisoners," I began to say.

"Jacob, what are you thinking?" Clipper interrupted. "We're in a bad spot. We can't save them ourselves. These rebels are dangerous and trained. I say we leave in peace and warn the right people. They can take care of this camp. Those people will get rescued."

"This is bad. If we don't save those captives now, they'll possibly die. Do you want that on your hands?"

Clipper took a deep breath and shook his head. I picked up a nearby stick.

"Now I have an idea. This is what we we'll do..."

With the stick, I drew markings in the dirt that resembled the building and the poles. I had arrows pointing hither and thither, this way and that. Clipper believed it was a complex plan for freedom, but it was not impossible. We both could do it. We *had* to do it. After I asked if he was ready, his nod signaled me to take off.

I ran around the perimeter of the camp, avoiding detection at all costs. Stealth was the key, and stealthy I was. I snuck behind various trees and bushes until I reached the back of the main building in the heart of the camp. Hiding behind the simple, wooden structure, I waited for Clipper to do his part. He moved like a specter around the building to find anything useful. He found a short rope, a container filled with kerosene, and, as odd as the weapons we saw, a small keg of gunpowder. I watched as Clipper filled a leather pouch he had with some of the gunpowder. It was the perfect mixture for a clever distraction once it was all together. He took the supplies and met me behind the wooden building. I peeked around the corner to see if the coast was still clear. The soldiers were at ease, sitting next to the fire. I guessed they were occupied for the moment.

The prisoners were helplessly standing, tied to the poles. Clipper gave me the supplies and waited beside me. "You know what I'm thinking with all this," he said. "Throw it nearby. Hopefully, it will divert them away."

I dipped the rope in the container of kerosene. I then placed the end of the rope into the pouch of gunpowder. It was nothing glamorous, but hopefully it would work.

"When I give the word," I said to Clipper, "I'll run past the rebels."

Clipper rubbed his hands together. "I can take your knife and cut the prisoners free."

I gave Clipper my small pocketknife and then took off with the homemade bomb, pinching the rope inside the pouch to keep it secure. I reached the corner of the building once again, got out a match from my side pocket, and struck it on the side of a tree. The spark produced a small flame that burned dimly. I placed it on the end of the rope. The fuse burned fast. I had to throw the bomb quickly before it exploded in my hands.

I threw the bomb into the air where it landed within the circle of soldiers around the fire.

It gave off a fiery explosion and the soldiers dove for cover. That explosion was my cue. I took off, dashing past the rebels. As planned, I made it easy for them to spot me. They immediately stood up and began pursuing me.

"There's someone here! He can't escape!" one of them shouted.

I started to pant. "Here it goes."

I ran out of sight of the rebels and left the path. There I concealed myself behind a big fern.

The moment the camp was clear, I watched as Clipper rushed up to the wooden poles and began cutting the prisoners free. "Don't worry," he said with comfort, "I'm a friend."

The prisoners responded in Indonesian. *"Syukurlah Anda berada di sini! Silahkan melepaskan kita!"* They looked relieved.

Clipper understood what they were saying. The prisoners were happy to see him. Clipper pointed towards the jungle, telling them where they could flee from the soldiers. They obeyed him and took off in a flash. As Clipper started to leave the camp, one of the guards from the compound caught sight of him and fired a warning shot with an ancient revolver. Clipper paused and slowly turned around.

From behind the fern, I saw the soldier grab my friend. I had a perfect opportunity to escape, but not with Clipper captured. Before I was able to move, one of the rebels yelled to me. He must have known where I was.

"You can't go any further," he called. "We have your friend. We will kill him if you don't return."

Without hesitation, I emerged from my hiding spot. The rebel gestured for me to come to him. He grasped my arm and forced me into the building. Another rebel tied me to a chair beside Clipper. The situation was grim. Even though Clipper and I were bound and trussed, we at least set the prisoners free.

Several minutes had passed when the leader of the small army returned. He spoke in a harsh voice. "You people stuck your noses in our business. You are fools for doing so."

Clipper cocked an eyebrow. "We didn't mean to come here. What are you doing in this camp?"

The leader slammed a fist on a small table. "Do not question me. You found us and now you must pay the price. You are now an enemy to the One Legion."

"The One Legion?" Clipper repeated.

The leader did not answer. He left us in the building. I could hear him speak outside, "These rifles and pistols are very effective. They're better than other weapons we have used. Organize an execution for them immediately. Use the plan of execution on them that we would have used on the other prisoners."

The other rebels laughed hysterically and did what their leader ordered. All but one left the camp. The lonely soldier stood outside the door, guarding us.

"We come to Komodo to gather the dragon's blood and here we are, imprisoned by an unknown group of revolutionaries," I said in despair. "Something's off about them. They say weird things. Effective guns? The One Legion? Who are they? They even speak English, but it sounds like some sort of Scandinavian accent. And just how they dress; I don't even know what to think of that."

"Whoever they are, we've got to find a way to escape," Clipper whispered to me.

"Preferably alive," I said. "We've got to finish our experiment."

"Jacob, quiet!" Clipper whispered harshly. "We don't want the guard to hear what we're saying."

Instantly, we heard a bang on the door. I licked my lips.

"Sorry. I'll be quiet," I called. I leaned to Clipper's ear and whispered, "Let's see if we can find a way out."

I scanned the entire one-room hut, looking for something useful to cut the ropes that bound us. Nothing seemed useful. The only things in the room were me, Clipper, the chairs we were tied to, and the table.

"Oh, what can we do?" I moaned.

Clipper looked at me for a split second then slowly stood up, still tied to the chair. I followed suit. We both stood on our feet with our chairs on our backs. Clipper waddled towards the door and cracked it open. The guard was drinking from his large beaker, unaware of our actions. Satisfied, Clipper silently closed the door and wriggled back to me.

"I have an idea," he said quietly. "Remember being in that school play a few years ago, the one where I was the pirate and you were the sailor? I had to strangle you off-stage, remember? You did a good job screaming."

I nodded as he explained his suggestion. I snickered in approval.

After a few seconds, I began screaming. "Help! He's… trying to… ah… strangle… me! Help!"

We both stomped our feet to add effect.

The guard opened the door to inspect the hysterical noises. Before he could do anything about the commotion, Clipper and I reared up into him. He fell back, his head colliding hard with the wooden floor. When I stepped outside, I began running with the chair still latched onto me. Clipper ran right behind me. We knew that the guard would alert the rest of the small army at any moment.

"We've got to get out of here," I said. "Follow me."

We headed down the western path. We were both in panic for our lives and when the path split, we mistakenly ran in different directions. Before we knew it, we were separated and lost.

I halted when I realized I had lost Clipper. I rolled my eyes. *How could this get any worse?* I thought. I was lost in the middle of the Indonesian jungle with a rebel force hunting me down! This was something I never thought would happen to anyone, let alone me.

I started to run again when my shirt latched onto the branch of a tree. I yelped from the unexpected grab. It took me a moment to calm down. Frustration became reprieve when I realized the rope that held me was shredded along with my shirt. There was no time to be angry at the sting on my side or at the fact that I had lost Clipper. He should be safe if he kept running. I removed the rope and the chair fell to the ground. Free to run with no resistance, I continued down the road. The tear in my shirt was so big that the shirt fell from my body. I tucked it in some vegetation and continued running.

After running for several minutes, I soon reached an old building. It looked like an abandoned church with a steeple pointing to the sky. The framework was of rotted wood and there was a giant hole in the roof. *What's this doing in the middle of the island?*

Despite the strange location, I thought it would be a convenient place to hide while I caught my breath, better than staying out in the open. I knew the rebels were still after me so I couldn't stay long. I heard them shouting in the distance. Without a second thought, I ran through the open doorway.

"I'll stay here until I aaahhh!" I jumped back out in terror. "I didn't know you were in here!"

Another Komodo dragon, what I believed to be the mate of the first one, roared at me. Komodo dragons were monogamous and the male was furious. I ran out of the building and scrambled up a tree. I had no idea I could climb a tree the way I did. The dragon looked left and right, finding nothing but the scent of me. He soon returned to the building. I began to climb down as silently as I could, but the branch that supported me snapped. I landed hard on the ground below. The dragon walked back out, glaring at me.

As he started running towards me, I dodged him and ran into the building as an idea had come to me. I quickly peeled off my shoes and socks and dropped them in the doorway as bait for the upcoming mob. Hopefully the dragon would distract them. I climbed the rickety stairs to the second floor. As I was about to take a sigh of relief, I saw the dragon following me. Surprised, I headed for a window. I bashed through the aged pane, rolled off the inclined roof, and fell into a patch of brush. The dragon stuck its head out of the pane, but it did not pursue me. I assumed it viewed me as some stupid creature, falling to the ground every few seconds.

I continued running down path just as the rebel mob stormed the perimeter of the building. One soldier found my shoes.

"Look at what I found!" I heard him yell to the others.

He ordered everyone in the mob to search the building. That turned out to be a mistake on his part. The Komodo dragon was after them in an instant. My plan worked. I was long gone.

I HAD BEEN SUCCESSFUL, BUT CLIPPER WAS GOING THROUGH A rough experience. The ache in his legs made him even more upset when he noticed that he was alone. With the chair tied to his back, he struggled up the beaten path until he was breathless. He took a step backwards but lost his footing. He landed hard on his back, crushing the spindly wooden chair. Crying out from the fall, he quickly got back on his feet. The chair was broken and he was free. He continued to run up the path while shaking his stiff arms. Dense vines seemed to reach out and grab at him. Fighting his way through, he did not see the sudden drop down into a misty, open gorge. Clipper caught hold of one of the vines and held on tightly as he fell. Groaning in fright, he shut his eyes and wished for it all to end. As he felt the bump on the opposite cliff, he reopened his eyes. He began climbing up the vine, refusing to look down. He knew he had to reach safety somehow, despite his strong fear of heights.

After the long, strenuous climb, he finally reached the top of the cliff. He scrambled away from the edge and looked down. Relieved, he took a deep breath. His feet were sore from the running and climbing, so he removed his shoes to give air to his feet. He rested until he heard yelling from the other side of the narrow gorge. He stood back up and began to put his shoes on again. Just as he slid his foot back in one of his socks, he heard the report of a gunshot. A sudden force bit him through the sock and pushed him back to the ground.

"Ow! My foot! He got my foot!"

Clipper clutched his foot and saw a lone figure across the gorge loading another round of into his revolver, the horns on his helmet clearly visible. Clipper feared for his life and crawled away as fast as he could, leaving behind a dark trail of blood. The distant rebel did nothing else once Clipper was out of range. When he reached a safe distance, he limped into the thick jungle and sat down to look at the wound on his left foot. The pain was not as bad as Clipper had anticipated, but he looked away in pure disgust when he saw the damage. The small toe on his left foot was gone, blown clean off by the bullet. The trail of blood ended in a pool that dripped into the soil. Clipper cringed in horror. He was just about to lie down and pass out when another gunshot was heard in the distance. He stumbled to his feet and hurried off as quickly as his injury would allow. He did not stop moving until he tripped again and fell into a small creek. Tiny fish surrounded Clipper's face. He quickly crawled out of the creek. Clipper hated fish. Besides the horrible taste, in his opinion, his face would get swollen if he ever ate seafood.

As much as he wanted to rest, he continued down the path. He shed a few tears on the way. All he wanted to do was find me. The encounter with the peculiar rebels seemed to have come out of nowhere. His life had changed in an instant. *How can my life change any more?* he thought.

THE PATH THAT I WAS RUNNING ON SLOWLY TRANSFORMED INTO A smooth but windy trail. I slowed down a bit, knowing that the mob was far behind me. I still kept my eyes open for any aggressive animal. Like Clipper, I was depressed from the recent turn of events. I did not know exactly how long I had been running on the trail. Before I stopped to catch my breath again, I noticed another path merged with the trail I was traveling. Was it the path Clipper had taken? It had to be. I was worried about him ever since I heard the gunshots. I called his name, not even caring about the risk of enemies hearing my voice.

"Clipper! Where are you? Clipper!"

I heard him respond. "Jacob! Jacob! I hear you! I'm coming!"

It was a miracle. His voice sounded like a victorious battle cry. I was glad he was safe. He came limping up to me and took a deep breath. I looked down at his feet and saw his missing toe. I was ready to cry out, but Clipper held a finger to his lips.

"You don't want any of those people or wild animals after us, do you?" he said. "We don't have time to worry over it. Now keep quiet and let's get out of here."

I nodded. Now all I wanted was to find the Jeep that had caused this misadventure in the first place. Clipper agreed. We searched along the trail while on the lookout for any more rebels. It was early in the evening when we finally heard the sound of the familiar machine. The Jeep came rolling into view and stopped next to us. We immediately climbed in.

"Where were you?" the guide asked. "It took me a while to fix this thing."

"We've got to get out of here," I said. "We ran into some rebel soldiers. I think they're planning something horrible."

"Here on this island?" The guide was confused as we were.

"It's true, and we better hurry," said Clipper.

The guide took our word and gunned the Jeep forward. Preoccupied in thought, the guide was caught off guard when a bullet struck the side of his seat. He tried to keep the Jeep away from the left side of the road. Another bullet struck right next to the steering wheel. He stayed down from then on. The rebels were still after us. If we got away, their little army could be exposed. They knew they had to get rid of us.

Clipper and I ducked, avoiding the flying bullets as much as we could. The guide made the Jeep go faster, eventually outrunning the rebels. When we were out of range, all of us sat back up. No tires were flat and the Jeep seemed to be running well.

Once we were away from the danger, we stopped. I examined the damage. To my surprise, there were not just bullets that struck the Jeep, but arrows as well. There were arrowheads and shards of wood.

Clipper pulled out a shaft from the back of the front seat. "They were using arrows, too." He handed it to me.

"I don't know what this is all about, but we made it," I said. "We're lucky we still have the knapsack. Our blood samples are safe."

"A knapsack for a toe," Clipper grumbled.

"Don't worry," I said. "We'll get you two to a hospital soon."

The guide kept looking behind us. "What about those rebels? They didn't look like rebels to me. Did you see what they were wearing? It looked like the clothing a band of barbarians would wear."

I looked back as well. "Whoever they are, they're gone. We don't have to worry about them anymore. Thank goodness."

It took a while before our Jeep reached the airfield. From there, we took a charter plane back to the city of Jakarta. After landing in Jakarta, we immediately went to the hospital. Clipper's wound was stitched together. He felt a little eccentric about having only four toes on one foot. The next day, we returned to our hotel room. We had transformed our room into a makeshift laboratory during our stay. When we entered, I set my knapsack down on the bed. Clipper opened it up and organized our new samples with the ones that we had gathered from different animals throughout the world. They were kept safe in our room. Clipper was also gently massaging the spot where his toe used to be. At least he received care and his foot was no longer bleeding.

"If my calculations are correct," he stated while working, "when we extract the genes, we have to put more Komodo dragon into the main formula than polar bear. But I may be wrong because I walked under a stepladder this morning. Should we add more polar bear?"

"Stepladders don't scare me," I said. "Superstition doesn't bond with reality. What do you want to do, give up and go home? If I was superstitious, I'd say the bad luck was losing your toe."

"I was only joking, but I get your point," Clipper said, cringing from a shot of pain in his foot.

Soon after we started working, we heard a knock on our door. I stood up, my eyes squinted. "I hope it isn't the maid. If she finds out what we did to this room, she'll have a fit."

I took a moment to stretch, then I moved to the door. I was still out of energy from the previous day's events. I opened the door to a familiar person holding a small bag.

"Sally?" I said in disbelief.

"Here I am," answered the young woman at the door.

"What are you doing here? You're supposed to stay at our lab in New York to get everything ready when we come home."

"Well, I don't like sitting in a chair for hours to protect something that's already secure," said Sally. "I hate desk work. Field experience is what I love. You have a clever security system at the lab that *you* created. You're a genius. I came to see how you two are doing. Are you on the verge of creating a monster?"

Clipper was surprised to see Sally as well. "We're not creating a monster. Jacob and I are compiling the genes of different living organisms across this planet. If you wanted field experience, you should have come with us to get the Komodo dragon's blood." He sat down and rubbed his sore foot.

Sally just gave Clipper an indifferent look. "The Komodo dragon. Well, I study zoology too."

Clipper told Sally about the situation with the rebels. Sally held her hands over her mouth when he mentioned the loss of his toe.

"I'm so sorry, I didn't know. I feel bad now."

"No need to be sorry," Clipper replied, still a little upset at the ordeal. "But we did get the blood sample, so we were successful in the end."

"What's in the bag?" I asked, trying to change the conversation.

Sally held up the bag. "Fresh ocellated flounder from the waters of southeast Asia."

Clipper stared at the bag in disgust. "You remember that I hate fish with all my being. Just anything that comes out of water makes my face swell up, you know that."

"I remember," said Sally, "that's why I brought you a boiled scorpion." She giggled at Clipper's expression.

Clipper sighed before making a single chuckle. "Just get that bag away from me. I don't have much of an appetite right now." He massaged his foot again.

I decided to take the scorpion. I bit into it. At first, I made a face of antipathy. But then I realized that it was very crunchy, just how I enjoy my food. Clipper did not eat anything that night. He stayed up until about two o'clock in the morning. When the sun rose on the horizon, I began managing the samples while he slept. I had samples of a grey wolf, a mountain lion, a billy goat, an African Spitting Cobra, a polar bear, a bearded dragon, and a Komodo dragon; just to name a few. Many different animals from many different continents. Many of them were dangerous beasts, yet we managed to collect the blood of those seven animals and more.

When midday came, Clipper and I were ready to travel back home. We waited patiently for our plane to arrive. I had my blood samples in my knapsack resting right beside me. I chose to keep it with me on the plane ride. I did not dare place it in the cargo compartment. The samples were much too valuable for me to lose.

Our plane arrived at last and we boarded. I was happy and excited. Clipper and I had big plans back home. With the proper uses of each sample, we planned to create a mixture and run tests on a lab rat. Sally decided to stay in Jakarta a little longer. She told us she would take another flight home.

We came this far, and we prayed that we would make it all the way. Peace spread through my body as I rested my head back into the seat. I wished the plane could fly faster. If I had wings, I would fly myself. We still had to cross the world's largest ocean and the entire North American continent. But alas, I had no control over the speed I traveled. I tried to remain patient.

To help the time pass, I glanced out my passenger window. I was engulfed in a blue world: the blueness of the Pacific Ocean and the blueness of the clear sky. I once caught sight of a small island. The island was so small and so green. It seemed like a slice of heaven, with all the rocks, the sand, and the vegetation inhabiting the area. I never knew simple pieces of Earth itself could be so beautiful. I felt like I was flying over another world. It was hard to imagine that a populated place like New York could be on the same planet as a place like this island.

As the hours passed, the state of California came into view. The world changed from sea to land, where the plane stopped in Los Angeles. We boarded another plane and headed for New York. Not long after we were in the air, we crossed the desert. It looked nothing like the ocean I had just seen. We eventually crossed Colorado. I found it amazing how the mighty Rocky Mountains spread across the west. And suddenly thereafter, the Great North American Plains took their place. They stretched out to the curve of the Earth. Right below me, I saw the many cornfields and green rolling hills of Kansas, not to mention some oil wells, too. Trees dominated the land in the state of Missouri. I was one to love the Missouri forest. We crossed over the Great Plains, catching sight of the swampy banks of the Mississippi River. The vision of the plains faded into the distance and the familiar eastern lands of my secondary home came into view. The plane descended onto the gray runway. As it slowed and eventually stopped, I closed my eyes, remembering the island of paradise back in the Pacific Ocean. This world was full of adventure.

Clipper and I were welcomed back to the city when we stepped off the airplane. We headed back to our college dormitories. *That's the last I'll deal with the dragons,* I thought.

CHAPTER 2

RETURNING HOME

Yes, the plane ride was long, but I enjoyed it. It astounded me how the world seemed so small, yet so big at the same time. One moment you would see a tropical island, next thing you see are the countless square miles of the Great Plains. When I crossed the cornfields and rolling hills, I had a vision of my youth. I wondered, *Could there be another world that was beautiful in its own way?*

On my way back to my dormitory, I thought about where my father was now. He must be looking out for me now as he had always done. He made sure that I would succeed at whatever I did. I remember shooting hoops on a bare basketball rim that hung above the barn door. And just as expected, as I was playing, my father was there having a great time along with me. He taught me how to make baskets from far away and how to become a likable athlete. Throughout that final summer with him, I learned to make three-point shots. At that age, I had visions of being the next basketball legend. Basketball was my favorite sport. Now that dream is gone. My father was taken away from me before I was even ready to take on life by myself. Angered and scared, I had fallen apart after the ordeal. But I still know even today that he watches over me wherever I go. I have faith that there is life after death, and that was what calmed me in times of fear.

I came out of the flashback as our taxi pulled into the parking lot of the dormitory. After Clipper paid the fare, I pulled my luggage to my dorm room. The dormitory building was old but well maintained. It almost had a Victorian feel to it, which I quite liked. I lived on the first floor near the entrance while Clipper lived on the second level. My depressed mood from the recent meeting with the strange rebels changed to that of a typical graduate student.

"Jacob," my roommate Lewis Chang called when I entered the room. "I'm so glad you're back! I was starting to get lonely without you. Sally called last night and told me about Clipper's toe."

"My foot's sore, but I'll be fine. Don't worry about me," said Clipper.

Chang was born and raised in China but had moved to Delaware at a young age. He once told me that he was fascinated with aviation, but he was especially enthralled by zoology after visiting a zoo during a school field trip. Of course, his name was changed to Lewis after he moved to the U.S., but very few people referred to him by that name. All his friends, including Clipper and I, simply call him Chang.

"Oh, you managed without me," I told him. "You had your painting above your bed to keep you company."

Chang turned to view it. The painting was that of a long snaky dragon that represented wisdom in Chang's native land. As I glanced at it, I had no idea what it would mean to me in the near future. I sat down on my bed without giving much thought to the painting.

"That dragon is very interesting," Clipper commented.

"Interesting?" Chang mimicked. "He's more than just *interesting*. He's a symbol of wisdom, luck, and doing what's right." He was about to give a lecture on how influential the painting was when he noticed my knapsack. "So I see you have your samples," he said. "I can't believe you did it."

"Well, it wasn't easy," I said. "I'd say either the polar bear or the cobra was the most dangerous to get. And other than the rebels, getting the Komodo dragon wasn't that hard."

Chang chuckled. "It must have been hard getting a sample of the cobra."

I handed him the knapsack to show him our progress before unpacking the rest of my luggage. I turned on the television in our room while doing so, watching highlights of what took place in Indianapolis during my flight over the city.

"The Pacers really blew it today," Chang observed.

"They were playing against the Celtics. I'm glad they won," I said.

"Watch out! The Knicks are doing well too," Chang said with a ghostly but playful voice.

"The Knicks? They haven't won a championship in decades."

Chang just glared at me. He had loved the New York Knicks ever since he moved to the U.S. As the highlights began showing other games I did not care for, I took a jersey and some gym shorts out of my dresser.

"Where are you off to?" asked Chang.

"Basketball practice," I answered. "I may have missed most of the season and traveled the globe, but my experiment is more important than my pleasure. Now that my expedition has concluded, I'm returning for the last few games of the season."

I grabbed my basketball and then headed to the practice gym. Since the college was not very big, being on the basketball team was no serious obligation. Throughout the long winter, they struggled without me. I assumed they were in dire need of a starting guard, so I decided to join the team for practice as soon as possible. Clipper followed me out.

"What are you going to do over there?" I asked him.

"I just want to watch you play. Besides, I need to use the hockey table out in the foyer to warm me up for real hockey when winter comes again. A true-blooded Canadian plays hockey."

"Indeed," I said, "but don't even try to play curling again. That silly game isn't even a real sport."

"We've been through this argument before, Jacob," Clipper grunted in good nature.

"Yes, and you should know that it's not a real sport. It's just a quick way to have fun on the ice."

"It is too a sport! It's in the Olympics!"

We had argued about whether curling was a real sport for a while now, but it was not a serious disagreement. We continued to bicker on our way. We first walked to the main campus to inform our professor that we had successfully returned with the blood samples before going on to the gymnasium. Clipper and I were still joking around.

"A college of biology and all you care about is basketball," Clipper said when we finished talking with the professor.

I rubbed my jaw back and forth. "My education comes first. I already told you that. If I cared more about basketball, I wouldn't have gone on this trip with you in the first place. Better yet, I would possibly be at the University of Kansas or Chapel Hill or something."

Clipper tapped his chin with his finger but did not say a word. He had a habit of doing that.

We passed two large, bronze statues of dragons that welcomed us into the main quadrant. I walked past them a million times without incident, but this time something had changed. As I ran my eyes over the two sculptures, blackness suddenly overpowered me, followed by a deep voice that spoke in my head,

"*You will become the dragon you truly are before returning to your true home.*"

The vision ended as soon as it came. The world returned as I knew it. I felt a strange feeling in my head. I dropped to my knees as several students nearby stared at me in concern. It took about a minute for the feeling to pass. I stood back up to see Clipper rubbing his forehead. He seemed to have experienced the same thing.

"Return to my true home?" he asked.

I shrugged. "I think we're still wound up from the trip. Let's carry on with our lives."

I was about to walk away when out of the corner of my eye I thought I saw one of the statues turn its head to stare at me. Was I seeing things? I did my best to get the image out of my mind. We crossed the campus, but the vision would not leave. I told myself that it was just subconscious triumph of the expedition and it was finding a way to reach the surface of my mind. This reminded me of the wisdom that a Chinese dragon represented. Chang's painting was interesting. Could it have a bigger impact later, during the tests?

CHAPTER 3

DAWN OF DARKNESS

As I remembered from what people said, Monty Victor was in an abandoned hideout a few blocks away from the gym on campus. Monty was a vulgar person. He was into zoology just as I was, but he had a dark soul and was a vile being. When I first came to New York, it seemed as if Monty had been expecting me. He had caused a lot of trouble for Clipper and me since then. He had lied, cheated, and stolen his way through life and had been angry at us since the day we first met each other. I had not known why at the time. He was a very cunning and brazen person. I often compared him to a tyrannical leader. But that was not the strange part. The strange part was the people who followed him. The rebels we had encountered reminded me of Monty's followers in a strange way. They were short, brawny, and foul mannered. Monty was taller than most of his followers and dressed a bit more formally than they did. His life was an enigma to me. At times, I could have sworn I had seen him practice dark magic. He was like no one else in the city. He had, should I say, more bizarre desires.

I originally thought that after gathering a few of the scoundrels he needed, Monty would travel to his homeland, somewhere foreign. His people possessed minds similar to that of Monty's. The malevolent lord found his men from all over the world, mainly in unknown corners of Europe.

In his hideaway, Monty watched his corrupt force while his most loyal servant stood beside him. His servant was originally named

Maroh, but Monty, as with his other followers, had renamed him. Maroh was called Raymond when they arrived in North America.

Monty and Raymond heard several different arguments ringing around the room. All were foul and vicious. Monty finally stood up and silenced them all.

"My noble followers, about an hour ago, I received word that our two greatest enemies, Jacob Draco and Justin Clipper, have returned from their mission!" He announced in a voice that easily carried across the vast room.

Once he finished his brief announcement, the arguing and fighting continued. The environment resembled a noisy tavern with all the hullabaloo. Monty walked to the corner of the complex and pulled out a map. He located my dorm, the practice gym, and most of the college campus. One of Monty's followers, who went by his new name Richardson, came to see what he was doing. Richardson stared blankly at the map.

"You told me they have their personal laboratory. Why is it not on the map?" Richardson asked.

"Their lab is isolated," said Monty. "They keep it so because they find it easier to work that way. That is why Draco's roommate has a car in such a city. Clever, if I may say so. But we can't let them succeed. I've told you why."

Just then, Wilson, another renamed member of the group, came up and grabbed Richardson's arm.

"Why are you tormenting, Monty?" Wilson asked.

"I'm not tormenting him!" said Richardson.

"Oh, no. You're not tormenting me," Monty said. "But now that I've told you about the lab, please leave me alone.".

"I just want to know what is going on," Richardson protested to Wilson.

"You don't need to know, you idiot. You just do what our leader says," said Wilson.

Monty told Wilson to stay out of it, but Wilson did not listen. He grabbed Richardson's arm again and began pulling him back.

Richardson slapped Wilson away. He disliked being touched. He angrily told Wilson to stop, but the problem just started.

Richardson took a step forward, brought up by his pride. "You're not my dictator!" he yelled.

Filled with rage, Richardson threw a punch at Wilson. Wilson saw it coming and dodged the blow. He grabbed Richardson's arms and twisted it. Richardson yelled in pain and kneed Wilson in the stomach. As Wilson bent down, Richardson raised a foot and kicked Wilson in the face. Wilson held his nose as blood dripped onto the floor. "You broke my nose!" he wailed as he pulled out large dagger.

Richardson realized that his enemy had a weapon and he did not. He began to flee when Wilson ran over, grabbed him, and wrapped his arm around Richardson's neck. He raised his dagger in the air and stabbed Richardson in his right side. Richardson fell over with a deep, bloody wound. He tried to stand up but he had no strength. Seconds later, he fell onto the cement floor. Wilson put a foot on Richardson's dead body in triumph. Monty then came up and pushed Wilson over.

"If you keep on killing each other, we'll be wiped out before Jacob and Clipper become what we fear," he hissed. "We must work as one legion. Now take care of this body before it smells. I have something for you to do afterwards."

He summoned one of his bearded minions.

"Sally Serene will fly back here sometime today. You and Wilson gather some comrades and bring her here. I have an idea on how to lure Jacob and Clipper into our hands." He reached for a scrap of paper and a tattered pen. "They will fall before they will change, with Sally's help."

CLIPPER GAZED THROUGH THE DOME, ONTO THE MINIATURE ICE rink below. He hoped his hockey team would score the winning goal. One of his players smacked the puck, but missed the net. It fell into the wrong hands, and the opposing team drove the little black puck down the rink. Just as Clipper's goalie was ready to block the upcoming shot, the puck slid right by it. The opposing team scored.

Clipper groaned in defeat as he leaned over the plastic dome. His opponent was his friend and roommate Joshua.

"You play real hockey better than table hockey," Joshua laughed.

"It's this particular table," said Clipper. "It hates me. I swear the red team is rigged just because I like the color red."

Joshua attempted to cheer Clipper up after the close game of table hockey. "I enjoyed hearing your Canadian accent. It makes the game more fun."

"You like my accent, *eh*?" said Clipper. He took a deep breath then looked out a window from the foyer. He stared into the gymnasium.

Inside, I was having a much more brutal experience. I never thought a scrimmage could be so strenuous. I was sweating a lot while running back and forth across the hardwood. I had not played basketball in a long time due to the expedition.

The coach finally blew his whistle and we headed to the bench.

"Great game," one of my teammates said as he cleaned his face with a towel. "I'm glad you're back. You must have all-stars in your family."

"This is my favorite sport," I said. "That's why I'm on the team."

My teammates walked into the locker room after the strenuous practice. I placed my towel on my forehead to absorb the sweat. I looked forward to the oncoming evening when my coach walked up to me. He handed me a peculiar envelope.

"This is for you," was all he told me.

Puzzled, I opened it. There was a note inside. I recognized Sally's handwriting. *I wonder what she needs this time,* I thought.

The note told me to visit a certain place at four o'clock. The address was at the bottom. I returned the note to the envelope and placed it in my gym locker.

I dressed into my casual clothing and decided to find Clipper, but he was nowhere to be seen. Joshua told me that Clipper had also received a note from Sally that instructed him to meet her at the same place and time mentioned in my letter. I did not think much about that. I stepped outside and took a deep breath, enjoying the air.

I pondered over my experiment as I left the gymnasium, fervently hoping the trip would be brief.

As I crossed an intersection on the street, a car missed a red traffic light and slid out of control. It swung straight for me! I had barely enough time to react. I jumped to my right, but I went too far. I hit a brick wall and was knocked unconscious.

SALLY STEPPED OFF THE AIRPLANE AND HEADED FOR THE SUBWAY. She was returning to her apartment. As she waited, she paced across the station platform. She decided to get something to eat during the wait, so she bought a snack from a nearby food stall. It was not long until the train arrived. Sally bit into her halibut sandwich, snickering at the flashback of Clipper's loathing of fish.

The train roared into the station and screeched to a halt. The doors opened and Sally boarded one of the coaches. She had no place to sit, so she grabbed a restraint while standing. The train started. As it picked up speed, Sally took another bite in her sandwich.

She was licking the sauce off her lips when a man, wearing tattered clothing, leaned next to her. Sally felt uneasy at being in such close proximity with him. The man was short and stubby, and smelled as if he had been surrounded by fresh-cut lumber his whole life. Sally did her best to ignore the stranger by biting into her sandwich again. She assumed that the man was just some lunatic. Her uncomfortable mood, however, suddenly turned into shock when the person grabbed her by the arm and whispered in her ear, "If you don't want to die, follow me."

Acting on an instinct of self-defense, Sally angrily nudged the man away. Grunting, the man returned to her side. She pushed him back farther each time he came close to her. After she pushed the man away for the fifth time he discretely pulled out a knife and pressed it in Sally's side. "Do as I say or I'll stab you."

Sally did not expect the knife. She wanted to yell for help, but she knew that if she did so, the stranger would possibly hurt her.

"*Oh, help me,*" she whispered.

She stood next to the stranger when the train stopped. Passengers rushed out and in before it started again. Sally missed her intended stop. Several tears ran down her face. She knew that her life was in jeopardy. All she hoped for now was that Clipper or I would come to the rescue.

The train stopped at an unknown station. The stranger nudged Sally to move. She glumly walked off, dropping what was left of her sandwich on the ground. She expected to see normal people at the station, but was surprised to see more strange folk staring at her. They all looked similar to her kidnapper.

"Look at the helpless woman," one mumbled.

"The others will fall for our Master's trick," another spoke.

Feeling embarrassed, Sally felt a pull on her heartstrings that felt like she was being dragged to her doom. She climbed the stairs beside her abductor and reached the surface. A cold, frigid wind brushed past her face. As they walked by an alleyway, she noticed more woodland people. Sally did not feel like she was in a shady part of the city. She felt like she was in a whole new world where nothing was as it seemed.

The long walk ended when they finally made it to their intended destination. Sally's captor threw her forward. Grunting, she fell to the ground at the feet of the one who was leading the operation.

"Monty Victor," Sally muttered in disgust when she recognized who it was.

"Ah, you remember me. I'm proud of you," Monty said. He thanked the kidnapper.

"How could I forget you? You cheated off my calculus test back in high school, I remember. And that was just one of many things you did. You're a worthless excuse for a human being. You seem to have something against Jacob and Clipper as well."

Monty chuckled. "Poor excuse for a human being, indeed."

To Sally, he did not seem like the bully she remembered. He had changed. His accent sounded different. His whole demeanor seemed different.

"If you're worried, you shouldn't be. Your friends will be here soon," said Monty.

Sally did not respond. She stood still and glared at him.

CHAPTER 4

STRANGE DREAMS

I felt like I had been asleep for days. I slowly opened my eyes, expecting to see hundreds of people around me. The answer unfurled as my vision cleared. What I saw was not downtown. Trees took over the biome. I stood up on a dirt road. This confused me; I was not dressed in the clothes I had on before. I was in armor, something a knight would wear.

Questions were scattered through my mind: What happened to me? Was I knocked out of time? Where on Earth could I possibly be? What is really happening to me?

I would have continued asking more questions had I not heard the sound of galloping horses. Before I could even move, a group of knights stopped in my path. An unknown person dismounted one of the horses and handed me a long, iron sword.

"We are relying on you," the knight said. "You must slay the dragon who lives in the cave down the road."

Before I could say anything, the knight and his company rode away. How strange. The knight said just two sentences and disappeared, yet the simple sentences scared me. I gulped as I slowly walked to the cave. Cautiously I stuck my head in the entrance before I entered. I began sweating even though I shivered with a chilling sense of fear.

Taking a deep breath, I gathered my courage and entered the cave. After advancing a few feet, a heavy wooden door suddenly dropped over the entrance behind me. I was trapped inside with a dragon somewhere nearby! I gulped again, hoping that if I did not make it, I would return to the intersection where I had almost been hit by a car.

I stopped dead in my tracks when a terror-ridden howl reached my ears, followed by a scream of horror. I held out my sword into the darkness. I could barely see a thing. I started panting. The temperature fell the deeper I ventured into the cave.

I stopped again. Further down the cave a dim light shone. It was so relieving. I never thought I would be so happy to see light. A brick lifted from my chest, making it easier to breathe. I ran towards the flickering light. When I reached it, I saw that it was only a torch on a wooden pole that stood in the center ground. Fear possessed me once more. I picked up the torch and walked deeper into the cave, expecting doom at any moment. I knew this dragon I was after could jump out and send my soul to the nether kingdom when I least expected it.

I continued moving. I walked and walked and walked some more and then… I stopped. I could have sworn I heard a voice calling my name; my last name at least.

"Draco."

I turned around. Nothing. I resumed walking when I heard the voice again.

"Draco!"

The voice was louder the second time. It was not a human voice. It sounded lower and rough, like a voice from a creature I had never known: the voice of a dragon.

"Where are you?" I shivered.

No answer came, just my name even louder than before, "Draco. Jacob Draco!"

I turned to the right. A set of glowing, amber eyes stared at me. I took one small step away from the eyes. When I saw a figure, I took another step back. I could not stop my arms and legs from trembling. A feeling of ice settled within me.

I pointed my sword at the figure. "S-Surrender, d-dragon!"

The figure jumped forward and landed next to me, causing me to fall to the ground in fright. I accidentally threw my sword to the side when I fell. Sure enough, it was the dragon. It was larger than me. It had long brownish-white horns, sharp teeth, broad leathery wings, and spikes along the back of its black-scaled body. I tried to stand up, but the dragon pushed me back onto the ground. Its tail flickered behind it. I did not know what to do.

"Just deal with me however you want," I cried. "I'm a dead man already!"

"It's not death," the dragon said. "I'm your greatest creation."

I tried to look away at the dragon's eyes. "I don't understand."

"You are me! I'm your greatest creation," it said. "Listen to yourself!"

I had no idea what he was talking about. I squirmed with all the strength I had left and freed myself from his grasp. I ran back to the entrance of the cave, yelling as I bashed through the door that was meant to trap me inside. Adrenaline pumped through me as I ran down the path. When I was far away from the cave, I slowed. I thought I had lost the dragon. I turned around to check, only to discover that I was wrong. The dragon was sitting like a dog right in front of me, its face composed in a very neutral expression.

Acting on instinct, I covered my head with my arms with just my eyes peeking through. I then heard a familiar noise. The knights on their horses came charging up to save me. But the knights stopped about ten feet away from the two of us.

"Don't just stand there," I yelled. "Help me!"

"Slay him!" one of the knights called. "Slay him!"

I stood up. I was about to run off when I realized the dragon was gone. It was *me* standing where the dragon had been! The duplicate of myself picked up his own sword, ready to kill me. Why was I going after myself? I did not even have my own sword anymore.

"Slay him!" the knight shouted again.

I turned around to see if the knights knew what was going on. They were looking at the other me, encouraging him. I suddenly realized what was happening.

I was the dragon! *I* had the sharp claws and black scales. I WAS THE DRAGON!

"Slay him!" the knight shouted once more.

The other me was ready to lower his blade. I was too cowardly to fight back or run away. I hunkered down, ready for the blade to pierce me.

"Don't!" I wailed. "Please put the sword down. I'm not evil. Listen to Chang. Listen!"

I WOKE UP IN HORROR. I SAW THE FAINT IMAGE OF A HUMAN BEING standing above me. Still caught up in my dream, I thought it was my counterpart about to kill me. I grabbed him and tossed him away from me. Guilt struck me when I realized that the person I had just thrown was a policeman. He stood back up, dazed and confused. Realizing that I was back in reality, I instantly apologized to the policeman. Luckily, he understood. I told him I was fine and that I did not need medical help.

"Sorry, officer. I really am," I said quietly.

"I'm okay. Just be careful," the officer replied.

I returned to my trek to meet Sally after answering a few more of the officer's questions. I was glad I had not been unconscious for very long, even though it felt like I had been. The officer told me I had only been out for a few minutes. I had no serious head injury, but the thought of me as a dragon would not leave my mind. Surely, I was the monster in my dream. I was the cause of my own nightmare.

It also confused me how the dragon kept saying that it was my creation, or why I had said, "Listen to Chang." Baffled, I continued on.

CLIPPER REACHED THE MEETING PLACE BEFORE I DID. HE LOOKED around the complex, finding nothing but a flock of pigeons. He wondered why Sally would want to meet him there. We had known Sally for a couple of years. Clipper knew that she was capable of something like this as a joke: leading him to a strange place for no reason.

"Sally, this isn't funny," Clipper shouted. "If you're not here, I'm leaving!"

Just as he turned around to leave, he realized that something was wrong. He paused as he heard a peculiar noise, as if someone was trying to squirm his or her way out of something.

"Sally, are you here?" he called in concern.

He walked around the complex. He froze when he found Sally tied to a chair with a kerchief wrapped around her mouth. A pile of bricks was stacked beside her. Gasping in horror, Clipper ran over to her and undid the kerchief.

"Sally, are you all right?" he asked.

"It's a trap!" Sally warned. "Leave now!"

Clipper tried to loosen the rope around Sally's arms. But before he made any progress, Monty's men encircled him. Some of them were armed with daggers; others had rusted revolvers or rifles. Most of them wore long, button-downed shirts and tattered trousers. Clipper wondered what these people wanted.

Monty stepped out of the darkness. "Sorry about this, Clipper. Life is tough. I know."

"What do you want, Monty?" Clipper demanded.

"Simple: the samples you and Jacob collected."

Clipper did not expect to hear that request. "Why do you want the samples? Even if I had them with me right now, I wouldn't dream of giving them to you."

Monty snorted. "Let's just say I do not want you to become what my, should I say, men have long feared. I'm trying to save you and Jacob both, Clipper. What you have could make something the world is not yet ready for. If you give them to me, I promise I will leave you alone."

"What? Us becoming what your men long feared? Jacob and I don't have anything like that."

"Wait until Jacob comes, then I will make you bring the samples," said Monty.

Clipper stopped protesting. Angrily, he picked up a nearby cement block and hurled it at Monty. With surprisingly good reflexes, Monty instantly dodged the block. "Get him Wilson," he commanded.

Wilson pulled out his old revolver and aimed it at Clipper. Clipper immediately reacted and smacked it out of Wilson's hand, then took off running out of the complex. He reached the alley in seconds. Wilson picked up his weapon and ran after him, all the while Sally watched anxiously.

"No!" Monty cried. "I told you, don't kill him! I only told you to get him, you sick rat!"

Clipper did not hear what Monty said. Glancing left and right, he found he had no route for escape. He could not run for long on his bad foot. He would be spotted if he tried to limp out of the alley. It was the incident on Komodo Island all over again! He had to find a place to hide, and quick. The only option he found was behind a nearby dumpster. Without hesitation, he limped over to the dumpster and crouched down, preparing to tackle Wilson when he came by.

Peering around the corner of the dumpster, Clipper saw Wilson leap into the alley. Monty came up beside him and smacked him on the back of the head.

"Where's Clipper?" Monty asked.

"I have no idea where he's gone," Wilson answered.

Monty smacked him again. "Then I recommend you go search for him."

Rubbing his head, Wilson slowly walked in Clipper's direction. Just before he reached Clipper's hiding spot, Monty pulled out a small dagger and stuck it in Wilson's back. Wilson was dead before he hit the ground. Clipper froze, keeping Monty unaware of his presence. He was not safe for long when he accidentally tripped over an empty glass bottle. Monty followed the noise.

At the end of the alley, Clipper saw a woman out in the street who had witnessed the scene. She fled immediately.

Monty must have seen her too. He ran back into the complex and ordered all his men to evacuate. "We must leave immediately. Wilson is dead. Someone has seen it and the police may be coming. Move now!"

The men scattered and ran out into the streets. Monty yanked Sally out of her chair and pulled her along.

Clipper furtively rose from behind the dumpster. Monty was gone, and if he was found there, he could be blamed for the crime. He escaped just as the first officers arrived at the scene.

THE WALK SEEMED LIKE AN ETERNITY, BUT I FINALLY MADE IT. I noticed flashing red and blue lights at the alley as I arrived. Something was wrong. Curious to see what the fuss was about, I watched as the body of an unknown person was covered and placed in a coroner's van. I did not know how to react to the scene before me. I became concerned about Clipper and Sally. They were nowhere to be seen.

What's going on? I thought. All I knew was that someone had been killed and Clipper and Sally were gone. I had to know what happened. I began fearing for my friends' lives.

I held my head in my hands. My mind had been on the strange dream, and now it was all over whatever had happened here. Leaving the alley, I searched up and down the street until I found Clipper sitting on a bench. He appeared upset. I was relieved to see him, but I was afraid of what he knew.

"Clipper, there you are," I called. "Do you know what happened? Where's Sally?"

Clipper ran his hands through his hair in agitation. He explained how Monty was holding Sally and how he had killed Wilson. The mention of Monty caused my hair to stand.

"I'm sorry, Jacob. I did my best," said Clipper. "Monty left before I could do anything. He still has Sally. I can't take this all in. We have to do something!"

I agreed. I did not care about my own life as long as Sally's was in danger. I worried for her. I did not want Monty to hurt her. He was twisted enough to make it very hard on Sally and see no fault in his actions. Sally had to be freed as soon as possible.

"Don't worry, Clipper," I said with more confidence in my voice than I really felt. "We'll find a way to rescue her."

Clipper and I immediately formulated a plan to free Sally. *Tonight may be well remembered as the day we saved Sally's life*, I thought.

My mind was reeling. I had Monty's killing, Sally, and the dream all in my head at the same time. For some reason I felt they were connected. No matter, I had to free Sally. It was going to be quite difficult if I was distracted by that dream. Why was the dragon not leaving my mind?

CHAPTER 5

RESCUING THE HOSTAGE

S ally remained blindfolded, tied up on a chair inside the complex where she had been hours earlier. As twilight closed in and the police finally left, the risk to her life increased. She did not know what was going to happen. All she believed was that if Monty's plan failed, she would die a horrible death.

Monty stood in front of Sally. He knew he was in control. He knew Clipper and me and was expecting us to try and break her out in our unique way of planning.

"Go ahead and do whatever you want. What is *your* life worth?" said Sally, knowing Monty was in front of her.

Monty crouched next to Sally. "Let me tell you what will happen if you attempt to escape while we're alone. If you anger me, disappoint me, or set off my fuse in any way, then you will suffer in a terrible way. You know me; I don't get angry that easily. But my blasted...er... men are too overwhelmed by this New York life. It torments me. I am calm now, but please don't add to my wrath. It's for your own good."

Sally remained silent. The idea of suffering scared her. If she was going to die, she wanted it to be a quick and painless death.

Monty clapped for the attention of Luke, one of his main body-guards. "Make sure Sally doesn't escape. That just might be a fatal mistake for the both of you."

"Right. I'll make sure she stays secure," Luke respectfully replied.

"Good. I'm going to watch out for the two people we are expect-ing. When they come, I'll have Raymond go to their home."

I WAS IN CLIPPER'S DORMITORY. HIS ROOMMATE JOSHUA WAS NOT home. We were glad we did not have to tell him about Sally just yet. We sat on Clipper's bed, laying out our plan of rescue.

"We have to be careful, Clipper. You won't have to worry about police custody if you're dead," I warned him.

"I'm aware of that," he said. "The thing we have to do now is rescue Sally. That's all what matters."

I took a deep breath. "Are you ready?"

"Absolutely. Let's go find her."

It was night when we returned to the old complex that Monty called home. We decided to make our move before the police launched another investigation in the area since they had yet to catch the true murderer. We heard the dripping of water and the haunting echoes of Monty's territory in the dangerous alley. I knew Monty, though. He liked to pretend he was elsewhere. Just when you thought he was gone, you should look over your shoulder.

With my brow sweating, I glanced around before slipping inside. I knew Sally was somewhere in the building. I also knew that Monty was more than likely on the lookout for me.

All was silent. I moved quietly around the building alone. Clipper was off taking care of his part of the plan. I hoped being alone was a good idea. The complex was spooky. But I could not back off now. There was a life I had to save. No matter the fear inside me, I could not let it slow me down. I would never avoid something terrifying and let my friend die. I could never have forgiven myself. Much as I wanted to keep Sally's rescue uppermost in my mind, the dream about the black dragon still bothered me. It would not leave my thoughts.

I reached the stairway and scanned the other side of the large room for any enemies. There was no sign of any living thing. I stepped away from the stairs and entered another portion of the complex. At this point it felt like I was trapped in a maze.

CLIPPER WAS ON THE ROOFTOP OF THE BUILDING NEXT TO THE complex. He waited there as the seconds ticked up to his next phase. He stood up and walked backwards, away from the complex, just a few feet away from the destined rooftop. Before he jumped, Clipper felt nervous. He remembered swinging across the canyon on Komodo Island. He closed his eyes, reopened them, and started running. He ran to the edge and jumped as far as he could.

He landed on his feet on the complex roof, holding his stomach. His fear of heights often nauseated him. He took a moment to rest his hurt foot before continuing. He found a door that led to more stairs. Clipper figured Sally was down there. As he descended, darkness engulfed the eerie location.

He just reached the bottom of the stairs when one of Monty's men came storming out. Clipper had been expecting this. "Here he comes," he muttered to himself. "Hey, what's going on? Where's Sally?" he asked, trying to catch the guard's attention.

The guard did not say anything. He charged Clipper with a knife. Clipper reacted quickly and tackled the guard, who went down flat on his back. Before he could get up, Clipper grabbed a wooden plank nearby and brought it down on his enemy's head. The plank snapped in two pieces. The guard was down, unconscious. Clipper was unharmed. He dropped the broken plank and continued on his way. "He wasn't expecting me to fight back," he snickered to himself.

AS CLIPPER WAS DOING HIS PART, SO WAS I. JUST AS HE DID, I TOOK out two guards with a wooden plank. Turning left and right, I had a hard time finding my way. It no longer felt like I was in just any maze. I felt like I was in the Minotaur's Maze, with danger lurking around unknown corners.

"I'm not trapped. I can find my way through," I whispered to keep myself in a positive mood.

Several minutes passed. I was still lost. I searched this room, but I found no sign of Sally. I debated whether or not she was even in the complex. As I searched through the many corridors, I found a long, dark hallway with railings alongside its walls. Sally could be down that hallway with Monty at her side, ready to ambush me. I would fight back if necessary. I had no source of light, so I slowly stepped into the darkness, ready for anything.

As I slugged along, I heard a low-pitched moan. I was unable to tell if it was real or in my head. It was followed by a voice similar to mine, "*Draco! Jacob Draco! I am your greatest creation. I have been a myth since the Dark Ages. You are your greatest creation.*"

Was this a dream again? It did not feel like one. I was not a knight in a cave this time. Growing tense, I clutched tightly to the railing. I continued to hear the constant moan. Then, in the darkness, I thought I saw a pair of eyes up ahead, glowing eyes. Moving closer, I realized they did not look human. They were the color of amber, just like the dragon's in my dream. I stopped in the middle of the tunnel as the ground began to quake. The vibration ran through my body. I did not know what to do. This was not a dream!

"Who's there?" I asked.

There was no answer. I was about to flee back the way I had come when the quaking stopped, the eyes vanished, and the moaning faded. I shook off the grim feeling and resumed my journey down the dark hallway.

What was going on? My mind was playing with me when I encountered the dragon statues, then the dream, and now this. The voice said that I was its greatest creation before saying that I was my own greatest creation. *What is with dragons?* I wondered.

It took a while, but I finally reached a dim room. And, of course, there was Sally, just as I figured. She sat on a chair, tied up and blindfolded. Monty stood next to her, holding a strange-looking dagger. The blade was clean and the handle had the image of a snake.

"You can't possibly kill her. You wouldn't do something like that," I said to Monty.

"Oh, I can, Jacob. I have killed before and I'll do it again," Monty replied, chuckling. "Say, do you know why I hold a grudge against you? You may find it baffling as to why I dislike you. There is a reason."

Monty had just started talking about my expedition around the world when a panel on the ceiling suddenly collapsed. Clipper dove through and landed on Monty.

"Nice work," I said.

I snatched the dagger from Monty and used it to cut the ropes that bound Sally. Our mission was accomplished. The moment her arms were free, she hugged Clipper and then me.

"Hey, you should be more careful who you hang out with," I joked.

"Very funny," she answered. "Now can we please go?"

"We're on our way. I know what it's like being tied up, too."

"At least you didn't lose a toe," Clipper added glumly.

I ignored his remark and tied the rope around Monty's wrists. When I finished, the three of us took off down another hallway and up several flights of stairs. We found ourselves on the roof of the complex. We sprinted across the roof and hurtled over the alley. We were on the building where had Clipper started out.

"We need to call the police, but let's get out of here first," I suggested.

From within the doorway, we heard Monty yelling for his guards.

Without hesitation, we descended the fire escape. I was satisfied with the day's events. It seemed so easy getting past Monty and freeing Sally. Now Clipper and I could continue on with our experiment. We jumped down from the lowest level of the fire escape and headed for home.

"I hope Chang remembered to pick us up," I said.

There was no need to worry. Once we left the alley, Chang's car pulled up beside us.

"Is Sally okay?" Chang asked as he opened the door on his side.

"I'm fine," said Sally.

I opened the rear door and ushered Sally in first. As Clipper was about to climb into the car, three of Monty's men came running from the complex.

My heart started to race. "We've got trouble!"

Chang set the car in gear. I kept the window to my door down as the car screeched across the pavement. The three men stood in our way and pointed their firearms at us. They dove for cover when Chang drove straight toward them. They jumped into a nearby car and, seconds later, were right behind us. I knew speed was not a big factor through the city traffic. Our pursuers just drove past and sometimes bumped into other vehicles. They caught up to us and swerved to the left, where they tried to bump Chang's car off the street.

Growing aggressive, Chang swerved his car toward theirs. Their car veered off to the side, but they were back on our tail a few seconds later. We had to get rid of them. I leaned forward so Chang could hear me clearly.

"Give me the brick, some napkins, and some matches! I know you have all those things. And that lighter fluid right there."

Chang was too busy dodging traffic, so Clipper gathered the items instead. The napkins on the dashboard were from a past lunch, the matchbox and lighter fluid were from a cookout at the college, and Chang had acquired the brick when vandals destroyed our window one night. We had half of a brick, to be precise. Clipper handed the supplies to me as the car skidded around a bus. I told Chang to get into the other lane to better my aim. The pursuing car was close behind us, making a good target.

I wrapped the napkins around the brick and, holding it out the window, poured lighter fluid on it. I clasped the napkins together so they would not blow away. Clipper then struck the first match on the box. It burned out instantly. He struck the other with the same result. It took him a few tries to get a good flame. He gave it to me and I held it out beside my diversion before it blew out. Oh, how I wished there was some other way to ignite my diversion. Finally, a small fire touched the napkin and a flame erupted, scorching my fingers in the process. With no time to waste, I hurled the brick into the air. The second it left my hand I blew on my fingers to ease the burning pain. The heat was too intense for my human flesh. The brick hit the hood of our pursuers' car before embedding itself in the windshield. The car spun out of control and crashed into a streetlight.

I was satisfied with my work. My distraction had done just what I wanted it to do. I cheered, but I kept my fists clenched from the burns.

"You should go to the police station while we return to the dorms," Clipper told Chang. "We'll join up with you soon enough so we can tell them what happened."

When we reached the dormitories, Chang drove off after Sally thanked us one last time. Clipper and I kept a sharp eye to see if Monty's men were still after us. There was no sign of them. We were very pleased with ourselves and our successful rescue.

"Next time, I go on the roof, and you go down the creepy tunnel," I said to Clipper.

"Oh, so *you* want the responsibility of falling through the roof?" he replied, laughing.

We continued to joke around until we reached my room. All joviality immediately ceased when we entered. My bed had been overturned. The knapsack was on the sheets. I could not believe my eyes. Who had been here? Why? It had to be one of Monty's people.

"Oh no," Clipper gasped. "The knapsack is here, but the samples are gone. Monty has our samples!"

My heart felt like it stopped.

CHAPTER 6

STEALING THE SAMPLES

Anger burned in my heart. All the work Clipper and I had done, all the work and all that time gone in a flash. I was very embarrassed. We had gloated about how easy had been to free Sally. Monty was sly. He had tricks up his sleeve as well. I should have seen it coming. Tears ran down my face.

"It's all right. At least we're all safe," said Clipper.

I ignored his attempt for condolence. I stepped out of the room to the front of the foyer. I kept saying to myself, "The samples are gone. The samples are gone."

Suddenly I collapsed onto the outside steps. Some odd force that felt alien mysteriously sapped my strength. I had the urge to sleep. I fought to overcome the temptation, but it was too strong. My eyelids grew heavy and closed.

IT FELT LIKE ONLY A FEW SECONDS PASSED. WHEN I OPENED MY eyes, I found myself running through the abandoned streets of New York City. There was no sign of people. All the plants were overgrown, making the city look like a large forest.

Why was I still running? Was this another dream? It felt like more than a dream. It felt real, but I had no way of telling. I stopped running and sat down on a marble bench. As I caught my breath,

I looked around. The sky was red and the air was humid. This did not feel like spring New York weather at all.

I stood up when I heard a roar echo through the city. It was an awful sound. The hair on my arms stood straight up. I covered my ears. Where was the eerie noise coming from? Maybe it was the reason I had been running in the first place. I resumed running. I ran far and fast. I did not stop until I came upon a polar bear standing in the middle of an intersection. I looked at it in curiosity. What was a polar bear doing here? It did nothing but stare at me with no hostility at all. A goat strolled by and a bearded dragon scurried past my feet. Even a Komodo dragon was present! More and more animals came and joined the group. All these were the animals that I had collected blood from for my experiment! They joined into one large group, staring at me with pleading eyes. They wanted me to do something. I stood still, frozen.

I decided to walk towards them. But before I got close enough to the wild group, they vanished into thin air. The roar came again.

"Where am I?" I cried at the top of my lungs. "Somebody tell me!"

I stood still, more confused than ever. Where had the animals gone? I sat down to think, but immediately stood back up. I had sat as if I had four feet. I began to sit down again, slower than before. Again, I did not sit like I usually did. I could not understand it. I stood up again. But when I stood up, I was on four feet.

This frightened me. I started to run again. I was running much faster now. I sped across the deserted streets until I suddenly found myself in a real forest. I ran until I came across a pond. Without thinking, I jumped in and paddled. I was usually a terrible swimmer. This time I swam swiftly through the water.

When I regained control of myself, I jumped out of the pond. Once the water calmed, I stared at my reflection. I did not see myself. I saw the dragon that had haunted my dreams before. I was the monster! I was the dragon!

JORDAN B. JOLLEY

My reflection was clear enough. I was a legendary, fire-breathing dragon. In panic, I flew into the air. As I glided over the green land, I felt thrilled. Flying was actually fun, save the burning in my chest. The pain started to increase to the point where it frightened me.

I had never felt fear like this before. I flew as fast as I could. I continued to fly until everything went dark.

I WOKE UP IN A COLD SWEAT. WHEN I REGAINED MY SENSES, I looked around. I saw the thriving college campus in the early evening. I stood up with a churning pain in my stomach. I held still, wondering why I kept dreaming of this black-scaled dragon.

A moment later, Clipper came out to join me. He seemed just as dazed as I was.

"We need to get the samples back," he said.

"You were calming me down a few minutes ago," I replied.

"Well, I didn't really want to say anything. But for the past few days, I've experienced odd dreams. There always seems to be a dragon in my dream. And sometimes I am that dragon, long sharp teeth and all. I know what I said, and I'm glad Sally is safe. But we need to get the samples back."

How was it possible that Clipper was having similar dreams as I had?

"I know what you mean. I've been having those dreams as well," I said.

"Anyway, I thought you would want to get the samples back more than I do. You were really upset."

"I do want the samples back, and I also want to know why we're having these dreams. They scare me!"

Clipper tried to keep the subject on the samples. "So how are we going to get our samples back?"

"The only idea that comes to mind is to *steal* them back," I said.

Clipper tilted his head. "And how are we going to do that? We fell for Monty's trick. I don't think this next time will be as easy as rescuing Sally."

"I don't know what to do, but I'll try to think of something." I was still very upset, but I had a little bit of confidence now.

We waited until dawn before we executed our plan, even though we did not sleep a wink. Chang and Joshua gave us some help forming the plan. I did not want to place them in any danger, however.

When morning came, Clipper finished a drawing of a map of the complex. I examined the map as Clipper explained the route, "If I know Monty, he'll have his complex heavily guarded this time, much more than before."

"He'll probably have his best guards - he calls them watchdogs if I remember - on the lookout for us. I don't think the roof is the best option this time. We can't go through, around, or over the complex without being spotted."

"What about under?" I suggested. "Take the sewer lines. They shouldn't be guarded."

"Sewer lines? Anywhere but that!"

"It's the only way. I'm not looking forward to it either, but it could lead to an opening where you or I could squeeze through."

"All right, all right."

"Maybe you can stay far out from the building. Be about three blocks away or so. I'll travel the sewer lines to the main complex. The watchdogs won't spot me at all. I'll just be a figure in the shadows. When I retrieve the samples, I'll break for the entrance of the building. By this point, I may be spotted. You come up the alleyway in Chang's car. I jump in and we escape. Simple as that."

Clipper sighed. "That plan sounds good, but how will I know when to come to the alleyway? And how will you find your way through the sewers?"

I retrieved a set of small microphones from a case. "We can talk with these. I'll keep you informed you of my progress."

Clipper nodded in approval. "I see. How will you know which way to go in the sewers? And what if a watchdog spots me?"

"Hmm. That's right." I thought for a moment. "Keep a safe distance away. Come when I get the samples, like I said. If they spot you, there'll be watchdogs around the whole block. If they notice even anything suspicious, they'll tell Monty. And while they do that, we'll escape. They'll expect us to come to him. But really, we are just leaving.

"As for the sewer lines...Let me think. Hmm. You can go to the library and find some maps. You can guide me through the sewers with them. And we really should let Sally know what's happening."

Clipper nodded and left for the library. I picked up my phone and dialed Sally's number. "Sally, this is Jacob. Where are you?" I said when she picked up.

"I just got back to my room," she answered. "Where are you?"

"I'm at my dorm and Clipper's on his way to the library. He's finding maps of the sewer lines. We've got to get our samples back from Monty."

"Monty has the samples?" Sally's voice was loud in the phone.

"Don't worry. We're getting them back." I said.

"That's a bad idea," said Sally. "You two need the police to handle this."

"We can't involve the police. This is our problem and we've got to take care of it. Please don't notify any authorities."

I heard Sally moan on the other line. "Jacob, all I know is that you are going to steal back the samples with no help. And why are sewer lines involved? Think about what you're doing."

I did not answer. I hung up the phone after saying goodbye. Clipper returned less than an hour later. He did not have the maps from the library, but he drew copies as he did with the complex. We viewed the lines and tunnels going in every direction. It took me a moment, but I found the pathway I was looking for. I drew a line through the correct path with a pen.

"Now remember," I said, "don't get too close until I'm ready. We don't want Monty's watchdogs to spot you and come after us before we have the samples back."

"You're not enjoying this, are you?" Clipper said with nerve in his voice.

"No, I'm desperate."

Clipper noticed how serious I was. "Don't worry," he said, rubbing the space between his nose and upper lip. "This is like our experience at Komodo Island. It seems unexpected and scary. But if we take it one step at a time, everything will work out."

Clipper was right. His words comforted my troubled heart. I looked down at the knapsack that hung on my desk chair. I took it with me. Once we were ready, Clipper and I walked out of the dormitory and climbed in Chang's car, with Chang's permission, of course.

"I just know I'm going to end up with bullet holes in this car," Clipper said. His voice sounded fragile; it was not often it sounded like that.

He parked the car alongside the street, a few blocks away from Monty's complex. I took one of the microphones and strapped it around my head. I would be able to hear Clipper in my left ear. Clipper activated his microphone, too.

"Ready?" he asked me.

I took a deep breath. "I'm ready."

I got out of the car, approached the manhole, and opened it. All I saw was a large stretch of mist in the darkness. I was quite nervous at first, but as I jumped in, I pushed it aside. The smell was strong; I had to ignore it. I stepped through the tunnels with a flashlight in one hand.

"I'm in the sewers," I said.

"I can hear you well," Clipper replied on the other end.

I made my way through the sewer line. With Clipper guiding me, I veered past twists and turns. I was glad Clipper had the map with him. If not, I would have been lost once I entered the sewers.

I sensed cool air and figured I was near another opening. I followed the cold air. All was well until I felt a small tremor.

"Did you feel that, Clipper?" I asked.

"Feel what?"

"The ground shook a little."

"I didn't feel anything."

I tried not to worry about the tremor. I chose to believe that the sewer lines quaked once in a while. I started walking again.

That was when I heard the strange voice again: "*Achieve your goal, make your creation. You will help many others.*"

I shook my head, believing that it was my subconscious mind talking. *Dragons again. I don't want to hear it,* I thought. Pressing on, I eventually rounded a bend. There was a dead end, with a ladder stretching to the surface. I told Clipper I was at the ladder. Clipper said it was the right place. I held the flashlight between my teeth and climbed. About halfway up, I heard a strange swishing noise in my left ear. It sounded like Clipper was moving.

"Jacob, be careful," he warned me. "The watchdogs out here are armed. They have old rifles. They haven't seen me yet. Keep a sharp eye, will you?"

I was up the ladder and just outside a small door to the complex. I heeded Clipper's warning and checked for anyone before opening the door.

I turned off the flashlight and slipped it into my knapsack. "I'm in the complex now," I whispered.

I spied on one of the guards near a hallway. He did not see me. As I did when I avoided the rebels, I slid past him. He did not even notice the slight sound I had made. That was one room gone by. I assumed the samples were in a room down the dark tunnel I had crossed before. I took off through the darkness once I reached the passage. I did not use my flashlight.

It was not long before I reached the other end of the tunnel. I scanned the different rooms, checking to make sure there were no guards. Not a living thing was in sight. Maybe this would be easier than I thought!

That thought did not last long. There was a guard in the room that I was about to enter. I saw him through the cracked door. How could I get past this one? With time to think, I had an idea. The guard was leaning against a wall, facing away from me. As he idled, I jumped up and down.

"Monty, is that you?" he said.

I did not answer. I wanted him to leave the room. Once he stepped out, he turned towards me. I attacked him before he could react, boxing him left and right. Blood drizzled from his nose and cheeks. I wrapped my arms around his, restraining them. No matter how much he squirmed, he could not escape. I opened a nearby closet door and threw him in, closing the door and jamming it shut.

With the only guard in the room defeated, I would easily find the samples now.

"What was all that noise? Are you all right?" Clipper asked.

"I took care of a guard," I murmured. "I'm all right."

"You're doing great."

I searched the walls of the room, expecting to find some sort of cabinet. There was nothing except for a painting. On the floor, I saw an imprint where something used to be. Whatever it was, it had to have been moved.

"Clipper, I'm stuck. I don't know where the samples might be. I thought that they would be in this room in a cabinet or something." I kept my voice as quiet as possible.

Clipper was silent for a moment. "If they don't want you to get our samples, they may have moved them to a basement. There could be a secret entry to it."

I scanned the room. There was no sign of a passageway any-where. I hoped I could find it in here. Then it came to me. There were small gaps in the room's far wall. I then looked at the painting. Such a random place for artwork. The gaps were next to the paint-ing. Yes, it had to be a door.

I tried to push it open, but to no avail. If it was a door, it was locked. I looked back at the painting and removed it from the wall. A small chamber was revealed. I slid my hand inside it where I felt some sort of stone handle. Maybe it was a latch to open the door. I pulled on it with much effort.

As expected, the more I pulled on the handle, the more the camouflaged door in the wall opened. I pulled out my flashlight once the door was open wide enough. There was a stairway leading down. Praying that the samples were down there, I descended the stairs.

At the bottom, I found a cabinet. I made sure there were no other guards near it. No one was in the secret basement but me. With fingers crossed, I opened the door to the cabinet. Sure enough, there they were. The samples were in there, smiling at me, encased in a wooden box with an open top.

"They're here!" I said in delight.

"You found the samples? Great job!" Clipper exclaimed.

It was official. Fate had taken our side. We could continue on with our experiment, and I looked forward to the day I no longer had to worry about Monty.

Just before I made my way out, however, I felt a funny sensation come over my hands. The samples… they did not feel like the samples Clipper and I had collected. They felt like an elixir of magic. *I'm too happy. It just feels this way,* I thought.

I pushed the feeling from my mind. Without a moment's hesitation, I transferred the samples out of the wooden box and into my knapsack where they had originally been. I had brought the box with me just in case I found a use for it. I hung the knapsack around my shoulder and headed up the stairs. All was well. Now it was time for the escape.

I returned to the room. The guard I had locked in the closet was still banging on the door. I left him and entered the dark tunnel. At that moment, a watchdog entered the room. Apparently, he had not seen me. I heard the two from the tunnel.

"Help!" cried the guard from inside the closet.

I heard the door open.

"I'm glad you're here," said the guard. "Jacob Draco, he's here. He came in and hit me. Now he has the samples."

"Jacob has the samples? Why didn't you stop him?" yelled the watchdog.

"I tried to capture him, but he caught me by surprise. The moment I stepped out of the room, he punched me. My nose may be broken!"

"Never mind your nose. Tell Monty that Jacob is here. He must not escape. I'll spread the warning. We'll make sure Jacob doesn't escape with the samples. Oh, and be sure to keep an eye out for the other one. If Jacob is here, so is Clipper."

I heard no more as I made my escape.

The two men separated. The first guard went to Monty, opposite of the dark tunnel. The rifle-armed watchdog went down the path I had taken. By the time I reached the other end of the dark tunnel, I knew he was following me. I looked around in panic, trying to find something to slow him down. I found a dusty shelf and quickly moved it in front of the tunnel, then continued running with the samples and the box.

I heard the watchdog moving the shelf aside. When I turned around, I saw him chasing me. The sight of his rifle made my heart skip a beat. One shot could kill me!

Clipper's voice became tense. "I hear something. What's wrong?"

I did not answer. I tried to stay as quiet as possible. Clipper understood as well and remained silent. He probably feared for my life, as I did.

As the watchdog chased me down the halls, Monty sat in his office. He was talking to Raymond, complimenting him for his service. Both jumped when the guard ran in.

"Have you seen Jacob and Clipper?" Monty asked.

"Yes! We found Jacob. He has the samples! I tried to stop him, but he hit me."

Monty clenched his fists. "You…idiot! You weren't doing your job properly. Go find Jacob. I'll alert the watchdogs. We can't let him escape. Move!"

The dazed guard stumbled off while Monty stepped out onto the balcony of his office. He yelled as loud as he could so all the watchdogs would hear him. "Jacob Draco's here! Find him now. Kill him if you must, but make sure the samples are ours."

He walked back into his office. "First they get away with Sally Serene, now this. Why can't my guards be like you, Raymond? Do you remember what will happen if they get away?"

Raymond cowered. "I don't want to imagine it. I will search for them immediately."

When Raymond was gone, Monty sat down with sweat on his forehead. He feared for the events yet to come.

I RAN PAST DIRTY WINDOWS AND THE DARK-GREEN COLORED WALLS, panting from exertion. The watchdog was right behind me, but he did not fire his gun. He must have known he would not get clean shot in the dim light.

I came to a split in the hallway. I could not remember which way to go. "I'm at the split Clipper, which way should I take?"

Clipper took a second before he answered. I heard him rustling through the maps. "Left," he said. "Go left!"

I took off down the left hallway. I traveled only a few yards then stopped. Two guards stood in front of me. Acting on instinct, I charged into them, knocking them both back. They rubbed their heads for several seconds then started after me. As I ran, I dropped the box. I turned around to pick it up. I raised it a few feet from the ground when one of the guards fired his revolver. The bullet destroyed the box, turning it into sawdust and splinters. I immediately dropped what was left of the box and began to move. I ran into a room with an opened door. I saw a bucket full of ice and glass bottles of some sort of drink. I picked up a few bottles, kicked over the bucket, then took off down the hallway again.

Waiting until the three men were closer to me, I hurled a bottle at them. It struck one of the guards in the sternum. I threw the second bottle. That one whizzed past the two pursuers and hit the same guard as before. I threw my third and final bottle. That one shattered in front of the two running men. The last guard slipped on the shards and liquid. The watchdog was still on his feet and still after me.

Looking behind me as I ran, I checked to see how far away he was. That turned out to be a mistake. The watchdog fired his rifle. The bullet missed my forehead by inches. I yelped from the close call. Clipper would expect the worse.

"Jacob!" he shouted. "Are you all right? Answer me!"

I did not answer. I was too busy wrestling the watchdog. He was big and tall, and a lot stronger than I ever was. He pinned me to the ground the moment I had charged him. Just as he was about to clout me, I raised my legs. My feet struck the watchdog in the back. He went rolling forward and bashed through a window.

His scream faded as I stood up. I looked out the window. The watchdog had landed in a garbage dumpster head first. He was alive but hurt.

I continued down the hallway, knowing that the other guards were still after me.

"Jacob, answer me! Please answer me," Clipper called again.

"I'm all right," I panted. "He missed me."

Clipper sighed in relief. "Thank goodness he missed. Next time you yelp, say something to me *then* go after the enemy, okay?"

"I'll do that."

I resumed running with Clipper guiding me where I needed to go. Finally, I was in the main area of the complex. I informed Clipper of my location and told him to get ready. Soon enough, I heard the car speeding toward me.

"When you get here, get in fast," Clipper warned. "Some watchdogs just spotted me and are after me. I don't want to die just yet."

JORDAN B. JOLLEY

When I reached the outside of the complex, I saw Clipper's car come into view. I opened the rear door and dove in. "Go now!" I shouted.

The tires squealed as the car raced forward. I looked behind. Two watchdogs were running after us. One fired his rifle, but missed us. Despite their desperation, it was too late. We were gone.

I took off the microphone and opened the knapsack once they were out of sight. The flashlight was in there, along with our prized samples. Nothing was missing or harmed. We had successfully escaped with what was rightfully ours.

BACK IN MONTY'S OFFICE, HIS MEN RELAYED THE NEWS OF OUR escape. With a simple sigh, he stood up from his desk and walked out onto the balcony.

"They have them. There's no need to steal them back," he said in a calm and defeated tone. "It's time we stop hiding. We must realize that our enemy has returned after thousands of years. If our one and only legion is to remain victorious, we need to take action now. Warn everyone from the Arctic southward. Jacob and Clipper will soon become what we most fear. I'm afraid I have to make a visit to my allies across the sea. There is only one way to stop them now, and that is with the master scepter. I will no longer hide. I have to show them who I actually am. Hhh, I will be going away soon to make sure everything is ready. We must make our move very soon."

CHAPTER 7

The Laboratory

The ride finally ended. Clipper pulled Chang's car into our dormitory parking lot. We decided to make sure everything was in order just in case Monty was after us again. Nothing in my or Clipper's room was misplaced or stolen, so we set off for our laboratory. When we arrived, I stepped out of the car while Clipper grabbed the knapsack that once again held our precious samples. I saw in his eyes that he was nervous. I did not blame him, for I was nervous myself, especially with the dreams of the dragon still haunting me.

"I don't know why we're so enthusiastic about this," said Clipper, "and I don't know if these tests will be useful or not."

"Same doubts here, but there's something deep inside that's urging me forward," I admitted. "Monty had a reason for stealing our samples. In any case, we should do this now. Hopefully, Monty will give up on pestering us for a while."

We entered the lab and began setting up for what would be the greatest work of our lives.

A few weeks passed. Clipper and I worked tirelessly, minutely checking and rechecking every detail. We meticulously recorded each and every activity. Our experiment could possibly create a new and interesting discovery, or create something the world was not yet ready for. What I did not see was that the boundary between what I thought was real and what I thought was myth was beginning to blur. The moment my spell would lift was only a heartbeat away.

On the fateful day, we approached the door of the lab. I unlocked it with a key. Only Clipper, Chang, Joshua, Sally, and I had a key to the door. I stepped in quietly after pocketing my key.

The lights flickered on. We set up for the final phase of the experiment. I brought out the glass tank where our lab rat was playing with a little, fuzzy ball. Clipper and I used the rat responsibly. We only conducted humane tests on it. I opened the lid and picked him up. The rat stared at me, disturbed from his fun. He did not squirm because he had seen me before and recognized me.

"Well, hello again," I said to the rat.

The albino rodent glared at me with his red eyes. I moved him over to a smaller cage. Clipper brought forth the newly created mixture of samples. By this point, the mixture had become something that puzzled us. The mixture was a thick liquid that would often change color. For a moment it would appear yellow, then purple, then green, then blue in no particular pattern. The mixture had been this way since we created it. It boggled me how the samples came to be so odd.

"Remember, I had to mix in some extra chemicals to stabilize the samples," Clipper explained. "I once put the samples together, and the genome of the most dominant sample canceled out everything else. Maybe the chemicals are causing the constant color changes."

"How will that affect the subject?" I asked.

"I have no idea, but that's what these tests are for. It's possible this sparkly liquid will make the animal a little sick, nothing more."

Clipper carefully drained a portion of the sample mixture into a vial. He held the vial out to show me. I nodded in approval.

"We can't give this mixture through a simple injection," I reminded Clipper. "It would give us wrong results. We have to shoot the mixture through the gun."

Clipper agreed. He placed the mixture into two separate syringes inside the specialized gun. The gun itself was strapped to the top of a pole and was aimed at the rat. One would think using the gun was a crazy idea, but the pressure was just right after calculations. It would only be a little poke. One shot would enough, but Clipper loaded the second in case the first failed. I climbed up an inclined ramp to view the test. Clipper prepared to fire the gun. He set the timer on it.

"Open the cage," I said, "but don't let the rat escape. And can we please hurry? I have a basketball game tonight and I have to show up an hour early."

Clipper opened the rat's cage and began tethering it to a bar in the cage with a piece of indigo string. I checked the gun. My eyes widened in shock. The timer was set too early. It was going to fire any second!

"Clipper, move! It's going to fire!"

Clipper did not move in time. The syringe sprang out and pierced him in the shoulder. He yelped as he fell, completely dazed.

I rushed over to him. "Are you okay? Did it hurt?"

Clipper groaned and rubbed his shoulder. It looked as if all his energy had been drained. I stood up to examine the gun, and the second syringe fired. It punctured the center of my chest, next to my heart. I also fell to the floor.

There I was, lying silently. I began hallucinating. Colorful, disfigured images flew around me. I felt heat throughout my body. A tingling sensation came over me and my limbs felt like they were shriveled up. A minute later, the feelings of tension and locked emotions were suddenly gobbled up by something. I again heard the voice from my dreams, "*Welcome, Jacob Draco. You will be one of us once again. You will be home.*"

"Who… who are you?" I asked the voice in my mind.

"*I am the spirit who has followed you. Now you will be as your true ancestors. They are smiling above you.*"

"What do mean 'true ancestors'?" I asked the spirit.

"*You will see soon enough. You will see…*"

The strange images vanished. The spirit was gone. My world returned to what it was before.

The entire experience lasted only a moment, but it felt like hours when I recovered. My eyesight was very unstable. I looked down at Clipper. He groaned and stood up. I started towards the door, needing outdoor air. When I reached the door, I found it was locked. I banged on it in frustration. This whole experiment had gone awry. I had to escape!

I went over to the empty gun and unstrapped it from the pole. Taking the pole with me, I banged it against the doorknob. I banged on it again and again until the knob ripped out of its place. I slid a finger inside the opening and pulled the door open.

Clipper struggled to his feet. Before he followed me out, he returned the rat to its tank where it had a supply of food and water. We both stumbled outside and breathed deeply. The fresh air helped clear our minds.

"What are we going to do about this?" Clipper asked, struggling to stay awake. "We might have done something really bad. These dragons from our dreams…maybe there's a connection. I think we need a doctor's opinion."

I checked the watch on my wrist. "We can't. I should be at the basketball court soon. Besides, we couldn't have dreams about this upcoming incident."

"But you can't just go play basketball after you changed yourself," Clipper protested.

"Hey, nothing has happened to us other than feeling dizzy, just what we predicted. And we weren't sure anything else would happen, right? I don't feel any different right now. If you're truly worried, we can go see a doctor after the game. Now come on, I'm going to be late!"

"All right," Clipper said as he sat in the passenger side of the car. "At least the rat will remain the same. I just feel a little tingly. I heard voices in my head about my true home. Augh! And my mouth hurts, too." He placed his fingers gingerly on his upper jaw.

"Oh, never mind your mouth," I replied. "I know things haven't been going well recently. But it'll soon straighten out. You'll see."

As we headed back to the campus, a strange image came into my mind. To this day I cannot describe it. I had a sudden feeling that I was about to head home, but not any home I would have recognized. Clipper already mentioned that. I blinked a few times and shook my head. Something was going on. I had visions of a strange place. What could it all mean?

I parked Chang's car behind the arena where the game was held. I jumped out, made my way towards the arena, and as I entered the locker room, I took a deep breath. A musky smell assaulted my nose, causing me to feel lightheaded. Usually the smell did not bother me. This time it seemed more potent. I quickly changed into my white uniform and placed a towel on my face. I decided not to tell any of my teammates about the incident. When I was ready, I came out onto the hardwood floor with the team and loosened my joints.

An hour passed, and we circled around for the tip-off. My teammates were optimistic. During warm up, I had not missed a shot. One of my teammates wished me luck as the referee tossed the ball up into the air.

The starting center from our team had control of the basketball. It was tipped directly to me. I caught it and dribbled down the court. Without wasting a second, I threw the ball into the air. It arched and sank perfectly through the net. Three points for my team.

As I played, my skills improved exponentially. They almost seemed to have improved too much. I caught the sidelong glances from the other players. When our team was on defense, the opposing point guard decided to pass the ball to the shooting guard. A split second before he did, my whole world seemed to slow down. I could see what was about to happen. The ball was going to the shooting guard all right. Just as the ball left the guard's hands, my own jumped in the way. It was a quick fast break down the court. For a point guard of six feet, I never knew I could jump so far from the hoop and dunk the ball. The muscles in my thighs felt stronger than ever. They seemed much more powerful than before. I intercepted another pass and continued to play at my highest performance. I was becoming more and more suspicious of the new abilities I had acquired.

Had the mixture actually have an effect on me? I wondered about this while I shot a free throw. It was very likely that the mixture was the cause of my aggressive play. At half time, my team was up by over thirty points. My abilities stunned the crowd as I played just as aggressively during the final minutes of the second half. I made more and more three-point shots from far off. Everybody in the arena was cheering me on, but the game was not foremost in my mind. The dreams, the visions, the spirit, and the accident were all flying through my head. I did not believe the experiment was connected to the dreams yet.

When the game ended, I still had more energy than ever. The team officials insisted that I should be tested for drugs. Luckily, I was clear. Everyone seemed convinced that I had miraculously improved my skill. I left the arena, feeling pleased with myself. I walked out to Chang's car. Clipper stood there, staring at me with a distressed look.

"Did that basketball game prove anything to you?" he asked.

"I felt more self-aware," I said. "I was thinking about it during the game. That may be the only effect from the mixture. I really don't feel anything else."

Clipper paced back and forth in agitation. "But you changed nonetheless! It's time to see a doctor. You said so."

"What's the doctor going to say? 'Oh, you've just genetically mutated yourself.' We can't go to a doctor."

"Then what do we do?" asked Clipper.

Before I could answer, a young woman named Cynthia approached us. She was a casual friend and had dated Clipper before we set off on our science expedition. Her smile told us that she was going to ask us something. I had seen that smile before.

"Hey, you really did well at the game, Jacob," she said, giving me a congratulating pat on the arm. "I was hoping you and Clipper could join us for dinner. My friends and I are going to Théo's Garden."

I remembered Théo's Garden. It was an elegant restaurant near the campus. It was the last place where I wanted to be at this moment, but I did not want to let Cynthia know about my small problem.

"Oh, sorry Cynthia. I can't. I'm…"

"Don't worry about Clipper," she interrupted, glancing at him. "He's coming, too. I just want to congratulate you on your basketball game and your little science adventure. Oh, please come. I won't take no for an answer."

"Okay, but only for a short while," I said, knowing there was no way out. "Clipper and I have… er… some things we need to do later this evening."

Cynthia beamed with amusement. "Great!" She turned her head and smiled at Clipper. All Clipper could do was nod. Leaving the car, we followed Cynthia to a taxi.

Once inside, Clipper leaned over and whispered in my ear. "What are we doing? What if some other change happens at the restaurant? Something bad might happen."

"Just run," I said. "We don't want Cynthia and her friends to see us change in any sort of way."

Clipper smirked. "So just run? Great."

Clipper and I entered the fairly large restaurant and sat at a white cloth-covered table. Many of Cynthia's friends arrived and we all waited with menus in our hands. Each of us ordered something when our drinks were served.

"I hope Sally doesn't find out about this," I said to Clipper in an attempt to lighten the mood.

"She's not jealous about my brief relationship with Cynthia. Sally's not that…" Clipper started twitching his nose. The smell of cooking food excited him. "Mmm. Something smells great. I can't wait to eat!"

I rubbed my stomach. "Neither can I. I didn't expect to have such an appetite."

The waitress brought each of us a delightful dish. Clipper had a beautiful salmon fillet. I was surprised, almost startled. I expected him to react to the fish like he usually did. This time, his eyes were glued to the food while his mouth watered with little control.

"Clipper, remember you hate fish?" I whispered. "You hate any seafood. It makes your face swell, remember? Why did you order it? And stop drooling! That's bad manners."

Clipper licked away the wetness. He then lifted a big piece of salmon on his fork. It hovered over his nose for a split second before he devoured the piece whole.

"Sorry, I just can't help…mmmnnphhhh. This is delicious! I smelled it and I couldn't resist."

Before anyone could stop him, Clipper tossed the rest of his salmon up in the air and caught it between his jaws. He swallowed it without even chewing, creating the impression of a carnivore after killing its prey. Everyone in the restaurant stared awkwardly at Clipper as he looked around the room. His head slouched to his shoulders in embarrassment.

"Clipper, can you…?" I sniffed my meal as well. "Ah! You're right! I can't help it. I…"

Just like Clipper, my shrimp was in my mouth with no time wasted. I swallowed the tails with no trouble, and I did not bother to use my silverware for the salad.

Silence fell across the restaurant as I finished. Everyone stared at me and Clipper, then at each other. I was about to break the silence when a sudden, sharp pain invaded my head, scaring me.

Clipper lifted his head. "I'm sorry," he said for me.

Cynthia simply smiled, shaking her head. "Oh, well. You've traveled the world recently, learning different customs, how to eat and all. I'm just relieved you actually ate the fish, Clipper. It seems that it doesn't bother you anymore."

Along with the headache, I felt a burning in my chest. "Why don't you two go out for a walk?" I said. "It'll be nice for you both to get reacquainted."

Clipper swallowed and placed his hand over Cynthia's. "I'd actually love that. Maybe the air will be good for me," he said.

He stood up and headed for the door with Cynthia beside him. I was alone with Cynthia's friends. I wanted to explain my embarrassing moment, but my vision seemed distorted. I leaned back on my chair and took a sip of lemonade from my glass.

"I'm so sorry. I know Clipper already said that, but I truly am as well," I said glumly.

"It's all right," one of the friends replied.

Moving my eyes around the room, I spotted a miniature bronze statue of a European-style dragon. It sat on a platform as a display for the ornate fountain. Its wings were spread, as if it was about to fly away. It appeared to be happy.

Ugh, dragons again, I thought. The sickness in its entirety stormed down on me once again. Each time I saw a statue of a dragon, I felt nauseated. Why? Why the dragon statues? It was driving me crazy. I rubbed my eyes, questioning myself. I saw that Cynthia's friends were concerned.

"Are you okay?" one of them asked. "You're looking a little green."

My stomach contracted. My head felt like it was spinning in circles. "I don't feel very well. I need to go home," I responded groggily.

With nothing left to say, I walked out the door. Reaching the street, I glanced back and forth, wondering where Clipper had gone with Cynthia. Despite how dizzy I was, I spotted them nearby. I could not help wobbling left and right across the sidewalk. I caught up with Clipper just in time to hear him complain about his own problems.

"I don't feel well at all!" he exclaimed in a bleary moan.

"I feel the same way," I said. "Maybe we should go home."

"I told it was… I told you… I… I told you… we've got to go to the… the…" Clipper found it hard to utter any word.

"Go where?" I asked.

Cynthia frowned as she took in our appearances. "Are you two okay? You both look pale. I hope this isn't something serious. Do you want me to take you home?"

Clipper took a deep breath. "I forgot what I was going to say. Let's go home, Jacob. I see a taxi just down the street. We can take that. You tell Chang to get his car."

Leaving Cynthia at the restaurant, we approached the cab and climbed in. On our way home, my stomach twisted and turned. I coughed several times. The cab driver turned back to inspect us. "Are you sick?" he asked.

"Fine," Clipper said. "I don't know what it is… but I…"

He was unable to finish his sentence. He coughed a few more times and then vomited on the floor. When the food was out of his system, he leaned back in his seat and stared blankly into space. The driver sighed in annoyance. "Drunks," he muttered to himself.

He let us out at the dormitories after I had paid the fare. He then turned on the "Off Duty" light on top of his vehicle; he was more than likely going to clean up Clipper's mess. Walking along an imaginary squiggly line, we opened the front doors.

"I'm…I'm going to my room," Clipper said. "See you tomorrow."

"Good-b… good… awe never mind." My mind had never been so scrambled.

Clipper hobbled up a flight of carpeted stairs while I turned and entered my room. Chang was at his desk, studying a textbook when I came in. He turned to me and noticed my sweaty, pale face. "Jacob, you're back," he said. "How was the experiment today? I also heard about your… are you all right?"

I lay down on my bed. "I just feel a little sick. I'll be fine tomorrow. Your car is still at the arena, by the way. Sorry about that."

Chang was not concerned about the car. "That's okay, I'll get it in a second. So what were the results of the experiment today with the rat?"

"Where's what and where?"

"Never mind. You need to sleep. You don't look well at all. I don't think you should go anywhere tomorrow; too bad. We're going to the campus lab when it's done…"

I did not even hear the rest of what he had said. I was already fast asleep.

THE NEXT DAY FELT A MORE PROMISING. MY SICKNESS FADED AND I felt healthy. Clipper happily trotted down the stairs. He was about to walk into my room when he was met with an unwelcoming bang against the wall.

"That's none of your business!" he heard me yell.

"What?" a voice asked. "I was just wondering if you..."

"Get out of my room! Right now!"

"Hey, I'm sorry. Couldn't you at least... Aaawwee! Okay. Okay, I'm going!"

A fellow student of mine opened the door and dashed out, grabbing Clipper's arms. "I don't know what's gotten in to him! He's acting like a maniac!"

I QUICKLY FOLLOWED THE STUDENT AND SHOVED HIM OUT THE MAIN doorway, slamming it shut when I was out.

"He thinks I cheated during the game last night," I grumbled. "I didn't! I'm sick and tired of everyone assuming that."

Clipper gave me an odd stare. "Jacob, are you okay? Why the hostility?"

My anger slowly drifted into confusion after I had cooled down. "I'm sorry. I don't know why I behaved like that. Hey, I noticed your face didn't react to the salmon last night, but your stomach certainly did. That's a good thing, nonetheless, I think."

While we stood there, Chang opened the door. He held two books in his arms. "I'm glad you're feeling better, Clipper," he said as he walked past us. He did not say anything to me.

We both watched him leave the building, on his way to the main campus.

"Joshua was worried about me last night," said Clipper once Chang was gone. He took a nervous breath. "I can't believe it. We injected ourselves with a strange substance. For all we know it could have changed our genes. I thought nothing would happen, but now I'm not convinced."

"Maybe getting sick last night was the main result," I decided. "I'm pretty sure we don't have to worry about a thing. Genetic mutations happen all the time in our bodies. Our cells are prepared for situations like this. Just live a normal life, but keep a sharp eye out. I don't know what Monty's going through right now. Just in case, let's just make sure Sally is on the lookout, too. We can go to our lab after basketball practice and see if these same symptoms affect the rat. Everything will be as it should."

We headed to the doorway when Clipper placed his hand over his mouth, wincing in pain. "Oh… Ah! My teeth have felt quite odd this morning. I think I need to pay a visit to my dentist later."

"You do that while I'm at basketball practice," I said.

After our conversation, the day treated us quite well. As time moved along, we found ourselves at one of the college's public laboratories. Clipper and I were mixing some substances inside a beaker when our professor came up behind us. "So, how goes your major experiment?" he asked. "I expect you didn't travel around the globe for nothing."

We both stayed silent for a moment.

"Eh… fine," Clipper said. "The test subject seemed a little sick but it eventually came out of it."

I nudged Clipper in the side and gave him a look that said, "What are you thinking?"

"Ah! An interesting effect." The professor chuckled. "Don't be discouraged. I believe you two young men are on the verge of discovering something great. Keep up the good work."

I held my tongue. The fluid that was shot into my chest did not feel like the mixture that Clipper and I had made. It felt like some strange elixir that was from a different world, something I could not even create.

Before the professor left, he gave Clipper a puzzled expression.

"Will you please open your mouth, Mr. Clipper?"

Without thinking, Clipper did as he was told. He exposed his teeth. The professor's eyes widened with shock.

"Some of your teeth look like they've grown! You look like a vampire!"

Clipper felt around his gums with his fingers. He was now vexed over his dental health. "I don't know what it is. It's scaring me!"

"Perhaps you should see a dentist, Mr. Clipper," the professor counseled, then left us to our lab project.

"I don't like this, Jacob. It's one thing after another," Clipper whispered in fright. "I'm afraid some major thing is bound to happen. For all we know, we could turn into some sort of hideous creature."

I felt around my own teeth. They felt pointier than before. I passed it off as my imagination. I was convinced there was nothing out of the ordinary.

"My teeth are fine. Clipper, I don't think it's anything. Can you please let everything go? Later today, we'll go back to the lab and fix our problem. We'll restart the experiment. Now let's continue our work and get on with our lives, okay? You're probably just worried over nothing. Trust me, nothing's wrong."

I meant what I said, but I noticed that I was more irritated than usual. Over the course of the day, even the slightest annoyance turned into a mild feeling of anger.

As evening approached, our daily routines shifted. Clipper set out for the dentist office while I headed to the practice gym. Not long after checking into the office, Clipper was greeted by the secretary.

"Dr. Weeks will be with you shortly, Mr. Clipper. Come on in," the woman said to him.

Clipper followed another woman into a cubical and took a seat on a cushioned chair. He leaned back on the headrest and relaxed.

Dr. Weeks entered the room a few minutes later. He greeted Clipper and scanned through a chart on a nearby counter. "So, you said that your canine teeth are bothering you? That's funny. There's no record of any real dental problems. Let's take a look."

Clipper opened his mouth to let Dr. Weeks have a look. In horror, the dentist stepped back. Clipper gave him a sturdy glare. "What's the problem? Is there something I should be concerned about?"

It took a while before Dr. Weeks spoke. "The teeth you said are bothering you are growing! Not only that, but all your teeth seemed to have gotten sharper; much like a crocodile's. I saw the change right before my eyes. You have fangs! And not only that, but your breath is really hot."

Clipper was spooked. "My breath is hot? And what do you mean my teeth changed before your eyes? My teeth can't…"

He left his sentence half-finished as he gazed into a nearby mirror. His incisors were not flat like a normal set of human teeth. His teeth had changed shape. Could this be the start of something bad, he wondered? He immediately rose and quickly walked out the door with his dentist following him.

"Mr. Clipper, where are you going? Don't you want to finish the appointment? I can get to the bottom of this!"

Clipper turned around. "I have to be somewhere. Leave me alone!" he snapped.

The dentist stared wide-eyed and open-mouthed. He inched a little closer before Clipper made a menacing growl. Not a human growl, for that matter. It was more of a snarl. He turned around and walked out of Dr. Weeks's sight. The dentist was left alone in front of the office.

As Clipper left the dentist's office, the burning sensation came upon him again. His face and arms started to itch, too. He scratched at what felt like spots of scales in his skin. He groaned. "What is this?"

THE SUN WAS ALREADY SETTING WHEN I LEFT BASKETBALL PRACTICE. Night was approaching, a night to remember for sure. I departed the gym with glee, clicking my heels together. I had been making threes all day. I felt unstoppable.

I skipped down the sidewalk, feeling very proud of myself. As I neared the dormitory, I saw Clipper running at full speed from a distance.

"Jacob! Jacob!" he shouted.

He lurched right in front of me and panted. "Jacob! Something's happening! We're changing! I feel it inside me. My organs feel like they're getting burnt to a crisp."

"I have a similar feeling," I said, holding a hand on my abdomen, "but I just got back from the gym and I always feel this way."

My opinion changed when I felt an actual burning. My happy mood switched to primitive fear.

Clipper rubbed his hands on his face. "Look at my face. Better yet, look at your face."

Red scaly spots were growing over Clipper's arms and face. They were slowly getting bigger. Stunned, I glanced down at my hands. My fingers had turned black as if death itself was scuttling on my skin. My fingernail tips morphed from round curves to sharp points. The black scaly texture crawled under my wristwatch, past my elbow, and up my shoulder. The dark-toned skin on my entire left arm had been transformed into a rich ebony color. I turned to a car window and gazed at my reflection. Black spots were growing all over my face.

"Oh no!" I howled.

"We've got to get out of here!" Clipper warned. "I don't want become a danger to the public."

We made a quick decision to go to our dormitory rooms. Along the way, we crossed the center of the college campus. In the front stood the metal statues of the dragons. They were looking as victorious as ever.

JORDAN B. JOLLEY

That was when the spark happened…

I had no idea what was going on. As I gazed upon the lifeless figures, some ghostly force seemed to have set off a psychological trigger. My head started pulsing. I fell to the ground. Clipper was kneeling next to me in a similar reaction. My vision started to wander without aim. This made my stomach queasy. I first chalked it up to a side-affect, but one of the statues seemed to have turned its head and give me a warm smile. A low voice spoke inside my mind, "*Welcome back to your true self.*"

Filled with overwhelming energy, I palmed my temples over and over again. The statue's fiery eyes opened, staring at me. "*Jacob Draco, you are returning,*" said the familiar voice.

I looked up at the spirit. "What are you doing to me, evil thing? Leave my mind! You're not even real."

"*You believe I am imagination?*" said the spirit who was inside the statue. "*Is this imagination?*"

The statue jumped off its pedestal and stepped up to me. It coughed out a ball of fire at my side. With my bleary vision, I avoided it the best I could.

"Spirit, you are evil! Dragons are evil and I want you to leave me alone."

"*For sure dragons are evil, but you don't have to be. I was once evil. In my lifetime, I had to learn the goodness of life so I could be here to talk to you.*"

"What are you talking about?"

"*You will see soon enough,*" the spirit said, coughing another fireball from the statue. "*My speech was much different in my time. But as time of the people had moved on, so have I. I learned to speak English.*"

"Stop it!" I yelled. "Enough with the dragons. Let me be!"

The spirit stood silent and moved back to the pedestal. "*As you wish, Jacob Draco. Once you have come to your senses, I'll be back.*"

"What do you mean by that?" I asked.

There was no reply. The dragon resumed its original position on the pedestal next to the other. Again, it was lifeless. I turned to see Clipper in as much panic as I was.

"I don't know!" he yelled. "Can you please leave? What do you mean I'm now fighting for what's right? Leave me right now!"

When his vision had cleared, he turned to me.

"Jacob... get... out... of...here...!" he stuttered.

I wordlessly agreed and slugged away. Unaware of each other's actions, we each went our own separate directions. I could not think straight. My eyesight started to cloud up. I turned right of the dragon statues, thinking that Clipper would follow me. Clipper lingered down the street on the left, thinking that I had followed him. I continued to make my way to the dormitories. My movements around the streets were crazy. Local people had the idea that I was very drunk. It was a good thing the darkness of the night covered the darkness of the scales. They did not bother to look too closely.

"What's the matter with him?" I heard someone say.

"I think he's had one too many drinks," joked another.

I ignored their assumptions and continued to my dorm. I wanted to warn Chang before it was too late. I could barely see where I was going when I felt a hand touch my shoulder. It startled me.

"Do you need a hand?" an elderly woman asked.

Instantly turning my face away, I was going to say that I could do it on my own, but it was hard to speak. "N-no. No. I-I'm okay," I managed to say.

"Are you sure?" she asked.

"Fine. O-Okay," I stuttered.

As she walked away, I rubbed the top of my head. I felt two large bumps under my hair, progressively getting bigger. That confirmed my worst fears: my whole body was transforming! No wonder my mind was playing games and invited that strange spirit. I had to do something. My body was changing. What should I do? What *could* I do?

I felt, not just on my arms, but my entire body changed into the scaly texture. With the last ounce of vision I had before I blacked out, I found a cracked mirror in a dumpster. What I saw gave me a sort of terror that I would never feel again. A muzzle formed on my face while the rest of my body was covered in scales. I had a white underside beneath my shirt. I wanted to scream. But before I could, I passed out and fell on the cold, hard ground.

My aciculate fingernails grew in length and turned into shredding claws. I grew a thick, spiny tail with a triangular tip at the end. Growing in size, my clothes ripped off of my body. I grew extra spikes on my elbows and kneecaps. My bones twisted and turned while my internal organs shifted into new shapes. Two large wings sprouted from my back. As I lay there, smoke escaped my mouth with every exhalation.

I was no longer a common man, lying unconscious on the black asphalt. My mind froze to nothing. I could not even think about what had just happened to me.

"*Welcome back,*" the spirit said again. "*You are now who you were destined to be.*"

I did not answer. My mind was dark. My own spirit may have even left my body for that moment. I did not know.

CLIPPER HOBBLED AROUND, UNAWARE OF MY LOCATION. SWAYING his head left and right, he found a butcher shop that was closed for the night. Instantly forgetting about me, he shattered the glass door and stepped into the closed store with no self-control. He searched around, smelling different things. He noticed that his canine teeth were again increasing in length, much longer than mine. Claws grew from his red, scaly fingers.

He finally found a refrigerator filled with various meats. Instinct called for some sort of food. He opened the door and stuck his head in. He pulled it back out with a ball of raw beef in his mouth. He chewed and swallowed the meat. After his brief snack, he fell to the floor. Like me, a long tail sprouted from his body and smoke escaped through his mouth as he exhaled. Large brown wings sprang up from his back as well.

Both Clipper and I slept as our bodies changed into something that came out of myths and legends. We changed into something that no one had believed in since the lost times of wise men. We changed into something that pleased those who inhabited a world in the heavens.

CHAPTER 8

DAWN OF THE LIGHT

The sun shone over the eastern waters the next day. As I was resting, the morning light woke me. I quickly opened my eyes, much faster than when I had closed them. My eyes glowed an amber-yellow color. I stood up in a quadruped fashion. My black spiny tail wavered left and right. My long, leathery wings pressed against both sides of the surrounding walls. When I awoke, my world seemed different. I did not remember the events from last night. I did not care who I was.

Forlorn as I felt, I stepped out onto the street, right in the path of a car that screeched to a halt. It emitted a startling honk. My head twitched and I stared at the metal automobile with eyes of anger. The driver's jaw dropped. He stared at me for a long moment. He did not see me as Jacob Draco; he saw me as a black monster. The man trembled in fear, then reversed back the way he had come. I used my new wings and flew to another car that was passing by. Landing on top of it, I clawed the roof open and roared with monstrous volume at the driver. The man screamed in horror and left the car to my mercy. He took off into a nearby building. I flew after him. He made a narrow escape through the door, yet I plowed through the delicate entryway with my horns, leaving a pile of glass, bricks, and mortar in my wake.

The terrified people in the lobby fled from the scene as I let out an incinerating flame. The fire spread onto the carpeted floor and the entire lobby went up in a blaze. I stood in the heart of the flames, looking for something else to do. I charged out of the building, again using my long, smooth horns. People saw me and ran, screaming.

Within a few minutes, I had destroyed the foyer of another building and soon the whole street. When the area was under my power, I ran to the end of the street. I was much faster in my new form.

Before I could do any more damage, a police car sped up to me with its lights flashing and sirens crying. The noise of the sirens only agitated me more. I lowered my horns and charged the car. The whole front end of the vehicle was crushed. Two officers tumbled from the disabled cruiser. They must have caught a glimpse of me disappearing into a hotel down the street, although I did not know it was a hotel at the time. Once inside, the foyer was abandoned.

From my vantage point, in one of the hallways, I saw one of the officers in the doorway holding his only weapon of defense. He did not see where I was. He stepped to the front desk and examined five deep claw marks in the top. Behind the desk was a shelf that I had already destroyed. He had just taken a step when I sprang from the hallway. In a dangerous rage, I clawed at the officer. He had just enough time to clear the desk and hide beneath it. I dug my claws into the side of the desk, then let two flames escape from my nostrils. Though the flames were small, the shelves and the front desk fed it. The fire grew bigger and bigger.

The officer climbed out from underneath the burning desk and fired his weapon at me. The bullet hit me in the chest. The impact forced me to fall backwards and crash out a window. I lay stunned, but not wounded. I leapt to my feet and roared at him. In terror, he fired at me once again. The bullets did not present any mortal danger to me. Shaking away the intense pain, I climbed up on top of the damaged police car and scanned the area. My body, much larger than before, pressed down on the car. The roof caved. Spreading my wings, I flew up to the sky and out of the city limits.

THE WHITE HOUSE STOOD IN THE CAPITOL CITY OF WASHINGTON D. C. Sergeant James Nelson was a trusted veteran. He sat in the oval office with the President of the United States. The talk was about the terror I was perpetrating. The President did not believe he had time for such nonsense. He was already up to his neck in many other issues.

"Mr. President, there are countless sightings of this dragon," James said.

The President sat still, confused about what he had just heard. "What do you mean dragon?"

"Residents all over New York are in a state of panic. They say that they have seen a dragon. Many say it is a dragon over anything else."

The President sighed in frustration. "Well, dragon or no dragon, see if you can find out what this really is. My guess is that it is something else."

"With all due respect, sir, how can this be something else? It was said that this 'dragon' attacked a police car and started a fire. There are no fatalities reported so far, but some people are in critical care. I can tell you, this is not something else. It's dangerous! No matter what it truly is, I see it as a dragon."

"I'm still not convinced," the President said, shaking his head with an annoyed frown. "I'm running a nation here. I can't go chasing after something from a fairy tale."

"All right," said James. From a briefcase, he removed several pictures shot from various kinds of cameras. "Can you explain these?"

What the President saw astonished him. Many photographs were blurry, but some of them were as clear as day. The President decided the situation was too much for him to leave alone. He knew he had to take action. "Something has to be done. But I'm still not convinced that this is actually a dragon," he said.

"Are you sure?" said James, wishing the President would change his mind. "Many have reported fire where the creature had attacked."

The President placed a hand under his chin. "Whatever this is, if the police cannot do anything about it, I suggest that the military should take action. I'm not exactly sure what this is, but we need to do something. Do you know where the…dragon is now?"

"We believe it is somewhere in Connecticut, but it hasn't been spotted in any towns in that state yet," James answered.

The President stood and went to a window, his hands clasped behind his back. "If we don't do anything, civilians *will* get hurt."

At that moment, the phone on the desk buzzed. The President picked it up and listened as the person on the other end of the line told him something that made him sigh. He gently set the phone back down. "There's another sighting," he said, "in Brooklyn. But this one is said to be red. This one is having some fun of its own. It has also set fire to several buildings. Now we've got one in Connecticut and one in New York. Sergeant Nelson, as Commander in Chief, I'm ordering you to send troops in and get to the bottom of this."

James Nelson saluted his leader sharply. He left the room and began to organize a full scale search. As he did so, he felt goose bumps on his arms. He had no idea what he was going up against. He did not know how powerful dragons were. None of his people knew what the outcome would be as they headed north.

CITY SKYSCRAPERS EVENTUALLY GAVE WAY TO BUDDING TREES. I had flown from New York and was now somewhere rural. I found myself in the environment I loved as a dragon: the forest. The city was not a place I enjoyed with all the people and buildings. I descended to the ground. When I landed, I felt the dirt underneath my scaly paws. I rested my claws in the earth and looked around. From afar, I heard the rumbling of thunder. For some reason, I loved the noise of distant thunder. It tickled my eardrums. I also heard the sound of a nearby road.

I jolted forward a few feet and ran up a tree. A feeling of freedom washed over me. No branch supported me, so I kept my claws in the trunk. Balancing with the help of my tail, I ran my keen eyes along the nearby road. I had enjoyed playing with the strange moving objects, which I should have known were cars. They were metallic and ran on wheels. The metal was so fragile and it was fairly entertaining for me to chase them.

While in the tree, a water truck came into my view. I waited. At just the right moment, I jumped out of the tree and landed on top of the truck. My long claws dug into the metal and water squirted out of the holes. With more excitement, I started digging through the metal as water spilled out all over the road. The truck pulled over to the side of the road. The driver stepped out of the truck.

The driver came into my view, complaining. His words were meaningless to me. The driver stopped speaking when he saw me. I stared back at him, waiting for him to run. The driver took a step back. This kept me calm. I eyed him as he slowly walked away. When he was gone, I jumped off the truck and looked for something else to do. I was not one who wanted to be bored.

As I moved along the side of the highway, I heard a peculiar buzzing noise. It sounded as if it was coming from the sky. I searched everywhere for it, looking this way and that. There were too many trees. I could not find the source of the noise at all. It was not long until I finally saw a large green vehicle slowly coming into view. What I saw was another giant metal beast, only this one was a lot bigger.

The large cannon was about to fire. Before it did, I jumped into the air and landed some distance from the landship. I then charged at it. I gained speed until I was traveling faster than a wolf after prey. I reached the vehicle before it was able to aim its large cannon. My horns rammed into the landship with such power that the whole thing slid, almost toppling on its side.

As I jumped onto my defeated enemy and looked back into the sky, I found the source of the buzzing noise. A large flying object hovered above me. I flew into the air and was preparing to attack it with fire. The men inside the helicopter saw me coming. The copilot fired a gun at me. The force of the bullets caused me to lose control and plunge to the ground, my wings bleeding in several places.

This green beast wanted to fight, so I took to the air again. More bullets sprayed at me and I was again forced to land. The next time I flew straight up, right below the green beast. It was quite exhausting, but possible. I reached the landing skid and destroyed it with my jaws after several tugs. After I spat out a piece of metal, I started to climb through the open door.

The copilot raised his foot before I could snap my jaws around it. He hit me square in the muzzle with his boot. I lost my grasp and fell back to the ground. The fight was not going well for me. I was just playing with the rolling vehicles until the one in the sky arrived. This was not fair! To show my dominant nature, I screeched a threat and instantly leapt back into the air, taking flight once again. I cast a flame from deep within my lungs. My fire engulfed the green beast. I then charged into its side. The hard impact caused it to spin out of control. It swayed hither and thither until it crashed into the ground. Parts of the green beast caught fire. The pilots jumped out before the crash.

Unharmed, I moved to the scene of the wreckage and saw the wounded pilot and copilot attempting to take cover in the forest. I was about to cast another flame when a second flying beast arrived. It fired at me as well. Flying back into the air, I let out another flame that covered the second green beast. The pilots jumped out the side door and opened their parachutes. Before I went after them, I noticed a third green beast coming after me. I was ready to attack it when I felt a sharp pain in my side. Falling to the ground, I turned around to see what was shooting at me. The aggressive landship was coming after me again. I regained my altitude and sprayed fire across the road as I passed over it. The flames did nothing to the metal. This annoyed me even more. I altered my direction. This time I dove headfirst at the landship. Horns pointed down, I struck the top with a mighty force. The top bent inward. I hopped off the vehicle, pleased that I was victorious once again. I bowed my head in satisfaction.

When I looked up again, I was introduced to more flying beasts. I hissed in disbelief. I had just finished fighting! Now I had to fight more? I decided not to battle them and ran back the way I came. Bullets struck all around me, many hitting my hide. Bullets did not threaten my life, but the pain they carried was too much to handle. I vanished into the forest so I would lose them. My wings were not as resistant as my scales. Though they were bleeding, I could still fly. I had to retreat or my wings might be too wounded to use.

Within an hour, I found myself back in New York. Some people saw me and dashed away in fright. I flew onto this and that building, trying to decide which way to go. Various policemen saw me and shot at me. Some hit me, some did not. I wanted to go back to the forest, but I knew the green beasts would be there waiting for me.

The battle in the city continued. I knew I should not fly away or else they might hit my wings to the point where I could no longer fly. I was lucky to have escaped last time. The first option that came to mind was to climb down. Once I did, I ran away from those who were after me. I wanted to chase an unarmed person instead. I found one luckless soul who did not have time to escape. He took one glance at me then ran inside an abandoned hospital. I chased him without hesitation.

The middle-aged man tried his best to stay away from me, but my sense of smell and sharp hearing led me straight to him. When he emerged from his hiding place on the third floor, I ambushed him. He was cornered. I took a step closer to him and exposed my teeth in a snarl. My claws dug through the surface of the floor.

Tears streamed out of the man's eyes. The smoke protruding from my nose stole the oxygen around him, making him cough and gag. He said something out of fear that I did not care to understand. I opened my mouth, ready to sink my teeth into his shoulder.

But as I was about to strike, my mind suddenly cleared. My former conscience returned.

I remembered who I was. I was Jacob Draco! My previous self regained possession of my body, which was now a dragon.

Realizing what I was doing, I immediately let the man go. The beast inside me cooled down. Once he was free, the man ran down the hall and down the flight of stairs. I did not chase him. I looked around, distressed. I walked to a window on all fours, which now felt normal. Police and armored vehicles surrounded the building.

What have I done? I thought. With anger subsiding from my mind, I yelled for help. But the only noise that came out was the eerie cry of the monster I had become.

CHAPTER 9

A NEW LIFE

My life was forever changed. I never thought that something like this would happen. My body was different, but in a strange way it felt completely normal. I felt like I had always been a dragon. The new muscles in my wings and tail felt natural, even though my wings stung badly from all the bullet wounds. I did not think I could speak anymore with the new shape of my mouth. In grief, I closed my eyes. I knew I would never return to the life I had known.

The man who I had chased into the hospital slowly came back up the stairs. He took a good look at me. He noticed my face as I gazed at the floor with wet eyes. The frightened yet curious man ventured closer to me. I looked up and stared at him, making him halt. I tried to say something peaceful, but I could not form the words flow with my mouth. My speech was gone. I had to let him know that I was not the monster he thought I was, somehow. For a second time the man came closer. He stared into my eyes. I did the same. My only idea to appear peaceful was to act afraid. I cowered like a lost wolf pup, my tail wrapped around my right-rear leg. The man was now standing next to me. Even when I sat, my head was above his.

"You weren't intentionally disturbing the peace, were you?" he said.

I continued staring at him. Calm as I was, he was still sweating with fear. He continued to speak to me, his body quaking. "I don't know what you were doing a few seconds ago, but that's in the past now. My name's Marvin."

I did not even attempt to talk. It would just end up as a horrifying noise. I remained silent. My tail uncurled and swayed back and forth.

"Well, are you from around here?" asked Marvin.

I nodded slowly. Marvin's eyes lit up, noticing that I had answered him. He was aware that he had broken a barrier between him and me.

"Can you understand what I'm saying?" he inquired. I nodded again. Marvin beamed. "Wow! Not only do dragons exist, but they understand English, too!"

He then appeared confused. I knew why. If I was a dragon from New York, then why has anyone not seen me until today?

"You know," he said, "it's a shame that you can't tell me your name. That is if you have a name."

I finally tried to speak. No sign of language came out, but I felt the sound of my new voice in my throat. Maybe I could speak after all, despite my muzzle! It would take some practice to completely restore it, but I could still speak. Finding something easy to say, I tried my family name. My dragon voice slowly bubbled out of my throat. "D-d-dr-drrrr..." The different shape of my mouth made speaking a challenge.

Marvin looked at me in amazement. "So you *can* speak!"

I continued trying. "Drac... Draca... Draco. Draco!"

Marvin raised an eyebrow. "Draco. That's your name?"

I nodded again. It *was* possible to speak after all! I tried other words. "Draco. I... am... Draco. Dacob... Jacob Dr... Draco." My new voice was a lot lower and serpentine.

"Jacob Draco," Marvin repeated. "Your name's Jacob Draco. How ironic, doesn't *draco* mean dragon? *Draconem* is Latin for dragon."

Thinking about my name made me smile. Marvin first took a step back before squinting at my teeth. "You're smiling, aren't you? That's interesting. Well, nice meeting you... eh... Jacob Draco. I think I should go now. I want to tell my wife that I'm okay. The news about this little debacle must be spreading. I don't want my family to worry about me."

After stretching his legs, he headed for the stairs. He waved his hand, wanting me to follow. "Come on now, let's get out of here," he said.

Knowing that the building was surrounded with soldiers, I shook my head. "No! No… Soldiers… No."

Marvin thought for a moment. "They will probably let me out with no problem. But now that you mention it, I am worried about you. They've surrounded the building. Here, let me go out first. I'll explain that you're harmless and they'll let you out, okay?"

I did not believe his plan would work in any way. "No. Soldier… try to… gill…kill me. Dey… They w-won't believe you. They try… kill me." It was becoming easier to speak.

"Don't worry. I'll be telling the truth," Marvin assured.

I wanted to talk him out of it, but I could not speak the correct words. I approached an open window once Marvin left. It was not long until I saw him walk out the door with his hands in the air. Some soldiers immediately ran over to him and escorted him away from the building.

My hearing was much improved as a dragon. I heard Marvin addressing the soldiers. "The dragon in that building is not a ruthless killer. He won't hurt anybody. He even spoke to me."

"Sir," the sergeant said to Marvin, "we can't risk that. That dragon has caused twenty-seven people to be hospitalized. It's dangerous."

Hearing Marvin protest, I expected that they were not going to listen to him. They would search the building and would be on my floor very soon. I had to find a way out without being spotted. I went to another window on the opposite side of the building and shattered the glass with a gentle bump of my horns. I climbed out with my wings folded so I could fit through. It was a tight squeeze, but I managed to make my way out. I was almost out completely when my rear foot slipped. I started to fall. As I did so, my claws latched onto the wall. My fall broken, I hung onto the side of the building. A soldier spotted me and alerted the others of my location. I was in no mood for more fighting. I scrambled up the wall until I reached the roof.

"After it! Don't let it escape!" The sergeant yelled.

I heard shots fire from all around the perimeter below. This made me afraid. I had to get somewhere safe, and quick! I stood on the edge of the building and spread my bloodstained wings. I looked down, wondering how I flew earlier. It was frightening to fly at this altitude! Acrophobia beat down on me. If I still had sweat glands, I would have been soaked. Nevertheless, I knew I had to escape. Shutting my eyes, I bounded forward with my hind legs. My wings flapped twice and, with luck, I stayed in the air. I opened my eyes to find myself soaring over my pursuers. As I flew, I saw that I was headed for the side of a dark window. I had to evade it. When I did, I soon had to dodge another building. Then I had to dodge another and another.

I did not want to go through so many twists and turns, so I flew even higher. I was soon above the height of even the tallest tower in the city. Everything appeared small when I found a comfortable thermal to ride. It was a beautiful sight seeing the city below. I felt like I was truly free. The ability to fly actually pleased me, amidst all my grief.

I tried to find somewhere clear to land where I could rest without having to fight or flee. I flew out over the bay. The only place I thought to land was the iconic Liberty Island. I planned to rest there for a moment before setting off somewhere else. I opened my wings to slow my descent, landing gracefully on the torch of the large statue. From there, I started climbing down. I found the copper very smooth and hard to grip. Down past the neck, I lost anchor. With my claws clinging to the side, I fell all the way to the bottom. I landed on the pedestal, rolled, fell again, and hit the ground with a hard smack. I would have broken several bones as a human from a fall like that. It would have killed me, too. As a dragon, I only had a sore back and some other odd pain that I had never felt before. Perhaps I strained my wings a little. They hurt terribly with all the damage they have taken. I felt guilty after noticing my claws had created many white, noticeable streaks on the front of the famous statue. Luckily there were no visitors to see it, being the early morning.

I stretched my tail once the pain subsided. Guilt left when I turned away from the statue. The city skyline presented a wonderful view. With my new vision, colors were sharper. I could spot movements in the distance as clear as if they were closer. Happiness washed over me, soon to drain into the waters below. I lifted my new forepaws from the ground. They were covered with black scales and white shredding claws. I made my way over to the water, noticing that I walked on four feet.

I reached the water. The reflection showed a murky image of my face: I saw yellow eyes, long brownish-white horns, and sharp teeth. I sat back down. There were other large claws coming from my kneecaps and elbows with more claws on my foot paws. My wings were a brown leathery texture. I guessed my wingspan was well over at least twenty feet or even twenty-five if I did not fold them.

I took a deep breath, letting a large flame escape my mouth. It flew out into the bay and disappeared in a cloud of smoke. Which of the chemicals in the mixture allowed me to breathe fire?

"What have I done? I'm now a monster," I whispered aloud. My speech was improving.

I stood back up and walked toward the statue. That was when I smelled something out of the ordinary. I sniffed the air, standing on my hind feet like a bear to get a clearer scent. I took a few steps forward, just in time to escape the sudden swoop of another dragon. This dragon was the source of the scent. I looked in amazement at the other creature. This one differed from me. This one had dark-red scales, not black as mine, and two sabered fangs coming from the top jaw that just reached below its lower jaw. I had sharp teeth as well, but no sabered fangs.

The dragon had a distressed look on his face as he tried to speak to me without success. I was met with strange cackles and calls. I looked down at the dragon's feet. Each paw had five claws except for one that only had four.

"Clipper, is that you?" I asked.

The glum dragon nodded. It was Clipper! My best friend had changed just like me, and just like me, he had barely regained his senses after his consciousness was hijacked. Clipper had grief written on his face. I asked if he was all right. He nodded again, then waved his forepaws in the air in an effort to communicate with me.

"Clipper, try to say a simple word. It will help you talk again," I said.

He attempted to talk. "Cli... Clivver... Cwivver. Cwivver!"

Embarrassed, he remained silent. I did not give up. I was able to talk, so Clipper must be as well. "You did well for the first try," I said. "Do it again. Sooner or later you'll get it. I learned how to talk the same way. I know the muzzle is making it hard. The shape of the mouth is different from what we're used to."

It took a little more time for Clipper to speak than me. Several minutes passed before he could say a few simple sentences in his new voice. His fangs made it difficult for him; I understood that. His speech eventually became much more coherent. Our conversation was about the previous events.

"So I guess de samples I added in de migsture mages up fire," Clipper said. "Now we gan orginicawy pwoduce it. But I s-*still* have no idea... *why* it is pwo... produced. We can now bwe... breathe fire and fly. We are dragons! I can't believe it! Hhh. I t-think I'm getting my language back."

"That's why everybody is hunting us right now. They think we're still aggressive. We've got to find a way to let them know that we are with them, not against them."

"How?" asked Clipper.

I did not answer. Thinking about the many people I had hurt made me upset. Clipper was upset, too. At first he did his best to keep a positive attitude. Whatever strategy he tried, he still felt depressed. He rubbed his snout on the ground. "I don't like this. That mixture shouldn't have done this. How did we turn into this? Dragons... out of every possibility! I don't want to be like this. I want to be normal."

"I want to as well," I said with a similar feeling. "If only we can change the past. But we can't. We have to live with it."

Clipper sighed. "I get what you're saying, I guess we have to learn to live this way now. Learn from the past to prepare for the future."

He blew some heat from his nose to dry the threatening tears. They evaporated off his face. Before he said anything else, I caught sight of a boat coming towards us from the mainland. I knew this would happen soon enough.

"I think we should get out of here," I said.

Clipper swallowed. "Where do we go?"

I looked around for an answer to our problem. I gazed at the water. I trusted dragons had amphibious qualities. I felt it in my internal senses. "Go underwater."

Keeping our wings folded, we jumped in the bay. I looked around once I was below the surface. I thought I would have to surface to breathe, but I felt fine. I guess I could hold my breath underwater for a long time. I started paddling forward, swimming as fast as any aquatic animal.

I swam quite swiftly, but I had to turn back for Clipper. He lost his way in all the filth in the water. He found me as I pointed to where we should go. He snapped his jaws shut and continued following me. The boat flew right over us, its occupants unaware of our presence. We swam on. We did not go directly to land yet, but to a shore where I thought we would be safe. By then the murkiness cleared up a little.

I crawled onto the shore and waited for Clipper. Not another soul was in sight. No one was out enjoying the spring air.

Clipper looked around. "It's too fine of a day for this place to be completely deserted. Maybe that's a good thing for us."

"Eh, Clipper?" I said. "Look directly ahead of you."

From the distance, I saw some soldiers wielding strange weapons that I have never seen before. They rushed onto the shore and stopped. One of them pointed at us and they continued running.

"We have to leave!" said Clipper. "I can't believe they are still after us. Everybody hates us! It's hard to believe that this is happening."

We raced alongside the shoreline in the opposite direction of the soldiers. The leader of the group, Sergeant Nelson, pointed at us. "After them!" he shouted.

The other soldiers fired at us. The rocks around our feet panicked from each bullet. I could feel some bullets biting my hind legs. I roared in pain. Clipper and I ran faster to avoid them.

When we were out of range, we spread our wings and leapt into the air. The wind from our wings created a storm of small rocks along the shore. The ground disappeared beneath our feet. In a matter of seconds, we were free in the air. Clipper was grumbling beside me as he beat his wings up and down. "With this new ability to fly, I thought I would no longer be afraid of heights!" he growled.

"Just get used to it," I called back. "Now where should we go?"

Clipper spoke a little louder to respond over the rushing wind. "If no one's around because of us, how about we go to our dorms?"

"It's worth a try. People have already seen us, so what are we risking?"

With the world below moving past us, we searched for our former home. It took us a few minutes to reach the familiar part of the city. Once we found the college campus, I dove to the ground and stepped up to the doors.

"Be careful. Try not to break anything," said Clipper after he caught his breath.

I gently grabbed the handles with my claws. Both doors opened perfectly, just as if I was still a human. When I entered, I tried to hold the two doors for Clipper to fit through. My claws slid across the window as a result. The screech was head-turning and the streaks were noticeable, like on the Statue of Liberty. I instantly lifted my paws from the glass.

"This isn't good for our first day," moaned Clipper.

I reached the door to my room and wrapped my claws around the brass doorknob. My claws were again causing problems. The metal was too smooth for me to grip. Peeved, I took a firmer grip and twisted it as hard as I could. The doorknob tore clean off, taking a large piece of wood along with it. I held the heavily scratched knob in my claws.

"Sorry, it was the only way to get in," I said.

Clipper ignored me. Thinking that there was no more use for the door, he used his horns and bashed right through it. The door ripped from its hinges and fell to the floor with two round holes through the middle. I tried not to mind as we struggled to fit our wings through the doorway. When we were finally inside, I tried not to touch anything. I miscalculated my size and my horns struck a low-hanging light. I spun around in fright. My tail slid across a study desk, pushing over Chang's lamp and some of his books. As I turned around to inspect the damage, my horns scraped across the plastered wall, creating two enormous gashes.

It was hard for us getting used to our bulky size in a small room. Many claw marks scarred the walls, the only window was shattered, my bed had been torn up, and the desk was leveled. We sat down in liberation, believing it was all over. Clipper took a deep breath. As he blew out, a mediocre flame spouted from his mouth, catching the window curtains on fire.

"Great, now we just burned down the dorms," Clipper slurred without panic.

"We have to put it out before it reaches the smoke alarm in the hallway," I said. "I don't want to have everyone leaving this building and seeing our room."

"How do we put it out? We *make* fire, we don't extinguish it."

At his words, I disappeared in the hallway. I returned shortly with a fire extinguisher between my jaws. I was about to drop the canister onto the floor and pick it up with my paw when I accidentally crushed the red cylinder. Growling, I spat out the disgusting foam and wiped my lips.

"So much for that," Clipper huffed.

I ignored him. I jumped atop a burning curtain that was once a silky green. I ripped it down and started stomping on the flames. Clipper's eyes widened. "Jacob! What are you doing?"

The lack of oxygen caused the flames to die out, but the weight under my paws broke some of the floorboards.

"The fire didn't burn me at all. It's like I'm immune to it," I said.

"Great, except now we have another problem. Your room is completely destroyed now."

"So let's never go into *your* room."

"Well, Joshua needs to know some time," said Clipper. "The best way is to tell him face to face, even if it sounds hard. Maybe we can do that while we're here."

I did not agree. "What do you mean? We'll scare out any bravery that has formed inside of him. That's a bad idea!"

Clipper glared at me. "It's not a bad idea. He needs to know eventually. The sooner, the better."

A minor argument broke out between us until I was struck by a sudden thought, "Where is Chang?"

Clipper fell silent. His eyes scanned the devastated room. "Isn't he at a lecture right now?" I was about to answer when our conversation was interrupted. Clipper moved over to the fallen door. "Jacob, do you hear that?"

My ears rose as I listened closely. "Sounds like footsteps."

"Whoever it is, he's coming closer!" Clipper whispered in alarm.

Wasting no time, I picked up the door and held it inside its frame with my horns. I held it tight as the vibration of the knock tickled the top of my head.

"Hello?" asked the unknown student. "Are you okay in there? I heard a whole bunch of crashing noises coming from your room. I heard there was some sort of monster loose in the city and I was wondering if you're all right."

The stranger's eye appeared through one of Clipper's horn-holes. Clipper placed his paw over the door, blocking out light. "This is Clipper. Don't worry about that noise. We're just watching… a movie."

I silently glared at him. Clipper shrugged with his wings. Stress was written on his face.

"Are you sure you're okay?" the student asked. "Your voice sounds hoarse, very hoarse. Do you have a sore throat? And what about your mouth? It sounds like there are popsicle sticks in your teeth. What are you doing, pretending to be a saber-toothed ti-?"

"It's nothing!" Clipper interrupted, trying to make a chewing noise. "I just have nmph… nmph… food in my mouth. There's nothing to worry about."

I shook my head. This whole situation was ludicrous. Whoever was outside would more than likely be concerned over our dragon, which were louder than before. They sounded nothing like our former selves.

"It appears that the door handle has been ripped off," the student said.

Clipper gazed down at the knob hole. He did not want the person to peek through that either. Without thinking, he covered that as well. He did not do a satisfactory job, as he was wobbling on his hind feet.

"What's this?" the student asked. "There's something strange right here."

He stuck one of his fingers through the hole and rubbed Clipper's scales. Clipper made a high-pitched yip and jumped. He toppled on the floor. His heavy weight caused more floorboards to shudder. I immediately placed my claws over the holes while keeping the door in place. I too was losing my balance. The student's presence annoyed me so much.

"He said everything's okay!" I snapped.

"All right, fine!" the student said. "If you say so, I'll go."

The noise from the other side of the door was gone as the person walked away. Clipper remained on the floor, sighing in relief. A cloud of smoke floated above him. "That was too close," he muttered.

"Hold the door steady," I said. "I have an idea."

Clipper took my place. I picked up the telephone that had not fallen off the broken desk. The claw on my finger created a large scratch on the phone. Dialing the number was not easy. I created several more scratches. At last I managed to call Chang.

"Hi, Chang. This is Jacob," I said when he answered.

Clipper closed his eyes. "This is not good," he groaned.

I heard Chang's voice without holding the phone to my ear. He told me how everyone in the campus was hiding, too scared to do anything else.

"What do you mean everyone's scared?" I turned the phone away, whispering to Clipper. "Chang's at the main campus right now. The whole college locked down, so are other public places all over the city. Chang says everyone on campus is terrified right now."

"All the streets around here have no people except for those who are trying to kill us. That's a swell fact to know," Clipper remarked.

I continued talking to Chang, "Okay, I'll be careful. Oh, Clipper and I have to go out of town. Yes, it's about our experiment. I know we just got back but something has come up. Nothing. Okay, see you in a few… days. Oh, and if our room seems to be in… hello? Hello?"

I looked down at the phone. It was damaged beyond repair.

I spoke to Clipper again after tossing the useless telephone off the desk. "We have to get out of here. Chang must know something's wrong now that he's heard my new voice. I don't even know where to go."

"We need to at least leave the city," said Clipper.

"All right, and we have to leave our life as students, too. Such a waste."

We sneaked out of the building and out of the city. When we were high in the air, we flew south, not yet knowing where to go. I had to admit that my life was taking a new course in order to ease the internal pain of change. I thought it all changed because of an accident, but I did not know what lay ahead.

CHAPTER 10

THE CARVING IN THE STONE

Two nights had come and gone. The third day showed promise as the sun peered over the eastern horizon. We traveled south. Far south. We avoided cities such as Baltimore, Washington, and Charlotte. That morning, we were in Georgia. The city of Atlanta came into view in the early dawn. The towers and other buildings ran by below us. They were not as tall as the ones in New York, thankfully. We seemed to be following some instinct. I could not smell anything that would attract me, but I felt something within my bones to come here. The problem was, I did not know exactly what I was sensing.

"What do we do next?" Clipper asked me.

"I'm not sure," I replied.

We landed on a quiet street on the outskirts of the city. Avoiding people the best we could, we climbed to the top of a red-bricked building. The two of us sat down and discussed our situation.

"Look, we've been shot several times and we were never seriously wounded," I said. "If we try to get away, they'll try to shoot us anyway. But if we show them we're not dangerous, maybe they'll give us a little respect."

"Great chance," Clipper muttered under his smoky breath.

"Hey, my first ideas are not always my best. I don't think this idea is so bad, though."

Clipper looked around. "I can hardly see anybody now. This morning is quite nice." I believed that he was trying to change the subject.

"I don't think it will be that way for long," I said. "They'll see us eventually. In the meantime, what do we do?"

Clipper had no answer. I spread my wings and eyed each of them. "We know how to fly. But what if we have to make sudden evasions from oncoming things like buildings? We need to be ready for that."

Clipper looked confused. "What are you talking about?"

"We'll train ourselves," I told him. "We can learn how to be a little more acrobatic in the air."

Clipper shook his head, taking a step back. "Oh no! I'm not doing that. I'm not ready for this! I'll crash into something. I have a fear of heights and you know that. Even now I do."

"That's why we need practice, so we can overcome that."

Before Clipper could argue any further, I took off running down the roof. I glided to the street below and landed still running. Clipper followed, not very thrilled with what I was doing. He chased after me and we gained speed. The street eventually met a T-intersection, bordered by a brick wall. At just the right moment, I jumped. I caught air and landed flat on the side of the wall. With my claws in crevices on the windows, I hung onto the wall. It was difficult climbing the brick surface, but with one paw in front of the other, I made my way up to the top. Clipper showed up behind me not long after.

"What's the matter with you?" he growled. "Someone must have seen us through a window. That's much worse than seeing us in the air."

"That's a possibility," I said. "We're going to have to get used to it. The people have got to get used to it as well."

Next, I dove over the edge of the roof, straight for the ground. Just before I hit, I flapped my wings. My drop turned into a glide, which turned into altitude. With enough energy, I aimed myself upward. I launched myself in the sky, arched, and landed atop a neighboring building. Clipper gave me an angry glare from the distance. "You're crazy! How can I do that?"

"Think up, not down!" I called. "You're telling yourself to hit the ground. You have to commit and execute the commands. Don't be afraid!"

Clipper's large body trembled as he peered over the edge to the concrete below. "This is impossible!" He remained still.

I flew back to the roof where he stood. "Come on Clipper! Just do it. Don't be afraid."

Just as he was about to lean forward over the edge, he backed off again. He inched his feet closer together from the sickness in his stomach. "I can't do it! I feel like I'm going to throw up."

Puffing out smoke, I did what I never thought I would do. I used my horns to butt him off the edge. Falling dangerously fast, Clipper roared in terror. He tried to spread his wings, but it was too late. He smashed into the middle of the pavement, leaving a crater. I jumped off and landed next to him. Clipper stood up in shock. "What were you thinking? Why would you do something that stupid? You *butted* me off!"

I held a straight, dragon face. "It'll be okay, Clipper. Let's do it again. Just follow me. Do what I do."

Clipper's gut wrenched several times until he regurgitated a puddle of green bubbling ooze in front of me. I stared at his vomit in disgust. "Dragon puke looks very strange," I said, grimacing. "I've never seen anything like it. Don't worry. When you get used to heights, you won't get sick at all."

We climbed back to the roof. I performed the exact same stunt to the next building. Clipper once again held ground on the edge.

Shutting his eyes, he started trembling again. It took him a moment before he gathered his courage. Growling, he leapt forward. He opened his eyes and spread his wings sooner than he had before. Taking the large flap, he hurled himself upwards. He reached my spot with no trouble. His landing was rough, however. Without slowing his speed, he rolled several feet. I had to jump to the side when he came rolling.

"That's good," I said, offering a paw. "You may need to practice your landing, but you've got the hang of flying. Now on to step number two: the Bank of America spire. It's one of the tallest towers in Atlanta. We'll spiral up there. Let's go!"

Jumping in the air, I flew to the tower in the bowels of Atlanta. Orbiting around the tower in an upward fashion, I reached the spire. I grasped onto it with all four paws.

Clipper soon landed above me. "That wasn't so bad," he said.

"You're doing great, Clipper. Now we'll dive straight down, using our wings to go back up. We'll make sort of a U-shape."

Clipper's jaw dropped. "What?"

I did not answer. Jumping off the spire, I fell several hundred feet. At the right moment, I shifted my wings to go in a straight, horizontal direction. Sure enough, the downtown area was full of people. And yes, many people saw me. I did not care for the moment. I did not want to hide for the rest of my life, but I did not want to present myself to the world either. I had to find some balance. Flying was a great option in my opinion. I could have a little freedom to myself, and people would only spot me for a split second. I was starting to enjoy myself, which felt great after three days of grief. Clipper, on the other hand, was frightened. He kicked off the spire and fell.

"Jacob! I can't believe you're making me do this," he yelled as he curved from the fall.

When he attempted to fly back up, I realized that he was in a dangerous position. He was just low enough to be in the path of a big supply truck. Roaring at the top of his lungs, his dragon voice echoed all around. I wished he had not done that. The truck was getting nearer. Just as they crossed paths, Clipper managed to get high enough to soar inches above the trailer. He kicked off the back of the trailer to give himself a boost. I zigzagged in and out of the paths of different buildings once Clipper was with me again. Reaching another flat-topped apartment roof in the outskirts, I slowed for a landing. I made a sudden stop in mid-air over the location where I wanted to be, giving me enough time to do a grand-ending front flip.

Flying was becoming a part of me. Being a dragon was not all that bad. Everything about myself seemed to connect. I felt like I belonged to a different place for I reason I did not know yet. Clipper dropped in as I was fantasizing a new home. Striking the sun-hot roof, he somersaulted and rolled, stopping just before he reached the far edge. He stood up, swaying in nausea.

"I'm not doing that again!" he bellowed.

I chuckled. "All in a day's work."

"I'm just thrilled all of Atlanta saw us during that little acrobatic performance," he said dryly. I was at least glad that Clipper's sarcasm had returned. He was coming to terms with his transformation as well.

"Well, we can follow through with my idea," I proposed. "We both realize our lives have been changed. There's no going back to before. As much as I don't like it, we must live this way for now on. It's going to be hard if we keep hiding from people. We need to show that we are not a threat to their lives. What happened before was not done by our choice."

Clipper finally continued my thought. "We *can* let the right people know. We need to find a policeman or someone like that." I nodded in approval as Clipper continued, "But can we do that later? My stomach hurts and my horns feel like they're pressing on my brain." He repositioned himself to see the entire street. "Hey, look where we are, There's a sign on the other side of the street. It looks like it's Chinese. Dragons are respected in places like China. I know we have sort of a European appearance. Hopefully that won't matter."

Clipper had a point. We had to introduce ourselves to the right person. Maybe this was a good place to do just that.

INSIDE THE RUNDOWN APARTMENT BUILDING, AN ELDERLY CHINESE man sat in front of a wooden table with the drawing of a dragon

JORDAN B. JOLLEY

on its surface. Some of his neighbors believed the elderly man had psychic abilities. The truth was, he knew things most did not.

His adolescent granddaughter sat next to him. "Grandfather, you're at the table. What do you see? What do you sense?"

The grandfather's hands trembled and quaked as his mind envisioned what he had hoped for. Awestruck, he explained his vision to his granddaughter. "The dragons are here. The day has come!"

"What do you mean?" the granddaughter asked.

The grandfather pulled out an ancient scroll with Chinese writing on it.

在你的生命，你會遇到龍的一天

There was more writing below it.

"It reads that before my life ends, I shall encounter the day of the dragon. It will be in the western world," the grandfather said.

The granddaughter was confused. "I don't understand."

"Since the dawn of time, dragons have given our ancestors luck and wisdom. Many gave us food, water, and shelter. Most dragons were evil, but they lived elsewhere. One particular dragon of light scales would visit us with peace.

"On one memorable day, they left. They wanted to go home. The words on this scroll were taken from a message written in stone, the same stone I hid in a safe place many years ago. I must see these dragons very soon. If one of them has a body that matches the image in the stone, then it must mean they are back. We shall meet them. The world will be reborn in the legends that are of the past."

Filled with excitement, the grandfather stood up on his aged feet and headed for his apartment door. "I must find them."

The granddaughter followed him down the battered stairs. "Grandfather, slow down! I don't think anyone will believe you."

The grandfather did not answer. When they left the building, he anxiously looked around.

"Maybe the dragon is back in China," the granddaughter guessed.

"No. They are somewhere near. They have come to us, despite being away from our homeland. This is the western hemisphere, or the western world as the message says."

He walked around, out into the street. Looking left and right, he could see nothing of interest. He was not a man to give up, though. He kept a sharp eye in the sky, unaware of the traffic in the street. He did not see a car speeding directly at him.

⸺◦/◦/◦⸺

CLIPPER NOTICED THE OLD MAN OUT IN THE STREET AS THE CAR sped towards him.

"Jacob, the car's going to hit that man!" he yelled.

Without thinking, I leapt from the edge of the roof. I kept my wings tightly against my back until I unfurled them at the right moment. With my claws, I seized the old man by his shirt. The car sped around a corner and disappeared. Circling around, I returned to where the man's granddaughter stood gaping at me in shock. Hovering momentarily, I set the grandfather back on his feet. He was bleeding a little, and his shirt was torn, but I thought that that must have been better than being hit.

After his heartbeat had returned to normal, the grandfather studied me thoroughly. "So you *have* returned," he said with a grin.

"I have returned?" I asked.

The grandfather's speech was slow, yet precise. "The era of the dragon has returned to this world."

I had no clue what he was talking about. At first, I thought he was talking about the Chinese Zodiac. According to the Zodiac, the year of the dragon was a few years ago.

"Can you please explain this to me?" I asked him. "But first let's go somewhere private."

"As you wish, dragon. We will go somewhere isolated. I know where to go." He was full of cheer.

As he climbed inside a battered truck, I flew back up to Clipper.

"He knew we were coming!" I said.

Clipper was as lost as I was. The grandfather started his weathered blue truck and sounded the horn. Just to keep him happy, I flew to the bed of the truck along with Clipper; it was a really tight squeeze. The truck lurched forward and we were on our way. I poked my nose through the opening in the rear window.

"So how were you were expecting us?" I inquired.

"Shouldn't you know?" the grandfather replied as he drove.

I looked up in the sky. "Last time it was the year of the dragon on the Chinese Zodiac was a few years ago."

"This has nothing to do with the Zodiac. Your kind existed long ago. Now that time has returned. You are here to give the Earth a whole new beginning. It's the rise of the dragon."

I was still lost. "I lived long ago and I represent wisdom in China, right?"

"You should know this. You have been on another world for centuries," he said.

"Listen, this isn't what you think. What happened was…" I would have continued speaking, but the truck lurched to a halt at the edge of a mucky bog. The trip was shorter than what I had expected. The grandfather and granddaughter jumped out of the truck as we hopped out as well. The truck groaned and wiggled as we did so. We stood on the road, away from the swampy water.

"Okay, if I am 'The Dragon', then who's the other?" I said, pointing to Clipper.

The grandfather continued smiling. "There is nothing wrong with two. Now, if I may ask, can you not ask questions to which you already know the answers?"

He continued the tale of an ancient dragon until I pieced together what he was talking about. Many years ago, a dragon ruled over China, bringing peace. This dragon had siblings who were evil. The good dragon had to escape them. But then one day he, along with his dark-hearted brothers and sisters, ascended to the sky, vowing to return someday. With this knowledge, I continued the discussion.

"I gave blessings to your ancestors and to the good people of China," I said, recapping what he had told me. "But then one day I left the Earth. The people no longer believed my existence. Now that I'm back, I am going to give this world a new beginning, right?"

"And how do we prove that we are the ones?" asked Clipper.

To answer his question, the grandfather made his way to a bulky, round stone next to the road. There was a tarp covering it. Pushing the tarp aside, he revealed the smooth face of the stone and uncovered an engraving of a message in Chinese. Below it was the carving of a dragon. The dragon was standing upright on three feet; one foot was in the air. What made it interesting was that it had no resemblance to the eastern ethos. The grandfather told me to strike the exact pose as the image. If I looked like the image, it would prove that the legends he told me were true.

Clipper studied the carving for a moment. He appeared concerned. "I'm a little worried. We have the appearance of European dragons: evil and terrible. If I'm right, Chinese dragons are long and snaky, far different from the western counterpart. I'm afraid we're actually enemies."

I continued examining the stone. "I don't know. This does look possible."

"I have no doubts," the grandfather said. "You are the two who have returned. Let me prove to you that you are the dragons. Now for the pose."

When I posed with one front leg raised, my body became an exact copy of the image on the stone. The grandfather clapped his hands with excitement. "Now, cast your fire as far as you can."

I did as he bid. I took a deep breath and exhaled a big flame that went farther than I ever thought it would go. The fire flew yards away from my jaws. My pose did not look similar to the engraving - it looked *exactly* like the engraving, as if I had stepped right out of the stone! I ceased my flame. A cloud of steam rose above the bog.

"Indeed, it is true. You have returned," the grandfather gasped in astonishment.

I could not even think how I had done it. My eyes were wide. I realized that I *could* be the returned dragon that was prophesied long ago. Happiness ran through my body. I no longer felt like a lost being with human enemies. I was no longer a monster. I was a fantastic creature. It was not an accidental science experiment that turned me into this. It did not feel like a prophecy, more like providence! It was, I would say, magic.

CHAPTER 11

A TRUTH LAID OUT

"It is true," Clipper said in awe.

The grandfather was right. He explained the differences between good and evil dragons to us. "The dragon we speak of was one good among many evil, as I have told you. His brothers and sisters were loyal to a king. I don't know much about this king, other than that he is on Elsov.

"The good dragon promised that his descendants would return to stop a dark force on our world. That is all I know about him, and the fact that he always left China before winter and returned in the spring. There is more to this true story than I can say, but the good dragon has kept his promise. He did not begin the dragon culture of China, but he surly enhanced it."

Stop the dark force? I thought.

Clipper looked down at his forepaws. "Our scales are dark. But I don't feel *that* wicked myself."

"You said Elsov," I said. "Elsov? Elsov. I think I've heard that word before, a long time ago. It sounds Russian."

The grandfather laughed. "Your ironic sense of humor. I love it."

"I'm serious, sir! I know nothing of this. I have never heard of this dragon until now."

"Yet here you are! I can't begin to describe how proud I am. No matter if you knew or not, you have returned."

The granddaughter ran up to me and hugged me. I held perfectly still and glanced awkwardly at Clipper. I knew the granddaughter was vulnerable to the claws and spikes all over my body. I still felt her warm hands on my dry scales. I was speechless. I had to take a moment with Clipper and talk about everything that had occurred. I told the grandfather that we needed time alone for a moment. With pleasure, he allowed it.

"You mean to tell me that all of this was *supposed* to happen?" asked Clipper once we were alone.

"He really thinks so," I answered. "If we tell him the truth about the failed science experiment, I don't even want to know how he'll react. I think we should play along. If we don't, he could be crushed. He'll die a depressed man. Do you want that to happen?"

Clipper sighed. "All right, we'll play along."

We returned to the grandfather. "Indeed. We are the dragons," I said.

The grandfather placed a hand on my nose. A ghostly breeze whispered by me. I felt something I had never felt before. The feeling was cool and peaceful.

"You have returned," the grandfather said. "The world has changed without you. I know you have been in the skin of our flesh recently and you are scared. That is something I know that is not written in the stone. But don't worry, you will learn."

I would learn. That sentence covered me like a sheet of truth. The grandfather knew what happened to me. I was a dragon. A dragon! I was wondering if I should really be playing along or if I should believe him. Was the world what I thought it was? Could there be more to my life than I know? I had to rethink what happened in the laboratory. I felt like I had been a dragon all along. This confused me. I came to be this way all because I had a fascination of animals. Were dragons as curious as I? Were they as adventurous as I? Were they as courageous as I? More questions flowed through my mind that I could not answer.

"You are accepting the truth," said the grandfather, evaluating my face. "You have lived with us for most of your life. Now you are your true self."

"I am," I replied. "I can see the truth."

I was a dragon. I kept telling myself that. The loving parents I remembered were my human parents. I did not question that fact for long. There was too much to consider. At that moment, I knew my kind once lived on Earth. And now Clipper and I had brought them back. I had many more questions that did not make sense, but the truth was the truth. It took me a moment to ponder on that.

The peace was broken when a strange bellowing noise came from up the road. It sounded like another vehicle. Clipper and I disappeared into the swamp. A brown Jeep roared into the clearing. The two newcomers did not even notice our presence. The Jeep stopped and they jumped out. They were both short and red-bearded. They reminded me of Monty's bootlickers. I wondered what they were doing out here. They seemed to have tracked down the grandfather.

"So, you're the Chinese psychic everyone is talking about," one of the men sneered. "You're the one who knows. I would have finished you off with the car, but you were saved by a particular creature."

"You mean you *tried* to hit me? You tried to kill me?" The grandfather's jaw dropped.

"Yes, or we could take you alive. Our leader wants to know more about your, should I say, knowledge. The Keeper of the Three will retrieve his scepter soon, and we'd like to know what saved you."

The grandfather appeared spooked. "You have come to kidnap me. How dare you!"

"Kidnap, indeed," the other man said. "We are Nibelungs. We've come here in disguise. And if you help us, we may think twice about killing you."

"Kill?" the granddaughter cried.

The grandfather showed no fear. "Monolegion Nibelungs, you are too late! The rise of the dragon has already come. It was a dragon who saved me. A dragon! They have returned to our world and they will end your filthy reign."

Both Nibelung people (I had yet to discover the meaning of that name) became wary. "They have returned?" one of them said. "We were warned about this. Ah, but face it, they are…mythical. What saved you could have very well been something else."

He stammered when he said "mythical". And why did he sound like he believed the old man? More questions were in my head, but there was no time to answer them. I had to save the grandfather again. I quickly stepped into the argument before violence took place. My feet were wet and covered in moss. There was no point to hide if they knew about my coming.

I gave a menacing hiss once I was close enough. "Actually, they are right behind you."

The men turned around and smiled, as if they knew I had been present the entire time. Something strange was going on. They knew about me, along with the grandfather.

I spoke to my enemies again to show that there was no fear inside of me, which was true. "You're not taking him anywhere."

One of the Nibelungs had a knife. I did not think a knife was a real threat to me. With my keen vision and improved reflexes, I grabbed his arm with the harmless weapon and clawed down gently. I did not want to hurt him too much just yet.

The knife slipped from the Nibelung's hand. Having more fun with my power, I stood up on two feet. I was much taller than he. Holding my front paws out, I knocked him flat to the ground, my claws pointed upward to prevent serious harm. When his partner ran up to me with his knife. Clipper, who had just joined us, instinctively spat at his eyes. The short man was down, crying in horror.

I stared at Clipper, curious about the spit. "That wasn't fire you used. What was that?"

Clipper licked the outer edges of his mouth. "I have no idea. It was some sort of venom, I think."

When the Nibelung I had pushed over stood back up, I tried the same thing. The venom formed at the back of my throat, not in my lungs like fire. I spat the fluid at my target. Now both Nibelungs were crying in panic. Where could this venom have come from? Dragons were not known to be venomous.

I walked over to my victim and gave him a close glare. "So, what is like having a potent venom on your face?" I growled.

"Forgive me, dragon. I do not wish to fight," he said, whimpering.

I laughed like a hyena at his remark. I never thought an enemy of mine would say that to me. I scoffed at him. "You people think you're powerful. But now that you're under my power, I'll show you what I do to my enemies. Stand up, NOW!"

The Nibelung stood with his hands over his ears, his eyes were swollen and red. "What are you going to do to me, dragon?" he quivered.

I continued laughing. "Here's what you should do: Either you give yourself up to the police, or come have a fun little flight with me."

Clipper glared at me. "Jacob, what are you doing?"

I ignored him. I grabbed the man's arms with my foot claws. With my wings spread, I soared into the sky, up to the clouds and away from the ground.

"Put me down!" he wailed. "I'll surrender. I don't want to fall. Please. Please!"

"That's more like it," I said, safely lowering myself.

The flight above the clouds was brief. In a few minutes, I again hovered just a few feet over the Earth's surface. I dropped the Nibelung in the bog before landing myself. I demanded that the two men get into their vehicle. I then turned to the granddaughter. "I'm sure you're old enough. You can drive if you want. I'll make sure these men mind their manners."

Clipper came up to me. "Jacob, stop. I think these dragon instincts are driving you crazy. You are too prideful of who you are. Snap out of it! They're done for."

I turned around to face Clipper. I enjoyed being a dragon. I felt like a king. If it was instinct, it had certainly gotten to me. It felt like something maleficent was taking me over. I remembered the spirit telling me that dragons were evil. Maybe it was right. The grandfather said that as well.

I took a deep breath to calm myself. "Sorry, Clipper. You're right. Let's not be too hasty, but we should at least take these people in. You don't want to let them run free, do you?"

"Okay, I get your point," Clipper said. "Just... just... awe whatever. I know how you feel. Let's deal with them, but let's not get carried away."

The two miserable men, one dry and the other wet and musky, sat in the back seat of the Jeep. The grandfather covered the great carving with the tarp and sat in the front passenger seat next to his granddaughter. Clipper and I flew above them as they drove back to the city. The drive ended before I knew it. We could not move any farther because the police swarmed the area. The Jeep immediately pulled to the side. Clipper and I landed next it. The police took cover behind their cars, aiming their weapons at us.

"Glad you're here!" I called as I landed. "These people in the back attacked this elderly man and his granddaughter."

The Nibelung men jumped out of the Jeep and surrendered to the keepers of the law. However, to my dismay, the police officers still appeared highly defensive against Clipper and me.

One of the officers called out on a megaphone. "You dragons are a threat to our peace. The military is after you. Release the hostages and stay where you are!"

The grandfather and granddaughter did not hesitate to protest. "Don't shoot!" they cried. "They bring peace to us all. They saved us!"

"We will shoot if we must. These dragons have terrorized areas in the states of New York and Connecticut."

I guess they were overwhelmed by our appearances. That did not surprise me. Still, I did not want to be captured. I knew I should surrender; Clipper and I had agreed on that. But at that moment, that seemed too cowardly. I wanted to escape. A sort of rage formed inside of me. It was hard to control.

"Stay clear of the Jeep," I told the elderly man.

The granddaughter and grandfather slowly climbed out the Jeep and stepped to a safe distance. I crept up to the front of the Jeep. I felt heat building inside my lungs as I breathed in. When I exhaled, my fire attacked the front of the Jeep. I leapt up into the air with Clipper following me.

The officers fired at us. I made a high aerial arch then hit the ground hard on the other end of the street. The officers ran after me. I raced down various streets. The wind blowing in my face felt nice. I halted and slightly lifted my front legs off the ground. The air rippled around my face; the sensation tickled me. It distracted me from the situation at hand.

The happy feeling ended when I opened my eyes again. I saw a small projectile land in front of me. When it exploded, it temporarily blinded me. I coughed fiery fumes everywhere. The officer who had fired the bomb rushed up to me and slammed a club into my gut. I roared and fell to the ground. The officer lifted me up by the horns to wrap a rope around my neck. With all my strength, I lurched back, biting the rope in half with one snap of my teeth. I then pushed the policeman down. I had to show him that I meant business. But as angry as I felt, I still knew better than to harm him.

More officers threatened to shoot gas. All of them were wearing protective masks. With their guns aimed at me, I wondered what most people would think of me if they saw this situation. No one had ever seen a dragon before. They did not know anything about me. I realized that these police officers feared me. With that in mind, my anger was pacified. I did not want my sense of power to be a burden on my back. So, I did what I had originally planned on: I surrendered. Even though I could easily escape or fight them, I did what I thought was right. What scared me was that I almost got carried away. My dragon mind was dangerous!

"Look," I said calmly to the police, "you can't kill me this way. There's no way you can catch me if I decide to flee. If I were you, I would fear for my life, but I won't fight back. I'm not that kind of being. I'm very sorry that I tried to run before. Do what you want with me, I won't fight back." I said this as peacefully as I could make it.

To demonstrate my submission, I took a step back, sat down, and lowered my head. The police officers glared at me. They could not bind me with cuffs, so they had to do the unthinkable and trust me. I met up with Clipper and the two of us waited together while the armed forces were notified of our capture. I did not hear the entire conversation when they came. What I did hear was that we were going to be transported to a place called Fort Sill.

Several days passed. I found myself back to the world that was familiar to me, Oklahoma. James Nelson arrived in Fort Sill shortly before we did. In the special cell made just for us, James spoke with Clipper and me. I knew James was questioning his conference when he was with us. He had nothing useful for defense should the need come.

"You two were once people like me?" he asked for the second time.

"Yes, it's true," I said. "I'll tell you why we attacked those people that morning. It was the after-effects of the transformation. They eventually wore off. At first, I didn't know who or what I was. I couldn't control myself. Now I can. I'm still a living being, aren't I?"

"Yes you are," agreed James, "and I understand your story. Luckily no deaths were reported from your attacks. I can't imagine what it is like having a completely different body."

"I know how it sounds," said Clipper. "But something is going on. I don't feel like I've ever been in another form. I don't feel like I've been changed at all. I feel like… I've just woken from a dream, if you know what I mean."

James nodded. "I see. I must admit you two are pretty dangerous beings. Look, I want to help you. If there is a threat, I fight it. If I can, I will use it to my advantage."

"Advantage?" Clipper asked.

"Yes," James responded. "Come with me. I want to try something."

He walked out of the building and entered a fenced-off area. Clipper and I followed him.

"Let's reenact the moment in the swamp when those strange people came," he said after the brief walk.

The two of us followed the sergeant's every command, hoping to avoid any suspicion of adverse behavior. We reached the site that resembled the bog in Georgia. Sitting next to us was the carving of the ancient dragon that had been transported, with the grandfather's permission, from the bog.

James wanted to make sure that Clipper and I could actually be trusted, and this was his chance. Being alone with us, he would know our true abilities. I wanted to give my best impression when I realized this.

"So, now the strange people show up?" James recapped.

"Yes, sir," said Clipper.

James carefully examined the carving in the stone. He seemed to be more impressed when he compared the engraving to me. I looked like the dragon in the stone.

"Where did this stone come from?" the sergeant asked.

"It was shown to us by the old man," I told him. "He said that some person from ancient China made the image. When we came, we would end a dark force. It's something like that."

James nodded again. "Interesting, very interesting. Maybe you are the dragon."

Clipper looked at me. *Does he believe all those legends?* He appeared to be asking.

James covered the stone with a tarp. As he looked back up, I heard the sound of a pickup truck. It stopped in the distance.

"Okay," said James, "I want you to hit this truck with your horns. I want to see what you can do with them."

I looked back at him. "Why?"

The two men in the truck jumped out while James was speaking to me, "You destroyed some of our well-armored vehicles with your horns. Now I want you to charge into this truck."

Obeying his order, I lowered myself into a charging stance. My back legs were spread while my wings were folded to prevent resistance. I raced towards the truck with my horns lowered. I collided with the truck and it twirled through the air before landing back on its top, the cab crushed. James gasped in surprise when I returned.

"Interesting. The man said that…" He was about to say something else, but instead stared silently into the round pupils in my yellow eyes. He was entranced in something that I could not explain. Maybe something spoke to him in his mind.

"Look, Jacob," he began, "not everybody is like you. You have the power to turn the tide in the fight for good. You said this elderly man claimed that your kind has returned? This may sound funny, especially coming from me, but I believe him. It may have started as a normal human life for you, but now you have found what your life here really means. This may be the start of something big."

"Turn the tide in the fight for good?" I repeated.

The sergeant looked at Clipper and me. "Will you join me, the head of a special branch in the military? It will only prove good for you and the world. Not everybody can charge into a truck and topple it over. Please, with your power, you can change the world as we know it."

"What special branch do you mean?" I asked.

"I run a secret, organized military. It's not something civilians know much about."

I looked at Clipper while he looked at me. I shook my head in disapproval. James raised an eyebrow.

"Why not? You will represent freedom. You'll also help the world through many struggles."

I again shook my head and bared my pencil-length set of teeth. "No. I'm sorry, but I refuse. First of all, Clipper's Canadian. Second, we're dragons!" I waved my front paws in front of his face. "Can you not see my appearance? I am a creature of magic! Everyone thinks I'm straight out of fairy tales! Ha!" I took a short breath to calm myself. "But you're right about one thing. We live in a dark world after all. Clipper and I became dragons to do something. We don't know exactly what it is yet. I won't be a soldier, but I'll still help you in any way. If you need me on a mission, I'll do it. I'll do what you want me to do."

James bowed his head in respect. "Okay. I won't force you, but I appreciate your willingness to help. There are a lot of thorns we need to get past. First, I need to test the *real* ability of you two."

Clipper squinted his eyes. "What do you mean?"

CHAPTER 12

TESTS AND TRAINING

We remained in Fort Sill for the next few days. Various experiments were performed to test our abilities. We were in an outdoor complex one morning, under the enormous blue sky that stretched across the rolling hills and was dotted with soft white clouds. To start off, a tester blindfolded Clipper. The piece of cloth was above his ears and tied in a special way so it would fit on his head. The tester then moved over to a basket. I watched the whole thing from the side.

"Your friend Jacob told me about your love for fish," the tester said, "so I'm going to use fish for this test."

Clipper exposed his sabered teeth in a smile. "I love meat in general."

Sitting with his eyes covered, Clipper waited as the tester took a fish out of the basket. Clipper's nose twitched as well as mine. All he saw was black nylon, I knew. The tester tossed the first fish at him. Clipper sensed it coming on his left side. He caught the fish in his mouth and swallowed it whole. The tester tossed another fish in the air. In order to catch it, Clipper jumped a few feet and caught it with no real effort. Fish after fish flew through the air. Clipper caught every single one.

After consuming several fish, he turned around and walked off, clawing away the blindfold. Still curious, the tester tossed another fish at the back of Clipper's head. Clipper again sensed it coming and twisted his head. The fish flew straight to his mouth and down his throat. The tester was astonished. I laughed at the whole scene.

NEXT, JAMES INTERVIEWED ME. HE WAS CURIOUS ABOUT THE desires of a dragon, and he asked me various questions on the subject.

"Do you view things differently as a dragon than you used to?" was one of the questions.

"Well, I feel like I want to strike fear into my enemies when I'm angry," I answered. "I want them to be at my mercy."

"You just love the attitude. You want to be the dominant one," James stated.

"Quite so. Deep down, I still care for others. I want to be as nice as I can be. But if trouble comes along, I want to get rid of it as soon as possible, whatever it takes. It feels like... I was born in the wrong time and place, and I've changed as I grew up."

"I'm glad you're on our side now," said James.

After the interview, I was given a bench bar. The shape of my body prevented me from using any other lifting equipment. I was much bigger than the average human, and I had spikes and claws in the way. My wings did not help either. Thus, I was only able to lift the bench bar from the ground. There were hundred-pound weights on both sides. All I had to do was lift the two-hundred-pound bar. I stood up on my two hind legs and wrapped my front claws around it. With some effort, growling while doing so, I lifted the bar high above my head. I quickly set it down before I toppled over.

For the next test, a fighting dummy was placed in front of Clipper. James wanted to see how he would fight against something humanoid. In a flash, Clipper jumped on the dummy. Claws from all four paws dug into the foam inside. He pushed the dummy back with his rear legs and it flew helplessly across the floor. When it was my turn, I simply tore it to shreds. It scared even me when I ripped its head off with my teeth. It felt like my adrenaline possessed me when I did that. In times of battle, I had little self-control over my actions. I was bothered by that fact.

Despite the mutilation of the dummy, James began looking up to me. I was glad that someone appreciated me like this. I remembered the grandfather's words; the time of the dragon had truly returned. It never occurred to me that the return was only the tip of the iceberg. At the time, I did not worry about anything beyond that moment. Life had taken a turn for the better. I would work to the best of my ability to make this world a better place. I would prove myself worthy to those I did not know, one step at a time.

As time went on, the tests continued. A martial arts trainer was once brought in. He stepped inside the carpeted arena. I could already see the fear in my opponent's eyes. If I were an ordinary human, he would have nothing to fear. Now the situation was completely different. He was going up against a creature that was thought to be only a legend.

A whistle from the sideline was blown, marking the beginning of the match. Nothing happened at first. The martial artist was too afraid to move. He stood still, staring into my eyes. I stared back. Without warning, he raised a foot ready to strike my muzzle. I ducked from the attack. I was not going to do any physical harm, so I dropped to the turquois rug. I kept my wings folded to my body. I swiped across the foot he was standing on and tripped him. It was incredible! I never thought I could make such swift motions with my size. I felt his weight drop next to me like a pile of bricks. I lifted myself up and pinned him down. All my victim could do now was squirm helplessly. I noticed that despite my care, my claws had ripped his clothing. Several harmless cuts were visible on his arms, but there were no critical wounds.

"Sorry I had to do this to you," I said, backing off.

The martial artist did not reply. He opened his eyes to find me sitting by his side. He sighed in relief. To show my sportsmanship, I held a paw out to him. At first, he did not know what I was doing. He moved his head away from my deadly claws. I did not say anything. I wanted to make sure that he knew I was his friend. Slowly, his hand quivered up to mine and he clutched it. I pulled my arm forward and lifted him back to his feet. The artist was my friend, not my foe. He smiled and stroked my head as if I was his pet. I simply walked away after the match was over.

Clipper sat alongside James outside of the fort. They were out on open grassland, surrounded by forest. Unaware of what the next test was going to be, Clipper patiently waited for a command from his new ally. He did not speak until James pulled a radio from his side.

"All right, send it over," said the sergeant.

Clipper was startled when a large landship came into view and stopped about two hundred yards away from him. The driver climbed out and ran for cover. Clipper turned to James in confusion. "What's this for?"

With a straight face, James pointed to the green beast and said one simple word, "Charge."

Clipper tilted his head. "You want me to charge with my horns?"

"Move," said James, stern in his voice.

Clipper shifted his body into his charging stance. He shivered, his tail slithering behind him. He had never tried to go up against this kind of metal monster before. He slowly lowered his head, his horns now aimed directly at his target. Just before he began his charge, he let out a small flame.

"What's the matter, Clipper?" James asked, pretending to be annoyed.

Clipper made a light growl. "I can't do this. I just can't."

James tugged on one of Clipper's horns. "Do it. That's an order. Move!"

Clipper returned to his previous position, horns straight. He blew a second flame out of his nose before moving. With his eyes shut, he ran at a disappointing pace. But as he gained momentum, he felt a strange sensation; a sudden burst of energy. Opening his eyes, he lifted his head. The landship was getting closer and closer. Clipper gained speed. His unconfident attitude morphed into aggression.

"I'm coming," he muttered to himself. "Look out. I'm coming. I'll do it!"

He shut his eyes again and lowered his horns when the time was right. By this point he was at a full sprint. Before he knew it, Clipper's horns smashed into the landship. The strong, blast protective metal bent inward as the helpless tank tipped to its side when Clipper lurched his head up. The landship was in ruins. James eventually arrived upon the scene, stunned at what had happened. "You took it out as if it was nothing!" he exclaimed.

Clipper sat on the ground, cringing from pain. "Sorry. Ow! Now I've got a bad headache."

MORE TESTS WERE EXECUTED THEREAFTER, ENDING WITH EXTRAORdinary results. At the end of the day, James told us that his opinion about forces beyond had changed. He was beginning to believe in more than just the existence of dragons; he even told me there might be more to our existence than what we saw.

"I'm quite impressed," he said. "You may not be members of my force, but I'll bet you two can help us. You can help anyone in need anywhere."

"I must ask, why are we in an *Army* base if you're in the Marines?" I asked while I had the opportunity.

"Oklahoma's the perfect spot for these kinds of experiments," James explained. "I had a talk with the right people. And I want to thank you two again for being on our side, fighting for what is right."

For the next few days, fortune seemed to finally find us. We were not Marines in any way, but we still helped them. They sent me into, should I say, bizarre situations. I had the capability to get past any obstacle. Bullets could not harm me, and my instinctive nature would get me through any melee, which led to the great escape in the Sahara when I rescued a pilot from desert bandits. But even though I felt great, I still wondered why I was a dragon. The grandfather said I was supposed to end some sort of dark force. I did not know the nature of this dark force. Not even the grandfather knew. Hopefully I would find out soon.

When I had finished my mission in the Sahara, James let us go on our free time. Clipper and I decided to head back to New York. James said he would stay near an airfield outside the city in case we needed his help.

The return to New York felt great. When I had left the city, the condition was terrible. It felt like everyone was trying to kill me. I had no friends except for one who shared my trouble. Now the tables had turned in our favor.

"Well, Clipper," I said once we were alone after midnight, "we're back in New York. Let's see if we can do whatever good possible. We can test ourselves to prove that we can actually do what's right. We can show these poltroons something about what's right and what's not. If we do, maybe we can find out what this dark force is that the grandfather was talking about."

"Poltroons?" Clipper tittered.

I chuckled at his response. "When we have to fly, stay high in the sky. Don't go low enough for people to see, and keep as much distance as you can from any sort of aircraft. The higher we are, the less likely we are to be spotted at night. Besides, people don't really take time to look up in the sky."

Clipper trembled. "Heights, eugh!"

We spent the next week searching for any clue as to what we must do. We did not show our faces and were only active at night. Over the course of those days, I longed to leave the city. I wanted to travel to some place where I did not have to constantly hide myself. Still, leaving the city was not my main worry. I was also bothered by the fact that I had not seen Chang or Sally in a while. I was wondering what they thought of me. I told Chang I would be gone for a few days. Three and a half weeks had passed since Clipper and I had become dragons.

One night, I sat on the roof of the dormitory building when Clipper returned from a flight. He did an acrobatic drop and landed right in front of me. Despite his smooth landing, he seemed ill again. This time he did not vomit the mysterious green slime.

I lifted my head when he arrived. "Clipper, thank goodness you're here," I said. "Chang is right below us, in my old room. Sally is with him. They're worried about us, I'm sure of it; especially since Chang has to have discovered our torn-up room by now. It's hard to believe that we've been to many places around the world in just two weeks. We've been doing many good things, but they don't know that. I just want to enter my room like I used to."

Feeling my sorrow, Clipper tried to lighten my mood. "I feel the same way about Joshua. I know he's looking for me." A grin formed on his face. "Hey! How about we do something crazy?"

I gave him an odd look. "Crazy? You used the word 'crazy'? What do you want to do? We can't disrupt the people. And my mind is on Chang and Sally. I'm worried about them."

"Just answer me."

"I don't know what to do." I paused for a second. "Life right now seems better than when we turned into dragons. Ever since we saw the carving in the stone it seems that everything flows easily. We are who we are, though I have something hidden deep in my mind."

"What do you mean?"

"Well, remember how we kept having those visions of that spirit before we changed? I'm having a reoccurring thought that maybe, just maybe, he was an actual spirit, the ancient dragon that the grandfather told us about. That visit to Atlanta convinced me that there is something that we must do. We were drawn there by some sense, weren't we?"

"Jacob, that spirit was just a mind-twister when we transformed. It's not like a spirit came out of nowhere and gave us m-ma…" He could not speak the last word.

"Magic?" I finished. "Clipper, you were just as amazed as I was when we discovered our similarities to the carving and what the grandfather told us. Something strange is happening. I want to get to the bottom of this."

Clipper tapped one of his fangs with his claw. "Okay, I see what you mean. But I don't think we're going to find anything ma-magical."

"Maybe," I muttered. "To think it all started when Monty got in the way of our experiment. With all the things he's done to us over the years, especially when he held Sally, I wish I could just… tear his bones out!"

Clipper's jaw dropped. "What? Since when did you have thoughts like that?"

I hesitated, my ears stood straight before answering. "I don't know, but I want to go after him. We have the upper hand, now let's show him that. And besides, remember those short men that attacked us in the swamp? It just seemed that those men might have known Monty. They may be the connection to this dark force we were told about."

Smoke floated out of Clipper's nose. "Those people again? I just feel like I want talk to Monty. I don't think there's an actual spirit or anything, but now that you've mentioned our enemies, I wonder if Monty is connected to all this somehow. We shouldn't hurt him or anything like that though."

I took a moment to ponder his suggestion. "You know, that's a good idea. Let's go talk to him."

That same night, we staked out the area near Monty's complex. If we wanted to find some trouble to take care of, this was a perfect place. As we approached, the scene became more familiar. On the complex roof was a person, armed with a rifle, watching over the area. He was a watchdog under Monty's orders, no doubt about that.

The two of us climbed the side of the wall. When we reached the top, Clipper let out a ball of fire. The ball could not be any more noticeable.

The watchdog rushed to the cloud of smoke. With his back turned to me, I moved past him. Quiet as mouse, I slipped up to the watchdog. As he turned back around, I mildly curled my tail around his neck.

"Stay where you are," I hissed in his ear. "Drop your weapon."

The speechless watchdog gently set his firearm onto the rooftop. That was Clipper's cue to join me. The watchdog gazed at both of us. I saw the sheer terror in his eyes. "The dragons have come for me," he squeaked.

"Oh, I'm not after you," I said. "Now if you tell me where Monty is, you will be bound on the ground. If you don't, you'll be dangling in the air."

"All right, he's in his chamber. He just barely returned here after... It is located down the stairs and-"

"I know where it is, thank you," I interrupted. "I've been here before."

The watchdog had a coil of rope with him. I picked it up with the hooks on my claws and wrapped it around his body. The watchdog sat still. He did not even try to escape. "My leader is right," he said, "you have become your true self."

When I finished tying the rope, Clipper smashed the door and squeezed his way down the stairwell, leaving the watchdog. I wanted to give the watchdog a little more grief for trying to kill me before, but Clipper was already on his way.

Outside Monty's office, Raymond paced up and down the hallway. He seemed to be avoiding the dark tunnel where I was staring at him. With a touch of courage, Raymond eventually decided to peep his head down the tunnel. My black scales blended into the dark, so he did not see me. He sighed in relief then turned around to pace down the other end of the hallway. As he did, I emitted a ghostly voice.

"You have done wrong against the dragon of old. Now you must pay the bloody price."

Raymond looked back at the tunnel in fright. "Who... who are you? Where are you?" he gulped.

Sweat shone on his forehead. He must have seen my yellow eyes. I found it fun teasing him; it was hard to stifle my giggles. "Come to me or I come to you in an unpleasant matter."

"What does that mean?" asked Raymond fearfully.

"Come to me or face the dreaded consequence!" I hissed.

"No!" shouted Raymond. "You're just a figment of my imagination. I'll... I'll..." Before he finished his sentence, I stepped out of the darkness. I flicked my tongue as I lifted my front paws and dropped them. In a split second, Raymond attempted to retreat.

He ran out of my sight and bumped right into Clipper, who was hiding at the other end of the hallway. At Clipper's roar, Raymond spun around again, back to me. He was trapped. All he could do now was cower.

"Raymond Maroh, the day of the dragon has returned! You must surrender your power or pay your debt the hard way," I roared.

"W-why do you expect me t-to pay your debt?" he stuttered. "I don't lead these people."

"We will tell you," said Clipper. He did not speak in a serpentine voice as I did.

Raymond attempted to run around me when I spat the venomous saliva into his eyes. Screaming, he fell backwards. He blacked out for a split second, but something worse started to happen. It looked as if he was hallucinating (I would know for sure from future events).

Raymond waved his arms in the air, crying while scrambling hither and thither. There was no escape from his hallucinations. I could almost tell what he experienced next. Raymond realized that he was working for the wrong side. What he was doing was wrong. He knew that he should either surrender or suffer. His panic subsided after a few minutes and he knelt down on his knees. His hallucinations seemed to have left. Clipper and I stood at his kneeling body.

Raymond breathed deeply after wiping the spit off his eyes. Sweat soaked his sorrowful face. In tears, he sincerely apologized. "I'll help you. Just don't hurt me!" he cried.

JORDAN B. JOLLEY

"Is Monty in his office?" I questioned. "I'd like to have a talk with an old friend."

"Yes, he's there," said Raymond, pointing to the door.

"If Monty has mentioned the name Jacob Draco or Justin Clipper, you'll understand. I'm glad you helped us," I said.

Raymond looked directly at me. "You are the Jacob he constantly talks about. You and Clipper. Monty was right, he knew you would become… no! I don't want the venom again! Please don't spit that awful poison in my eyes!"

"You will get it again unless you leave," Clipper warned.

"Okay, I'll leave. To make sure I don't do anything, you can lock me somewhere like a closet. Or chain me to a-" Raymond stopped talking as I pointed to the dark tunnel. "Okay, I'm leaving."

We had gotten past Monty's guards with no trouble. Now it was time to talk with Monty Victor himself.

I cast a flame at the door to Monty's office, then I used my horns to push it down. Just as I hoped for, Monty was inside. The heat did not bother me one bit as I walked over the fallen door. Clipper followed close behind me. Monty seemed frightened at first, but then he casually sat down in his chair.

"Remember me?" I asked.

"Jacob, you're back," he said. There was no alarm in his voice. "I heard your encounter with Maroh out there."

Clipper bared his fangs. "You don't seem to be shocked to see us like this. How did you even recognize Jacob?"

"Recognize? Ha! Since the first time I saw you two, I knew you were going to be who you are right now. I knew this would happen to you. That is why I tried to steal your samples, except you got away, along with Sally. But your conflicts with me have not ended yet, I'm sorry to say."

"What are you talking about?" asked Clipper.

Monty offered a fake smile. "Far off in the forests of Europe, there are creatures and people that most think are mythical, just like you. You're not alone. And if you're worried about me, think again. When the time is right, an ugly plot will be revealed."

I grew concerned. "What plot are you talking about?"

"In a short amount of time, this human race you know of will dissolve to an inferior power. I've met these different people when I left after your escape. I will return again shortly."

Defying all my expectations, I could tell Monty was speaking truth. I saw light behind his eyes. If he was right, then this may lead to something so unearthly that it could cause great trouble. Clipper and I had already caused trouble in New York. I had to stop whatever Monty was talking about. I said nothing to him and left the complex immediately. Clipper followed behind me.

"The dwarves will conquer you," Monty said through an open window as we flew past. "I know you don't believe me, but you'll see who you really are soon enough."

We reached my dormitory room after we told Sergeant Nelson about our concerns in Europe. Chang was not at my dormitory when we arrived. He had a part time job at a local restaurant on some evenings. In my room, my section was neat and tidy. This time I hardly touched a thing (I was getting used to being a dragon). Looking around, I found the new telephone on Chang's desk. When I managed to get to the spot I wanted to be, scratch marks were all over the floor once again. Messages haunted the phone's answering machine. I replayed the messages.

"Jacob, this is Sally. I don't know where you or Clipper have been. There's no answer at his place either. I haven't seen you since the basketball game. Let me just say, if you go on vacation, don't forget to contact me. And please be sure to tell us where you're going next time. Oh well, see you soon."

A second voice took Sally's place. "Hi Jacob, this is Chang. Where are you? You called earlier. You didn't really tell me what caused your voice to change. I was a bit bewildered when I saw what happened to our room. I know you mentioned that before the phone line broke up. I've taken care of it, as you can see if you're hearing this. I haven't seen you in a while and I'm worried. If you happen to get this message, please call me. Thanks."

I had to contact Chang if I was to go to Europe. I dialed Chang's number on the phone. Clipper chuckled; it still amused him to see me using a telephone.

It was difficult for me to dial the number. "This is one thing I'm not getting used to," I huffed.

I managed to dial the number after a few tries. "Hi Jacob! Where are you?" asked Chang on the other line.

"Oh, around," I said. "By the way the experiment was… okay. How should I say this? Clipper and I had some complications. So, we were going to Europe to see to some things. It's kind of hard to explain."

"You two have been gone for weeks now! You just got back and you're going to leave again? Ah well, I know what you mean. I still notice your voice is different: low and rough. What happened? You sound nothing like yourself."

"I'd rather… I can't really explain right now," I stammered.

"I see. Well, good luck. I sure do miss you two. Thanks for calling me, that means a lot."

Clipper headed for the door after I hung up the phone. Before I followed him, I took out a pen and wrote a message to Chang on a sheet of paper. It took a moment to learn how to write with my paw. My penmanship was terrible.

A few minutes passed before I wrote the following:

Dear Chang,

Clipper and I unintentionally transformed ourselves at the lab. We were turned into dragons, the same dragons you may have heard about earlier. Don't be shocked. I am still your friend. Please understand. I know you won't believe this right now, but hear me out. There is something strange going on somewhere in Europe. That's why Clipper and I going. I won't blame you if you think I'm ridiculous. Thank you for being my friend. I will never forget you.

- Jacob

I placed the note on his bed and left the room. Clipper and I then flew to the airfield outside the city for a special plane ride to Europe. Sergeant Nelson understood our concern once we told him. We were ready to confront the unknown that Monty had spoken of. The trouble was that Monty mentioned dwarves. Was there something else? What kind of force would we be up against? Somehow, I knew this was the dark force that the grandfather had mentioned. It all fit together.

As we were about to leave, a voice came into my head, "*I am the spirit of the dragon of old. I am here. I will always help you.*"

I licked my teeth. Something did not seem right in my mind. I did not know where I was going, nor did I know if the spirit in my mind was real or not. I was going to find out soon enough.

CHAPTER 13

ARRIVAL IN CANTERBURY

The British Isle was much too far for us to fly to under our own power. That did not present much of a problem, though. James was our friend, so we had access to much more than we might otherwise have had. We ended up flying in a cargo plane, one that two dragons could fit in, of course. It took hours to cross the Atlantic Ocean. The plane landed at a private airfield near Canterbury, in the district of Kent, with permission from Her Majesty's Royal Air Force.

We landed on the flat gray runway in the late afternoon. The side door opened, and we jumped out. Thanking the pilot, we walked off the runway. The British airfield was informed of our arrival, yet the guards were still astonished. I did not worry about them. I was thinking about Monty. I did not trust him, yet I knew he told the truth. His words were on my mind under the dark, stormy clouds that hung over the airfield.

During the flight, a critical question plagued my thoughts: What could possibly be out there that Monty knew about? I knew it was in relation with the dark force that the grandfather had mentioned. For the moment, I was just glad that I was in England so Clipper and I could begin finding answers. Instinct told me that I was not going up against anything I knew, or anything I was familiar with.

Canterbury was not as big as New York, and its layout was much different. We decided to climb a nearby hotel after we decided not to wait until nightfall. This threat was too real to wait. We got a good view of the city from the hotel roof, especially the cathedral.

"Where do we go now?" asked Clipper.

I searched any other tall buildings. "The tallest place I can find is the cathedral," I said. "I don't think we should land on it, though. That's disrespectful. Let's try someplace else."

We flew to a less populated area outside the city. Our location was a good spot. I was in a shaded area where nobody could see me (my black scales in the storm helped). Clipper landed beside me.

"So, what do we do now?" I questioned. "We can't stay here for long."

"Well, Europe is a big continent. It'll take forever to find what we're looking for," Clipper said. "If only we knew exactly where we need to go."

After thinking hard, I came up with a risky solution. "Is there a library near here?"

Clipper cocked his head. "Why the library?"

"Let's do some research," I answered. "You never know what you can find in a book."

Clipper almost laughed in disbelief. "We can't go in the library. How do you think the people would react if a couple of dragons just walked in there and asked for a book?"

"Who said anything about walking in?" I responded.

Clipper's protests were useless. The only way to find what we were searching for was to research it. A library was the best idea at the moment. Flying high above the land of Kent, we eventually found a library. We landed by the back of the building. There were five large windows, each about seven or eight feet wide. I peeked in one of them. I saw an empty area of the library, a perfect spot.

"You do the honors," huffed Clipper.

He helped me reach the window's latch with my foot on his head. I stuck my claws into the rough brick wall. Dust fell on Clipper as my markings remained on the side of the library. Climbing up to the grimy window, I began opening it. The window screamed as it fought back. I quickly leapt to the ground as a librarian came to examine the source of the noise.

JORDAN B. JOLLEY

As soon as he walked past, I opened up the window all the way. I folded my wings snug to my body in order to fit through. Once I wriggled in, I fell forward with a thud. I found myself in the unoccupied portion of the library. First, I stretched my wings and other limbs, then I peeked around a stack of books. I saw a pair of computers sitting on a clean, solid table. I heard footsteps nearby, yet no one was present. Keeping my wings folded, I cautiously made my way to the computer and sat down next to the chair. I pushed a button on the keyboard as gently as I could. The computer hummed with life. I withdrew my paw and raised my ears. The computer wasn't locked, I had access. I reached down to push the Enter button, but my claws proved too sharp. The Enter button shattered, causing a startling zap.

Using the computer was a terrible idea, I thought. I yanked my paw back again. My elbow blade slashed the back of the chair beside me. I removed my blade from the chair and looked to see if anyone was coming. I heard footsteps heading my way. I returned to all four feet and looked for an escape route back to the window. As I scanned the room, a book caught my attention. The title on the spine read, "Unknown Places in Dark Europe". *That might be something*, I thought. Maybe whatever Monty was talking about was mentioned in that book.

Just before I was able to grab it, I heard voices accompanying the footsteps.

"I was reading silently when I heard a funny noise," a patron complained. "I also heard peculiar breathing, as if it came from an animal."

"I simply don't understand it," said a second voice. "These computers are the best our library has to offer. What is this? It looks as if someone took a knife and slashed the keyboard. Same here in the chair."

The voices continued ranting. I took advantage of the distraction and, from behind the shelves, I reached around to retrieve the book. Again, I bumped into random objects, forcing me to pull my paw to safety. At least I had the book now. With the two people still distracted, I crawled away with the book in my mouth. I headed for the open window with my reward. I moved quickly around another shelf, only to be greeted by a large study table with thick encyclopedias stacked in several neat piles on top of it. It was too late, I bumped right into the table. I heard the footsteps coming my way after my error. Wasting no time, I jumped onto the table and over to the open window. The encyclopedias tumbled to the carpeted floor as I crawled through my escape route. I landed in front of Clipper and we immediately raced around the corner.

"Did you get the right book?" he asked after taking a deep breath.

I triumphantly dropped the book onto the ground. "I think I did." I picked it up again with my paw for Clipper to see.

With our spot of cover, Clipper and I made ourselves comfortable against the wall as I opened the book. Leafing through it, I found what appeared to be poetry.

To meet the enchanted one, you'll go
Up North into the frozen land of snow.
Bevoktet Skog is the forbidden land,
In there marks the end of Man.

I frowned. "The end of man? Where would this lead? It's just a poem."

Clipper squinted at the text on the page. "It's a riddle. Do you remember traveling to the Scandinavian region during our experiment? *Bevoktet Skog* is Norwegian for *Guarded Forest*, I know that. My guess is that this place Monty told us about is in the Guarded Forest... in Norway!"

I nodded in satisfaction as I searched in the index. Coming across "Guarded Forest", I flipped to the right section. It was on the page after the riddle.

"The Nibelungs, or Niflungs in the Old Norse language, are the names of dwarfs in Norway, according to legend. The name originates from the Germanic epic, *The Nibelungenlied*, and *Der Ring des*

Nibelungen by Richard Wagner. In recent years, these dwarves are also named the Monolegions. Legend has it that the Monolegion tribe is planning to spread their influence throughout the world. It is said that the beginning of the conquest is currently taking place. Some of the Monolegions are in the Guarded Forest, while others are establishing stakes across the world."

Reading further, the book explained that the strange forest, where the Nibelungs were thought to exist, had been involved in so many unexplainable incidents that the area had been declared unsafe. The Norwegian government had built a fence around the forest in an attempt to keep its citizens safe. The mystery surrounding the forest remained unsolved.

"Hmm… This is interesting," said Clipper, scraping a claw along one of his sabered teeth. "This looks like a guidebook. This section right here sounds like it's speaking truth, even though they say it's a legend. Dwarves discretely establishing stakes? Does this have something to do with Monty's people?"

I looked at the cover, the author's name was Andrei Blue-eyes.

"Blue-eyes?" I said. "His first name sounds Russian. Who is this person? Some sort of elf or something? Who knows."

Clipper shook his head. "I'm not buying into that. I know we're dragons, but that doesn't prove that everything else is real. Dwarves are possible. Elves and magic? I don't know. I'm not even sure I believe in the 'ancient dragon'. My life is devoted to scientific logic. We should figure this out in a reasonable way."

"Hey, we matched the qualifications set by the dragon of old," I said. "We know that much of the story is true. Also, remember Monty's followers? They seemed quite… short. I even think Monty mentioned dwarves at one point, I can't remember exactly. I remember the old man said Monolegion Nibelungs to the two guys that grabbed him. I'm still as into science as you are, Clipper, but there may be something else we don't understand. And besides, I'm not going to risk it. I'm taking Monty's word and I'm going to stop this trouble. And *you're coming with me!*"

"Okay, okay," Clipper huffed, still rubbing his claws on his fang. "So we now know that this place is somewhere in Norway, but where? It could take years to search the whole country. Not as bad as searching all of Europe, but still pretty ridiculous."

Without saying a word, I flipped through the pages and eventually found a map with a caption below, stating that this was the map of the area where the Nibelungs, or Monolegions, were believed to live. I studied it until it was written in my memory.

"Now we don't need this book anymore," I said.

We returned to the window. Once more, Clipper hoisted me up. I tossed the book through the window where it came to rest near the pile of encyclopedias. As I dropped to the ground, the voices of the reader and the librarian reached my ears. We glanced at each other and quietly departed.

A little under an hour had passed. The idea of hiding slowed us down too much, so Clipper and I gave up the undercover stance. We found a quiet, neighborhood street. We knew people would see us, but we hated living in the shadows. We longed to walk in the open.

The first people who saw us were a mother and her young child. The mother was preoccupied and completely failed to notice to what was in front of her. When she did, the mother screamed in horror and ran. The child just smiled and walked towards us. Clipper and I stared at each other. Neither of us knew what to do.

To make sure I did not frighten him, I did my best to make a convincing smile that a human would recognize. The child jumped up and grabbed my lowered horns with his small, sticky hands. I closed my eyes in embarrassment. Clipper pretended not to notice. He casually stared into the wet, cloudy sky. The child kept holding of me, yet I remained calm. He grabbed the side of my mouth and pulled down. He took a good look at my teeth then suddenly stuck a finger up my nose. Startled, I lurched back and sneezed a ball of fire that dissolved next to the child. Despite my annoyance, I lowered my head again. The child instantly ran back to me and pulled down on my horns again. I reminded myself that if I hurt him, even accidentally, it could be the end of the recently restored happiness in my life. I sat still when the mother returned to the scene.

"Alfie! What are you doing? Those are dragons! They're dangerous. Come here at once!" The fear was clear in her voice.

Her son did not listen. He grasped me again by the horns. I could not do anything about it. The mother had a horrified look on her face, so I decided to break the silence.

"I think you should listen to your mother," I said to Alfie.

Even with a fast-beating heart, I stayed as calm as a leaf on a gentle autumn day. It was not easy. The child did not want to let go of me. I had to show the mother that I did not want to harm her little boy.

"I wove you, dwagon. You be my fwiend!" Alfie yelled.

I took shallow breaths. "Okay, I'll be your friend. But first, you have to go back to your mother."

The child cheerfully ran to her. The mother took his hand that had grasped one of my horns. She was shocked and relieved. "Who... who are you?" she asked me nervously.

"I'm just another living thing like you," I answered in a civil voice.

The mother became calm. I managed to smile, convincing enough. The mother smiled back. At that moment Clipper tapped my wing. I looked back at him as he pointed behind us. Several armed police officers came into view and halted.

"What's going on?" I asked them.

"You hold it there, you monster!" one of the officers shouted.

The police officers' hostility was quickly irritating me. First the police in the United States, now the United Kingdom! This did not look good. They seemed to pay no attention to the mother and the child behind us. I did not want them to get hurt, yet something happened inside of me. I felt threatened. My blood began to boil. I tried to hold back the rage, but it came with such a strong force.

Clipper nodded at me. Without a second's notice, I spewed fire at a nearby car. While the police stared at the car, Clipper and I raced forward. Some of the police fled the scene. Others tried to stop us. One attempted to hit me with a club. With extreme force, the club came down and landed on my midsection. With my own strength, I pulled it away with my teeth and bit it in two. I then pinned down the officer, careful not to harm him. The officer could not free himself from my strength. The mother nearby held her hands to her heart while Alfie cheered.

I roared to the other police officers before they fired their guns. "Are you people crazy? There is a mother and her baby behind me. They could've gotten hurt!"

"Why should you care about another's life? You are just a blood-thirsty dragon!" one of them yelled.

That remark offended me. I was not looking for trouble. I had to let them know that.

"I'm not who you think I am!" I announced. "If I was a savage monster, I would have killed this man under my power, but I won't. I know it's hard to believe, but your government knows I'm here."

A military truck arrived within minutes. Now I could prove my point. A young British soldier jumped down from the truck. I released the policeman when I saw the soldier. The officer ran to join his comrades, shaken and humiliated.

"Hear me!" cried the soldier. "These two dragons are not our enemies. By order of the Prime Minister, I command you to let these… er, dragons free."

Grudgingly, the police lowered their weapons.

"How do you know the Prime Minister?" one of the officers questioned me.

Clipper and I both stared at each other. "Dragon's business," I said.

It took a while for the commotion to fade away. The street soon returned to normal after Clipper and I had left. We sat on a grassy slope outside the urban area. Clipper had his nineteen claws dug into the rain-moistened ground. The only thing I heard were a few passing cars on a nearby road and the bleating from a flock of sheep.

"What are we waiting for?" I asked to break the silence. "We know where to go now."

Clipper kneaded the ground like a cat. "Jacob, I've been thinking. What kind of dwarves, or whoever they are, do you think live in this 'guarded forest'?"

"I haven't a clue," I said, "but Monty said that there was something in the forest that no one believes exists. Dwarves for instance, and not the kind of dwarves we know. Soon they'll do something horrible to the whole world, apparently."

"Yeah. Not the kind we know, especially if they're trying to do something horrible."

"Exactly. We also believe Monty is in on this whole dark force thing. Let's just say the world has more magic than we thought. Life is full of mystery, you know. All we need to do is take out the evil on this world of ours."

Clipper sighed.

"I know you still don't believe in magic, but I do," I gnarred. "Right now, we can't let something like this go. We both have to assume the worst."

Clipper swallowed. "I'm not convinced about this magic deal, but I'll follow you. I'll say it's real."

"That's good," I replied. "Now we better go. We're losing time. To Norway. These dwarves and whatever else there is won't wait for us."

CHAPTER 14

THE CHUNNEL

In a large, dark tunnel, there was a faint rumble, followed by a ghostly light in the distance. The rumbling grew louder and louder. The ground started to shake. A passenger train suddenly came roaring out of the tunnel, grinding to a halt. Clipper and I kept well hidden. I peeked out from our hiding spot to find passengers getting off and on the train.

We could have flown across the English Channel to mainland Europe with no trouble, but we figured the Chunnel would be faster. We also decided to travel through France so we could fly over land the whole way to Norway. When we had the brief opportunity, we leapt up on top of one of the coaches.

"What do we do now?" asked Clipper.

I explored the top of the coach. "Well, if we don't want to cling to the top of the train for dear life at a high speed, maybe we can find an emergency hatch somewhere on the roof. We just have to make sure it's not to one of the main compartments. We don't want to startle the passengers."

Before either of us said anything else, the train started moving back down the tunnel. Unprepared for the sudden movement, Clipper and I tumbled from the metal top.

Clipper panicked as we stood up on the platform. "Jacob, the train is leaving!"

"Jump!" I roared.

Leaping anxiously, I caught a hold of the side, my claws creating twenty gashes in the wall of the coach. As the train increased speed, I slid backwards, shattering an entire window. Clipper made his own nineteen marks in the coach as well. We frantically tried to climb back to the top of the train when my rear foot slipped. I quickly gripped the coach's side. I already knew I was exposed, for I heard passengers screaming in disbelief. As I reached the top of the coach once again, the train was already traveling quite fast. All I could do was hang on with the hooks of my claws.

"Well, so much for finding a hatch!" Clipper huffed. I could barely hear him over the rushing air.

The train traveled even faster. I really wanted to get off the roof. I slowly crawled down the chain of coaches until I reached a car towards end of the train. Hissing with dismay, I realized that there was no way in from the roof.

"We can't stay on here forever!" roared Clipper, his voice racing past my ears.

"Use your instinct," I called back. I doubted that he had even heard me, so I trusted mine. Lifting myself up a few inches, I clawed the roof as hard as I could. Scratches appeared, followed by a ragged hole that continued peeling back. Sparks spewed out as I struck electrical wires. One spark landed right in my eye, causing me to flinch. The strong force of moving air caught my wings like wind to sails and pushed me on my back. I slid on my wings towards the edge. Acting out of sheer panic, I jammed my claws into the top of the train once more.

The wind tossed Clipper aside. He managed to latch onto another window. The glass instantly gave way to his claws. Clipper now hung by only his front paws. Reaching as far as he could, he embedded his claws into the roof of the coach and flung himself back to the top of the train. He slowly made his way to the hole in the roof, clawed at it until it was large enough, and dropped inside. He lay on the floor stunned, but unharmed.

I remained on the roof as the train sped along. Grunting, I scrambled for the hole I had created. I fell through and landed next to Clipper. The lights throughout the car were off.

"That was too much," Clipper panted. "I'm never doing something like that again."

"Maybe we should wait here throughout the ride," I suggested. "Hopefully, no one will come in here. It looks like a supply car. Yeah, we'll wait it out."

Clipper took several deep breaths. "You're right. Wait it out."

We then sat in silence, while our wings pressed against the sides of the car. All was well for the next several minutes. I was about to fall asleep when the door suddenly flew open. A man entered the car. He did not seem startled to see us at all. He rather had hostile stare.

"Who are you?" Clipper demanded, baring his teeth.

"The one you call Monty sent me," said the stocky man. "He knows you are coming. My people will be waiting for you. It seems that I myself do not have to wait."

"If Monty sent you, then I must ask; how involved is Monty to this Monolegion tribe?" I asked.

The man ignored me, so I took immediate action. Eying his face, I blew a little fireball that was too close for his comfort. The man yelled in pain. I did not notice that he a gun until it was too late. There was no time to question how he smuggled the gun onto the train. He pulled it out and fired. The bullet struck me in the chest. I fell over, feigning death. My eyes were open, but were motionless.

"You killed him!" yelled Clipper, catching onto my act. "You murderer!"

He immediately stood up and approached our enemy, his expression furious. The man stumbled back, terrified at the sight of Clipper's bared fangs. Wrapping his claws around the gun, Clipper yanked it away and tossed it out the hole above him. The man plucked up his courage and glared back at Clipper.

All I saw was too much for me to hold in. I stood up, cackling like a hyena. The man was confused. "I thought I killed you!" he exclaimed.

"You did shoot me," I said, "but did you know that dragon scales are thick? They may even be impenetrable. Your gun is powerless against us. Nothing on Earth can get past my hide. And by the way, I hate to see people killing each other with these stupid guns."

Wasting no time, the man tried to take me down. I realized that he was a well-trained fighter, but his experience was not enough. My size and stamina gave me a big advantage. When he attempted to clout my eye, I ducked and he struck my horn, cutting his hand deeply. At the right moment I gently butted him. We went crashing out the door, into the adjoining coach. The passengers wailed in horror.

"It's the dragon from America!" someone shouted.

"I knew something was going on in there!" cried another.

"*Coup d'oeil! La bête s'attaque le pauvre homme!*" yet another person screamed in French.

The man got to his feet with blood on his hands. He took out a knife that even he knew was useless. This frightened the passengers even more.

"That man has a knife!" someone cried.

I grabbed my foe's arm that held the harmless knife, and he simply dropped it to the floor. A security guard hurried over and grabbed the man. The guard explained that he had heard of our coming from the British authorities and said he would help us in any way he could.

"All you need to do is take this man away," Clipper said, emerging from the supply room.

The passengers stared at us in awe, at a loss of words.

"Sorry for the commotion," I said, feeling awkward.

I was on my way back to the supply car. Just when I thought it was over, the man struck the guard in the ribs with his elbow and stole his gun. He waved it in the air as he yanked an innocent woman to her feet. Screaming and squirming, the woman tried her hardest to regain her freedom, but to no avail.

"Surrender this instant or she dies!" the man growled.

My tail and wings dropped to the floor. The fight had unexpectedly turned in his favor. I did not want the woman to suffer because of me.

"All right," I hissed lightly. "I surrender."

"Good, I knew you would listen to reason," the man said.

His arm was wrapped around the woman's neck as he backed towards the supply car. Just as he reached the door, he pushed the woman forward. She tumbled into the aisle, effectively blocking my way as he retreated back into the supply car. Nearby passengers rushed to the woman's aid. I tried to go after my enemy, but my path was cramped. I saw him climb up to the hole. He was going to jump out of the top of the train! I had to stop him or else he would get sucked out. I tried to warn him, but he did not listen.

For a moment, he clutched at the sides of the hole, then he helplessly rolled to the side and towards the edge. Luckily, a neighboring train, going in the other direction, roared past. The man jumped with as much power he could muster.

Watching from the window, Clipper's mouth was wide open. "Oh no! He might be… wait… I see him! He's on the other train back to England!"

That was the last we had to worry about him. I was glad he had not hurt anyone. The passengers took their seats; none of them spoke. It was not long before the train slowed down when it reached the other end of the Chunnel. It came to a stop and the doors opened. Passengers flowed out into the station. I saw more people queuing on the platform, waiting for the coach to empty.

A man stared awkwardly at me as I strolled alongside him. When I left the station, I rejoined Clipper in a place out in the countryside where we were alone. We took a moment to stretch our limbs and wings.

"Well, we're in France. What do we do now?" asked Clipper.

"I don't know, head north?" I said dryly.

"I know that," Clipper sniffed. "My question is, '*how*' do we get there? Do we fly, hitchhike, book a plane, what?"

"Whatever we need to do," I answered.

We started walking down a rural road, away from the city. More time passed. We found ourselves in the middle of rural France. It was a great place to just spread our wings and relax.

"This is a lot easier than I thought," said Clipper, "but we don't really have a fast pace."

I took a deep breath. "You're right, we need to fly high in the sky. Everything is okay now, it's not like we're over dangerous territory and... wait. I hear a car coming."

Sure enough, a small car came into view. Several other cars of similar design were behind it, followed by a large armored truck.

"Clipper look, police. Maybe they can help us. The British authorities must have mentioned our coming to the French."

The police cars rolled to a stop. Two policemen stepped out of the main squad car, along with those from the other cars. They formed a line, facing us. Despite their uniforms, something was off about them. They smelled suspicious. I tried to brush the scent to the back of my mind; they looked like police to me.

"*Bonjur*," I greeted.

"Good day to you," said the policeman. He had no French accent to speak of. "You are the dragons who have been mentioned."

"I hope that's a good thing," Clipper said in a cheerful voice.

"Very good now. You are under arrest," the policeman announced.

At his signal, every police officer in the line drew their gun. I knew they could not harm Clipper or me in any way. Escaping would be easy, but I remembered how we dealt with the police back in the U.S. Fleeing would not help our cause. Besides, I did not want to feel the sting of bullets again, especially in my wings.

"May I ask why you're doing this?" I said.

"We're not causing any trouble," Clipper gently protested.

The police ignored our comments. The leader of the group ordered us to go in the truck. They tied ropes around our feet and wings, while our mouths were belted shut.

Clipper found a way to speak around the belt. "Is this even

necessary?" he asked me when we were alone in the truck.

"Something tells me this is not part of their regular duties," I said. "There's something strange going on here. Let's wait and see what this is."

Chang paced back and forth in his dormitory room. He could not believe what had happened to us. Once again, he read the note on my bed. The latest information he had was from Sergeant Nelson. We were in Britain and were last seen near a train station where the line headed to France.

He continued to pace until he had an idea. If he took a passenger plane to France, witnesses may give him clues as to where we were.

After a few more moments of pondering, he decided to sacrifice most of the savings from his part-time job to purchase a plane ticket to Paris. It was a quick yet important decision. Hours later, he was high in the sky. As his plane flew over the Atlantic Ocean, thoughts ran through his mind. His friends were dragons! How was this possible? He would not have believed the note had he not heard about the sightings. Dragons. Dragons! How could everything go so wrong? No matter the answer, he knew we were still his friends. He would not let us down just because we were different. Now was the time to become a true friend.

CHAPTER 15

IMPRISONED IN FRANCE

Paris was beautiful as we passed by the city early in the evening. It was a majestic place, like the gateway to Heaven itself. The armored truck did not go deep into the city, however. It turned onto a road that headed out to the countryside, far from Paris. We may have even been closer to Orléans or Dijon; I did not know exactly where we were.

The truck turned onto an unpaved road. We approached a rotting, rundown prison. Not many people knew the ugly penitentiary existed. Slavery and captivity were written all over its walls. It was large, dull-colored, and had bars over most of its windows except for three. Four towers with ramparts atop looked out over the prison grounds. To me, the building looked as if it was once an acropolis or a castle. I could see the resemblance.

Clipper and I were forced off the truck. There was no more time to view the prison before we entered the main office. We sat on the cold, stone floor with a wooden desk in front of us. Behind the desk sat the warden. He was a stern looking man with a ragged silver-gray mustache.

The warden glared at us with a pencil in hand, examining us, for he likely had never seen a dragon before, let alone two. We could have fought the warden and made an easy escape, but that would have just fed our bad reputation. We hoped to gain as much information as possible from this situation before making a clean escape later. I had my suspicions about the origin of the warden's authority. Nevertheless, we sat motionless, except our tails, which swayed back and forth.

The warden looked down at Clipper's feet. "You only have four claws on your left foot, I see," he said, pointing.

"Yes," said Clipper. "When we were in Indonesia and still human, a rebel soldier shot me from across a ravine. The bullet hit me right in the small toe. Funny how those rebels looked like Vikings if you ask me."

"Rebel soldiers in Indonesia? I have never heard such nonsense," said the warden. "Indonesia is a peaceful country. A rebellion there is unlikely." He seemed to be hiding something about his conclusion.

I was livid about this ordeal. Choosing to surrender and not fight was going against my natural urge. I tapped my forepaws on the floor as I held back the fire I wanted to cast. "Impossible nonsense is lighting a bonfire under her deck," I said, mocking the warden's claim.

The warden stood up and stepped around his desk. "You two have set all of France in panic. You have even attacked one of our citizens. Because of your actions, you must stay here until my supervisor comes."

"Attacking French citizens?" I growled. "We didn't do anything like that! He told us Monty, our nemesis back home, sent him. We haven't caused any panic in France! We barely came here!"

"Words can spread. You attacked people in New York City. Then you were seen in Canterbury, England. The your victim told me that he was just an innocent bystander and that *you* attacked him."

Clipper seemed upset as well, except he held in his anger much better than I did. "He was lying," he said calmly.

A guard burst through the door before I could add to Clipper's truth. "I heard one of them yelling at you. Is everything all right, sir?" the guard asked.

The warden swished his fingers. "Take these two creatures away. We need to keep them here until the supervisor arrives."

Clipper and I both hissed in dismay. What was really going on here? The warden assumed that we were just savage beasts looking for trouble. If we were, we would have fought our way to freedom. I almost did, to be honest. In my rage, I felt like turning him into a pile of ash. It was only Clipper with his calmer nature that had spared the worthless prison keeper. It angered me how my promised coming had arrived and yet had already sparked hatred in so many. Like the man in the train, Monty and his people, and now the warden, they were all distrustful and suspicious. What struck me was that all my enemies seemed to look alike. They were short, most of them muscular. I really started to believe that they were the dwarves of the Monolegions.

INSIDE THE AIRPORT CHANG PICKED UP HIS BAG AND SLUNG IT OVER his should. It had been a long flight and he was tired, but he enjoyed every moment of his time in Paris. He decided to have a snack before starting his search. He sat at a small table under a green umbrella and munched on a tasty éclair. It was a wonderful experience.

When he finished half of his pastry, Chang noticed that the person sitting on the chair next to him was listening to the radio. Chang had studied French before and understood some of the broadcast. It reported that two dragons had been captured and taken to a special prison. The location of the prison was not mentioned. The report ended with words of comfort, so that the people's fears could be put to rest.

Many people nearby stared incredulously at the radio. They offered a wide range of comments.

Chang started to sweat. Not only had his friends been turned into dragons, but they were now trapped in a French prison! Chang was relieved to know that he was at least in the right country, but he was still aghast at learning of the whirlwind transformation. He had to find us sooner rather than later.

He racked his brain for ideas on how to find us. It would be crazy to *visit* us in the prison, that is if he knew which prison to go to. It took him a second, then it struck him. Two policemen had come into his view. What caught Chang's attention were their appearances. The policemen's uniforms looked different from what he had seen earlier after leaving the airport. They had a belligerent look different from real enforcers of the law.

Now for Chang's plan.

He took the rest of his éclair, along with the plate, and sauntered in the direction of the two constables. When he approached them, he threw the éclair at the officer on his left. It landed square in the policeman's face. The other officer walked angrily up to Chang. To ensure something awful would happen, Chang took a glass of wine from a nearby table and poured it on the officer's head, not saying a word.

Several of the people watching laughed hysterically. The two policemen, embarrassed and furious, grabbed Chang and tossed him in a police car. It seemed like his plan was working. Chang fervently hoped that he was headed to the right prison. He inwardly chuckled at getting himself arrested.

With no due process, Chang was taken directly to a special bus. He sat in the front seat, all alone save the guards and the driver. The bus left the city headed a desolate place. Chang stepped off the mud-splattered vehicle when it reached the prison. It looked like a prison that should have been abandoned decades ago. Chang took a dry, deep breath as he eyed the small, bastille penitentiary. The feeling of something unearthly came to his senses. He felt sure we were nearby.

Chang began to look around. *It shouldn't be hard to spot a dragon*, he thought. As his eyes wandered, one of the prisoners approached him.

"*Bonjur*, friend. My name is Byron," the friendly man said, shaking Chang's hand. "I have been here for years, but I do not think you will be here for so long."

Chang felt happy to meet someone so friendly. He took the opportunity to glean as much information as he could from the man. "My name is Chang, pleased to meet you. So, where are we? This is not like any prison I've ever heard of," he said.

Bryon leaned close to Chang's ear. "Between you and me, this is no real prison. The guards who run this are not real guards. They speak no French. I understand English, and I hear them speak that language. They also speak a northern language, too. I believe it is either Swedish or Norwegian."

Chang nodded. "Interesting to know. I live… er…lived in New York."

"Welcome Chang," said Byron, smiling. "Sorry for the trouble. I know you are not a real criminal. I am not a criminal myself, you know. Don't worry. But if I may say, you look like a man on a mission. Why are you really here? An inside job, perhaps?"

Chang explained to Bryon why he was at the prison. "…so I intentionally got myself arrested because I'm looking for a friend. Two friends, actually. Jacob and Clipper. Have you seen them?"

"I have never heard those names," Byron replied.

Chang sighed, running his hand through his hair. "Have there been any visitors here who are unusual?"

Byron looked skeptically at Chang. "I know you won't believe me, but there is something here you may have never seen before."

"Are they dragons?" Chang asked with a lump in his throat.

"I know it is ridiculous, but it's the truth."

Chang's heart raced. He felt like he was going to burst. "Yes! I do believe you. Those dragons are my friends. I've known them for years."

Bryon cocked an eyebrow. "You have?"

"Yes! Can you tell me where they are? I need to see them!"

Just then, a bang rang out behind him. As Chang turned to look, the doors to the main complex swung open.

CLIPPER AND I SPRINTED OUT, GIGGLING, WITH THE ANGRY WARDEN behind us. Chang was both frightened and excited. With my speed, I easily outran the warden. When I reached Chang, I skidded to a stop, astounded to see my roommate in the prison. A small flame left my mouth in surprise.

"*Du elendige drager! Fortell det aldri igjen!*" the warden shouted in his native tongue.

Chang had to catch his breath as well after seeing me. "Hi... ehh... Jacob? Clipper?"

I did not believe my eyes at first. Chang stared straight at me, not even blinking. I never thought he would be here in France.

"Chang! What are you doing here?" I asked.

Chang gulped. "After I discovered what you and Clipper did to yourselves, I had to find you. Your voice... I didn't recognize it before. If you're wondering how I knew you were in France, I talked with Sergeant Nelson. He told me that the last sign of you was in the Chunnel."

"How did you get thrown in this prison?" inquired Clipper.

"Simple, I intentionally got myself arrested. That part was fun, too. I had to make sure I was tormenting the right police or else I would've been taken to a different jail. I picked out two officers that stood out from the other police I'd seen already since I arrived in Paris. By the way, that man who's yelling at you, what's his name?"

"Oh, he is really starting to push us to our limits," I said. "We just wanted to have a little fun with him. That's the warden. I guess he doesn't have a good sense of humor."

The warden caught up to us, his face red. "Who do you think you are, trying to be smart with me and then run off? How dare you!"

"I can enjoy myself, can't I?" said Clipper.

"Hold, *kjeft!*" the warden shouted. "Will you please stop talking? I cannot bear it! Just wait when my supervisor arrives. He will properly deal with you two!"

I gently touched the tips of my claws to his back. He quickly batted my paw away.

"Listen," I said. "I don't want to accuse you or anything, but you're not being fair. Is it my appearance? You have no reason to fear us."

"What do you mean by that?" grunted the warden.

"What I'm saying is that I haven't killed anyone. I've been telling you that for days."

"I do not believe that one bit!"

"It is actually true," Chang said.

"Is it?" said the warden, turning to Chang. "What does a Chinese man know about these dragons of, should I say, a European appearance?"

Chang folded his arms. "Okay, let me tell you something. These dragons have known me for a while. They're my friends!"

The warden did not like the truth one bit. "Stop it, now! Just for that, you three will be locked in your cells for two weeks. No privileges for any of you! How does that sound, newcomer?"

He was red in the face, so we decided not to bother him for the moment. The three of us did what we were asked to do. As we made our way back to the prison, I glared at my keeper. The warden simply returned the glare. There was pure hatred in his eyes. I turned my head forward as I retired to my cell. He, like the grandfather, knew the rise of the dragon had come.

I SAT NEAR THE WINDOW. CHANG WAS BESIDE ME. MY FRIENDS AND I discussed our situation all day. Chang did not know how to react to the tip of my wing tickling him. I did not do it intentionally, but I had to stretch my wings.

"So, now that we're reunited, should we try to escape?" asked Clipper.

"I'd really like to leave this house of offal," I said. "This will take careful planning."

Chang tilted his head. "Offal? Since when did you use words like that?"

I thought about his question for a moment. "Hmm. I get what you're saying. I said 'poltroons' a few days ago."

"I feel that way too," said Clipper. "I've said words lately I rarely use as well. No matter, let's focus on the task at hand. How about we just wait until the guard opens the door and when the time is right, we run right out of here? Easy as that."

"Yes, but what about me and Byron?" asked Chang.

Clipper lowered his head. "Oh, I forgot about that. Sorry. The plan will have to be a bit more complex, I'm afraid. It just needs to be quick yet effective. We still have to go north."

At that moment, Byron came into our cell with a tray of fruit. "Dinner," he said. "For a nasty prison, the food is not so bad."

"Thanks, but food is not what I'm concerned about," I said. "We're going to get out of here. You can come along with us if you like, Byron."

"Yes, please," Byron begged. "I want to get out of here and see my family again."

"You may come with us," I said, "but we have to make a fool-proof plan. I don't want anyone hurt or killed."

Clipper thought as I refolded my wings. "We need to create some sort distraction," he suggested. "That way the guards will be more focused on the diversion than us. Next thing we know, we're home free!"

I nodded. Clipper was right, we needed to form a distraction. If only I could get my paws on something that would explode. Explosions could be a very effective diversion in a prison. The guards would think that a riot had broken out or something like that. When they went to investigate the four of us could escape. But there was still another obstacle: the outer walls with numerous guard towers surrounding the perimeter. If it were just me and Clipper, escape would be easy. It was Chang and Byron I worried about.

I thought for a moment until I had an idea. I asked Byron if the prison had a weapons facility. He mentioned a storage shed that held guns and other arms. There were two doors to the shed. If I waited until nightfall, my plan could be put into action. I knew there were guards nearby. It would have been stupid of the warden not to have them on duty. As angry as the warden was, he was not dull-minded. My advantage was that the guards were never near the cell door for their own safety. They stood watch at the end of the hallway.

Night soon fell, granting a new moon. The only light outside came from the searchlights on the four towers. It was time for my plan. My three friends stayed in the cell. All I had to do was evade the guards and head to the shed without being spotted. I was the chosen one for the task because my black scales would help me camouflage with the darkness.

"Ready?" Clipper asked.

"I am," I replied.

"There's just one small problem," said Chang. "The door is barred. How do you get past it?"

Without answering, I stepped up to the door. I latched onto one of the bars with my claws and bit down on the center bar. Flames spat out as I clamped my teeth. The bar glowed from the heat. I bit down on the hot metal and the bar soon gave away. I spat out the remaining steel, then moved on to the next bar.

In no time at all, three bars were melted and removed. I used my horns to dig away the soft metal. When I finished, I turned back to my friends. "Well, I'm off. See you in a bit."

The hallway was dark. I knew the interior walls were made of fine wood (a bad place for a misguided flame). I figured the guards would be down the left side of the hallway, so I moved like specter to the right. If I was to remain unnoticed, I had to walk slowly. Moving too fast would result in the clicking of my claws. That would give me away.

I slowly made my way to the open window at the end of the hall.

The window was about ten feet wide with the help of the eroded stone. It did not look safe for the guards or prisoners, and possibly violated a few safety codes. At least it was bigger than the window in the library. It had no glass or bars either.

My wings brushed against the sides as I scrambled out. Once outside, I found myself dangling on the jagged wall about forty feet in the air. With my claws, I started climbing down. All was well until saw a searchlight heading in my direction. I immediately leaned close to the wall. Sure enough, my black scales did the trick. The light flew right below me. Not even my brown wings were noticed.

With the coast clear, I continued to make my way to the shed. When I reached it, I found a padlock secured the door. Had the prison been more kept up, the weapons shed would have probably been much more difficult to break into. Similar to the bars on the door, I bit the lock. This time, I used no heat. The light could make the guards on the towers suspicious. I had to bite much harder, but I destroyed the lock. Quietly opening the door, I shut it behind me just as the searchlight slid over the door.

As I looked around inside, I spotted an envelope resting on a crate. Curious, I opened the envelope with one swipe with a claw. I removed a sheet of paper. My pupils dilated as I focused on the note.

It read:

Triathra, our trusted Leader
From the country of France.

This is a WARNING! The dragons have finally returned. They show a true threat to the One Tribe. If something is not done immediately, the Nibelungs will be in grave danger. Please come once you have read this.

- Your loyal servant, Greyhair

I almost laughed at the names of Triathra and Greyhair. Could those names be translations of something else? And the Nibelungs. They were the same men we had encountered in Georgia, the Monolegion dwarves! This note was an alert of my and Clipper's coming. I read the document again then slid the note back into the envelope. With a single flame, I incinerated it.

As I continued to explore the eerie place, I found old and rusted guns, crossbows, and composite bows. I hissed at the sight. Vile weapons, modern or not, did not please me one bit. However, I could use them to my advantage.

I gathered a few crates full of ammunition. I opened shotgun shells and other bullets, which spewed gunpowder. I gathered the gunpowder and looked for something to put it in. Ripping off the barrel of a double-barrel shotgun with my teeth, I used a claw to bend one end of the barrel.

Next, I found a crate of classic grenades. If I used a grenade itself, the explosion alone would be too strong. All I wanted was a little burst. Heads would turn, but no skin would burn. I removed the detonator from the main section of the grenade. I then removed the red paste inside. Taking the detonator with me, I made my own makeshift firework. My Molotov cocktail was ready, though I had doubts it would work. It was worth a try. I could always find something else if my bomb failed.

There was one minor problem. I could carry the gunpowder in one paw, and the detonator in the other. I would just have to shift to being bipedal temporarily. I would have to crouch, but that was not an issue. The main problem was the explosive pre-workout. Where should I carry that? With a number of ways to do so, I found the most efficient but riskiest solution.

Before I picked up the detonator, I placed the cellucor in my mouth. Any disturbance and it would trigger, so I had to bottle up the heat from my frenzied lungs. With the plugged barrel of gunpowder, several detonators, and the cellucor in my mouth, I waited for the right moment to exit the door.

When the searchlight passed again, I had the cover in the darkness. It would be hazardous trying to climb the wall with only my back claws, so I spread my wings and lifted off the ground.

I spiraled in the air to gain altitude, then flew to the ruined window, flattening my wings against my back at the last second. My three friends waited patiently for me.

"Looks to me like you were successful. How did it go?" Chang asked when I reached the door.

I nodded before carefully spitting out the cellucor. "It went very well," I said when my mouth was empty. "I might have the makings of a good distraction. I couldn't be in there for too long, though. Byron, can you find some paper and some tape?"

"I'll see what I can do," Byron said as he slipped through the door. He was careful not to touch the hot metal.

"So, you're going to wrap the red paste and gunpowder in the paper and tape it together," said Clipper with a hint of doubt in his voice. "When that's finished, you connect the detonator to the main portion of the bomb. When you pull it, it should be engulfed in flames for a few seconds before it explodes. Right?"

"It should if we're lucky" I replied and complimented Clipper's observation.

It was not long before Byron returned with the paper and tape. I began the process of creating the bombs. When I finished, I showed it to Clipper.

"Pulling the pin on this thing you made won't work," said Chang.

"What do you suggest?" Clipper questioned.

Chang thought for a moment. "Replace the pin with a fuse?"

I reasoned with that idea. "We'll try it. Just remember, the supply truck will come early in the morning tomorrow. Clipper and I will fire the first few bombs. If they go off, you two should be at the edge of the window. If they don't, Clipper and I will use our own fire for the distraction. We will come back to give you a ride down. We jump in the truck and take off."

Chang scoffed. "Ride on you? You want us to ride on you?"

"I'm not looking forward to this either, but it has to be done," I said. "When dawn breaks, the plan goes into action."

Clipper liked that idea. He gave a long yawn and sat in the corner of the cell. "It'll be a big day. I recommend we try to sleep."

"Good idea," said Chang, yawning as well. "It's been a long day. I was also wondering, Jacob, why does Clipper have sabered teeth and you don't?"

I ran my tongue over my top row of teeth. "To tell you the truth, I don't really know. Your guess is as good as mine."

Chang lay in his bed. "That should be something to think about as I sleep."

Enough was said. Bryon slept on the top bunk. Chang slept on the bottom. Clipper and I curled up on the floor. It took a moment before I drifted off to sleep. I did not realize how tired I was before I shut my eyes. The room became silent, quiet before the events of the next day.

CHAPTER 16

THE ESCAPE

I was lost in a thick forest. I looked this way and that. There was no sign of the prison. As I explored the forest, I heard a distant noise. It sounded like a low huff. I did not know what to think when I saw another dragon land next to me. It looked somewhat similar to me, except it had brass-colored scales. I could not tell if the mysterious dragon was a physical being or an apparition.

"The rise of the dragon has come. Swear that you will never fall into evil, the natural mind of a dark-scaled dragon," the dragon said.

I assumed it was the spirit again. "You told me that dragons are evil, but I don't have to be. I can overcome my natural heart and be who I should be, right?"

A warm feeling came over me.

"If you replace the evil in your heart with what you see is good, you will fulfill a promise," said the spirit. "But be warned: you will be tested. The dark force you seek is in the forest of the country you know as Norway. Be aware, they also strike elsewhere in this world. As you progress, you will see a glimpse of your true home."

I was confused at what he had told me. "I understand that these Monolegions have already set stakes in other parts of the world. Monty was right, and it's already begun." I started to breathe heavily. "But what do you mean I will see my true home? Did I live somewhere else?"

"You must understand," said the dragon, "you must do all you can to defeat the Monolegions first. You will understand what I say about your true home soon enough."

That answer set my mind in a spiral. "True home? What do you mean? Was I born somewhere else? Was I a dragon when I was born?"

"You will learn in your own due time, Jacob. Right now, you must find the leader of the Monolegions. He is a strong and powerful sorcerer."

"A sorcerer? My enemy is a sorcerer?" I almost did not believe what I had heard. "You said he was a strong and powerful leader. Where do I start if I want to defeat him? I know nothing of magic or sorcery."

"You will be guided by the following steps," the spirit explained. "First: find the Guarded Forest. Your first questions will be answered there.

"Second: there is an emblem of your return. The emblem is the representation of you. Find it and protect it with all your power.

"Third: destroy the Monolegion power. Cut off the main body of your enemy.

"Forth: find your way back home. I believe you will stand as a key of opposition to the Vesuvian crown.

"Work hard in these tasks. Do not use your abilities for evil. Use them for good and for what is right. I was a dragon in my mortal life, and I know we are wicked creatures."

I started to feel scared. "What is this Vesuvian crown? Was it responsible for my life as a human? Is my life really what I think it is? Tell me more."

The spirit ignored me. I continued to gasp heavily when the ground began to quake. A large crack opened in the ground and the dragon glided down the chasm.

I heard his last words. "I will be a part of this Earth. Defeat the sorcerer, and you will return home."

I watched him disappear down into the abyss as the forest went up in flames. The sight was awful. I gazed back up into the sky where I saw another dragon in the sky. This one definitely had a physical body. It was large, red, and had glowing orange eyes. It was well over twice my size, maybe bigger. As it flew off, all my fears seemed to vanish. All the noise around me faded into silence. The fire around the ghostly trees dissolved in a mist of black smoke that tattered away in the warm wind. I felt comforted as I took another look at the sky. Oh, the sky was so lovely! I felt like I was on another world. I could see a violet nebula, many stars, and even a blue ringed planet that looked to be about the same size as the Moon! The celestial sight brought me to tears. I felt like I was home. I stood in awe until I realized that I was in a dream. I was still in the prison. That did not upset me much.

My eyes blinked open. Fatigue gave way to pure energy. I turned to see Clipper wakening as well. We were both ready for the day.

"What a dream." I yawned. "I dreamt that I was visited by the spirit of the dragon of old. He told me about my true home. It was strange."

Clipper seemed as refreshed as I was. "Well, you seem ready for today's events. Now for us to get out of this prison. It's funny, I had a dream like yours. And this wasn't the first time I had it. You know, I'm starting to think this spirit is real. I know it sounds crazy, but I guess there really is more to this Earth than we know. Being dragons just shows a part of the road."

We were still talking about the dream when Byron and Chang woke. Their eyes opened with several blinks. Once they were up, all four of us knew that our plan of escape was ready to happen. Only one thought came to us: "prepare ourselves". I gathered up the bombs I had made the night before while waiting impatiently for the supply truck to arrive. Byron had told me that the truck came to the prison once every week. It was either now or never for our escape. We could not wait another week.

Clipper's ears perked up after several minutes. "I hear the truck coming. Get ready," he said, huffing smoke from his nose.

It was not long before I heard the truck rolling through the open prison gate. That was my signal. No guards had come by our cell since last night. With some bombs in my grasp, I climbed through the hole in the door once more and out the open window. This time I climbed to the top of the tower. Clipper followed me. I had a good view once I was on top of the roof. The breeze gave me a sour-sweet scent.

What interested me did not come by smell, but by sight. Down below, I saw the warden speaking with an unknown person. I told Clipper to wait for my first bomb to make sure they worked. I lit the fuse with a small flame from my nostril. The bomb burst into a small yet feisty blaze. The flame would reach the grenade's cellucor in just a few seconds, so I hurled the bomb into the air. It landed with a thud behind the warden on the ground below. He went to inspect the strange object when it exploded with a loud bang. The warden jumped back in fright.

I could hardly believe it. It worked perfectly! I had my doubts that it would work, but the bomb had detonated against all odds. Unfortunately, I had no time to stand amazed. I roared as a signal to go.

I ignited another bomb after Clipper ignited his first. They both blew. An alarm sounded after my second bomb's explosion. Guards swarmed around the grounds. They did not know where the bombs were coming from.

From the window, Chang threw a rope down the side of the tower, opposite from the main grounds (I guess the rope took place of the riding). He and Byron climbed down before anyone spotted them. When they safely reached the bottom, Clipper jumped off the tower. I followed with the bombs in my claws. We landed next to our friends with dirt flying around the disturbed ground.

"Sure beats riding dragons," Chang said to Byron.

We ran around the building and headed for the truck. Chang reached the driver's seat while Byron sat in the passenger's side. Clipper and I climbed into the covered truck bed with the tail-end open. We dropped our bombs in the bed, ready to use them if needed. Clipper tore out the cover around us so we could fit our unfolded wings in comfortably. Chang started the truck and the engine roared to life. The driver, who was cowering from the disturbance, recognized the sound and immediately rushed after us. He would have had enough time to catch up, but I spewed a warning flame in his path. The former driver jumped away.

We were home free by the looks of it, so I cast a larger, victorious flame out of the truck.

My dragon laugh rang out. Clipper bared his sabered teeth as he hooted aloud as well. Our laughing died down when I heard Chang's voice coming from the cab, "Jacob, I can't believe this worked. Those bombs actually work! I've got to say I'm surprised you found all those things to make your bombs."

"You know, all the people we have run into lately do the strangest things," said Clipper. "They all look like they came from the same place. This prison must be run by those Monolegions. All these incidents have to trace back to the Guarded Forest."

"We'll see when we get there," I replied.

Chang frowned, keeping an eye on the road. "What forest? Is there someone who's sending all these weird people?"

"It may even tie in with Monty," I said. "That was why he tried to steal our samples in the first place. He captured Sally to do so." I did not want to say anything about the sorcerer that was mentioned in my dream just yet.

Chang started to pick up speed when Byron pointed at something ahead. I looked at where he was pointing. The warden was off in the distance with his arms in the air. He appeared to be holding some sort of stick or wand. Something did not feel right.

"How did he get there?" Chang exclaimed.

My puzzling was cut short when one of the truck's front tires suddenly blew. The truck veered left and right then tipped on its side in a nasty crash. I lost my balance, toppling onto Clipper, who roared in shock. We crawled out of the back, both of us wobbling in a dizzy state. Chang and Byron climbed out the upturned door. Other than a small cut on Chang's arm, they were not harmed.

Three guards surrounded the overturned truck. Knowing the nature of ranged weapons on my scales, be it guns or crossbows, I prepared to cast a flame to ward them off. But before I could, one of the guards held a gleaming dagger at Byron's throat.

"One finger of fire I see and your friend will die!" the guard screamed in sheer anger.

I could not let anything happen to Byron after all we had been through. Like Marvin, he was a man who trusted me since we first met. I did as the guard commanded and let out a dry growl instead.

The warden stepped between Byron and me. "There's a good dragon. I already know that a bullet won't pierce your heart from the outside, but it can on the inside."

"There seems to be no available transportation," one of the guards said. "We will have to walk back to the prison."

"It's two kilometers away," the warden said, shaking his head. "You dragons should not have attempted an escape."

With the dagger still pressed against Byron's throat, I cooperated. We took the discouraging trek back to the prison. I was depressed. Our escape had been going so well! How had the warden caused the truck to crash? All I had seen was the man pointing to the heavens with a strange stick. It looked as if he had used some sort of magic. That would not surprise me at this point.

We reached the prison about twenty minutes later. The warden ordered us to go directly to his office. I obeyed, still aware of the dagger against Byron's back. The other two guards walked behind Chang. They were armed as well.

"Sit down, you four," the warden commanded when we were all in the office.

We silently sat down, unaware of our fate. This was going to be a matter of life and death for my friends. The idea of the warden using magic was on my mind. Monolegions might be more dangerous than I first thought.

The office felt different than when I first came here. At least none of my friends were seriously injured, but my anger for the warden was building nonetheless. I had a dire urge to simply rip him apart. Then my recent dream came to mind. I was naturally evil. I had to overcome my natural desires. To hold back this feeling of violence, I decided to try teasing the warden, hoping it would help calm me.

"So the penalty for escaping prison is going back to prison?" I asked smartly.

"Enough of your silly words, Draco! If you keep talking like that, I will pluck your eyes out," the angry warden said.

"Isn't that illegal?" I inquired. "I thought the French didn't use torture these days. I thought that there were rights here. I love France; it's a great place to be. But I wonder, what kind of representation do you think you're making of such a lovely nation?"

"Yes, but you're a dragon," said Clipper, realizing my intentions.

"Yes, I am a dragon," I began, "but I still act like a human. I've been a human for almost nineteen years. Do I get the rights of a human? I still am technically human. And even if we were just random dragons out there in the world, we're an endangered species. Why? Just take a look at us. How many dragons are on the Earth this very moment? Two. And last time I looked, it's illegal to kill an endangered species. It's also illegal to kill in circumstances like this. So there are, let me think, three reasons why you shouldn't pluck my eye with a knife. Besides, it's just vulgar. And if…"

"I've heard enough!" the warden shouted. He ran his hand through his silver-gray hair. "You may be a different sort of human, but one thing you should learn is that you are in *my* prison!"

As he finished speaking, he took out the long, wooden wand he had before. He pointed the wand at us. That was when it came to me. Greyhair! *He* was the writer of the note I had found in the shed. My beliefs were confirmed: the strange people we were seeking in the Guarded Forest were on our trail. The warden's name, funny as I thought it to be, was Greyhair! It made sense, too, because of his grayish colored hair. The truth was very uncomfortable. He had to have flattened the tire with... magic!

I pondered until Greyhair spoke to me again. "What's the matter, Jacob Draco? Nothing smart to say this time?"

I could not take it any longer. The teasing was over for me. "Sir, I don't want to play this game anymore. I've just figured it out. Your real name is Greyhair, and you're frightened now that we've come. You're from the Guarded Forest, aren't you? The forest that Clipper and I are looking for. You're a dwarf!"

My words seemed to have crossed Greyhair's boundaries. He stood up, red in the face. "The dragon knows! Kill him!"

Two guards burst in. Each had useless revolvers.

"What are you doing?" Greyhair yelled to the guards. "Bullets won't do any good!"

The guards had nothing else other than their revolvers. Even though the bullets held no threat to my life, I had to take action before they turned on Chang and Byron. The last few times I battled, I fought gently because I did not want to critically injure my opponent. This was a different circumstance.

With adrenaline pumping through my body, I felt my wrath return. This time it was a wrath I had never felt before. I was not going to let a few little revolvers hold me back. Besides, it was not evil to protect the lives of my friends. With my abilities, I cast a flame; a flame that was too big for the small office. The doorway was ablaze and the two guards were on fire. They rolled along the hallway floor in panic. With them out of the way, I turned to Greyhair. Baring my claws, I swiped them over Greyhair's shirt. He fell to the ground with several holes in his shirt. Chang and Byron stood by the office window, staying away from the flames and watching me in fear and uncertainty.

I stood directly over Greyhair, while Clipper attacked the two guards outside the door. He ran through the spreading flames like a fiery spirit and tackled them both. I kept my attention on Greyhair. I cornered him at the far side of the obliterated office. The warden had nowhere to go. His last chance was a rapier that was strapped to his leg. But before he could pull it out, I cut the strap with a single swipe of a claw. The rapier fell to the ground with a humiliating flop. Knowing that Greyhair was weaponless, I wrapped my claws around his arm. With my paw on his stomach, I pressed him to the floor. I was ready to sink my teeth into his shoulder when I gazed in his eyes. There was no pride in them, only fear. I really wanted to punish him for imprisoning me, but I hesitated. It did not feel right. Nevertheless, I was still angry; and the anger of a dragon was no light matter, I had come to notice.

"Killing is my first instinct, and I don't like it when rats like you think you can defeat me," I growled. "But today you are lucky. I have no need to kill you any more."

My claws tore through what remained of his shirt, then they crossed his chest and up to the right shoulder, leaving three large claw marks etched into his flesh. Greyhair yelled in fright. I made the scratches deep enough to be permanent but not life-threatening. He gasped for air with my paw on his chest. I relieved the pressure when Clipper ran back into the office.

"Jacob, this place is burning. Those are wooden walls out there, and we're on the top floor," he said. "How do we get Chang and Byron out of here?"

I turned my head. My two friends stared out the window, then back at me. The window had a glass pane that swung out if unlatched. That reminded me of the open window I had used already, so I made my way to the window at the end of the hallway. Chang jumped over the flames to the window. He gave me a concerned stare after peering over the edge. "Oh, no way," he moaned. "I know what you're thinking, Jacob. I can't do that."

"I don't want to either, but the only possible way out is for you to ride on my back."

Chang was restless. "No. There's no way."

"It's the only solution," I said. "Now do it!"

Chang moaned again. I felt his leg go over my back. Byron and Clipper came to the window. When they saw what Chang was doing, Byron jumped on Clipper's back.

Chang yelled in pain when he sat down. "Ow! I just sat on your spikes!" He lifted himself a few inches, his legs cradled in the joints of my wings.

I knew he was going to react to my spikes. I gave no apology. I just told him to hang on, then I jumped off the window's ledge, spreading my wings. Chang's weight and mass were affecting my flying in a very bad way. I flapped as hard as I could, but no progress was made. Chang's awkward position was rushing me. I rapidly glided down to the ground below. After I landed, Clipper fell on top of me. It was a very strange experience.

"I'm not taking you on my back again," I muttered to Chang. "It'll never work for me."

"Now you understand," replied Chang, still panting.

As I shook myself free from the dirt, numerous police cars and a few fire trucks surrounded the prison. One of the policemen approached me. This constable looked much different from the police who had brought Clipper and me here in the first place. I could tell he did not want any trouble. He was taller than those I had confronted before. He was no Monolegion.

"Are you Jacob Draco?" he asked, nervous of my presence.

"Yes, and over there is Clipper. Justin Clipper," I said, pointing to my friend with my muzzle.

The policeman spoke in a thick accent. "Jacob Draco, I have been informed about you. The police who have captured you and sent you to this prison are corrupt. You may have noticed that. You may have also noticed that there are not many prisoners here. Most of them are not even convicts. So you see, you are now free. But I must ask, what are you dragons doing here in France? I thought you were from America."

Clipper looked at me.

"Our business here is of a personal nature," I said. "Sorry."

The officer understood and concluded his business. My three friends and I watched as the firefighters tried to douse the fire that invaded the inside of the prison.

CHAPTER 17

SALLY'S SEARCH FOR ANSWERS

Digging through desks and under the bed in my room, Sally searched in determination for just one clue as to where I could be. She felt a slight sense of guilt, wishing she had helped more with the experiment. After twenty minutes Sally decided to take a break. She felt exhausted as she sat in Chang's desk chair. *Something seems wrong here,* she thought.

Sally had not seen us in over a month. Now Chang was missing as well. Sally sorely regretted making the decision to not visit Clipper and me before we had dinner with Cynthia. Had she done so, then maybe she could have had more information. Then Sally thought about Cynthia. That was it! Cynthia might have some valuable information

Sally replaced everything in the room. When she was done, she took a taxi to the mansion where Cynthia lived and told the driver to wait before going to the front door. The grandfather clock chime of the doorbell rang throughout the house, summoning Cynthia's father. He did not recognize Sally. "Can I do something for you, miss?" he asked.

"Yes, sir," Sally responded. "I'm looking for Cynthia. Is she here?"

"Oh, I'm afraid not. She's down at the college labs. Are you a friend?"

"Yes, I'm a friend," said Sally. "You say she's at the labs? I'll go there right now. Thank you for your help. It means a lot."

THE TALES OF DRACO   185

She returned to the taxi and told the driver to take her back to the college campus. Sally hoped that she could find some answers from not just Cynthia, but from other people as well. She knew that Clipper and I had many friends, and the chances that someone would know something seemed great. As Sally made her way to the laboratories, she stopped at the front desk. She asked the receptionist where Cynthia might be and was informed that she was on the second floor, room 223. Thanking the receptionist, Sally took the stairs up to the next level. She entered room 223 to find test tubes and opened notebooks. There were several students present; among them was Cynthia.

"Cynthia!" Sally called out. "Can I speak with you?"

Cynthia placed her notebook on a nearby table and followed Sally out into the hall. "Hi, Sally. What is it?" she asked kindly.

Sally gulped, thinking of what to say. "Did you know Jacob and Clipper are gone?"

Cynthia frowned, causing a rain of worries to drench Sally's thoughts. It was clear Cynthia did not know anything of value. Sally shared what she knew about the science experiment and the disappearances.

Several tears rolled down Cynthia's face when she recalled the night at Théo's Garden (Cynthia was one to express her emotions). "The last time I saw them was at dinner after Jacob's basketball game," she said. "I'm worried about Clipper. We dated before he and Jacob left on their expedition. I was a bit nervous about them leaving alone that night. Now you say they're gone?"

"Did they continue their experiment after that dinner?" asked Sally.

"I don't think so. I was a little confused. You know how Clipper never liked fish because he was allergic to it? Well, something was out of line that night. He and Jacob scarfed down their food. And what's funny was that Clipper enjoyed his salmon, *and* his face didn't swell one bit. Stranger still, they just…well… ate like animals! I don't know why. Something strange was going on that night. After dinner, they both said they were feeling dizzy and had a burning in their chest. I let them go home. That was the last time I saw them. Oh, I'm worried now. Do you know where they are?"

Sally sadly shook her head. She and Cynthia stood in silence for a moment. Sally pondered the idea of talking to others who were close to Clipper and me. Thanking Cynthia for her help, she returned to the dormitories and questioned Clipper's roommate, Joshua.

"The last time I heard anything about Jacob and Clipper was when Chang called me and said he was going to meet them," said Joshua, "but I don't know where he was going. He didn't say. It's funny, Chang sounded worried over the phone, like he'd just seen a ghost or something."

Sally did not find any useful answers. The various clues from Sally's other friends were diverse and unrelated:

"I've haven't seen Jacob and Clipper in a while. I wonder where they are."

"I would *guess* that they're on vacation, but the semester is ready to end."

"It's true, Jacob's gone. And I'm pretty sure Clipper's with him. If one is gone, the other one is gone as well. They're the best of friends."

"Last I heard, they were in their own lab out of the city."

"Last time I saw Jacob was at his basketball game. One of his finest games, too. I've seen him play well before, but not *that* well."

Each response took Sally nowhere. *I hope their disappearance didn't have anything to do with their science project,* she thought. Chang told Sally that something had happened to us before he left, but he was not clear in his explanation.

"This is as mysterious as the panic over those dragons a while ago," she told Joshua later that day. "You know, that happened about the same time Jacob and Clipper left." Sally felt a chill run down her spine when she said that. "I hope Jacob and Clipper didn't get hurt from whatever was out there."

Wondering if the two incidents were related, Sally's questions led her to a man who claimed to have run into one of the dragons.

"Do you think I believe in the sightings?" the man exclaimed. "Everyone saw the dragons, even me! I saw one of them up close. I thought it was going to attack me, but for some reason it didn't. One moment it was it was ready to kill, next thing you know it's as gentle as a daisy."

"You're telling me that the alleged dragon *chose* not to attack you?" Sally asked.

"Yes. And as hard as it is to believe, it even tried to speak to me. It had a hard time doing so, but it was like he had talked before. I'm sure he remembers me, Marvin."

Sally grew uneasy. "Do you know what the dragon was trying to say?"

"Oh, he was stuttering at first. He eventually said his name was Draco. Out of all names, too. Jacob Draco."

Marvin's remarks froze Sally from the inside out. The locked door inside her mind opened. Things started to make sense for her. We, her closest friends, had turned ourselves into dragons!

It was too much for Sally to take in. Her heart felt like stone. She needed to find us and quick! Slim as it was, she finally had a lead. The only thing she had known about the dragons before was the first incident in the city. Since then, Sally had not believed the stories one bit. But when Marvin explained his encounter to her, she had second thoughts. Now it was time to do some research. Using the Internet, she tracked the dragon sightings throughout Europe. It did not take her long to trace us to a corrupt penitentiary in France. Like Chang, she wanted to take an airplane to France. But first, she had to do some extra digging to see if France was the right place to go.

CHANG AND BYRON RESTED BESIDE THE DULL WALL OF THE PRISON, relieved that they were safe. The prisoners and most of the guards, who surrendered to the proper authorities, were out as well.

Clipper and I sat with Chang and Byron when a policeman approached me. It was the same officer who had spoken to me before. "Jacob," he said, "we believe that there are people trapped in the fire up there. We can't get to them. Can you get past the flames and save them?"

"No problem," I said, though I was reluctant to do so.

Without any further encouragement, I stood up with my wings spread. Up I flew towards the high tower. I latched onto the wall below the open window where the flames were reaching out with their flickering fingers. I grabbed the sill and climbed through. Flames encircled me once I was in the hallway. If I were not a dragon, I would not have passed the flames without getting burned. I searched for any victims in the fire my anger had created. I was still a little angry, but I did not want anyone to die.

"Anybody here?" I called.

I heard an answer coming from a room down the hall that was not yet touched by the flames. There was Greyhair, crouching in the far corner like a lost kitten when I came in the office. He could not go through the flames like I had.

There had to be a way to take him through the fire unharmed. I returned to the hallway and began stomping the flames. It was much harder than stomping the small fire in my dormitory room, but I eventually created a smoky passageway. I then went back to the warden's corner in the office.

"Come on, Greyhair or whatever your name is. Let's go," I ordered.

The warden just trembled in fear, not saying anything.

I roared at him. "Would you rather burn to death? Come on!" I almost wanted him to stay and suffer. After all he had done, he definitely deserved harsh punishment.

I edged Greyhair out to the hallway using the sides of my horns. He could not go around me. The only place to go was the window. With another gentle bump, Greyhair fell out of the tower. Clipper, who was down below, caught Greyhair with his strong wing, protecting the warden from sharp spikes and claws. Clipper flapped his wings up and down once Greyhair was safely on the ground, which told me that all was well down below. I was about to jump out myself when two arms suddenly latched onto the back of my neck. I did not hear anyone approaching because my ears were pointed frontwards. In reflex, I jerked my front leg back. My elbow blade scraped the side of my unexpected attacker. I heard him grunt and fall over.

I turned around to find that my attacker was the guard whom Clipper had taken down earlier. He fell into the fire after my slash, screaming as his clothes started to burn again. Acting quickly, I pulled him from the fire. I stood up on two feet and fell forward on top of him, covering his body completely. The fire could not get the oxygen it needed, so it died.

The guard lay gasping for breath after I stood back up; his skin turned purple from the burns. With the fire out, I grabbed him and headed for the window. The guard began to pant in fright.

"Hey! Don't do this! I don't like heights... yyyyyyaaaaahhhhhhh!"

He tried to stop me from pushing him out the window, unaware that Clipper was at the bottom and ready to catch him with his wing.

"Out you go," I said as I pushed him forward.

The guard screamed as he fell onto Clipper's wing. His wing gave way to the man's body and he dropped to the ground. Knowing it was clear down there, I searched the hallway for anyone else who was trapped. The other guard that Clipper had fought was not present. I remembered seeing him below, meaning he got out safely. I did not find any more people in the building, so I jumped out the open window, gliding safely to the ground.

"Right, we're no longer prisoners. We can leave now," Clipper said happily after I had landed.

"Where are you going?" the policeman asked as we climbed into the supply truck.

I thought of an answer that would not give away too much information. "There's something lurking in the north. We're going to see what it is."

The policeman understood and swished his fingers, saying no more. We bid Byron farewell, happy that he could return safely to his family. Chang drove the newly repaired truck away from the prison while Clipper and I sat in the bed, letting the wind blow past us. Dust flew high behind the truck as it sped along. The last thing I saw from that awful prison was the policeman and Byron waving to us.

The quest for seeking the Guarded Forest would continue. A sense of freedom returned to me, but one thing was for sure: Greyhair was a Monolegion. Whoever these Monolegions were, dwarves or Nibelungs or anything else, they knew that Clipper and I were coming for them. I did not know what was yet in our path, though.

CHAPTER 18

HEADING NORTH

Sally had received word of our last known location in the illegal prison that was no more. It was suspected that several police officers had been involved in the unlawful activity, and those people had mysteriously disappeared. Sally did not wonder about the prison for long. The revelation from Marvin alone shook her enough.

Sally was still not exactly sure where she should go in Europe. Days had passed since the incident at the prison became known, and Sally wanted to leave as soon as possible. Luckily her knowledge of geography and calculation gave her the upper hand. Keeping a close eye on the current events in Europe, she realized, through reported sightings, that we were gradually moving north. Still, she was not certain of our destination. She knew nothing about the Guarded Forest or the Monolegions. She sat in the library with a computer in front of her, her hands shaking in anxiety.

"If I'm at the right place at the right time, I might intercept their path," she whispered to herself. "But what are the chances of that? If only I knew exactly where they were headed."

Sitting back in her chair, Sally mindlessly looked at the books on the shelf beside her. That was when something caught her eye: the spine of "Unknown Places in Dark Europe" by Andrei Blue-eyes tucked away on a shelf. Curious, she decided to take a look, unaware of what she would find inside the book. She had no idea it was a copy of the same book I had read in England. Thumbing through the pages, she came across the riddle; it did not take her long to figure it out. She read about the Guarded Forest and was excited at the results. Looking back at the computer, she noticed that the string of dragon sightings was headed to Norway.

"I'll go to Oslo," she decided. "I can travel to that forest from there. I have a feeling they'll be there."

Leaving the library, she returned home and began to prepare for the important trip. Like Chang, she was determined to help her friends. She was ready to leave for Europe after a day of preparation.

UNLIKE THE BRITISH, THE NORWEGIANS DID NOT KNOW OF OUR coming. This was what we wanted, so we could enter the Guarded Forest with as much cover as possible. There was no way of telling if these Monolegions were monitoring us. Chang, who had rented a car back in France, could enter the country with no problem once we reached it. He figured that a car would be easier for me and Clipper to track than if he had taken a train. It was not too difficult cross national borders if we took to the air above the clouds and kept an eagle's eye on Chang, who would be inside the car. We rose above the low, stratus clouds, occasionally descending near the surface to check Chang's progress.

"We've just crossed the border," Clipper said over the passing wind. "We're no longer in Luxembourg. We're in Germany."

"We're making good time, then," I replied. "We've traveled a long way."

Chang sped down the road, driving fast to make up for lost time. We watched as a silver car came up right behind Chang. An arm waved outside its window. It looked as if the person wanted Chang to pull over. Chang seemed to be ignoring it. The car sped up a little and bumped Chang's car from the rear.

"What's going on?" I asked, watching from above. "They better not be Monty's people or those Monolegions."

"If they are, Chang better not stop. He needs to keep going," said Clipper.

With the small economy car that Chang was in, the chances of them stopping him were very likely. There was something else that caught my attention. I could see the same arm holding some sort of glowing stick or baton. Chang's car soon slowed down; the engine looked as if it was smoking. The other car was quickly catching up.

It could not be, but there it was! There was no more guessing about it anymore. This was magic. With that on my mind, everything made sense.

It took some time to accept what I saw when a lightning bolt suddenly appeared above me. The small bolt caused me lose control and land on the ground, next to the road. It was no dangerous zap, but one that stunned me.

My vision blurred for a split second before clearing again, just in time to see the wand in the car glowing brighter. I knew it was no simple lightning bolt that struck me. Thinking quickly, I flew back into the air. It amazed me at how much faster I was than the pursuer's car traveling at its fastest. I landed on the hood of the silver car, causing the spooked driver to slam on the brakes. Due to my weight on the front, the car tipped forward. It spun this way and that until it went off the road. Clipper landed behind Chang's car on the other side of the road. Chang's car looked as if it had been burnt. Chang emerged from the damaged vehicle, miraculously safe.

"I'm not sure what happened," said Chang as he freed himself from the wreckage. "I saw the car chasing me, then I felt some surge of electricity strike my car. Was it lightning?"

"Chang, there is going to be a lot we need to find out," Clipper stated. "I think that was a spell that came from the ones following you. It looked like they used a wand."

The two people who had come out of the second car, a man and a woman, stood in front of me with expressionless faces. I kept my eyes on the wand in the passenger's hand. With a growl and a roar, she dropped the wand in fright. I blew a small flame to keep them away from it. When the flame cleared, I grabbed the wooden wand with a single claw and prepared to snap it in two.

"Don't!" yelled the former keeper to the wand. "You could unleash pure destruction if you break the albore!"

I balanced the wand on my claw. He called it an albore. That must have been the true name for it. I stared into the poor woman's eyes; I could tell that she was pleading for her life, so I dropped the albore and clenched my scaly fingers.

I then glanced at Clipper. "Take this... albore... far out and bury it."

Clipper picked up the albore and flew away. Finding a thick tree, he buried the albore several yards away from it. He returned shortly, empty-pawed. Now that my enemies were powerless, I gave them a threatening hiss. "Now I'm new to all this magic or whatever we're dealing with, and I'm not about to be defeated by it," I said. "Now don't start making stories. You people are from the Guarded Forest, aren't you?"

I had my suspicions about them. Their height was no obvious clue. The obvious clue was their questionable clothing of fur and leather. Save the missing horned helmets, they looked like the rebels from Komodo Island; and the two Nibelungs in Georgia.

They both started whimpering.

"Please, mighty dragons, we were not after you," the woman said with a Scandinavian accent. "We have mistaken you for another being."

I roared back. "Don't start that kind of talk! You mistook me for who, another dragon? In case you haven't noticed, Clipper and I are the only dragons on this world!"

"What about the dragon that was said to return?" the man asked.

"*We* are the dragons who have been said to come, and we have the proof," Clipper hissed. "An elderly... prophet or something from China said *we* were the dragons. He had a stone carving of the first dragon."

The Monolegions started to shake and quiver as Clipper continued speaking, "The carving in the stone matched Jacob's appearance. It shows that we are the ones whom the dragon of old mentioned. If you're still in the dark about this, I can explain more."

"Stop!" shouted the man, covering his ears. "We've heard enough. Those people never gave up hope for your return. We admit that we are not the people we want you to believe. We are among the Nibelungs of what you call the Guarded Forest. Take us back there, please!"

Clipper responded by slowly stepping back in a merciful manner. I did not give up my defensive stance.

Chang approached the silver car and looked it over. Moving to the driver's side, he tried the engine. It roared to life, much to my relief. In spite of the damaged hood, we decided that we should continue on our journey as soon as possible. The glum dwarves climbed in the back seat. Clipper and I resumed our surveillance from the sky once Chang was on his way.

"These dwarves are nasty little boogers, aren't they?" I said to Clipper when we were in the air. "I don't think *all* dwarves are bad, but these ones sure are. I believe all of the enemies we've fought since Indonesia were Monolegions. You know, I thought they'd be shorter. They don't seem too small."

"Hey, we've only been dragons for about a month and just discovered the tip of the nature in magic. Life is full of mystery," said Clipper.

The low-hanging stratus clouds faded the farther we went. I laughed as a spontaneous burst of energy pulsed through my muscles. "And we're here now! Long live the enchanting! Long live the enchanting!"

"I feel great," said Clipper. He began yelling the same words. "Long live the enchanting!"

As we continued north, a strange thought went through my mind. Ever since Clipper and I had arrived in England, I had had strange feelings. It felt like all that was familiar was becoming unfamiliar, as if I had lived somewhere else my entire life. Placing more attention forward, I continued to fly alongside Clipper. We were both chanting again.

"Long live the enchanting! Long live the enchanting!"

High in the air, I was thoroughly enjoying myself. I gazed down at the German landscape. Everything was green and beautiful. With a sense of peace, I felt the spirit return.

"Jacob Draco. Your true life is touching you. I'm pleased that you believed the albore's abilities when you saw them. Again I say, when you defeat the dark forces of this world, you will return home."

I grew up on the plains, I thought. The grandfather said Clipper and I came from another world. If Oklahoma was not my true home, what was?

CHAPTER 19

THE GUARDED FOREST

We finally made it to the country that we were seeking a few days later: Norway. We had traveled north through Denmark and Sweden. Chang and our two dwarf companions used the ferry while Clipper and I decided to swim underwater. We were tired of flying at that point.

Norway was certainly chilly, and despite the spring season, several feet of snow blanketed the ground. A frigid wind blew across my face, but I enjoyed it as I did any other breeze. I let out a smoky breath of pleasure.

When we reached land, Chang purchased a heavy coat in preparation for the bitter weather. The cold did not bother me or Clipper, though. Our internal heat warmed us enough. The dwarves seemed to not mind the cold either. The furs they wore suited them well.

Clipper and I were back in the air after a short break. The open land turned into a thick, conifer forest mile after mile. This seemed like a welcoming spot for… well, dwarves! Most of the fir and spruce needles were covered in snow. The trees themselves emitted a pleasant, pungent smell to my keen senses.

In the thick of the woods, Chang had to leave the car on the lonely road. Clipper and I dropped to the ground and we all walked away from any sign of human civilization. The atmosphere changed. I noticed that the dwarves seemed to be growing more and more anxious. We continued into the forest when Clipper suddenly stopped us. "Take a look ahead," he said.

I squinted my eyes, noticing a large, electric fence nearly hidden within the trees. After researching the forest at the library, I understood that the land we were seeking was fenced off for protection.

"Getting Jacob and Clipper over the fence will be no problem, but I have to find some other way to get in," said Chang.

"Is it up and over in a 'shocking' way for some of us?" asked Clipper, sniggering.

I looked down at my claws, remembering how quickly Clipper had buried the albore. I shook my head and told him it was just the opposite. We both examined the fence carefully. It was electrified all right. I could hear a low hum singing its grim song of danger. There was a three-foot concrete base below the fence. We nodded at each other and started digging through the snow and frozen mud in front of the base. We dug as fast as we could. Dirt and rotted plant roots took flight. About ten minutes later, we created a wide hole leading beneath the concrete footing.

"Hurry," I said. "There's no way of telling if some sort of guard will appear. Electric fence, ha! Blue-eyes's book was certainly right about this."

"I guess the Norwegians have no control beyond this fence," Clipper said thoughtfully.

"That's true," said the female dwarf. "We as Nibelungs don't use outside technology."

"Sure. That explains why you were driving the car behind Chang," I scoffed.

When Clipper and I finished our tunnel, Chang and the two dwarves quickly crawled through it. With all of us on the other side, we disappeared into the unknown woods. The dwarves seemed to know their way, so we allowed them to be the vanguards.

Clipper began griping several minutes later. "Something's bothering me. We saw these Monolegions use magic already. How much influence do you think they have here, Jacob?"

"We'll see soon enough," I replied

"We'll see," Clipper repeated. He sounded nervous.

Several hours passed. Sally was still apprehensive. She had landed in Norway and made her way to the border of the Guarded Forest just before the sun set. Approaching the fence, she stepped carefully to it. It was definitely electrified. *They have got to be close,* she thought.

It was not long before Sally found a clue. She came across big hole that ran under the fence. Dropping on her hands and knees, she scrambled through it and came out on the other side. She examined several strange footprints in the snow once she was free. Sniffling from the cold, she quickly picked up our trail, sorely hoping that the trip would be worth it.

Time passed slowly. Sally knew it would take multiple days to search the woodland, but she was prepared. She took off the backpack she was wearing, built a small fire, and then ate some trail mix she had in her pack. Looking around, she found a suitable spot for her sleeping bag. She unrolled it and crawled in.

"For a New Yorker like me, I think camping isn't that bad, even in all this snow," she said aloud. "I could get attached to this lifestyle."

For some reason, she and nature clicked. The freezing atmosphere annoyed her some, but she did not care after watching the stars twinkle in the night sky. She was especially swept away by the green and purple of the aurora's enchanting dance when she saw it. The dazzling sight soon made her eyelids grow heavy. With sleep sneaking up on her, she closed her eyes and entered a surreal dream. She lay in her sleeping bag, surrounded by the crystal white snow.

The peace was broken by a sharp snap in the distance. Sally woke up with a start. The gibbous moonlight, with the help of the aurora, gave her barely enough light. She could see a figure moving through the trees ahead of her. Taking out a flashlight, she shined it on the shadow. She was startled to discover that she was actually surrounded by many people: five men and two women. They were dressed in brown fur coats and the men had sharp, horned helmets. Sally's heart began to race. She stood up in a flash. "Who are you? Tell me now or all of you are going to get it!"

The Nibelungs did not respond. Not hesitating another second, Sally picked up a stick from the fire and swung it at one of the dwarves. The stick struck the dwarf right in the face, sending him down with a cry of pain and a cheek full of hot embers. His nearby comrade came to his aid while the rest of the Nibelung band advanced on Sally. They tried to get their hands on her, but Sally fought back with fierce aggression. A stick of embers served as her effective weapon. She downed three more dwarves with two head strikes and a solid whack in the gut. It seemed that Sally could fight the rest off when she suddenly felt something smack the back of her head. It felt more like a rock than a stick or club. She fell in a dazed state.

A male dwarf stood behind her with an empty sling. "A woman, all alone."

A female dwarf placed a hand over the bump on Sally's head. "Take her to the village after we care for our injured," she said. "Let the sorcerer deal with her."

Sally, gaining her senses after the attack, found herself hanging upside-down from a pole like a hunted deer. Struggling and squirming, she attempted to fight her way to freedom, but to no avail. The rope was tied tight to her wrists. She knew that she could not free herself. Instead, she focused on where she was going. In the distance was a diacritic glow. The next thing she knew, she was in a village. She passed houses of different sizes, small shops, an arena, and the town square; most of the houses either resembled log cabins or stone cottages. Whatever she had gotten herself into, she was not prepared for it!

Sally continued guessing about what had happened until the dwarves holding the pole dropped her. She landed hard while one of the dwarves cut her free. She rubbed her back from the fall as she stood up. There were red marks on her wrists where the ropes had been. She looked around to find the villagers; men, women, and children staring blankly at her. Many of the adults, not all of them, wore either horned helmets or stocking caps.

A stranger approached Sally. He was taller than the dwarves, even taller than Sally. He had a thin gray beard and wore a long black cloak. In his hand was a shiny staff with a green jewel on its top.

"A woman like her hasn't set foot in this forest in centuries," the robed man said. "Now we come across two of her kind in one day."

"Who are you?" Sally asked him.

"Who am I? Why, I am the sorcerer, Triathra. I'm the keeper of the three worlds: this world, the enchanted world, and the underworld. My magic gives me the most power on this Earth. I am leader of this Nibelung tribe – the last that has survived through the centuries. Now our fate awaits us. We have received the emblem of the dragon's return one moon ago. Now they have come, two dragons to be precise. A man and two of my own people followed them. But we have shown them our power. We have captured the dragons. Now we have captured you. I'm afraid now that you are here, you can't leave. I don't want anyone who is not of our tribe to have knowledge of our recent intentions, if you know what I mean."

"Wh… what are you going to do to me?" Sally gulped.

Triathra chuckled. "I have been planning this for a while. I talked with my captives. They swore to follow every command I give. I told them they would either fight the intruder who followed them to the death or die themselves. They did not think anyone was following them, but I knew otherwise."

Sally's eyes widened. The voice of Triathra sounded quite familiar. It almost sounded like Monty's, only in a different tone. But Monty had no beard.

The sorcerer nodded. "Yes, Ms. Serene, you will have to battle them. Does it surprise you that I know your name? I know who you are." He ran his fingers over his chin. His beard looked shorter and much neater than many of the dwarves'. "Take her to the arena," he told Sally's captors. "She'll die for our entertainment. I'm dreadfully sorry, Sally."

A rope settled around Sally's neck and she was dragged to a small, torch-lit stadium where her captors mercilessly threw her inside. As she rolled on the ground, she was still puzzling that Triathra knew her name. She was sure his voice was familiar. Had she met him before without knowing it? She removed the rope after she got to her feet.

Sally stood in the center of the arena with the tribe surrounding the open field. Several dwarves rolled in a large iron cage on wheels. Inside was the dragon that Sally had to face. As the dwarves opened the cage and left, the dragon jumped out. Sally did not know how to react. She stood still and did not move. The red dragon walked towards her then stopped only a few feet away. Sally panted. She remembered what Marvin had said before. She stared into his eyes and the dragon blinked.

Sally noticed the creature's feet. There were five claws on each foot, except for the rear left paw. Sally knew who had a missing toe. "Clipper? Is that you?" she asked.

The dragon bared his teeth. At first, Sally thought it was ready to attack, but the dragon did not even move. Sally looked closer at the dragon's expression. It was not snarling, it was smiling!

Clipper grunted a few times before he said, "Sally! It's you! What are you doing here?"

The two stepped closer to each other. Sally placed her hand between Clipper's horns. She felt Clipper's tough red scales. A trail of spikes began at the top of his head, each as smooth as his horns. Tears ran down Clipper's and Sally's faces. The crowd of dwarves booed. They wanted to see a fight, not a touching and heartwarming moment.

"Clipper, what have you done to yourself?" asked Sally.

"It's a long and dull story," said Clipper.

He gave her a brief summary of what had happened. Sally was glad nothing horrible or fatal had occurred. It was a miracle in her mind. As Clipper finished his story, the sorcerer appeared with an expression of disappointment etched in his face. He held his glamorous scepter in his right hand. "Cowards don't fight. I knew this would happen," he said softly. "Take them away."

⎯⎯⎯❦❦❦⎯⎯⎯

THREE DWARVES WITH SHARP SPEARS FORCED THE TWO INTO A small cabin. The door slammed shut behind them. Sally and Clipper both sat down. I had been hiding in the shadows, but I revealed myself when I saw Sally. She was again frightened, yet she quickly realized who I was. She ran over and hugged me.

"I can't believe you two are with me right now!" she cried. "But now all of us are imprisoned here. Why don't you attack these dwarves? They seem perfectly harmless to you."

"Sally, did you see the staff the 'sorcerer' had?" I asked her.

Sally nodded. "Yeah. It had a funny handle with a jewel on top. Some of the others had wands or something like that."

"Those 'wands' are called albores," I said. "As for the staff the sorcerer carried, that's what keeps us here. It's a scepter. If we make one wrong move, he'll use it against us. I don't know what the scepter can do, except we know that it's really dangerous."

Sally pondered for a moment before she realized what I was talking about. "You don't think that wands or the staff are *enchanted* or *magical*, do you? Jacob, you've been a science bug your whole life. Think about what you're saying, please!"

I clawed the floor, thinking of a way to say what was on my mind. "I have. I was told that the rise of the dragon has come. There is a reason why Clipper and I became who we are now. Not only that, but I saw magic happen right before my eyes. I *saw* someone use an albore to create lightning. That is science I don't understand.

"Also, I'm been having second thoughts about my past life. My father, despite how much I love and miss him, may not even be my real father. I'm sorry, Sally, the world is a lot different than the one we know. Monty told me about the Monolegions roaming this very forest. He mentioned that they would rise in power. They are a true threat to our civilization. Your race, Sally, *our* race, is in jeopardy. These dwarves have already started and no one has noticed. They controlled the prison in France, and remember those mysterious rebels I've mentioned in Indonesia? That was them, too. Yes, I am a scientist. All my life, I've been fascinated by the behavior of animals. I love animals. That's what led me to this. Science led me to the truth. I'm sorry, Sally. I truly am."

Sally sat still in the darkness of the cabin. "Jacob, this is too much to take in," she said, sniffling.

Clipper turned to face his friend. "I wasn't convinced right off either, even after all this happened. I thought it was some phenomenon I could eventually explain. I was a little more stubborn than Jacob. Often when someone hears something they don't believe, they reject it."

Sally frowned. "What are you trying to say?"

"If a person wants to know the *real* truth, he will search for it. He'll gather all the facts, not reject them. I rejected the fact about the existence of the Monolegions, these dwarves. Now look where we are. I personally saw what an albore could do right before my very eyes."

Clipper's reasoning moved Sally a little. Of course, it was hard for somebody to believe what we told her without witnessing it for herself. Sally sat silently. She licked her lips, she sniffled, she whimpered, then finally she smiled.

"All right," she said with confidence. "Let's get out of this place. So these dwarves, these Monolegions you say, are real. Monty told you this and you believed him?"

I scratched the back of my ear as I answered. "I knew he wasn't lying. I could see the truth in his eyes. And he was the last person I'd trust, too. That means a lot."

A lonely hush fell over the imprisoning cabin. Sally had to adjust to her senses. When she did, she stood up and prepared herself for the next turn of events. "We're here to stop these guys. Let's do it!" she exclaimed courageously.

The door suddenly swung open and Chang rolled into the cabin amidst the angry shouts of the villagers. "You get back in there!" a dwarf yelled as he slammed the door behind him.

Sally was again surprised. "Chang! You're here. What was that all about?"

Chang panted. "Hi Sally. I didn't think you'd be here. They were interrogating me. After they realized I was just an ordinary person, they got pretty upset." He brushed filth off his leg when he climbed back to his feet. "Funny. They said if I followed Jacob and Clipper, then I would fight their king in some Elsoovey place." He made small chuckle. "I don't know what they were talking about."

"Elsov," I said. "We've heard that word before. Well, it's time to get out of here. I have a plan that shouldn't have this place swarming, though we will make some noise. This will involve... a personal touch."

We formed a quick plan and immediately executed it. The guard of the cabin was awakened abruptly from his sleep by the sound of Sally's scream.

"Oh no! Stop doing that! Help! Somebody, anybody! Help! He's going savage!"

The dwarf peeked through a crack in the cabin wall. I glared at him with a piece of a torn shirt hanging from my mouth. The dwarf was about to leave, maybe to inform Triathra. If my plan was to work, he should open the door instead of leave. I banged my horns on the door.

"Somebody! Please, help!" Sally shouted again. "Oh! Ahhhh! I can't breathe! I can't breathe! I'm going to die!"

Before the guard left, I gave one good smack on the door with my horns. The door fell into the snow in splinters. To the dwarf, Sally was gone except for her bloody arm in Clipper's jaws. I held the piece of the shirt that once belonged to Chang. The dwarf was shocked at the sight and was about to run. Before he could, I ignited and tossed one of my bombs over his head. As it exploded, the dwarf was thrown forward. I released Sally's arm and she stepped out from behind the door. We quickly rushed over to the dwarf. Sally defeated him with a single punch to the side of his head. Clipper aided Chang's intentional wound. We heard voices ringing throughout the village in response to the echoing bang, but no one came to the cabin.

"I'm sure glad I had the guts to cut myself on the arm with one of your claws," Chang said as he eyed Clipper's bloody teeth. "It wasn't a deep cut."

Sally groaned as she dragged the dazed dwarf into the cabin. "Next time you bite my arm, Clipper, don't bite down so hard. I still have teeth marks with Chang's blood all over them."

"Sorry, I was being as gentle as possible," Clipper said.

I chuckled when I saw Sally's look of disgust. She obviously did not feel comfortable with someone else's blood on her skin.

"Well, at least this part worked," I said. "We've just broken out of this prison without any noise, sort of. When Chang ties up this poor dwarf, it'll be time for the next phase."

Chang tied the dwarf to a wooden beam in the cabin with a piece of cloth around his mouth so he could not spread the news of our escape. One by one we slipped through the darkness and to the side of a bigger cottage, where we had reason to believe the emblem was kept. We had to keep a sharp eye out for the sorcerer and his scepter.

"That's an incredible bomb you've made," Sally whispered to me.

"Those are powder bombs," I whispered back. "Chang carries them around. But you can't really use them without burning your hand. I call them powder bombs even though they have cellucor instead of gunpowder. I like the sound of the word 'powder.'"

"Jacob, hush!" said Clipper quietly. "We can talk about the powder bombs later."

Inside a luxurious cottage, Triathra the sorcerer sat in a comfortable, cushioned chair. His eyes were closed and his enchanted scepter leaned against the wall. A cauldron filled with some sort of broth bubbled over a fireplace that lit the interior. I peered inside through a window. I looked around to make sure there was no other company. Since there was none, I opened the front door. Chang and Sally walked in. I could not fit through the doorway without causing any damage, so I decided to stay outside unless Triathra awoke.

All was going well until Chang accidentally stepped near the scepter, bumping into it. The relic fell over and hit the ground. This awakened Triathra. Startled as well, I immediately took action. I charged into the cottage, destroying a part of the doorway. Sally picked up the scepter and moved it away from Triathra's reach.

"Very little power without your scepter," I taunted to Triathra.

"Give it to me!" he demanded. "You don't know how dangerous it is!"

He stood up and rushed over to me. With the butt of the scepter, Sally struck Triathra's foot. The young warlock took a step back and rubbed his foot. He was not prepared to fight without the scepter. Chang tripped him and placed a boot on his back. Sally made her way to the fire. She was about to throw the scepter into the flames.

"Sally, don't!" I warned her. "If it's destroyed it could unleash something we don't even understand. That goes for any other albore the dwarves may have."

"The scepter's metal though," said Chang.

"I don't want to risk it," I replied.

Sally dropped the scepter. The metallic handle clanked on the ground. I did not really think it would melt in the fire, but as I have said, I did not want to risk it. Lowering my head to examine the scepter, I noticed the interesting artwork etched in the handle and the green crystal on the top. The design alone created the possibility that this object in particular was special, as it differed from the albores that the dwarves have used. Before I was placed in the cabin, I remembered a little of what Triathra had told me about the handles on albores. He mentioned that the symbols and a particular spell was what gave the albore its power.

"Let's tie up Triathra, then we can search for this emblem," said Chang.

He quickly searched for some rope, binding the sorcerer when he found some. Triathra did not say a single word during the process. Sally locked him in a room upstairs when Chang was done. With the most dangerous of the Monolegions out of the way, we sniffed around his home. There was a strange scent for sure. It smelled a little like Clipper, but it was much more potent. There was something else that was different, too. The worrisome thought of someone in danger was on my mind. I could not explain why.

"This is a waste of time," said Sally, unaware of the scent. "We're looking for something, and we don't even know what this something is."

"We'll find it, just be patient," I said. "I smell something strange."

"I do too," added Clipper.

As we searched, my ears perked up. I heard a strange noise. It sounded like a crying infant, not unlike a human cry. Clipper's ears twitched as well while Chang and Sally stood still in confusion.

"What was that?" Clipper asked, looking around.

I did not answer. We instead followed the sound of the cry. Opening a closet door, I found that the cry was coming from a closed, woven basket with several holes in the lid, possibly used for breathing. When Sally removed the lid, the four of us froze. A small creature lay on its bed of wet straw, crying. It was on its belly while its small wings were sprawled out on the bed.

"It's a baby dragon," I said in amazement.

CHAPTER 20

THE LIVING EMBLEM

The tiny brown dragon lay on its belly with its front paws covering its short horns that were yet to be sharp. Tears ran down its snout. I guess the commotion had frightened the little bambino, which was no surprise. It looked like a poor, neglected soul for the first month of its life. Now it was facing something noisy and loud that it had never experienced before.

Sally carefully lifted the infant out of its basket, staying clear of its spikes. Still crying, the infant stared at her. Clipper and I sat perfectly still, watching them. I did not know what to do in the presence of the baby. My mouth was slightly opened but I could not speak. Sally handed the dragon over to me. I raised my forepaws from the ground to take it.

"Why are you giving it to me?" I asked.

"You're a dragon. It's your responsibility," she said.

"This baby isn't mine," I protested. "I can see what it is, that doesn't mean I'm its father." I puffed a small cloud of smoke. "This is an emblem all right. A baby. That's why we need to protect it from Triathra!" I recalled the dream I had in France.

"Jacob, just shut up and hold it!" Sally quietly demanded, placing it in my arms.

I wobbled on my rear feet as I held it in my grasp. The crying reduced to a constant sniffling. I gazed down into the baby's eyes. It seemed to have finally found something to be happy about for the first time in its life. The corners of its mouth rose above the rest of its snout. I smiled back. Eyeing its small body, I took note of its sex. "This dragon's a girl."

Clipper poked his head out from behind my wing. "It sure is," he said.

"How can you tell?" asked Chang.

"Details aren't important," I stated.

Sally beamed at the heartwarming event as the little dragon rested her head in my forepaws. I continued to huff smoke from my nose. It was hard to believe the emblem was a young, female dragon. When she looked up at me, the little infant finally stopped sniffling. She made a chattering noise that I recognized as laughter. She stretched her arms and started to climb on me until she reached the top of my head. Her front paws grabbed a hold of my horns.

Clipper grinned, rubbing his fangs with a claw again. "Aww, she's so adorable. Look at her. Why would this sorcerer enslave a cute little one like this?"

Chang also smiled. "Hey, she already knows how to climb around. Are you going to name her?"

Before I could say anything, Sally answered for me, "Yes he will, won't you Jacob?"

"Ehh, sure. She'll get a name," I stammered.

Different names for her scattered through my mind. My best strategy was to look through my memories. I remembered the name of the nearby city where I grew up in Oklahoma. I thought it was a good name. "Her name will be Reno, after the town I grew up in, El Reno," I announced.

My three friends watched the dragon playing on top of me. She was a picture of happiness and joy. The three all agreed; Reno was a good name. She was still climbing on my head when she lifted her little brown snout toward Clipper and blew a small flame at his face.

"She is cute for sure," said Clipper. "She's adorable when she blows fire."

Reno climbed down from my head and onto the floor of the cottage. She started to run around the rest of the building. She seemed to be sensing true freedom and open spaces for the first time. The people she had known earlier where no longer imprisoning her in the basket. Before she could jump out a window and onto the snow below, I caught her in midair.

"Whoa, let's not go outside just yet," I cautioned her.

Clipper was walking towards me when he noticed an aged parchment rolled up on a nearby wooden desk. Curious, he picked it up. His claws made it difficult to unroll, so he silently handed it to Chang. Chang unrolled it. It was some sort of map.

"Hey everybody, come over here and see what we found," Clipper called.

Placing Reno on the floor, I went to see the parchment. It was an odd map of an unknown forest, certainly not the Guarded Forest. Near a sketch of trees were drawings of castles and caves all around. In the top-right corner was an image of a galloping unicorn. The page was fragile and faded. It looked as if it was hundreds of years old. Chang flipped the page over. He read a message that was discovered on the back.

He spoke aloud: "The date is the eleventh day of the fifth month, in the year of our Lord, thirteen hundred and fourteen. The map is of a wood in England. Castle Saint Cassius is in great danger. Three dragons were observed in the area. One black, one red, and one young and brown. They were seen along with a woman and a man. They are plaguing the wood and taking the lives of our people and the natives. His Majesty the King is searching for them now. The three dragons have mysteriously disappeared." Chang stopped reading. "What is this? They practically described the four of us, I mean, five of us. How can we be there and here at the same time? He said May of 1314. I would think that this message would be written differently for its age."

I thought for a moment before it came to me. "Do you think *we* were cursed to wander many centuries ago? Like Chang said, they described us quite well."

At that moment, I noticed a dwarf peering through the window. Spooked as he was, he held out the albore for defense and began to run.

"We've got to stop him before he casts a spell on us!" yelled Clipper.

I sprinted after him, preparing to spit venom into his eyes. The sweating dwarf, stopping and turning around, held his tool of protection in front of him. Before I could spit any venom, a large purple warp appeared behind me. I stood still as the warp grew bigger and stronger. The instant I was in the warp, it was too much for my eyes to see.

A powerful force yanked me back into the center of the warp. My friends and I helplessly vanished away from the runt figure as the warp dissolved into thin air.

TO THE DWARF, I WAS OFF LIKE A FLASH. HE QUICKLY CLIMBED THE stairs and freed Triathra, then gave him his scepter.

"They almost got away with the Master Scepter," shivered the sorcerer. "I was almost defeated."

"They were coming after me," the dwarf said. "I used the first spell that came to my mind. They are now in an era of the past."

Triathra rubbed the jewel on his scepter. "If they find another albore from the past, they may find their way back to us. That is why many dislike the curse of time. It does little good for anyone. But we can't change that now. There is a chance that they will come back. Before they return, I must hide the scepter. I do not want them to steal it if they learn of its true power. It has to go somewhere far away where only I know where it will be. It will hide itself if I cast the right spell. Then I'll travel back to North America and find it. I'll send a clue to the dragons as well so they will come to me. I can't let them roam free. With my power and preparation, I will crush them. I was not prepared before and I almost lost the scepter, which is why I must leave. They will come to me and I'll be ready for them. But where should I hide the scepter?"

He stepped to the side and picked up a map depicting the entire Earth. Scanning his eyes over the western hemisphere and North America, he pointed his finger at a spot in the western region over the Rocky Mountains. He turned to his servant. "Gather the whole tribe together. One half will follow me back across the Atlantic Ocean. One quarter will stay here while the last quarter will help the children to evacuate."

Triathra knew I would return very soon, but I was not aware of that myself. I spun helplessly through a swirling vortex and landed hard onto the leafy ground, next to a large tree.

CHAPTER 21

THE BRAVE KNIGHT VERSUS THE FIRE DRAGON

I stood back up on all fours as I regained my senses. I found that my group was still together. Clipper had held Reno tightly through the fiasco. The baby had started to cry again through the moment of horror. Chang and Sally seemed okay, too. I looked around once I knew that no one was badly injured.

Our environment had changed. We were no longer in the frigid Guarded Forest. We were in a green temperate marsh with various trees here and there, and a withered path that led to an unknown destination. A cool breeze blew a dull gray mist blew along the ground. My limbs quaked after such a sudden experience. I was in a new and strange land. That was when I realized what had happened. The documented sighting of three dragons many centuries ago mentioned on the ancient parchment had described Clipper and me accurately. It even mentioned little Reno! It was crystal clear why the appearance of the dragons mentioned on the script had happened. It was because of the cowardly dwarf that was simply protecting himself. *He* was the reason we were here!

Chang rubbed the back of his head. "Oh, my head is killing me," he groaned. "How do we get back? Didn't the scroll say that we mysteriously disappeared? I believe that we *do* find our way back to the present eventually. But how?"

"Good question," I said. "Maybe we can find one of those albores to transport us back. It's just that we need to know what we are dealing with. Triathra the sorcerer told me a little bit about albores before we were locked in that cabin. First of all, he said that the reason they contain magic is because of the rune on the gold handle. Only someone like Triathra can carve it. It looks like a character in the Chinese alphabet."

"Except it isn't," Chang mentioned.

"Right, it's something else," I continued. "If a sorcerer or wizard does not carve it, it'll not contain any power. Second, the way to cast spells is to simply hold it in front of you. You don't have to say 'hocus-pocus' or anything like that. The albore connects with your mind and will do what you wish. Third, every single albore is made of fine wood with a golden handle."

"Well, we know that much about the albores," said Sally. "Now we have to find one. I don't know how powerful they are, though."

"Just remember to not ever break one," I added.

I was about to say something else when Clipper held up his paw. I lifted an ear in response. I could hear the clomping of horse hooves coming down the long path.

"Uh oh, we've got company," said Sally. "I see a group of horsemen in the distance. I can't make out who they... oh no, they look like... knights! Royal knights! Jacob, Clipper, hide in those trees, quick! They'll try to kill you if they see you. Take Reno as well."

Taking Reno from Sally's arms, I jumped and briefly caught air on my way to the trees to hide. Clipper was just seconds behind. When I found the cover I was seeking, several armored men on horses raced up to Sally and Chang. The lead knight drew his sword, but realized that there was no real threat. He slid the double-edged sword back into its sheath.

"What is your homeland, unknown travelers?" the lead knight asked.

Chang tried his best mimicking the accent of the knight's to avoid suspicion. "We are but peasant citizens who... err... were brought here by the dwarves of the Monolegions. We are in need of your help. Please, aid the poor."

The knight was shocked at Chang's words. "I like this not at all. Your race is uncommon in this land. I believe your home is in the land of the Chine. What is your task here? And what in the name of Noble Charles persuaded you to state you're coming from the Monolegions? They are the only tribe of Nibelungs known to our kingdom. They are passive and live in the north. They are our allies until time itself grows old."

"But sir, the Monolegions have plans of invasion!" said Sally. "They will hide themselves in the forest where the fjords are. Many will blend among our own people. Their descendants will overtake our sovereignty."

"Do you speak of events yet to come? Have you gone mad?" the knight snapped. "The Nibelungs are our friends. They have lived in peace with us, especially since the dragons have departed."

Sally and the lead knight continued to banter words while I watched from the trees. I felt Reno squirming on my back, starting to create a ruckus. I had to keep Reno still. After her attempt at freedom failed, Reno's whimpers changed into pure wailing. The knights turned in our direction. I was distressed as the lead knight dismounted his horse and made his way to us. I had no idea what to do. I did not have any powder bombs with me. Chang held them in my old knapsack around his shoulder.

As I stepped sideways to view the knight's progress, my foot paw struck a rock. I yelped. My hiding would be of no more use to me after that. Taking a deep breath, I stepped out in my quadruped fashion and calmly sat down in front of the knight. With my tail swishing back and forth in the tall grass, I nodded, my horns moving up and down.

The knight was instantly on guard. "I believed that the dragons had left us. What manner of monster is this?"

"Good sir, we were brought here by a time spell," I said as kindly as possible. "We are from the days to come. But please do not judge us so harshly. My friend Clipper and I were once men like you. We are now dragons who wish to befriend you. I hope you now know that these Monolegion dwarves are not to be trusted."

"What manner of evil has given the dragon the ability to speak? Clipper? That name sounds despicable for your kind. And your accent - what is your land of origin? You are but a vengeful dragon who seeks trouble."

"Actually, there are few dragons in existence who work for the good of mankind. We're among those few," I explained with my limited knowledge of the subject. "You see, years after the dragons have left, people no longer believed in us. They thought we were merely legendary. Now that we are back, we are here to show who we really are. I must tell you, my comrade and I *do* help people. We're with the two people you've met on the path, actually."

The lead knight did not seem impressed. He ordered his band of knights to dismount and attack. Raising their long swords with both hands, the knights advanced. I knew this was not going to be good. I refused to shed innocent blood, but I had to defend Reno and myself. Taking a swift jump, I scraped one of the knights with my claws. I heard the screeching of his metal armor. When he fell onto the ground, I pressed my large paw on his chest to keep the knight down. As I was about to let go, the sharp edge of an unexpected blade pressed on my neck.

I lurched back, gasping for air. This was a costly move for the knight who had attacked me. Reacting reflexively to the sword on my neck, my elbow blade ran across his shoulder. Not even his armor protected him. It peeled away like the skin of a banana. As I turned back, I saw blood dripping from my blade. The knight's shoulder had been cut and he was bleeding badly. Mildly bumping him with the flat sides of my horns, I knocked him over. The other knights did not back down, so I continued to fight. Clipper fought beside me. One knight raised a boot and kicked Clipper in the bottom jaw between his sabered fangs. Clipper held the bottom of his mouth, cringing from the blow.

"Get Reno out of here!" he roared to me through the commotion.

Clipper was right. Reno could not defend herself so easily. She had to be saved. Digging through the vengeful knights, I found her curled up against a rock. To my horror, a nearby knight lifted his battle-axe over her head. I puffed out two waves of threatening fire from my nose before charging forward. The knight dropped the axe and took a step back. I glared at him, hissing in fury. The knight held still in surrender.

With over half of the knights defeated, the rest soon tried to flee on their horses, back the way they came. As they readied to leave, I glided in front of the line of horses and let out a big flame off to the side. The spooked horses took off in the other direction.

"That will make sure they don't warn anyone any time soon," I said, puffing out smaller yet threatening flames.

I turned to check on Reno. She was sitting on top of the dropped battle-axe, grinning. I smiled back, glad that she was unharmed. Sally and Chang brushed dirt off their clothes that were now out of century. They noticed my victims on the ground. Most of them were wounded, none were dead.

"Lucky I didn't have to kill any of them," I said. "I'll only kill if absolutely necessary."

"How about we find out where the knights came from?" Chang suggested. "If we do, we might find a clue as to where we could get our hands on an albore."

"We should," said Clipper, "but this time let's make sure that we're prepared to deal with any unsuspecting passers-by."

"May I recommend making tracks now? It'll only benefit us," I said, eager to leave.

After aiding the knights we had wounded, we were on our way to the castle mentioned on the parchment. Chang, who had kept a hold of it, unrolled the map and examined the path. As we approached a fork in the road, Chang examined the roads carefully and pointing to the right. We ventured down the road he indicated. After a few minutes I stopped in my tracks and sniffed the air. I could smell smoke. The smell of meat also came to me.

"We must be getting close," I said, twitching my nose. "I smell something delicious."

Clipper licked the teeth between his fangs. "Smells like pork. I'm definitely in the mood for swine right now."

"Clipper, we can't eat now," said Sally. "We can stop for lunch later. I remember seeing a pond about a mile back. Cynthia told me how seafood doesn't bother you anymore. Do you still hate the taste?"

"I happen to love seafood now," said Clipper.

I was about to step in the conversation when I noticed something about a mile away. It looked like the castle we were looking for. "We should keep quiet," I said. "I think I can see Saint Cassius in the distance. But I don't think that smell is coming from the castle. It's much closer than that. Maybe you can check it out, Sally."

Everyone became silent. Sally slipped past us, rounded a bend, and disappeared beyond some trees. Waiting patiently, I knew Reno could smell the food as well. I picked her up and set her down under my belly so that she would not escape.

Not even a minute later, I heard the voice of a man. "My, what outlandish clothing you have! What is the purpose of your strange attire? I apologize if that brings offense, but I have never seen such clothes before in my life. Ah, never mind that. Could I offer you some roasted pork?" My guess was that the man was a friar.

"Oh, no thank you," Sally replied. "Is the castle ahead Saint Cassius?"

"'Tis so, stranger, 'tis so," said the friar. "Saint Cassius has stood with pride for many years. King Adam is the ruler of the land now."

I was pleased. Other than the fight with the knights, finding the castle had not been hard.

"My thanks to you," said Sally. "I have been lost. I am in the search of a... an albore."

I heard the friar grunt in surprise. "Oh, I am afraid those are quite rare these days. My brother told me that they could only be made by an enchanted being. One can always tell if it contains magic if it has a rune carved in the golden handle. I have never laid eyes on an albore myself, but I have heard that it protects a man better than a suit of armor. Now let me see… if you want to find an albore, you need to see the Nibelungs. I would recommend the Nibelungs of the north. You are but a few days a journey from their nearest settlement. But you must hurry. Day after day their numbers dwindle. I dare say they will be of legend quite soon."

"There are Monolegion dwarves near this kingdom?" asked Sally. "They must be heading up to Norw… I mean… the north."

"Yes, they are north. But first you must gain permission from King Adam to cross his land. Saint Cassius Castle is his home. The poor place is in ruin, sadly. I fear the unicorn will no longer visit us in the future. Our land is protected when it runs by. Oh, why can our kingdom not be as honorable as Camelot?"

"Thank you for your help," said Sally. "I'll be on my way."

Sally turned and rounded the bend back towards us. We retreated to the trees to make our plan of action.

"I think Sally can get past the friar and head to the main gates of the castle," I whispered.

"You, Chang, and I can sneak around and make our way up the wall," said Clipper. "Jacob and I can take Reno, fly up to the top of the wall, find a rope, and toss it down for Chang. With all of us on the wall, we can watch Reno while Sally is inside getting permission."

I liked Clipper's plan. "I'll find some other way in. If Sally has trouble, I can be nearby. If she can peacefully get permission, it's home free back home. If not, I can offer help."

"I hope all goes well," said Chang.

Sally again met the friar on the side of the path. I did not hear the friar say anything as she passed. He was possibly getting suspicious.

Sally headed for the front gates of the castle. The entrance was open, so she walked in. When I finally saw the friar, he was standing up from a tree stump and was examining the area around the path. He started coming towards us. Placing Reno on my back,

Clipper, Chang, and I carefully stepped around the thicket. When we reached the friar's campsite, Clipper stuck a claw in the pot and pulled out a chunk of meat. He placed the claw in his mouth and nodded in approval. Quickly, he grabbed another chunk and gave it to Reno who sniffed it then happily chewed on it.

The distracted friar looked around as if he believed he was not alone. We waited until just the right moment. At my signal, we took off towards the castle wall. We then went around the corner and out of the friar's sight. I blew a small flame of triumph once we made it.

"I'll wait down here with Reno until you drop a rope or something for me," said Chang.

Clipper and I silently nodded. I snuck along the perimeter of the wall, moving away from the spot where the friar had returned to his soup pot. Chang petted Reno's head while he waited.

The jagged wall was perfect for climbing. I did not have to fly up. All was going according to plan until an armored guard came into view. Luckily, he failed to spot us. I climbed halfway up the wall with Clipper close behind me. He was trying not to look down. With my claws digging into the crevices, I waved a paw to warn Chang. Grabbing Reno, he jumped around the corner and hid from the guard. He sloppily buried himself with nearby sticks and grass. Reaching into my bag, he took out one of the powder bombs. He was about to ignite the fuse, but hesitated. To keep himself from burning his hand, he took a piece of string from his pocket and tied it around the bomb, creating a longer fuse. Lighting the string, Chang threw it as hard as he could. He peered around the wall to see if it would explode. There was a sudden BOOM! The guard and the friar looked up at the commotion and the two rushed over to see where the sound had come from.

With the two out of the way, Chang, with Reno in his arms, ran through the castle's open gate. This bought Clipper and I enough time to climb over the wall. We soon reached the parapet on the other side of the ramparts.

"Well, it looks like Chang doesn't need rope anymore," said Clipper.

"Right," I said. "I'm going to find another way to get inside. You stay here with Chang when he gets up here. Make *sure* Reno does not escape."

Clipper tapped his fang. "I'll do that." He gazed back over the wall. "Looks like the guard and the friar are back where they were, so don't worry about them. If they make a move, I'll let you know. Easy as that."

After a single nod, I jumped down from the parapet to the main grounds. Glancing around, I found that all the windows to the castle were shut. A balcony atop the tallest tower had a way in. I began a vertical flight up the wall. It was strenuous, but I made it with no real trouble.

INSIDE THE GREAT HALL OF THE CASTLE, A MERRY FESTIVAL UNDER-way. King Adam had never been happier. With a hand resting on his big belly, he chuckled in his jolly way. His daughter, Princess Rohesia had finally found a worthy suitor to wed. The festival was being held for the anticipated arrival of the prince, which made Adam very excited. He had always cherished his daughter and wanted her to be happy. As he sat in his throne with a goblet of wine, he leaned over to his wife the queen.

"Is this not wonderful, my love? Our daughter will be wedded soon," he said.

"We still have to meet our daughter's true love," the queen reminded him. "He has to prove himself worthy to be the prince of Saint Cassius. But do not worry; I am certain he will be a worthy suitor. But I must ask, where is that daughter of ours? She is taking an awfully long time to prepare for the occasion."

As they discussed the arrival of the future prince, a guard escorted Sally into the main room. Nearby servants stopped to look at Sally's unusual clothing.

King Adam, in his cheerful mood, spoke warmly to Sally. "Welcome to Saint Cassius, stranger. You look as if you have traveled a long way. Come sit here. Everyone is welcome. I believe in peace and prosperity. I do not allow torture or any vulgar practices under my rule."

Sally smiled back at Adam. "Pleased to meet you…er…your Majesty. I've come from a land far from here. I hope you don't mind, I'm all alone. I'm here to get permission to travel north to the tribe of the Nibelungs, again… if you don't mi… never mind."

Adam spoke kindly to Sally still. "You are free to go anytime you wish. But you are also welcome to our festival as well. Come join us! My daughter's true love will arrive shortly, and we will have a celebration for the upcoming wedding!"

Sally acted excited. "That sounds lovely. I can stay for a few minutes, but I am in a hurry and I cannot stay long."

"Great!" boomed Adam. "Now where is my daughter? She should be down here."

UP IN THE TOWER, PRINCESS ROHESIA WAS IN HER CHAMBER. SHE was supposed to be dressing for the celebration, but the vision of her love was in her head. She sat on a stool and daydreamed instead, the open breeze making her coffee-colored hair flutter. She thought of playing with her love out in a meadow. Life could not get any better. Standing up with her hands over her heart, she stepped behind a curtain so she could dress herself for the celebration.

As she idled behind the curtain, I landed on the balcony. I was not expecting anyone to be in the chamber.

"Man, that flight felt great," I said to myself. "I enjoy using wings. I could fly all day if I wanted to…" I stopped talking when I smelled Rohesia's presence.

I heard the footsteps from behind the curtain. "Is someone there?" the princess called.

I froze, realizing that there was someone in the chamber. Still on the balcony, I hopped over the edge and took flight. I forgot about the spire that was on the roof. Just before I flew into it, my front paws latched onto the shingles of the round roof. With me out of sight, Rohesia did not see any soul.

"Hmm, I must be hearing things. Flight? Wings? What did I hear?" Shrugging, she resumed dressing. A few minutes later, she stepped back out onto the balcony and started daydreaming again. Her back was to me.

"Oh, Roger, my dear sweet Roger," she mumbled dreamily. "When we are married, we shall live together until the time comes for us to take leadership of our united lands."

My heart was touched. I twisted my head sideways so I could see her more clearly. She turned and re-entered the chamber. I made my way closer to the balcony. Thinking she was alone, she did not bother to use the curtain to dress. I turned my head away to give her privacy. I hung there for about a minute when I felt my claws slipping from the roof. My eyes widened. I could not hang on much longer! Before I slipped, I kicked off the wall. I landed on the edge of the balcony and tripped forward. In the middle of the balcony, I held still, waiting for a scream of terror. The scream was just as I imagined it. I saw Rohesia dive behind the curtain. She stammered. "Oh my! Y... you... you are a... a..."

"A dragon?" I finished.

Without a second thought, she screamed again and immediately threw on her former apparel. Filled with fear, she did not think of a simple solution like fleeing out of her chamber. She decided to fight me off, grabbing a nearby dagger and waving it at my eyes. "Stay away from me, black beast! I dislike hurting others, but I shall if necessary!"

"I don't want a fight either," I said, trying to calm her. "Just take it easy, I won't hurt you."

"I have no trust in you. You are a *dragon*! I will never trust you! NEVER!"

She screamed once more. Tears poured from her eyes. I did not expect anything when she suddenly ran up to me and kicked me in the chest. Barking from the hit, I fell to the ground. The kick was not painful, but the impact of someone's foot could still take my breath away. I tried my best to not fight back, or her assumption of my hostility would be correct. I had to lie down on the ground as she kicked me again and again while waving the dagger near my face.

"Keep away!" she warned. "You stay back! Help! Some soul who cares for me, help!"

SALLY STOOD UP ALONG WITH THE OTHER PEOPLE IN THE GREAT hall and applauded when the prince arrived. He walked over to Adam and bowed. "Good day, your highness. I am looking forward to marrying your daughter. My name is Prince Roger, and I have ridden for days to reach this glorious place known as Saint Cassius."

"Prince Roger!" bellowed Adam. "Pleased to meet you. I am looking forward to calling you my son-in-law. I hope you are patient enough to wait for Rohesia. She should be down here any moment."

As they cheerfully chatted with each other, a guard that was supposed to be out patrolling the area around the castle interrupted the two. The guard whispered quietly into Adam's ear. Sally noticed that Adam's smile drooped to a frown. Something was wrong. When the guard was done with his message, King Adam stood up and addressed the visitors of the castle.

"Everyone," Adam announced, "I have just received word that our patrol has been attacked by two monsters that were said to be legend: dragons."

Numerous gasps were heard across the hall. Adam turned to his guard. "Have the pages tend to their knights."

The guard left to gather the pages while the inhabitants in the great hall were in a state of shock. Among the small crowd, Sally began to sweat. The message that the king received might ruin her plan, for the knights knew what Sally looked like. She quietly slipped out of the main hall and onto the castle grounds. As she did so, the friar she had met earlier showed up. He held the heavy pot of soup.

"Are you feeling ill?" he asked.

"I'm fine," Sally answered. "I just need to get a breath of air."

The friar nodded, though Sally believed he was suspicious. He said no more and waddled into the castle with his arms around the pot. Sally stared at the tall tower. When the friar left, she heard a faint scream.

"Is Jacob up there?" she wondered. "Oh no, he must have been seen."

Sally turned around and saw Clipper hiding on the elevated parapet that encircled the ramparts. Clipper noticed Sally and waved. Sally waved back. All seemed well for them.

SADLY, ALL WAS NOT WELL FOR ME. ROHESIA STOOD BACK UP AFTER repeatedly kicking me while waving her dagger near my face.

"Your kind is not welcome here, you devil!" she scowled. "Leave or I slay you!"

I stood up as well and stared at her, breathing heavily. I swallowed my pride and spoke with the most humble voice I could make. "I'm not here to make trouble, honest. I have a friend downstairs talking to the king this very moment. A human friend, for that matter. We're friends."

"You are deceitful," she said. "My father has told me stories about our brave knights battling the dragons until the beasts have disappeared. If you try something, I shall…"

Her sentence was cut short as I took swift action. I swiped the dagger away from Rohesia's hand with the tips of my claws. I closed my fingers together and the blade folded in half. Thinking she was powerless, the princess crouched down and began sobbing. "You are going to spill my blood before I get the chance to wed. Go and take my life! I would rather it be now than later," she cried.

Dropping the useless dagger, I tried to assist Rohesia back to her feet. "Look, if I was that kind of dragon, you would've been dead by now. But look at you. You're alive and well. It's just as I said: I'm friendly. I won't hurt you."

Realizing my intentions, Rohesia stopped crying. I gently returned the dagger to her. Trusting me, she placed the bent weapon on the nightstand where she had found it. She took a deep breath of relief and sat down on her bed. I sat on the floor next to her.

"You said that you're engaged or something?" I asked her.

"Indeed," she said, cheering up a little. "The love of my life has ridden to our kingdom. He should be here even as we speak. Ah, I have been reminded! I must join my parents."

She quickly stood up and dressed behind the curtain before heading to the door. She turned around to me and wished me luck that I would not get caught. I was pretty sure her father would never approve of me. A few seconds later, I was alone in the chamber. Assuming Sally's step in the plan was going well, I stepped out onto the balcony and jumped off the edge. With my wings out, I flew to the south parapet where I reunited with Clipper, Chang, and Reno.

"How did it go?" asked Clipper when I landed. "I saw a little of what happened over there."

"It's all right. I take it Sally's still inside?" I rubbed my claws on my broad white chest. I looked down near Clipper's feet. "It looks like Reno's happy to see me."

CHAPTER 22

BUTTERFINGERS

King Adam smiled at the sight of his daughter descending the stairs in her bright violet dress and silver bracelets.

"It is good to see you, Father. I'm sorry I am late," said Rohesia.

"Is there a cause for the delay?" asked Adam, caring not about the answer.

Rohesia thought about telling her story, but decided it was better to not say anything about me. She answered with a twitch in her eyes, "I had trouble fitting this dress. I found a solution to the problem. Thus, I am here."

The queen placed a hand on her chin. "Dearest me! Your dress does not fit?" she questioned. "I've spent months making sure every detail of the dress was correct."

"There is no problem," Rohesia said, comforting her mother. "It fits well. I apologize for the time I have spent."

Roger joined in. "I was beginning to believe the dragons have captured you. Then I would have to slay the beasts!" He laughed.

Rohesia was thrilled to see Roger. Roger kissed Rohesia's hand in greeting.

"Oh, Roger! You are here!" said Rohesia. "I must say, what is this of dragons? I have not heard of dragons in this kingdom."

King Adam answered, speaking softly, "Rohesia, I am sorry to say this, but our knights have said that they were attacked by two dragons. One was as red as blood with daggers for fangs. The other had black scales. I am sorry to frighten you, my dear."

Rohesia realized that I fit the description of the black dragon her father had mentioned. However, she did not believe that I had attacked the knights. She herself was not attacked, after all. She wanted to argue, but knew that it would do no good. Instead, she said nothing of my presence. "Well," she said, swallowing, "as you can see, I have encountered no dragons. I... I will just remember to close my windows at night."

"Worry not, my love," said Roger, courageously. "I shall find these dragons and slay them!"

"No!" Rohesia blurted out.

Roger turned and stared awkwardly at her. "I beg your pardon?"

Rohesia covered her mouth at her unintentional interjection. "I meant that right now I would like to enjoy our festivities. Please forgive me."

Sally, standing near the prince, heard the exchange. She felt apprehensive. Looking left and right, Sally turned to again leave to the castle grounds.

"Who was that woman?" Rohesia asked. "She was wearing odd clothing. None that I have ever seen before."

She looked down to admire her own elaborate ball gown when she realized that she had forgotten something important in her chamber. "Oh dear, I forgot my grandmother's brooch! I must go find it."

"I will come with you," Roger said. "I have not seen you in such a long time. I want to be with you."

"No!" Rohesia again blurted.

The several nearby guests again looked up in surprise. Rohesia flushed and caught herself. She had to think of something so she would not ruin the upcoming celebration. "Please, do not bother. I will only be a moment."

Roger wrapped his fingers around her smooth hand. "Nonsense, Rohesia. I want to be with you." His smile dropped when he noticed her distress. "Is there something wrong?"

He was unaware of my presence inside the chamber, and

Rohesia had no intention of letting him find out. Hoping that I had left, Rohesia pasted a small smile to her face. "Nothing is wrong," she answered.

The couple climbed the stairs and entered Rohesia's chamber. I was nowhere in sight. Rohesia felt as if something heavy had lifted off her chest. She removed the brooch from its box and pinned it to her dress. Roger spied the balcony and wandered out to look over the castle grounds. Rohesia stepped out to join him.

"It is so beautiful out here," said Roger. "But it's not as beautiful as you. You are my dream come true. Ever since I was a young man, I wanted to wed a woman like you. When we are together, we will live in peace."

Approaching the railing, Rohesia saw someone below. It was Sally. "I noticed that woman in the great hall. Where did she find the funny clothing? She looks… rather unusual."

Roger stood next to Rohesia. "Never mind her. I love you. I will always be with you. Never will I let you stand alone. If you have troubles, they will be my troubles. It will be that way until the day I die. I will never let the dragons or anything else harm you."

Rohesia stared into the sky. "If a dragon ever does come, I sincerely hope it will not be wicked. I hope at least a few of them are kind."

"Do not worry. If you are ever in trouble, I will help."

Rohesia turned to the prince. Her eyes twinkled. She leaned against the railing with the wind blowing her hair back. As she shifted her weight to a more comfortable position, her foot slipped on the smooth stone of the balcony. Losing her balance on the rail, she fell backwards and over the edge. Her quick hands grabbed Roger's arms just in time. The princess panicked as she hung over the edge.

"Oh no! Hold on!" Roger shouted.

Rohesia wept. "Help! Help me please!"

Down below, Sally caught a glimpse of Rohesia hanging over the balcony. Frightened, she darted back inside the castle to alert the king.

It took less than a minute for everyone to flood out onto the grounds, watching as Roger held the princess. From atop the parapet, Clipper saw Rohesia dangling before I did. He unfolded his wings as he watched in horror. "Jacob, look! It's that princess you were telling me about. She's going to fall!"

Clouds of smoke escaped my nostrils when I looked over. "She's got butterfingers. She'll slip. I've got to rescue her." I jumped up and down in anticipation.

Clipper's jaw dropped. "What? Why would you do that? You know that the whole castle is going to see you. Besides, I can see someone already up there with her."

Chang observed the sight as well. "He won't be able to hang onto her for much longer. If she's to survive, someone else needs to save her."

"That's true," said Clipper, grabbing Reno's tail to keep the playful dragon nearby. "I just hope it's someone *other* than Jacob."

On the balcony, Roger held as tightly as he could to the princess's hands. One slight mistake would send Rohesia to her death. Roger's precarious position through the railing made it difficult for him to hold on. Though Rohesia was hanging on tightly, her hands suddenly slipped from Roger's grasp. From my spot, I saw her fall. I ran to the edge of the parapet and hurdled over. All Clipper could do was watch me fly to the tower to attempt the rescue. We both knew this would reveal us.

The crowd below stood in horror. They screamed as Rohesia fell. About thirty feet from the ground, I intercepted Rohesia's fall. When she landed on my wing, her body-weight disrupted my flight. I pumped my other wing as hard as I could to regain control while keeping Rohesia up by not dropping the wing under her. I spun in circles then slammed into the side of the castle, ricocheting off the wall. The ground jumped up at me as I crashed onto the dewy grass. I rolled several yards and stopped. Rohesia was flung slightly further, catapulting off me.

When I stopped rolling, I saw Rohesia in front of me. She stood up on wobbly feet. It did not look like she was seriously injured. Realizing that she was all right, I turned my attention to the other problem I was facing. The shocked crowd had witnessed the whole thing. Many of them backed away from me.

Rohesia collected herself. Despite the numerous cuts she had from my spikes, she was happy to be alive. I slowly stood up, my world spinning. Several royal knights surrounded me when my vision cleared. They had shining, double-edged swords that were pointed at my nose. Adam pulled his daughter out of the circle and spoke to her, relieved that her daughter was not seriously harmed.

"You are a girl of great fortune," Adam said to her. "It's a good thing you did not fall to your death or get eaten by that horrible creature."

I stared at the king in disbelief. "What do you mean horrible? I wasn't trying to eat her."

The king appeared surprised. He seemed to have expected a loud, wicked roar. But that was not the case. Though my voice was rough and loud, I had nonetheless spoken. It took him a moment before he answered me. "I mean… well…you tried to abduct my daughter. Yes! You may take my life, but you will never take her to your vile home. I will die and you will never enslave or harm her. Thankfully, you have failed!"

"No!" I cried. "I was saving her!"

"Do not lie to me! I know about your kind. You are vicious beasts who have plagued this land before. You have especially plagued the Nibelungs. You will not leave them alone, will you? They are our friends and you tried to destroy them."

"Let's not get off the subject. I was saving her! I would never try to hurt the princess of your beautiful kingdom."

Adam did not listen to anything I had said. He ordered one of his knights to take my life. A knight that was standing in my blind spot took me by surprise. He jabbed his blade towards my heart. Though the blade did not pierce me, a tremendous pain shot through my chest. I cried out, letting an involuntary breath of fire into the air. With anger building inside me, I wanted to fight back. I lowered my horns and threatened my assaulter. The knight knew I meant business and backed away from me.

The princess could not take it any longer. She had known what I had intended to do when she fell. She stepped in front of the knight just as he was about to lunge at me again. Another knight quickly kicked me in the stomach just as Rohesia had done earlier. I fell back to the ground. Before I could get back up, a ring of iron, attached to a chain, was fastened around my neck. The other end of the chain was embedded into the wall of the castle. Another servant to the king wrapped a belt around my snout to prevent me from casting my fiery breath. I was not going anywhere. To demonstrate my passiveness, I tried my best not to fight back. That proved to be a challenge, however. My anger still got the best of me. I screeched and growled as my neck pulled back and forth on the chain. It started to become weaker and weaker on the wall.

"Stop! I don't want you to hurt him. He is telling the truth: he saved my life," Rohesia cried, getting in her father's way.

Adam stared at her daughter with startled eyes. "Rohesia, what has come over you? Do dragons have the ability to control the mind? I cannot believe this! Very well. If the sword through the heart does not kill the drake, then it certainly will through the eye. If that fails, then we will have to find some other way to execute him. He will not be allowed to live."

The king ordered his knight to kill me. The knight, reluctant to do so, advanced again. I was chained, but not completely helpless. With my heart pounding, I jerked harder and harder. This time the blade was heading for my eye. That would be fatal! Just as he was about to thrust his sword, I puffed a small flame at him through my nostrils. The knight backed off again. I slid the leather belt off with the swipe of my claw then bit the chain into two fiery pieces, like the prison bars in France. With the broken chain swinging on the iron ring around my neck, I jumped into the air. Several armed knights charged at me. I used my wings to create a stiff wind that would at least blow them off their feet. With no one else after me, I flew away from the crowd, landing near Clipper on the wall a safe distance away. I noticed Chang was not with Clipper.

"Look! There are two drakes!" someone shouted from below.

"After them!" ordered the king. "They must not escape!"

I saw the castle's defensive force charging up a stairwell and onto the parapet where we stood. Placing Reno on my back again, I jumped off the edge with Clipper following behind me. We flew to the nearby woods, perfect for cover.

KING ADAM LOST PATIENCE. HE ORDERED HIS WHOLE ARMY TO find and kill us. As the army marched out on horseback, colorful banners waving on short poles, the friar came to Adam. "Your Highness," he said, "I suspect the mysterious woman is with the dragons."

"I believe you may be right," replied Adam. "Find her and send her to me."

The friar searched all around the castle grounds but did not find Sally anywhere. She had taken advantage of the distraction to sneak away with Chang while I saved Rohesia. The four of us, along with Reno, were long gone.

"I cannot find her, Sire," the friar said to Adam a few minutes later. "She is gone."

Adam clenched his fists. "Resume your duties," he ordered, sighing. "I shall deal with the drakes myself, God help us."

Rohesia approached her father just as the friar left. She had the countenance of a harmless little girl. Just as if she was pleading for her own life, she pleaded for mine. "Father, please. That dragon saved me. He did not even try to kill me. You must know the truth. I met him in my chamber while I was preparing for the grand meeting with Roger. That was why I was late. The dragon said his name is Jacob. I believe that he is as kind as you or I. I can tell he did not want to harm me. If he did, I would have been dead by now. Please believe me, Father."

Adam finally swallowed his pride and felt Rohesia's sympathy. He bowed and turned to the queen. "My dear, I have heard the pleadings of our daughter. In order to make things right, I must find this dragon. If you will pardon me, we will ride north. The mysterious woman said that she will find the Nibelung people, so there we will go."

The queen would lead the kingdom by herself for the next few days. After a hard farewell, Adam and Rohesia, who had left her grandmother's brooch in her chamber, left the castle, escorted by a group of knights. The two had their horses prepared by servants and they rushed out into the woods, down the path that led north. Roger was left behind. Dreading Rohesia's possible fate, he took out a piece of parchment and sketched a map. He then gathered information from the knights who had first confronted us.

"They took the woman I loved," he murmured in fury as he wrote the note on the back of the map. "I will get her back! Hopefully this message will help spread the truth about the dragons."

CHAPTER 23

THE MONOLEGIONS' TRUE COLORS

Days passed since our departure from Saint Cassius. We traveled north, though I did not know how far, considering the fact that I did not know where in Europe we were. On the first day out, we stopped next to a lake to rest. Chang and I sat near a campfire that I had easily created with a single breath. After a long silence of sitting, Chang spoke up, "I don't get it. You mentioned your experience with the old man in Atlanta. You told me about his respect for you. I know that dragons have a good reputation in Asia. But here in Europe, you're not appreciated at all. All these Cassians want to see your dead body."

"Thanks for pointing that out," I sighed, scratching the ring on my neck.

"So let's get on the same page. Back in the Guarded Forest, you told me that that the dragon of old practically predicted that you would accidently transform yourself. That's amazing. But how did you know about tracking down the Monolegions in Norway?"

I summarized my knowledge. I explained to him that the Nibelungs had nearly been wiped out before. The dragon of old had nearly defeated them long ago. When the dragon left, there was only one tribe of Nibelungs remaining: the one legion. Blue-eyes's book explained that their central place of order was in the forests of Norway. They stayed there for hundreds of years with spies stationed around the world. It was only a matter of time before the sorcerer would begin the infiltration. Whether it was by arms or the pen, I did not know.

Chang's eyes widened with awe. "So now all we have to do is find the Monolegion dwarves, get ourselves back to the present, and stop them from doing who knows what, right?"

"Simple as that," I answered, though I did not think it was that simple.

After we had finished our discussion, Sally returned to the fire with Reno beside her. "This little bug sure loves to explore," she said. "I had to chase her down a couple of times."

I laughed as Reno blew a small flame from her mouth into the already burning fire. I could tell that she had been happy all day. Her whole life before her rescue had been dark and closed in. Now she was enjoying her freedom. While our attention was on Reno, Clipper emerged from the lake with another fish in his mouth. He chewed and swallowed it, then licked his large fangs with his thick tongue.

"Clipper, you were supposed to bring fish to the fire to cook for *all* of us, not eat them raw yourself," said Sally, glaring at him. "I can't trust you or Jacob to go fishing. You two just eat them before we have the chance to cook them. You're like two children eating a batch of cookie dough."

Chang stood up and broke a branch off a tree. He honed one end to a sharp point with the small knife in my knapsack. He was going to use the stick to harpoon fish. Over the course of the evening, he caught five, cooking the first two of them over the fire. When the fish were ready, he snacked on one and gave the other to Sally. He then gave one of the raw ones to Reno. I could not help but be impressed with how fast Reno ate her supper.

When she finished eating, Sally sat next to me. She examined the iron ring on my neck. Chang assumed that Sally wanted to get it off and offered to help. He grasped the broken chain on the ring and lurched it back and forth. The tight ring pressed hard on my neck.

"Ouch! Stop! That hurts," I coughed.

"Hold still," grunted Chang.

Sally immediately stopped Chang. Pushing him back, she pulled out a small key.

"Where did you get that?" Chang asked in surprise.

She inserted the key into a small keyhole and unlocked the ring. I waited a few seconds to take some long, smoky breaths.

"I took it back in the castle from one of the guards while they were putting the chain on you," she answered.

"Thank you for that," I gulped, scratching the back of my neck with a foot. "Now I can sleep in peace."

"That's a good idea," said Clipper. "We better get some shuteye soon. I'm quite tired."

"I didn't mean it that way but sure, I guess I can sleep. It'll do us good," I said.

It did not take long for the darkness of night to replace the light of day as the five of us lay next to the fire. Sally and Chang were buried the previous autumn's leaves while the other three of us used our natural heat. Sometime during the night, I heard Reno sniffling with sadness again. Awakened, I did not have the energy to move. The whimpering continued, so I crawled over to her. Poor Reno was feeling lonely and wanted someone to be with her. I lay next to the baby dragon.

Knowing she was with someone, she curled up against me and fell back asleep. I shut my eyes and went back to sleep as well. When I did, I was reminded of why Reno was with us. She was the emblem of my arrival. In my sleep, I also envisioned a mystical and magical forest that for some reason seemed like home to the both of us.

It felt wonderful to finally get some rest. I had not slept at all the night before. At dawn, I opened my eyes. The smiling sun spread over the hills and gave life to the land once more. I rose to my feet and stretched like a cat. Clipper and Sally woke up shortly after, followed by Chang and finally Reno.

"I've never felt so relaxed in my life," Clipper yawned, exposing his shorter teeth.

I could not agree more. It did feel good to finally get some well-deserved rest. But now the sun was up, and someone would be tracking us again. We had to move.

The days flew by and I was quite sure we were making good time. We walked across the scenic countryside. I would have patrolled from the air, but the wind was traveling with us. Clipper and I would smell new visitors from over a mile away, even on the ground. When we headed into a small marsh, I started smelling something nearby.

"I think there's someone over there," I said, facing the trees.

Sally decided to check it out. I began to feel paranoid. What I had felt in the Guarded Forest was beginning to return.

"This is it. We're in the land of the Monolegion dwarves," Clipper announced.

The happy day had somehow turned into a haunting afternoon. The thick mist did not help. It felt as if we had entered a hostile environment. I could not hear singing birds or feel the breeze. Even Reno looked as if she had seen a ghost. She would not leave my side.

Sally returned. "I didn't find anyone, but I don't like this place."

"That probably means that we've made it to our destination," I said. "I feel like we're being watched. I felt that way after we crossed the fence into the Guarded Forest."

I kept a cautious eye when I saw a strange person approaching us. He did not look like a dwarf, rather a man who was trying to hide from someone. At the sight of him moving towards us, I took Reno in my grasp and followed Clipper to a spot out of sight although I thought the man had already seen us. Sally and Chang were left alone when the strange man caught up with them. When he reached the duo, he collapsed, exhausted. From the distance, I noticed that he had a large wound on his side.

"The Nibelungs are imposters," the man said in a weak voice. "They are not friendly as the people of Saint Cassius believe. I make but a simple trek to their closest village and I am beaten. They have planned a nasty plot. I overheard them and they attacked me. Please believe my words!"

"What you say is true," Chang said respectfully.

The fallen man smiled. He shut his eyes and rested his head on the ground. His wound was too critical for him to live. Sally and Chang knew that all he wanted to do was warn someone about the evil Monolegions. Now that his task was complete, he let himself die in peace. Clipper and I joined them and stared at the man's body. Sally pulled a kerchief from the man's pocket and placed it over his face. "Rest in peace," she said reverently, tearing up.

"There's proof," said Clipper. "That man won't die in vain. Now let's find a dwarf, preferably one with an albore. We have to travel back as soon as possible. Hopefully, what we do now will send them up to the far north where they are in our day."

I sank my claws into the ground. "Just be careful how you handle them so we don't get knocked to an even deeper time in history."

Clipper closed his eyes in a cringe. He was as concerned as I was. Getting an albore was going to be risky. The chance of a time spell or anything else an albore can do was something I tried not to think about. In any case, we had to get an albore one way or another to return. This was a risk we had to take.

As we were about to continue down the path, Reno made an alarming screech. Looking behind us, we saw a group of knights approaching us. I rolled my eyes and huffed. There were enemy dwarves at one end of the path and hostile knights at the other!

"Clipper, stay here with me," I said. "Sally and Chang, take Reno and go behind those trees. I'll keep the powder bombs with me. Hurry!"

All three were off. Chang gave me the knapsack that held the powder bombs. I laid the bag down in front of me. Sally left with Reno in her arms.

"I've got to be careful holding her," said Sally. "Her claws are a little sharp."

I took out a powder bomb and waited for the knights to get closer. At the right moment, I lit one of the bombs and let the blazing missile fly through the air. With a neat arc, it landed near the horses and exploded. The spooked horses bucked most of their riders off their backs and fled out of sight. As for the grounded knights, some fled while others charged at me with their double-edged swords.

Clipper hissed. "Here they come."

We both got into a defensive stance. I ignited another powder bomb and the attacking knights ducked for cover. As it exploded, they were left vulnerable for me and Clipper to do our fair share of attacking. With my front claws ready to shred anything it could reach, I leapt forward. Clipper stayed behind and used his fire. When the knights realized they were powerless against us, they fled, along with the other knights who had retreated earlier.

"They're out of the way," I said to Clipper. "Find Sally and Chang while I scout out the area ahead. I'm pretty sure some of the dwarves heard the commotion."

Clipper escorted our friends from their hiding place while I ran at full speed down the path. Noticing the thatched roofs of houses ahead, I knew I reached the village. I planted my paws into the ground and slid to a stop. I made a chirping noise to signal the rest of my friends to join me. I gave Chang the knapsack of powder bombs and examined the village.

"Okay," said Clipper, taking lead, "let's hurry and run them out of here. Let's do it as fast as we can so we can return and stop Triathra. And remember to keep an eye out for any albore."

We were returning to the site of our recent battle when we saw two horses racing up to us. Clipper chomped his teeth. "Oh, no. Not *him.*"

"Him" referred to King Adam of Saint Cassius Castle. Riding alongside him was the beautiful Princess Rohesia. They halted next to us and dismounted. Adam drew a clean, steel sword and held the tip of the blade up to my eye. He was red in the face with anger. Infuriated myself, I held my ground. We stood face to face. I, the black dragon, growled at my bitter rival. The monarch held his sword, ready to use it at any time. There was tension and the risk of violence.

"Did you not see that, Princess Rohesia? These dragons attacked our men. Our finest men! They are evil and they must die!" shouted Adam.

"No, no, no! For the last time I am not trying to kill you *or* your daughter!" I roared back. "It was just a matter of self-defense. I'm trying to help in case you haven't noticed. Remember a few days ago? I *saved* your daughter's life. SAVED!"

"Father, listen to him!" begged Rohesia.

Adam did not relieve tension on his sword. "I'm sorry. I cannot let you live."

With the point of the blade coming to my eye, I dodged the sword and batted it away from Adam's grasp with my horns. Adam, knowing there was no way out, prepared to run. Chang picked up the sword gently by the golden hilt.

"Oh, go and let your friend spill my blood. I know you will do it," said Adam as he closed his eyes, waiting for the blade to strike him. Sweat rolled down his face. He waited, but the blade did not strike him.

"Now that we're even with each other, I can explain," I said. "If I was going to harm you, I would have done so by now, but I won't. Chang, give him his sword."

Chang held the sword with the blade pointed down. But just as he was about to return it, the sound of a collapsing tree stopped us all. I noticed from the corner of my eye that a big willow was giving way. It was going to fall on the king. I pushed Adam out of the way and dodged the trunk as well. The willow smashed onto the ground, the branches flailing all about like cruel whips. I emerged unharmed.

Call it luck or cruel fate, I turned around to see an albore in the hand of a nearby dwarf with an uneasy look on his face.

"An albore," Sally said quietly.

"I believed the dragons were gone!" the dwarf cried. "Now what is this? I thought the return of the dragon would be taking place thousands of years from now."

Clipper took a step forward. "What are you going to do? Are you going to curse us?" he growled in a mocking tone.

"Have you gone mad?" inquired the dwarf. "These albores do not have the ability to do that. Only the scepter wielded by the sorcerer whom I'm about to send for will get rid of you. All these albores can do are simple spells."

He was surely lying. It was an albore that had burst the tire. It was an albore that had summoned a bolt of lightning. It was an albore that had thrown us out of time. If I only had one in my grasp, I could show him what an albore could really do. Without warning anyone, I flapped my wings up and down. The disturbed dirt blew everywhere and the dwarf shielded his eyes. I exhaled a large flame into the air. The dwarf must have known I meant business and calmly stepped back.

"So, can these albores throw a being out of time?" I asked harshly.

"Most certainly," answered the dwarf, exposing an innocent smile. "'Tis an unexplainable ability. This albore has extra power with the help of sorcery. One can transport himself to another location as he chooses so with it. Most albores have no such ability."

That was all I needed to know. The dwarf was not lying about that. All I had to do was get that albore in order to get back to the present. Now was my chance. I grabbed a powder bomb out of the knapsack and ignited it. The dwarf jumped for cover.

Just before it exploded, I hurdled the bomb. It landed right next to the dwarf. When the dust cleared after the explosion, I jumped on the small victim. He tried to squirm but became motionless as I pressed a paw down on his chest. Clipper joined me and reached for the special wand. With a good hold on it, he pulled it away from the lone dwarf. I let loose of the unarmed Monolegion. He scurried over to the fallen willow, hoping that this ordeal would soon be over.

"Get out of here. And tell the dwarves to move away from here or we will return," I ordered. "Now move!"

The dwarf summoned his courage over my roar. "Never! I will never do what you say. You will slay me no matter what I do. My people will stay here. End of that!"

I roared again, this time much louder. He noticed my clenched claws and took a deep breath. "Eh… what's my fate? If I move my people, you will kill me. If I do not, you will kill me and everybody else."

"You will certainly die if you don't!" I hissed.

Clipper slightly bumped me with his horns. "Jacob, there's no need to say that. Let him go peacefully and we'll take care of him if he double-crosses us."

Angered, I let the frightened wretch go. Clipper stepped in front of him before he could escape. "No tricks now," he growled. "I'm not one to hurt others, but I will if you force me to."

"I'm not going to trick you. I will comply," said the dwarf, covering his wet eyes in embarrassment. He immediately stood up. "We come from the far north. We will return there immediately."

With that, he took off running back to the village. I knew he would spread the news of our existence.

Clipper took a deep breath of relief. "Don't worry about him. I could smell his fear. He knew if he tried something, he wouldn't like the results."

"Clipper, you handled that very well," said Sally, setting Reno down. "You chose the better path. Who else would react the way you did?"

What Sally said made me realize how harshly I had behaved. "I'm sorry, Sally." I said. "I didn't know what was going through me. When confronting someone I don't like, something inside me wants to act aggressively. Sometimes I win and I hold ground. Other times I lose and my instincts take control. The dragon part of me will act like I did after I transformed."

"It's a war I face, too," said Clipper, "but I won't kill unless I must. Just remember, pride is a powerful thing in all of us. It can get so strong that you can't hear the ancient dragon's spirit."

"You're right," I replied. "I just need to control myself. I won't let my pride control me. Hey, at least we did it. We just sent the Monolegions away, *and* we have an albore!"

I gathered my friends together. Chang held up the wand. "Evil, cowardly, stupid. These are pretty much opposite of what I thought a real dwarf would be. Ah, well. What should I do with this?"

"The albore reads your mind," I explained. "Just wish for something in your head. You don't even have to say anything."

Chang understood and shut his eyes, waiting to be transported back to present-day Norway from the medieval world. He stood there for several seconds. He opened his eyes again, but we were still in the marsh with Adam and Rohesia watching. Chang was confused. "What's wrong?" he wondered.

"If I may say," Adam began, "the albores only work for those who are from that time. You say you are from the days yet to come. You cannot make this one obey. If you are to go to your present time, you must have someone from the time of the albore to go with you."

I was a little frustrated upon hearing this, but I remembered what I had just said. I tried not to show my disappointment.

Chang looked around. "Okay, maybe Rohesia can transport us back."

All of us looked at Rohesia. She stared at her father. "I will do this," she said.

Adam shook his head firmly. "I will not let you go. It could interfere with your marriage and ruin your life. You may never see Prince Roger again. I forbid you it!"

"Father, if all goes well, I will return here to this exact spot at this exact time. If you let me go, I will return within seconds, I promise. If I do not go, and Jacob speaks truth, those of tomorrow will be in ruin."

Tears ran down Adam's cheeks. I could tell that he was pondering Rohesia's plea. After about a minute, he nodded slowly. "Enough said. I will let you go, Rohesia, but take care for yourself. Great care, hear me. May the Lord our God guide you down the straight and narrow path in your endeavors."

Rohesia and Adam hugged each other one last time. After the touching moment, she joined the circle with the rest of us. Chang handed her the albore. It was satisfying to feel the wind rush past me.

King Adam stood by himself in the marsh. Her daughter was ready to leave. She was going to help what he had once thought was the foe. Now we were after the *real* foe that he had thought was trustworthy.

"Farewell, my child," he spoke as another tear formed in the corner of his eye. "Bring peace and prosperity to the land yet to come."

Rohesia and Adam stared at each other when the vortex formed. Just as before, we were sucked inside.

It was the middle of the second day since our departure. We were not in a joyful situation.

CHAPTER 24

BACK TO THE PRESENT

I opened my eyes to find a circle of Monolegion soldiers surrounding the cottage where we had returned. I huffed a cloudy breath of skepticism. The princess and Sally, keeping Reno close by her, stood behind Clipper and me. Chang was off to my right. Rohesia cradled her arm that held the albore, as if her hand was sore. Each of my human friends shivered in the icy wind.

Rohesia stared nervously at the threatening men and women. "What are we doing here?" she asked, shaking the albore-wielding hand.

"Princess Rohesia," I said, "I would like to introduce you to the descendants of those who deceived you."

Clipper tried to be as peaceful as possible with the dwarfish mob. He spoke to the hostile beings in an effort to avoid a fight. "Where is your sorcerer, Triathra?" he questioned.

"He is overseas on the American continent," one of the dwarves answered. "He is prepared for your coming; that is if you can make it there. When he recovers the hidden Master Scepter, the Nibelungs will triumph for good."

I recalled the staff that Triathra kept at his side: the scepter that gave the sorcerer his power.

Clipper tapped a fang. "He's in North America? I didn't know he traveled outside this forest. If we can just leave in peace, no one will get hurt. I mean no offense, but I doubt you can beat us."

I leaned over and whispered into Clipper's ear, "What in the world are you doing?"

"I'm trying to talk our way out of this pickle we're in," Clipper huffed back.

I growled at his remark. "Talk won't do any good. We've got to get rid of them. They won't live in peace as long as we're here."

"Jacob, remember what I said earlier," said Clipper. "Don't let your pride control you. You need to calm yourself. Don't let the natural dragon overtake you."

"He's got a point," Sally whispered from behind me.

Clipper's words did not combat my anger. Just as before, my blood felt like it was boiling. Rage was building up inside me as I took a deep breath, ready to spread a wave of fire over the enemy. Clipper read my emotions and tried to get in front of me. "Jacob, don't let your natural dragon control you. Keep it cool."

I was about to release the flames of fury when Clipper gently placed a paw over my mouth. Snarling with anger, I knocked him to the side with my horns. "Get out of my way!" I bellowed.

In the blink of an eye, I exhaled my fire. My friends could do nothing except watch. Several dwarves jumped to the side while the rest in the center rolled in the snow to suffocate the flames on their fur coats.

"Kill me if you can!" I roared.

I charged at one group of dwarves who had dodged my flames. With no real knowledge of dwarves, I did not know every capability they had. It turned out that they were incredibly agile and fast. They could move in and out of places better than most people I knew.

The pile of living dwarves vanished from my path. I found myself running straight into a Norway spruce. My head smashed into the thick trunk, sending it straight to the ground in a loud crash. Seconds later, several of my enemies jump onto to my back. One grabbed both my horns while the others started jabbing me with small daggers. The miniature blades did not sting as bullets did, but it was next to unbearable. I started bucking like a wild horse. This only resulted in one or two dwarves flying off my back. One was tossed over my head. He landed several yards away. With the remaining dwarves on me, I dropped to the ground and rolled in the snow. Many of them let go under my weight. I felt their squirming slowly die down. Those who did not come across the spikes on my back were not dead, just dazed. I stood back up, teeth unfurled, facing Chang and the rest.

"Good to see you're okay," Clipper said as he finished up a second battle on the other group of dwarves. "But will you please not be so violent? Just fight them, you don't need to cause any real harm."

"We've got to find a way out of here!" Chang interrupted. "Monty was right. There is danger here. Maybe we can do something about it back home. The dwarves are infiltrating more and more places if the sorcerer is gone. We need to find this scepter he has."

I started digging into the snow to calm myself, taking several deep breaths. "You're right. Here in Norway, the prison in France, and possibly on U.S. soil! They're everywhere!"

"U.S. soil?" Rohesia repeated. "I'm confused."

"No need to be confused," said Sally. "Just stay with us and you'll be all right. I'll try to explain things to you as we go."

We were about to leave the scene when we heard the crunching of snow nearby. A dazed dwarf stood up and held an albore in the air. A ball of light blasted out of the wand and struck me. I flew backwards and struck the trunk of another spruce with excessive force. The tree fell, landing on the cottage and destroying it. Albores could do much more than what the dwarves would reveal, no question about that. I would have been furious if he had sent another time spell.

Before I stood up, several dwarves stood up and again jumped on me. I let out a flame, only blowing one of them off me. The rest grabbed me and tried to pin me down. I swatted enemy after enemy off of me. It was overwhelming.

"Clipper! Get the others out of here, now!" I roared to my companion. "We can't let them get hurt!"

Clipper touched his nose to Reno's side. "Take care of Reno and get to safety," he told Sally. "I'll stay and help Jacob."

Sally again picked up Reno. Our human friends moved as fast as they could through the deep snow. Rohesia dropped the albore on her way out, but didn't notice in all the confusion.

Back at the fight, some of the dwarves I had squashed under my back spotted Clipper and decided to attack him. Clipper attempted flight and managed to land on top of a tree. He clawed through the branches until he could hook onto the trunk. The dwarf with the only albore used it to destroy the upper-half of the tree. Clipper jumped off before the trunk fell and caught an air current. He flew in a circular motion around his grounded enemy. The dwarf below secured the albore underneath his belt. Making his way to what was left of the cottage, he found and picked up a rifle. He loaded it and fired the first bullet, but missed badly. After a few more attempts, he found out that hitting Clipper would prove to be a challenge. He fired more bullets, all whizzing past his red target.

The last bullet raced straight to Clipper's stomach like an angry hornet. Clipper coughed out a ball of fire and lost control, but soon regained it. The dwarf immediately took out his albore. As he gazed into the sky, Clipper dove after him, roaring. The dwarf dropped the albore so he could cover his ears. Clipper landed and stood over the albore. "I'm not going to break it," he said. "And I'm not going to kill you… that is unless you force me to. Here's a little reminder in case you forget."

Clipper raised his claws and struck the dwarf above the wrist. Yelling in fright, the dwarf clutched at the scratches on his arm.

Clipper placed his paw back on the ground. "The scars will be red, just like me. When you see your scars, you will think of me and you will remember not to upset me."

The dwarf did not say anything. He only nodded. Clipper scraped the snow with his tail and left. Not a moment passed before he lowered his head in regret. He realized that he almost let his natural side win as well. When he was calm, he buried the albore in the frigid ground and went to help me.

The battle was turning in my favor. Fewer and fewer dwarves were able to climb on top of me. I finally had time to stand back on my feet. Using my horns, I took out the dwarves who attacked me. I did not even look up, I lowered my horns and waited for a fateful dupe to run into them. It was not long before I felt no impact on my head. I raised my head to find the majority of the dwarves down, with Clipper's help.

"Let's get out of here while we can. If we escape, we can contact the Norwegian government and warn them about these poor invaders," he suggested.

"Are you sure they'll believe us? No stranger has actually *trusted* us yet," I huffed angrily. I forgot about Marvin, the grandfather, or Byron.

"We won't give up until they do believe us," Clipper said. "We can't afford to have Monolegions regain power here."

Our conversation was cut short by the few remaining dwarves. One loaded a small stone into a sling and flung it, hitting me on the nose. The force of the stone hurt. I held my paws over my nose.

A whole new wave of rage washed over me.

"Ouch! You idiot! Do that again and I'll cut your heart out."

The dwarf and his neighbors suddenly stopped their attack when Clipper slowly turned to me. "Don't... even... think about it! We've already killed many."

As I marched towards them, Clipper blew a warning flame in front of them. They swiftly disappeared.

"Jacob, they're gone. No need for a fight now," Clipper said to me.

Fighting the adrenaline as hard as I could, my rage quieted down. It was no easy task. "I'm... I'm sorry, Clipper. My anger is acting up again. It's not easy to control."

"I started to feel that when I gave one of them some scars. Now I feel bad I did so. It's interesting, my rage seems easier to control than yours. It's a challenge for me, but it's not impossible."

"Well, with these dwarves down, we can leave," I said.

With no sense of hurry since the dwarves were gone, Clipper asked a question that was even on my mind. "What do you think makes the Master Scepter so important?"

I thought a moment while I walked. "Well, you know the staff that Triathra kept with him all the time? Remember how he held it almost reverently? That's it! I'm sure of it. If we can get that, maybe we can wipe out the Monolegions. The dwarves said Triathra was finding the hidden Master Scepter."

"Triathra was pretty nervous when we took it that first time. Of course, we didn't know how powerful it was at the time. All we knew was that it could kill us. That's why we surrendered."

"And now we know that it's a key to the Monolegions' destruction. That explains why he left for the Americas somewhere."

"Question is, *where* in America."

We were following our friends' footprints when Clipper decided to search for them from the sky. I spotted something in the snow and stopped him just before he left. "Hold on. I think Rohesia dropped the albore."

I picked up the powerful albore before I jumped into the air along with Clipper. We searched the ground below for Sally and the rest.

"Where are they?" I asked. "I can smell them."

Clipper sniffed the air. "Right below us. I can see them."

We stopped flight. I free-fell back to the ground, hovering right in front of Reno's face. Reno chirped with joy. I gazed back up in the sky as Clipper spiraled down, unlike my style of free falling.

"Sorry," he said when he landed, "I still have a thing about heights."

"Never mind that. We need to go to Oslo now," I stated.

"Oslo? The name of a kingdom?" Rohesia asked. "I apologize. I promise I'll not question names or cultures."

"Why do we need to go to Oslo?" Sally asked me.

"We drove most of these dwarves from their place here. Maybe the government can flush out the rest," I said.

"Jacob's right. And we need to hurry and go," Clipper urged.

After I gave the albore back to Rohesia, we all made our decision final. We then crossed through the tunnel under the electric fence once we reached it.

A few days passed. Like before, Clipper and I flew high in the sky while Chang and the others drove in the rented car. We managed to reach Oslo soon enough. The ambassador, who had heard about me, gave me permission to speak with the Prime Minister of Norway concerning the trouble in his land. Clipper and the rest waited while I conducted business with the Prime Minister.

Looking back to this day, I knew the Prime Minister did what he thought was best. I now wished I had not been so spiteful. But at the time, my annoyance made me believe that the Prime Minister did not want to listen. All he seemed to do was ridicule my suggestion. At first, I kindly asked him. When he said no, the argument slowly became louder and louder.

"You've got to take care of this now," I told him.

The Prime Minister avoided eye contact with me. "I can't order my soldiers to attack this restricted area. It does not work that way. People have disappeared there before."

"If you don't do something now, you may be overpowered," I barked back. "Why won't you listen to me? Is it because I'm a dragon?"

"No. You're a human, right? The ambassador said you have accidentally injected yourself with some fluid."

Losing my patience, I leaned closer to him. "Well, I'm a dragon." I huffed out a fiery cinder in front of him. Smoke blew out of my nose. My eyes were next to his. "I am not trying to cause trouble. That thought never crossed my mind, but I can lose my temper really easy." Once I said that, I realized how cruel I was behaving. I blinked a few times and took a step back. "Listen, I'm trying to be friendly. It's just hard for me at the moment. Please understand me."

"Okay, fine. If this is to help my people."

I sat down. "Good. I'm glad you see things as I do. I really am sorry I got mad. I didn't mean to."

JORDAN B. JOLLEY

The Prime Minister smiled. "I'm glad you spoke with me, Mr. Draco."

The entire confrontation took about five minutes. I returned to my friends afterwards.

"Well, did he do it?" Chang asked.

"I had to raise my voice, but I got him to do it. I think victory is on our side."

"You *yelled* at him?" Clipper said in shock. "Now I know you've got anger problems. How do you think he feels now? I mean a dragon trying to tell him what to do."

"It's all okay. At least we achieved one thing. The central part of the Monolegions' land will soon be no more. Now we need to find other dwarf locations, take them out, and, most importantly, find Triathra's scepter."

"Sounds like an adventure. Where do we do now? Return to New York?" asked Sally.

"Yes," I replied.

Clipper pointed to the albore in Rohesia's hand. "The dwarf who had this albore said this can take us from one location to another. Not all albores do that."

Rohesia gazed at the albore that Clipper had retrieved. Sally explained to Rohesia where we wanted to go. Without saying a word, Rohesia used the albore to transport us back to New York. She used her mind, despite never having been there or even having heard of New York. The albore did the rest of the magic.

I shut my eyes. The howling wind again gathered speed around me. The air was warmer now. When I reopened my eyes, I found myself standing on a field of grass, surrounded by a large body of water. I turned around and noticed the statue that I had visited before: The Statue of Liberty. My friends were getting to their feet.

"Is everybody all right?" I asked.

"We're fine," said Chang.

Reno had landed on top of Clipper. She jumped off as he stood up. The princess looked up at the statue in sheer amazement. Sally and Chang sighed in relief now that they were back home. Sniffing the air, I kept an eye out for any tourists in the area. It looked like the island was closed for the morning.

"What are we doing here on Liberty Island?" asked Clipper.

Rohesia winced again while cradling her hand. "I had no knowledge of where we would be. And the magic I make gives me pain." She looked across the water to the skyline of New York City. "Is that your home? It is truly magnificent!"

"Thank you. I wish we had time for sightseeing," Clipper said gently, "but we have to find Triathra."

Rohesia shook the rest of her pain away. "And how do we get off this island?"

"By ferry of course," I said. "A tour boat should arrive here soon. It comes at around ten in the morning, I believe."

Five minutes later, I was as good as my word. A ferry full of tourists appeared. The six of us hid. Since it was the first tour of the day, there were no returning passengers. The humans of our company merged with the tour. Afterwards, they boarded the ferry. Up on deck, Rohesia was delighted by the self-produced power of the boat. Clipper and I swam under the boat. Reno was following us with no trouble. I was happy I could keep my eyes open under the water. Near the Hudson River, the bay was very murky. I could barely make my way through the bothersome litter.

We soon reached the mainland where we decided to split up. Sally and Chang would teach Rohesia what to do to blend in the best she could. I took Reno and followed Clipper up the side of an apartment building.

"I'm thinking, Jacob; we have to clear some things up. I want to know how Monty is tied in to all this. I really think he's related to Triathra somehow."

We stood at the edge of the building. There was no need to dodge skyscrapers for a while. I had to get used to them again. With Reno hanging on my back, I jumped off the edge and soared to another building of similar height. I repeated this

JORDAN B. JOLLEY

process several times. I knew many people would see me, but I did not have time to play the hiding game. I did not worry about the people below.

As I approached downtown, the buildings became taller and taller. Now was the time to actually fly. I flapped my wings and gained altitude. I flew in and out of different places in the city. I gained height until I found a good place to land.

Clipper dropped in at my side. "Before we go, do you really think we should visit Monty's hideaway? I think that's exactly what he wants us to do. Come to think of it, that place felt more like a dungeon than a warehouse, remember?"

"I know," I said. "Monty *wanted* us to go to the forest. I do believe he wanted to show us why we are who we are. Like you said, Monty and Triathra might be related. Monty could be Triathra's brother or cousin. I noticed a resemblance. Anyway, I'm thinking we need to go to Monty's complex. But first we should go to the dorms and meet Chang and the rest. I want them to know where we're going."

"I wonder if we can get in without tearing the place apart. And we need to remember to be quiet."

Reno stood at the edge and blew small flames over the building.

Clipper chuckled. "She's so funny."

I lifted her up and placed her between my wings. "Reno can stay with Sally while we go to Monty's complex."

Chang, Sally, and Rohesia allowed us into my old dormitory when we arrived. The room looked quite nice, considering how I left it before.

"You are back," said Rohesia. "Do you have an idea where to go?"

"Clipper and I have decided to go to Monty's complex to see if we can find out where Triathra's scepter is," I said. "If you don't mind, we'll leave Reno here."

Everyone was okay with that. Chang said he would keep an eye out for any danger near the dormitory, just in case.

Familiar with the way, Clipper and I flew to the complex in no time. But when we reached the building, something felt different. There were no watchdogs on duty. It was too quiet. Not a footstep or a breath could be heard. We both looked at each other, then soared to the roof. Not a soul was in sight. The building was as silent as a tomb. We crept down the stairs to Monty's office. The room was bare except for the dusty, wooden desk. There was a piece of paper pinned on its top with a small knife.

I stepped around the desk to examine the paper. I pulled the knife from the desk.

Clipper stepped up behind me and read, "The feature or features of an area of the Earth or a portion of the heavens."

The words on the paper made me ponder. "A feature? What is Monty trying to say? This is another riddle. It's just as bad as the one in the library." It took me a moment before I thought of the answer. "It's a map. A map is a feature of an area of the Earth or the heavens. This is more like the definition for a map."

Clipper flipped over the paper to find another crudely drawn map. We carefully examined the drawing and quickly realized what the map depicted. "It's a drawing of North America," said Clipper, recognizing the many landforms. He squinted his eyes. "There's a dot over the western part of North America. And there's some writing here. It says School of Preston. Below it shows an arrow pointing down with the number forty beside it."

I studied the map. "What does 'Preston' mean? And what does the arrow represent?"

"Is Preston the name of a person or a town?" Clipper thought. "It says 'School of Preston,' so I think it's a town. Chang will be able to help with this. Let's get back to the dorm room."

Flying back was no trouble. When we returned, we showed the map to Chang, who pulled the dust-covered atlas out from under his bed. He opened it up and flipped through the pages. Passing various states, he kept his sights on locations on the western half of the continent.

Sally pointed to one spot in particular. "Look here. Preston. It's a town in Idaho, by the southeast corner. It looks like the spot where the map is pointing. And if 'school' is written on the map we found, maybe we should find a school."

"What if we go to the school there and find a clue?" Chang suggested. "Then we can find out what the arrow and the number mean, but it seems that Triathra has more than likely relocated himself there. If so, why would Monty leave this map here?"

"He wanted us to find it," I assumed. "Triathra's waiting for us. It's a trap by the looks of it. We're the dragons of this era. Then there's the sorcerer's Master Scepter. If we can get a hold of that, we can defeat him. But if he kills us, there is no stopping him. The Monolegions will win."

There was a brief moment of silence.

"He's waiting for us," said Chang. "That's a scary thought. But if we don't do anything, his plan will work. It may be dangerous for all of us, but we've got to stop him. We need to defeat the Monolegions."

"It's worth it," Sally added. "I can stay here with Reno here and tell Sergeant Nelson of our return. I'll call him."

"I'll go with Jacob and Clipper, along with Princess Rohesia. You'll need me," said Chang.

I would have argued with Chang, but he was right. He could be a great help. "You can come, Chang. Like you said, Princess Rohesia will come with us since she's the only one who can use the albore. We'll get there in the blink of an eye."

Rohesia was baffled. "Call? Can you explain this?" She held up her hand. "Forget I spoke. I promised I would not question this age in time."

"Well, we know where to go. We better move," said Clipper.

I handed Reno to Sally. Reno started to whine, not wanting me to leave her. I stroked the back of her head.

"She'll get over it," said Sally. "She's starting to like me. Good luck, you four. You'll need it."

Rohesia stood inside a triangle made up of Clipper, Chang, and me. She held out the albore and shut her eyes. Once again, I felt the wind blow past me, ending in about a quarter of a minute. We found ourselves in the middle of a community park, quite out in the open.

"Quick, get somewhere private," Chang told us.

He looked around and saw a structure nearby. It looked like a church. He pointed at the yellow-brick building. The rest of us followed him there. The church appeared to be empty. It would be a perfect hiding spot for the moment. The glass door was locked, as I expected. I did not think Clipper and I would fit inside anyway. Besides, I did not want to damage the door out of respect for the church. We instead sat under the roof beside the door.

"How will we find the Nibelungs?" Rohesia asked. "I hope we are able to know when we see them."

"We were supposed to find the school," I said. "I'll look for it."

"No, leave it to me. I need to get used to heights." Clipper stepped out onto the parking lot and took off.

We waited patiently as he flew through the sky. I knew he was risking his cover. Chang, being the least conspicuous, stepped out to the sidewalk to track his progress. It was not long before Clipper began circling over something. He was only a block or two from where we were. Chang noticed a library across the road, but it was the red brick athenaeum beyond that held Clipper's attention.

I saw Clipper land on top of the school and signal us to join him. Making sure I was clear, I took flight to the school. Chang and Rohesia walked down the block and circled around to the main entrance of the school. Clipper and I climbed down the side.

"Are the Nibelungs in here?" Rohesia asked.

"Possibly. We have to go inside," said Clipper. "Remember to stay alert."

With his horns, he knocked away the metal bar that split the two main doors so he and I could enter. Chang, who held one of the doors open, caught it before it clanked onto the floor. Classes were in session and there were no students in the hallways. The four of us crept silently past a long row of lockers to the right.

JORDAN B. JOLLEY

"I don't see any Monolegions," I whispered. "I don't think they're here, but they may be nearby. I can feel it."

Clipper sniffed the air. "They're close by. I know it. Keep moving and don't make a lot of noise."

"I will have no difficulty doing so, but you may," said Rohesia. She waved the folds in her purple linen dress with her hands. "My clothing may stand out, but at least I am not a dragon."

I sniggered a little bit at her remark.

We continued farther down the hall and up a stairwell when, at the worst possible moment, the bell rang. Students started streaming out of the classrooms. Without thinking, I turned for an open set of adjoining doors. My wings caught on the frame and slowed me down, feeding my irritation. I bit off a part of the frame so I could fit through. My friends followed. Chang, who was the last one in, closed the doors behind him.

"This was a bad idea," Clipper muttered. "This is a classroom. At least no one's in here."

I looked around the room for a place of cover. The room had three elevated rows that had desks and music stands on them. The three rows, along with a piano near the chalkboards, told me that this was a choir room. I let out a silent hiss; the other doors I could see were too small for me to fit. I heard the main doors creak open, followed by adolescent laughter. I overheard light comments about the damaged frame. The next thing I saw were three girls staring at me, each with wide eyes and open jaws. I gave an innocent stare back and greeted them in a composed tone. "Eh… hello."

I should have known my peaceful greeting did not match my deep, dragon voice. One girl gazed at me for a split second before running off. A terrified scream echoed out in the hall. "Ahhh! Help! There are monsters in the choir room!"

Both her friends ran out after her, also screaming. The other students who did not see us had blank faces. All they heard was that there were monsters in the choir room, quite a puerile assumption if I was in their situation.

I then heard the voice of an adult woman. "Dearest me! What in the world is going on?"

The first girl wept the loudest. "There are monsters in the choir room! One was black; it had horns and giant wings. The other one was red. They had sharp teeth. Oh, it was horrible!"

More students started screaming, but it was not because of me. Rohesia, wondering what was going on, gazed down the hallway with her eyes squinted. She looked back at me with a worrisome frown. "I fear I saw a Nibelung, my friends. Stay here while I investigate."

She left the choir room to offer some sort of explanation amidst the confusion, quite clever in my opinion; until I heard students running in various directions. I peeked my head out the doorway to see the commotion. To my horror, I saw a woman dwarf attacking the princess with a knife! Avoiding the dreaded weapon, Rohesia spun her leg under her attacker's and tripped her. The vicious little dwarf jumped right back up. With a clinched fist, Rohesia struck her in the jaw then tripped her again. The dwarf stood back up, this time avoiding Rohesia's fist. She pinned the princess to the wall with one hand and held her knife high in the air with the other. Just as she was about to lunge, I charged out of the choir room. The great force of my horns destroyed what was left of the frame. Keeping my horns low, I sent the ruthless Monolegion sliding down the hallway.

"Where did you learn to fight like that?" I asked Rohesia in amazement.

Rohesia gave a charming smile. "A good princess is one who is trained to defend."

When Rohesia was out of danger, I rushed over to the dwarf to make sure she did not get back up. My claws kept her arms from going anywhere. Squirming, the dwarf yelled in panic. "The dragons! They're here! Help!"

There was a reply from the first level. "I hear you! Stay there and don't get killed! We'll be up!"

Feeling her under my claws made my heart beat faster, and faster. I realized that my anger was building again. Before the dwarf could shout any more, I snapped my teeth. The dwarf stayed silent, sweating and shivering. I was concerned about whom she had alerted. I looked up grimly when Clipper left the choir room, along with Chang.

"Go to a classroom and look out the window," I told Chang. "See if there's anything going on outside."

Chang vanished into the nearest classroom. The students in the room were frozen from hearing the turmoil outside. The teacher, who was erasing her board, frowned. Chang went to the window and gazed down at the street. Instantly, he whirled back to the class. "Get down!" he shouted.

It was a very brief warning. The students fell to the floor as the windows of the classroom shattered all about. When everything quieted down, Chang looked back out the window. Gasping, he ran out of the classroom. "Jacob, I saw several Monolegions run inside!"

Rohesia held her arms close together. "What was that frightening sound?"

"That's bad news," said Chang. "I just saw about eleven Monolegions enter the school. More are waiting outside. I don't think we can make it out as easily as we came in."

"Not if we fight our way," I huffed. "It's obvious they wanted us here. They were waiting for us."

Down the hall, someone caught my eye. I watched as a familiar figure, dressed in slacks and a shirt and tie, headed for the stairs. He scratched his bearded cheek and furtively slipped out of sight.

"It can't be," I whispered.

It was Triathra. It seemed as if he had disguised himself to blend in at the school.

Rohesia looked up and down the hall. "We cannot leave! We're trapped!"

"Don't worry, we can get through this," said Clipper.

I jumped down a different stairwell to the bottom level. Triathra was nowhere to be found. The students that remained in the hallway wailed in terror at my presence.

"Everybody take cover! There's going to be trouble!" I cried.

The students scrambled for hiding places. Some of them banged on locked classrooms, begging to be let in. Others simply hid themselves behind litterbins and under water fountains. The rest ran up the stairwells.

It was not long before the Monolegions arrived. They were armed to the teeth with revolvers, crossbows, knives, and the like. Red stripes were painted on their faces, and they wore the expected horned helmets with iron caps. None had albores.

"They're coming," I warned.

"They're here," said Clipper.

CHAPTER 25

THE NIBELUNGS ATTACK

Sally yelled into the phone. "I told you already, I need Sergeant Nelson. This is about Jacob and Clipper, the dragons."

The official questioned her further. Sally moaned, thinking the inquiries were not important.

"Jacob and Clipper my friends!" she exclaimed, though not in a rude manner. "I used to go to school with them. Now please, will you get Sergeant Nelson?"

The person on the other end of the line agreed at last. Sally waited impatiently for an answer. She also kept a close eye on Reno, who was playing nearby with a durable toy ball. She soon heard an answer on the phone.

"Yes, I'm here, Sergeant," Sally said. "I told you about my friendship with Jacob and Clipper, remember? Well, we're back from Norway. I need to warn you about an upcoming conflict. We found out that there is a tribe of dwarves in Norway. I know this sounds crazy, but that's not the strange part. The strange part is that they practice magic. Jacob found this out. They have numerous spies around the world as well. They infested a prison in France, but are elsewhere, too. Jacob and Clipper are now in a town in Idaho called Preston. They have a lead on a sacred scepter and a major artery of the Monolegion dwarves. Can you to send someone out there and find out what's going on? Forgive me, I know this sounds crazy, but… You will…? Oh thank you, thank you so much!"

Sally nearly wept with relief. She hung up the phone. She would never have thought a sergeant in the military would reason with magic. It sounded as if he had tremendous faith in Jacob and Clipper. Now Sally was worried about other things. She walked out of the dormitory with Reno at her side. Reno was curious about how her new world worked. It was a different way of life for her.

"Don't worry, Reno," Sally said to the infant. "They'll be okay. I'm so relieved that Sergeant Nelson listened. What are the chances of that? Well, the Norwegians are taking care of business in their land, and now here we are with our friends far away. Jacob was right; it's hard to believe all this. But once you broaden your mind, anything's possible."

Reno made a playful growl in response.

SALLY, SATISFIED AS SHE WAS ABOUT NELSON'S RESPONSE TO HER call, wondered what was going on many miles away in Idaho. She had no way of knowing about our current situation. In the midst of the fight, our foes were ruthless. Shots, pangs of enemy fire, and my own roars reigned domain as the primary sounds that thundered throughout the school. I thought I would have frightened off the Monolegions with my appearance by now, but it did not seem to affect them one bit. They behaved as if they battled dragons every day.

Standing unguarded was not a good idea for me. I could not charge with bullets and arrows flying about, neither could I use fire since it was too destructive. What I needed was some temporary cover. Searching nearby, I found a broken table that I could use as a shield from the oncoming missiles. As I tipped it over, arrows embedded into the table like darts; and bullets began biting through the metal like angry little devils. Through the assault, I took care to shield my wings, which were already riddled with several bloody wounds. How festering they were!

Chang crouched next to me behind the table. I was more concerned for his and Rohesia's safety, considering that they were more vulnerable than Clipper or me.

"Powder bomb, quickly!" I ordered with a paw held out.

Chang provided me with an explosive. I ignited it and tossed it in the air. Two dwarves jumped for cover as the bomb exploded, leaving a black crater of tiled floor in the middle of the hallway. The fire alarm sounded its piercing cry as the smoke rose. No students or teachers left their classrooms, though. Chang warned me that there were only a few powder bombs left.

"What do we do now?" called Clipper, who was standing in the stairwell.

"Manual labor," I responded.

I pushed the table with my horns along the industrial tiled floor. Picking up speed, the table crashed into one of the revolver-armed dwarves, knocking him over. This gave me the opportunity to attack the vicious Monolegion.

Clipper emerged from his cover in the stairwell. He charged at one of the dwarves, sending him sliding. Clipper was about to seek another enemy when a sudden arrow struck him in the roof of his mouth. Clipper howled in pain and shook his head. The dwarf who had shot the arrow advanced on him, cautions of any oncoming fire. Princess Rohesia jumped out from her spot in the stairwell, wielding a wooden bat. She first struck the dwarf in the stomach, then on the back. The attacker fell, out of breath.

Rohesia held up her choice of weapon in triumph. "'Tis an effective club, indeed. I will only use the albore if I must. I want to avoid the pain it inflicts."

"Whatever works," Chang remarked, monitoring the battle.

With the small group of Monolegions out of the way, I helped Clipper to his feet. He was quite upset, but not badly wounded. I yanked the arrow from his mouth, making him wince. My help was cut short when Chang interrupted us. "Hey, the rest of them are retreating!"

Chang pointed anxiously at the fleeing Monolegions. I followed them to the east doors of the school. Before I could exit the doors myself, two dwarves with rapiers ambushed me from behind a corner. One ran my way and instantly dropped to the floor, sliding neatly under my feet. His swiftness kindled the fire in my lungs. *I've got to know Nibelungs better,* I thought. The stereotypical dwarf was a fat, merry miner. Maybe that was true depending on the dwarf. These ones were muscular and incredibly agile. They were able to do things that I have never even dreamed they could do.

Slowing down, my enemy grabbed the upper half of my tail and started slashing at my scales. The sensation felt like a red-hot needle being driven into my tail. Acting on reflex, I spun in circles in an attempt to drop him, but he clung on to my tail like a monkey to a banana tree. Bashing my tail into the side of the wall barely loosened his grip. Swinging to the opposite wall gave me a good result, for my tail collided with a trophy case. Three trophies, shards of glass, and sawdust rained down on us. A basketball on display rolled away safely. That and the trophies were not badly damaged. What was displayed did not concern me, however. I felt the weight on my tail drop, but my freedom did not last. The dwarf climbed back onto my tail the second he had slipped off. My thick layer of scales started giving way to blood with all the slashing.

Thinking of another solution, I stood on two feet and fell on my back. I was anchored to the floor with my spikes. With my broad wings flat on the once clean floor, I raised my hind legs and kicked the dwarf off. His short journey ended after falling through a double doorway into the gym. I caught a glimpse of the dwarf standing up again when the doors closed on me. Using my horns, I sent the doors flying down the gym floor in multiple pieces. The debris made my rival cower, giving me the perfect time to use my claws. I took a wide-aimed swipe over his shoulder. Indeed, this proved that my scales were several times more durable than dwarf flesh. He fell to the floor in pain.

He was not defeated yet. With great tenacity, his sword switched hands and he waved it madly in front of my muzzle. The Monolegion would not surrender! Enraged, I procured a chunk of what was once a door and smashed it down on his head. All I heard was a simple *thud*. The section of the door broke into two smaller halves. He was out cold when his cohort, who also had a rapier, showed up. The second dwarf! I had forgotten about him. I huffed in anger.

I took a step forward with my horns at the ready. The dwarf's quick nature gave him the time to make the first move. Hand down, blade up, he was aiming straight for my eye. I did not want to even think what would happen if he succeeded in his attack.

My strength again gave me the upper hand. In one swift motion, I grabbed the blade with my paw. My large body versus his stumpy self gave me an advantage. Not only that, but I was a lot, should I say, bulkier than the little fool. With more muscle capacity, I was able to push his pathetic blade back. As I did so, I felt a strong heat wave behind me. The dwarf panicked and fled the scene. He was replaced by Clipper's open mouth, releasing a hot yellow flame.

When Clipper found out that he was flaming me and not his target, he closed his mouth, his sabered fangs resting just below his mandible. The Monolegion, who had fallen victim to Clipper's fire, rolled frantically on the hardwood beside us to smother the flames on his clothes.

I gave a furious glare into Clipper's eyes. "What's the matter with you?" I growled, turning to view the holocaust. "Now the gym's all torn up and on fire!"

I felt my blood boiling. Buckling my claws, I prepared to finish off the cowardly Monolegions. There was no need to attack, however, for the dwarf whose clothes were burnt jumped on me and jabbed at my already wounded wings with his stupid little rapier. Roaring in fury, I spun around and wrapped my paw around his neck. Hissing, I tossed him to the floor. My first idea was to spit venom at him, but I felt like doing something else.

"You can't run anywhere!" I taunted. "You think you can stop me? I'm much stronger than you!"

I listened to the sound of my voice. I never thought I would say something like that in such an awful manner. My natural self was controlling me again. I fiercely tried to calm myself. I could tell I was feeling too vengeful towards my enemy. Displeased and disgusted, Clipper butted me away from my victim. The dwarf cried in shock. It did not take long before his body could not take the stress. He took one more breath and gave up his ghost.

With his enemy out of the way, Clipper's concern turned towards the spreading conflagration. As the fire ate up more and more of the painted wood, the more anxious Clipper felt. Rohesia, standing in the doorway, watched in awe at the destructive sight. Without thinking, Clipper called to her, "Rohesia! Get a fire extinguisher!"

Rohesia tilted her head in confusion. "I don't know what you are trying to tell me!"

Before Clipper could explain, I began rolling around on the flames to stop their expansion. Holding my wings to my side, I rolled back and forth, making strange noises. "Yaaaaaaaak!!! Grrruummmmph!!! Heeeaaaaahhhh!!! Ya! Ya! It's okay Clipper! Leave it to me!"

It took some time, but I finally suffocated the fire. Though only a quarter of the gym was damaged, the section lay smoking. Three of the six basketball hoops were stained black. I stood back up and wriggled my body. My behavior was now different than it had been a few seconds before. Clipper noticed that as well. After the brutal battle, the sensation of boiling blood changed into that of surprise and sorrow. It was a feeling of despair. I was ashamed for what I had done. Bowing my head, I silently sat down in front of my friend.

"You did the right thing to hit me off of the dwarf," I said calmly. "There needs to be a way to control myself. I almost attacked you after you hit me."

Clipper shook his head regretfully. "Like I said earlier, when you become angry... you know, it's all right. I felt a little vengeful myself. We can both learn how to control our anger in time."

Before I could reply, I saw something move out of the corner of my eye. I turned to the high post on the other side of the basketball gym. A lone student, wearing a white jersey, stared at us in astonishment. I knew he was no threat, so I remained calm and watched him run off the court in fright. Like the rest of the students, he did not leave, even with the fire alarms going. I stepped into the hallway and outside the building just in time to see the rest of my enemies jump into a car and speed away. I felt my heart racing again, only this time there was no anger. Determined to not let them escape, I bit whatever arrow shafts were stuck in my wings, then I took flight. My wings stung with all the wounds in them.

Chang ran out of the building with Rohesia. "What are you doing?" he shouted.

"You two stay here and help if you can," I called back. "I can't let these Monolegions escape! I need to know where they came from and if they were sent by Monty or Triathra."

High in the sky, I saw several police cars, two fire trucks, and an ambulance racing towards the school. Keeping a sharp eye on the Monolegion car, I saw it leave the city limits and into a flood plain. The car crossed a bridge over a river and then turned onto a dirt road at the river's bank. The two Monolegions got out and approached another group of their kind. I landed near the river. Moving with care, I listened to the conversation while hiding in a thick grove.

"What happened?" a voice inquired; it sounded like Monty.

"We are the only ones remaining," one of the Monolegions answered. "Everyone else has been killed. We have injured both dragons, though."

"I see," said the voice. "No albores and only you two survive. Every death costs, I should remind you. Oh, don't worry yourselves. I'm not mad. Everything's going according to plan."

"Our firearms and crossbows have fared well, but we would have done more if we had albores," said the second dwarf.

"There were no albores because I didn't want any mistakes that you'd be bound to make," the voice replied. "That attack wasn't meant to kill Jacob and Clipper. And I don't want them to be cursed out of time again. I need them under my power. That way we can have leverage on the Second Earth."

Second Earth, I thought. What was he talking about?

I heard the helmets of the two Monolegions drop in the grass. "You have control, Lord Triathra," they said in unison.

"And you are loyal to the end, my nobles, and I expect more in the near future."

I listened closely to the voice. Strange, I first thought it was Monty speaking, but it was actually Triathra.

"I'm no longer able to stay at the school," Triathra continued. "I'm sure I have been recognized. However, I've concluded my business here. I'll locate the scepter as quickly as I can. You two stay here with the rest. When I return, we'll find the infant dragon. We must get her back."

I put it all together then and there. *Monty* was the sorcerer! *He* was the keeper of the three worlds! *He* was the black-cloaked figure back in the Guarded Forest! Monty was Triathra! My mind was reeling. I had many questions, yet I knew that I had to find the scepter before he did. I remembered the arrow on the map pointing south. It must have been pointing to the Master Scepter. The number forty could have meant the number of kilometers. There was a city, I remember, about twenty-five miles south of Preston, and twenty-five miles was about to forty kilometers. With this knowledge, I left the grove and stood on the bank of the river. Sneaking around was actually easier than I thought. In the current environment, moving with silence proved no challenge. I saw the sorcerer wearing the same clothing he had on when I saw him in the school.

The dwarf band broke up. Monty was left alone. He stepped

into a cluster of trees. When he returned, he was once again in his black sorcerer's cloak. He pulled out an albore and held it above his head. A gray whirlwind formed around him until he was no longer visible. The miniature tornado was there for about ten seconds before dissolving into thin air. The sorcerer was gone.

Baffled, I moved over to inspect the spot where Monty had vanished. I really hoped he was not after the scepter. I sniffed around the spot when I heard the honk of a horn. I raised my ears. The dwarves had spotted me! I should have stayed hidden.

"There's the black dragon!" one of them shouted. "He must have heard us!"

Spraying a threatening flame, I took off into the air and headed back to rejoin Clipper and the others. Below me, the car was on its way back to Preston. Since I had been spotted, the search turned into a race to see who would reach the scepter first. The dwarves did not bother me; I could travel a lot faster in the air than they could on the road. My true concern was Monty. I sailed back to the school and landed beside Chang and Rohesia. The street in front of the school was jammed with police cars and other emergency vehicles. Clipper glided down from the roof of the school. I quickly brought everyone up to date, how Monty was Triathra and not just a brother or a twin.

"Well, what town is forty kilometers south of here?" Clipper asked.

"When I examined the atlas, I saw a city called Logan," Chang explained.

I raised my wings, ready to leap into the air. I looked at Chang and Rohesia. As they stared at each other, a student pulled up to the curb in a silver car. He leapt from the car, leaving the engine running, and walked up to a policeman on guard. Clipper and I looked at each other, then looked at the car. A slow grin spread on Clipper's face. I approached the car and tried to open the door nicely, but I was in a hurry. I ripped the door from the car.

"Get in here!" I told Chang.

Chang ran to the car and jumped in.

Rohesia hesitated. "Perhaps I should stay and explain what has happened if Sally communed with the Sergeant?"

She had a point. Sally should have contacted James by now. I let Rohesia do her own bidding.

Chang threw the car in gear. He pressed his foot on the gas pedal and the car shot forward, its tires squealing. All the police saw was Chang in the car with me and Clipper, the two dragons, flying behind. The owner of the car did not chase us. All he did was yell in fright.

Chang, Clipper, and I were long gone. Soon after finding the main highway, the black car came charging up behind us. We knew we were in trouble as Chang sped down the highway with our foes on our tail. I was pretty sure other people on the road would be quite startled. Someone driving a car that had a door missing and two dragons flying above it was something not many saw every day.

This was turning into a real high-speed chase. Now the fun had really started (I say this out of sarcasm). We had to beat the dwarves while racing to Logan to find Monty. I could see Logan in the distance; it looked bigger than Preston. I looked down at the car that was gaining on us. There were two threats that had to be dealt with. A feeling of urgency washed over me. We had to find Monty and quick! I told Clipper to go ahead and search for the sorcerer. The Monolegions were mine!

CHAPTER 26

THE FEARFUL SURPRISE

The car chase was aggravating, yet exciting at the same time. All I wanted was to find the scepter before Monty could do anything dangerous. The dwarves were just another obstacle. The next county we crossed should have been warned of our coming. I assumed there would be extra company soon. The police were not my main worry, though. The car with the dwarf legion was close behind Chang. Sooner or later they would hit the rear end of Chang's car. I had to get them off the road. The dwarves would be much more powerful than the police if they had any magic left.

I had to talk to Chang if I was to get the dwarves off our tail. This time I was not so angry. I wanted to get them off the road without killing them in a brutal manner. I did not want to use fire, and I could not land on their car because of their crossbows. They did not fire any revolvers; I guess they used all their ammunition.

Very carefully, I landed on the roof of Chang's car, where I clung, spreading my legs and wings to make sure the roof did not collapse under my weight. I lowered my head so Chang could hear. "Try to get more distance," I called.

"I don't think I can," Chang cried. "They keep gaining on us."

I wanted Chang to get a bigger lead, so I could jump off the roof and charged into our pursuers. They would not be able to aim well with the bulk of their crossbows going out the side window, and I would not be coming from the air either. Chang sped up. Before the gap closed, I kicked off the roof. The Monolegions veered left and right at the sight of my charge. I felt the car's side graze my horns. It ran off the road and toppled in a ditch.

I laughed and blew a flame in the sky. Sadly, the fun did not last long. We had to worry about the police cars that were after us, followed by a helicopter in the distance. I flew up to Chang's slowing vehicle. "We can't run from the police," I said. "It won't do us any good, but don't mention the scepter. Clipper's tracking Monty."

"You're right, we shouldn't hold him back."

Chang pulled over and climbed out. We stood silently, facing the police, who were well armed and not afraid to defend themselves. Just as I was about to give them an explanation. I heard a voice coming from the line of police. "Draco! Jacob Draco! We were sent here by Sergeant Nelson!"

I turned around to find more officers purposefully striding up to me. One of them ran to the other group of officers and told them our story. Some went to aid the dwarves inside the destroyed car, leaving one officer to speak with me. "I received a message from Sergeant Nelson about you. I know who you are. The sergeant said that a young woman informed him of the latest turn of events."

"Thank you," I replied. "I hope you understand that we're on a personal errand at the moment. It's of the utmost importance and we need go quickly."

"You are free to go just as soon as we wrap things up here," the officer said. He stood still and eyed me in awe. Another police car soon appeared. Rohesia emerged from the passenger side. "I was told that we are not being ,held accountable for the damage," she said.

Chang looked at the car he had used. "That's good to know."

I took a deep breath as I waited for the police to allow me to leave. I sorely wished they would hurry. Hopefully, Clipper was doing his part in our search for Monty.

To help clear my mind, I looked out across the valley. Green fields covered the land from mountain range to mountain range. The valley looked so peaceful, considering the fact that a terrible

Jordan B. Jolley

sorcerer was not too far away. I would hate to see this land if Monty and the Monolegions spread their dark sorcery over it.

Apparently, I was not the only one staring out over the valley. The officer beside me looked troubled. I decided to see what was bothering him.

"What's wrong?"

The officer blinked. "All my life, I believed your kind only existed in fairy tales. But here you are talking, breathing, living right in front of my face. Where did you come from?"

"Well, I actually used to be a normal person... I think. I was born and raised in Oklahoma. Though sometimes I think I came from somewhere else, some other world."

"You were born a human?" the officer asked.

"Maybe," I began. It took me a moment before I could finish my sentence, "but there's something else, too. I've discovered that there is possibly more to our lives than we know." I left it at that.

Chang interrupted our conversation. He looked distressed. "Jacob, I was talking with the police. The Monolegions that were in the car are missing. There's no sign of them, no footprints in the field they crashed into."

"That doesn't make sense," I huffed. "How did they get the albores if they didn't have them earlier?"

There was no time to ponder the question. I heard a high-pitched screech in the sky. Clipper appeared in the distance and landed beside me. "Jacob, I found Monty's scent. We've got to leave now. I don't think one of us should follow him alone."

My internal heat felt like ice. I told the officer in charge that I was leaving. To make up for lost time, I instantly took flight.

"Get to Logan and meet us there!" I called to Chang and Rohesia. It worried me to leave them alone and unprotected, but we had no choice. We flew as fast as we could southward.

"Where is he?" I asked Clipper.

Clipper beat his wings a few times then sniffed the air. "I remember where he is. Follow me."

I continued to fly behind him, both of us flying as fast as possible. Clipper led me to a city park. I landed in the nearby parking lot. From there, I could see Monty attempting to climb a tree in the middle of the park. Gazing at the tree itself, I saw the Master Scepter. It was resting high up between two branches. I had to get it away from Monty before he climbed to the top. I knew I could not approach him directly; his albore made sure of that. Looking around, I saw an empty car parked on the side of the street.

"Stand back," I warned Clipper.

Clipper moved to the side. I lowered my horns on the side of the car. My strong horns struck the its side. When I jerked upwards, the car twirled through the air. Monty saw the car flying towards him and jumped out of the tree just in time. When he got back up, he saw me in the parking lot. My cover was blown. I sprang at him with fire spouting from my mouth. There was no other choice. Monty took out his albore. He created a shield from the intense flames and started climbing again.

"Your fire has no power!" he shouted.

I reached the tree when Monty jumped down. The scepter had slid from its resting place and lay on the damp grass.

I was quick, but not quick enough. Monty reached the scepter a split second before I could. At that moment, the ground started to rumble. An invisible force pushed Clipper and me back. When we stood up, Clipper charged after the evil sorcerer.

With the mighty powers of the Master Scepter, Monty sent a dizzying whirlwind in my friend's direction. Clipper had no time to use fire or venom. After spinning helplessly in the air for several seconds he thudded hard to the ground. Just as I was about to take action, Monty placed the scepter on his back, where it stuck right to his cloak. An unearthly green flash of light encircled him. I stared at the scene in complete terror.

Monty had turned himself into some sort of monster.

He had some characteristics of a dragon. He had large wings and sharp horns. However, he was almost twice the size of me or

Clipper, had no muzzle, and stood on two legs. His black cloak also grew in size. It appeared to be tattered and torn and was flowing in an unnatural breeze. I was shocked at Monty's new appearance. He was a thing of evil! How could I compete with this? He did not look like a demon; he was a demon!

Clipper was shaken as he stood back up. All he could do was cower in fear. Monty turned around and glared down at him. When Monty turned away from me, I saw the Master Scepter was attached to his back, as if it was glued there. Monty yelled in fury at Clipper. He raised a large hand, ready to strike. Clipper jumped out of the way in the nick of time. The impact on the ground left a large crater of dirt. I stood frozen in the street when Clipper darted towards me.

"He's a demon!" exclaimed Clipper. "A demon!"

"We've got to stop him," I said grimly.

Monty, now the monster he was, charged after Clipper. We were both intimidated by his size, but Clipper's bravery soon rose to the surface. Facing him directly, Clipper raced toward Monty. Both of them were sprinting head to head at each other. As they clashed together, Clipper was helplessly tossed in the air by his contender's strength. Rushing in to help my friend, I let my fire of defense surge forth. I was pleased to see Monty back down. He was not immune to fire like I was. I took a deep breath and released another flame. It was working! The demon was diminishing! *Now should be a time to show my aggression. I need that wrath right about know,* I thought.

I sucked in another breath. Just as I was about to attack him again, he struck me from the side. I crashed into the tree. The intense force caused the trunk to snap and fall. Monty watched me groan and wobble on trembling legs. He laughed like a diseased hell-dweller. The sound made me want to vomit.

"As I've said, Jacob, your fire cannot stop me."

He was about to strike me again when Clipper jumped on him from behind. His sharp claws dug into Monty's jade flesh. Using brute force, Clipper tore into his archenemy. This gave me time to regain my senses. Letting out another wave of fire, Monty dropped on his back and rolled. His heavy weight crushed Clipper beneath him. Instantly getting back to his feet, he batted me with his horns. Fighting Monty as a demon was not going to be an easy task. I expected his advance, but he did not come. Instead, he backed off.

"No! It's not time yet. I would like you to get past the dwarves, you two. If you want me, you have to go through the Monolegion tribe. Maybe I can even give you a vision of your true home."

Using the power of the scepter, he cast an earth-bending spell my way. The ground shook from the inside out. I bounced in the air before landing on a pile of smoking dirt.

"The number of your allies are very rudimentary compared to mine," he said. "I must admit that there are dwarves who would fight me, but they have no power in this world."

I shook the pain away before I responded. "What is my true home? What are you talking about?"

Monty did not answer. Using his magic, he transformed back into his former self. He had the gray beard and an unblemished black cloak, looking like the Triathra I remembered from the Guarded Forest.

"I am the sorcerer!" Monty snapped. "You can't beat me. Humans here are weak and powerless. They don't deserve to rule this Earth. What they need is a powerful ruler: a king!"

At that moment, I prepared to pounce on him and tear him to shreds. Just like the time on the riverbank, a whirlwind formed around him. He disappeared to parts unknown.

Clipper emerged from the crater and observed the upturned park. "Ugh. This place is ruined. I think we put up a good fight."

"When he turns into that demon, he's dangerous," I said. "We can still beat him. He mentioned that we must defeat the Monolegion tribe first. I just wish we had some help. Monty *did* acknowledge the existence of good dwarves."

"If that was so," Clipper said, his attention elsewhere. "In the meantime, let's focus on defeating Monty. He has the Master Scepter. That is not good."

I nodded in agreement just as a police car drove up to the destroyed city park. Chang jumped out the door to the driver's seat.

"I saw what happened," he said, looking spooked. "What was that thing?"

"That thing was Monty," I answered.

Chang buried his face in his hands. "Oh no! I don't believe it."

"Fighting him will be harder, but not impossible," Clipper stated. "There has to be a way to stop him."

Chang lifted his head. He had an expression of guilt. "I'm sorry."

I was confused at first. It was not long before I realized what he was talking about. Two men climbed out of the car. Monolegions. Each had a nocked bow aimed at Chang. I could have sworn I had seen them before.

Clipper appeared more surprised than I was. "Aren't you the Monolegions that attacked us in Georgia?"

The men had eyes of evil and hate. "Silence!" one on the left spat. "Dragons cannot be defeated by the bullet of the gun, so now you must deal with us, or your friend dies. Don't you have something funny to say now? Maybe spit venom at us and fly us in the sky. That's worth a laugh or two! Ha ha!"

The second dwarf pulled out a knife and held it to Chang's throat. Chang was ashamed. "I'm sorry. When the police left the scene of the crash, they came out of nowhere and attacked me."

Rohesia was not present, so I guessed she was safe. But if I made any sudden move, Chang would be killed. I bent my knees and lowered myself in pure shame. The humiliation made my chest hurt. The moment I blinked, my eyes became cloudy. I felt as if I had been struck on the top of my head. Was it another spell? The other Monolegion must have picked up the albore that Monty had used before he grabbed the Master Scepter.

"What have you done to me?" I groggily asked them.

Before I could hear an answer, I was out like a light.

CHAPTER 27

COMING AND GOING

Sally got off the airplane in the Salt Lake Valley. She was headed north to reunite with Clipper and me. But something did not feel right. Everyone around her seemed to be in distress.

Sally sat down at a bus stop and set her suitcase beside her feet. On her other side was a pet crate. She looked in to see Reno, sulking with boredom. Reno could barely fit inside and her wings were cramped down next to her body.

"I'm sorry, Reno. This was the biggest crate I could find," Sally crooned. Reno ignored her and huffed a smoky breath. Sally finished what she was saying, "I can't let you roam free. You'll scare everybody. That's right, you're big and scary."

Reno giggled as she listened to Sally. Though she did not understand Sally entirely, the sound of a friendly voice soothed Reno and made her forget about her discomfort for the moment. To make the little dragon happier still, Sally reached into her bag and pulled out a can of raw sardines that she had acquired back in New York. She inched the door open and tossed a few small sardines inside. Reno pounced on a fish and swallowed it whole.

After Sally closed the door, she noticed a newspaper stand next to the bus top. Curious, she bought a copy of the Salt Lake Tribune. She read the article aloud to keep Reno entertained.

Her mood darkened as she read: "A large creature has been sighted in city of Logan. It was first reported to be one of the suspected dragons sighted in New York a few weeks earlier. That idea has since been proven wrong. This monster, suspected of being much larger, and described as a 'demon' by witnesses, was last seen in a city park, which was where the dragons were last seen as well. They have not been seen since that sighting. Many have chalked up the demon and dragons as something else. The majority of Logan's residents do not believe that demons and dragons are real."

Sally placed a hand on her cheek. Perhaps this was the cause of the distress she felt around her. She could not believe what she had just read. She knew that Monty was there. What about the demon? What if Monty found the Master Scepter?

Sally gasped. "Oh, no. It can't be. What if Monty used the scepter to turn himself into some sort of monster? That... that's scary. How powerful is he? Can Jacob and Clipper beat him?" She took a deep breath. "I can't let this happen, Reno."

She wanted to do something to help. She knew that the police were playing down our existence the best they could. But whatever Monty became, there was no denying that more trouble lay ahead.

THE CAR ARRIVED IN THE CENTER OF LOGAN. ROHESIA STEPPED out of the car and thanked the driver for picking her up. Even after having seen New York City, the sight of the smaller city center still astonished her. She spun in circles, amazed at every enchanting aspect. Understanding her new environment was not too difficult, and she did her best not to be overwhelmed. Her happiness did not last when she asked for help. After asking various questions to random pedestrians on the street, she still had no idea what to do. Some people treated her rudely while others repeated what they had heard from others. All she discovered was that there was some green monster fighting two dragons. Others said that they had heard about someone taken hostage by two men dressed like Vikings.

Asking someone for a final time, she finally received some information that got her attention. "That car with the hostage?" a woman said. "I heard that they found the police car that was stolen here in town, but they didn't find the hostage or the kidnappers."

"So those men must still be here," said Rohesia.

The princess was grateful for the information. The problem was that she did not know where to look. She searched different blocks and shops; neighborhoods and churches, but found no clues. Exhausted, Rohesia sat down on a bench. Her legs were sore and her head ached. The albore remained safe in her sweaty hand throughout the day. Rohesia did not wait long when a large, flat-nosed vehicle bellowed up to a curb. The princess watched as people got off the bus and others lined up to board it.

"Princess Rohesia!" a person in the exit line called.

A new tide of energy filled Rohesia's chest. "Sally, what a surprise! What are you doing here?"

"I'm looking for Jacob and Clipper. I heard of their fight at the school, then I read about a green demon. I think it's Monty. Does that make sense to you?"

Rohesia groaned, not answering Sally's question. "Oh dear! We must find our friends. I was told the stolen police car was found in this town."

"Then they might be here," said Sally. She looked down at the crate. "Don't worry, Reno. Your friends will be safe."

Reno grunted inside her enclosed space, still angry with Sally for placing her in there. She puffed a small stream of fire out of her nose. Sally tapped the crate. "Now Reno, stop that! You don't want anyone to notice you."

Reno snorted. Sally felt sorry for her. She and Rohesia began their search together, unaware of the two people that were following them.

I woke as a pail of cold water splashed on my face. I found myself on the floor in a dark room with my four legs bound in chains. I saw Clipper and Chang waking as well. Both of them were bound the same way I was. My vision was a little blurry and I felt very groggy. Another bucket of icy water splashed on me.

"Awaken, you dragons," ordered one of the Monolegion captors.

When the three of us were fully awake, the dwarf continued speaking, "We are the Nibelungs, not like the dwarves of the other worlds. Dragons drove our people into a dense forest thousands of years ago. However, some of our people have managed to survive in the east."

"We are not the short, bearded, mining fools you've thought us to be," the second dwarf concluded. "We are more powerful with Triathra on our side and our King on his side. Now it's time for us to show it. We will soon take over this world. All people will bow to the throne."

"You won't get away with this," Chang shouted. "Now that the dragons are back, they'll stop you. No one will bow to Triathra or whoever your dumb king is."

The first dwarf smacked him on the cheek while the second continued speaking, "We dwarves have a gift of magic, more magic than you've experienced. With the dawn of a new era, we will attack this world. With help of our most powerful member of the Nibelung tribe, Lord Triathra, we will prevail. He has the Master Scepter and it is time we make our move. The people here are powerless. They are sheep. Their freedom, as they consider it, comes at the expense of corruption and greed."

"People deserve agency," I said. "They freedom to make mistakes and consequences for their actions but you want to take that away."

The dwarf ignored me. With his speech finished, he laughed aloud and walked away with his comrade following him. Chang, Clipper, and I were left alone.

"What do we do now?" asked Clipper.

I looked down at the shackles that strapped me down. They were locked together with an iron padlock. I gazed around the room to find anything useful. All I could find was Chang's knapsack that no longer held the powder bombs, which I assumed the dwarves had taken. Despite that, there could still be something useful inside. I scooted as close to the knapsack as my chains would allow. I was able to reach a strap of the knapsack and pull it towards me. Feeling around inside, I found a pen. I could not take it apart without breaking it, so I gave it to Chang.

"How good can you pick locks?" I asked him.

"I'm not an expert, but it's possible," he said.

Chang slid over next to me so he could reach the pen. It took several minutes for him to work. The padlock was eventually unlocked, and I freed myself from the chain. Chang freed Clipper as well. All three of us were ready for action.

"Couldn't you just bite the chains?" Chang asked.

"We may be impervious to the heat, but you aren't," Clipper told him.

"Well, we're free now," I said. "What's next?"

"We now have the upper hand," Clipper replied while evaluating his surroundings. "Hopefully, we can take our foes once we find them."

"Then let's go," said Chang, "but with care, please."

We stood in front of a window. Clipper, with a single swipe of his paw, shattered the glass and climbed to the roof with me behind him. Chang, who left through the doorway, emerged from the main entrance below and joined in with the people on the street. We kept an eye on him from the rooftops. He gave us the thumbs up and strolled into the nearby multitude of townsfolk. There was nothing of concern yet. Clipper and I scaled the buildings on top, keeping an eye on Chang. I wondered where the Monolegions were.

Chang searched hard for the ones who had captured us. Sometimes, he would discretely look up to the rooftops to make sure we were there. He kept his primary focus on the streets around him. As he rounded a corner onto a side street, he finally found his suspects. The two Monolegions were sauntering down the street, not caring about their appearances. Some people stopped and stared at them. Chang discretely followed them.

I hissed when I saw the two. Clipper shook his head before I could unfold my wings. "Easy, Jacob. We'll only go down there if they go after Chang."

My legs started trembling. A cloud of smoke formed around my head. I was lucky my wrath was not provoked to its limit. I took a deep breath. "I'm fine."

Down below, the dwarves suddenly stopped and turned around. Chang froze in his tracks.

Watching the whole scene from above, I felt anxious. It was not wrath; it was the need to help Chang. There was no need to hide anymore. At that point, I did not care about being seen. This was a life or death situation. I leapt off the edge of the roof and landed in front of the duo of Monolegions. The people nearby fled the scene, screaming in fright. If I intervened with the dwarves before they used any magic, fighting them would be less troublesome. I knocked both of them on the ground with the flats of my horns.

As I flipped one of them on his front, I felt a rope latch around my neck. Gasping for air, I coughed out fire and smoke. The second dwarf had roped me after standing up. Placing my front two paws on the ground, I raised my rear legs and kicked the strangler like an agitated donkey. He flew several yards and struck the side of a wall.

I dropped on all fours in triumph until I heard an unfamiliar cry behind me. The dwarf I had let go grabbed a bystander by the neck, the albore in his hands. One decision could make a serious consequence.

"Make a move and this woman's dead!" the dwarf hissed.

I was about to surrender to him when I saw Clipper coming from behind. I nodded in approval as Clipper pounced, tearing holes through the dwarf's shirt. One of Clipper's wings bumped the bystander and sent her to the ground, although without hurting her. I joined Clipper. The dwarf who Clipper had attacked dropped his albore. It rolled away and fell into a storm drain. Our enemies were powerless without their source of magic.

I looked around the area. There were parked cars on the sides of the street, but there were no people besides the woman. They had all fled the scene in fright. I was glad there was no crowd for the moment. The next person I saw was an approaching policeman.

"I don't know how you came to be," the officer said, "but I'm glad you did. I've been told about you."

"You have no need to fear us," I responded. I did not mention the trouble with Monty or the Monolegions.

Another officer appeared with a worried face. "Sir, I've just got word of a bus that's been hijacked. It's now on 10th West."

I would have worried about the bus more if Monty did not bother me.

"We have time to get to that bus," Clipper said unexpectedly. "You know, these dwarves are really getting on my nerves."

"How do you know they're Monolegions?" I asked.

Clipper growled. "I *know* they're Monolegions."

A van's engine revved nearby. I turned my head to find Chang sitting behind the van's steering wheel. He shouted to us to fly overhead. We followed him as he drove off. The police broke for their car.

Clipper had a point; we should go after that bus. If they were Monolegions, they had to be dealt with. I did not know how many of them were out there.

CHAPTER 28

A JOURNEY UNVEILED

Reno would not stop crying in terror as the dwarf at the wheel of the bus cut across the road like a madman. The two Monolegions had forced Sally and Rohesia in the bus back at the stop. The hijacker's companion stood at the front of the bus, armed with a crossbow and dagger. Hearing Reno yet again, he stomped over to Sally's seat and pointed his dagger at Reno's crate. "If you don't quiet her, she's going to face severe consequences. Yes, I know it's our little emblem in there!"

The dwarf bent down at the crate and peeked in. Reno growled at him, saliva dripping onto her feet. Before the little dragon could produce a flame, the dwarf snatched the crate from Sally's grasp and took it to the front of the bus. Rohesia went after the infant dragon. When she reached the front, the dwarf smacked her in the arm with the butt of his crossbow.

"Get back in your seat or you'll know what real pain is!" he sneered.

Rohesia scrambled back to her seat with her hands over her sore arm. She sat back down, her lips pursed in utter hate.

Sally put an arm around her shoulders. "Are you all right?"

Rohesia nodded as she fought for her temper. "I want to cast a spell with the albore," she mumbled to Sally. "But whatever spell I think of, I am unable to cast it. I do not want to expose the albore to the Nibelungs. It's hidden in my dress as we speak."

She and Sally knew there was no way they could take on the armed dwarves by themselves if they could not use the albore. All they could do was hope for a miracle. There was no escape.

The hope for a miracle soon reached them when they heard the driver say in a nervous voice, "There is a van following us. I can't get rid of it."

Rohesia looked out the window. A green van was beside the bus. The tinted windows of the vehicle prevented her from seeing the driver. Windows! Windows were made of glass. That gave Rohesia an idea.

⟞⟐⟐⟐⟝

THE VAN SLOWED, VEERING BEHIND THE BUS. CLIPPER AND I WERE in the air above it. We were not flying at our fastest because it was hard to fly in a straight line at our current speed. Instead, we stayed over the van by circling it like vultures.

Chang, rolling down the driver's window, yelled the rest of the plan to me as we flew, "Remember, get on the roof and I'll distract them."

"I hear you," I called back.

Doing my part, I descended to the roof of the bus. Chang accelerated, passing the bus and pulling ahead of it. I made my way to the bus's front, waiting for the opportune moment.

The armed dwarf opened the passenger door and leaned out with his crossbow aimed at the van's tire. Before he could fire an arrow, I lunged down and pushed him back in the bus with a blunt paw. With the rest of my claws anchored on the roof, I dipped my head down in front of the windshield. The driver, shocked at my presence, swerved his vehicle back and forth, trying to loosen my grip. I almost jumped off in a start when a bright yellow flash burst from the bus's interior, nearly blinding me. Every glass window, including the windshield, exploded in all directions, as if falling victim to an ear-splitting coloratura. I shut my eyes just in time before tiny shards of glass peppered my face. My scales protected me just fine. When I opened my eyes again, I saw Sally and Rohesia hunkered down inside, shielded from the glass. It looked like Rohesia was responsible for the flash. Now I understood why the dwarves have hijacked this bus.

The driver wailed as blood ran down his face. It looked like he and his companion were both blinded. The bus screeched to a halt. Reno's crate fell to the floor and its door swung open. Sally rushed over to her when the brown dragon got to her feet. Sally picked Reno up and ran out of the bus. Rohesia followed, striking the armed dwarf and taking his crossbow. She clenched the albore between her teeth.

Reno caught sight of me once she was outside. She squirmed in Sally's arms. I placed a paw on Reno's head, savoring the happy reunion. Chang arrived and escorted Rohesia to safety. Police cars soon sped in and officers aided our friends and the dwarves. They treated most especially the cuts from broken glass. Sally and Rohesia had the cuts on their faces and arms bandaged. We left in peace several minutes later. There was little cover where we were, so we found a quiet place outside of town, across the road from a calm and peaceful marsh.

"Not badly hurt, I assume?" I asked Sally, only half serious.

Sally shook her head. "Princess Rohesia got hit, and she says her hand is sore, but she's okay."

Rohesia shook away any pain she had left. "I have no mortal wounds, thank God. I found the perfect spell to break the windows."

"Well, I think the Monolegion dwarves are headed for a downfall," said Clipper. "I mean we haven't had any real losses yet."

Clipper was right. We joked and laughed about our recent adventures. The mood was comical and delightful.

Until the ground began to shake.

It shook so hard that it threw us off our feet. My light heart quickly changed to trepidation. When I stood back up, I beheld Monty in his demon form, wearing the tattered cloak. I felt a pang of fear, but I was not going to let him see it. "What do you want, Monty?" I hissed calmly.

The sorcerer chuckled in a disgusting manner. "It's amusing how you still call me Monty after knowing who I truly am."

"I still see you as that prideful boy you've always been," I replied.

"I see. You think have power over me now that you've returned to dragon form," he said. "You thought you defeated the Nibelungs in the Guarded Forest. You're wrong, you know. We're now spreading our reign across the world, one nation at a time. I had spies follow you in Europe before you found us. A true stake of ours lies in Indonesia. You may know the place if I've heard correctly."

"Why Indonesia? That's quite a random place," Clipper commented.

"I have my reasons."

I remembered meeting the Indonesian rebels a few months ago. I already knew they were Monolegions. I was not surprised.

"You want to defeat me?" Monty said. "Defeat the Monolegions first. If you do, I'll reward you."

I glared at Monty. "You'll reward us?" There was obviously a catch.

With his big green hands, Monty snatched Sally and Reno. They both screamed in fright. "I assume you know what I mean," Monty laughed.

I tried to save them, but it was too late. Monty had them and once again formed a whirlwind around himself. I pounced on the spot where Monty had been standing: a patch of mud and reeds.

I dug through the ground in vain, roaring. "No! Triathra, you coward! You stupid coward! Aauuggghhh!"

"It's the scepter!" Clipper growled. "It's making him invincible! Oh, Sally."

I restlessly paced back and forth. Sally was gone, along with Reno. Both their lives were at risk. I continued pacing for several minutes until an idea came to me. There was no time to think of anything else. "Chang, call Sergeant Nelson," I said firmly.

Chang scratched his head. "Why?"

"We may be the ones who will wipe out the Monolegions, but it'll take more than just two dragons, especially if they're in other parts of the world. I want Sergeant Nelson to speak with the President. I know where to go from here."

Clipper stood on his hind legs and protested with his arms high in the air. "We can't have Nelson involved in this!"

"We're helping this world. We have to stop the spreading sorcery. Now please call him, Chang. Monty has Sally and Reno. He's not going to win. He'll pay for this!"

"Will this call even work?" Chang asked.

"I trust Sergeant Nelson. He's a sergeant in the Marines. He's sympathetic and he trusts us. There's no one else that we can count on."

I looked at Clipper. I could tell he was trying to stay positive, believing that Sally and Reno would be safe. As I took a deep breath, I thought about my true home in an effort to clear my mind. I remembered what the spirit had told me. Wherever my true home was, I believed it was far from the world where I stood. That thought was easier to believe now that I knew my task here on this Earth.

CHAPTER 29

FALL OF KOMODO

We sat in the cover of the marsh, out of sight from the road. The singing birds helped to calm me a little, but my mind still raced no matter what song they sang. I did not want the military involved in my problems, but these problems were of concern that called for their help. I wanted this Monolegion conflict to end. The anxiety made me loath Triathra even more.

"Even if Sergeant Nelson does talk to the President, I don't think he'll help," Chang said. "He's not going to declare war on some foreign entity he doesn't even know about."

"I'm not looking forward to it either, but it's the only way," I argued. "Besides, the country will not technically go to war. We just need a bit of assistance. Sergeant Nelson will help us."

Chang resigned his position. He knew I would not change my mind. He remembered that I was very stubborn as a dragon, so he asked how he could contact James instead. I told him the sergeant's special telephone number. He left the marsh to make the phone call. Clipper followed him as far as the road.

Princess Rohesia and I were alone for the moment. Both of us remained silent. As I waited for Chang and Clipper, I observed the Wasatch Mountains to the east of us in the late noon under a perfectly clear sky. The people in this valley were completely unaware of the impending Monolegion threat. It was a good thing, too. I did not want any radical reactions over the Nibelung dwarves. Most people would never believe it anyway, considering the sorcery involved.

Clipper returned a few minutes later. "I told Chang to mention the people in Indonesia," he said. "After a good talk, Sergeant Nelson informed Chang that a special helicopter will pick us up at the airfield in a few hours. We have permission to go back to Komodo Island."

Rohesia did not speak but looked at me fearfully.

"That's not all," Clipper continued. "I think we need to get Princess Rohesia and Chang out of sight. I don't want anything bad happen to them."

Rohesia scraped some mud off her dress. "Worry not for me and Chang. I do not believe the Nibelungs will be after us soon. We may stay at an inn, if there are any in the city of Logan. If there is trouble after all, my albore will protect us."

Chang eventually returned as well. "I assume Clipper told you all what's going on?"

"I did," Clipper replied. "Let's take a short break and then go to the airfield. I hope the helicopter's big enough for us."

Chang wiped his eyes, checking them for tears. "Good luck when you leave, my friends. I'll be with Princess Rohesia while you're gone."

Rohesia gave each of us an awkward hug. "Please take care of yourselves," she said. "May you succeed in your endeavors."

A few hours later, Clipper and I flew straight to the airfield northwest of the Logan. The helicopter was waiting for us there. We climbed in and it took off. The helicopter was large and spacious enough that we were not crammed in. We headed back to Indonesia where the trouble had begun, to the same island where we had gathered the last sample of animal blood.

We crossed the Pacific Ocean once again. During the flight, I thought of the paradise island I had seen what felt like so long ago. Such a symbol of peace in a darkening world. Just looking down at the ocean almost made me forget that there was dark magic I had to deal with. The paradise island, wherever it was, was good to think about. With the exception of a different island here and there, the color blue surrounded me, as if there was no sorcery at all.

A few more hours passed. We arrived at Komodo Island in the middle of the night, landing near the dark, inhospitable jungle. It was hot and mucky, just as I remembered it. Spending the previous morning in the frigid, Norwegian forest, it was very odd being back in the hot and tropical wilderness. We jumped out of the side of the helicopter and were met by James. Only he and a few comrades were present.

"Hello again, Draco. You, too, Clipper. You've both made it," the sergeant said. "Follow me. Don't worry about the locals, they're not in any danger. They've been evacuated until this is all over. I don't know how strong these Monolegion people are.

"There are only four others here. I know you two are familiar with this area, so I'm sending you two in alone. It's for the better."

I nodded and followed Clipper down the road. We kept on the trail until I found a peculiar black spot on the road. A few sniffs told me that oil had been sitting there for a while. The scent was very cold. I realized this was where the engine of the guide's Jeep had blown up months ago, the same Jeep we had ridden in during our expedition. We were at the spot where Clipper had fallen off. I made a motion with my paw to tell Clipper to stay extremely quiet. We crawled down the slope. Another scent reached my nose; it smelled like the camp in the Guarded Forest. The scent formed a trail in the jungle. I would have been blinded by the night with human eyes, but my dragon vision and smelling guided me where I needed to go.

Sure enough, we found the camp. The building where we had been held captive was still standing, just as the way I remembered it. This time we saw several mounds of dirt and leaves throughout the outpost grounds. The stakes where the two prisoners had been tied to were gone. Silently, we continued down the slope until we reached the bottom.

I smelled something else. It was a scent I had never smelled before. This boggled my mind. If I was to compare it to anything, it smelled like burnt gunpowder from a used firework; something like sulfur. I tried to locate the scent when I heard a strange hiss. A bright violet beam of light shot up from the ground, exploding in the air in the form of many green lights. The dazzling sight nearly hypnotized me.

Then it happened.

The evil dwarves swarmed out of their hiding places. Some remained up in trees, down inside foxholes, or behind dirt mounds covered with some liquid; possibly a flame retardant. They fired guns and shot bows. Some of the soldiers had albores. More of the violet beams burst around me, showering me in green lights. I began to feel invisible forces weighing me down like solid ingots; then came zaps from lighting balls that materialized above me. These zaps did not feel like real lightning bolts, thank goodness, but they hurt just as bad as bullets. The battle had elements I had never experienced before. It overwhelmed me. I looked over to see Clipper snapping at the green lights between surges of electricity. If I were to overcome these violent spells, I had to eliminate the source.

I cast fire and spat venom at the dwarves. Indeed, the battle that changed my life had officially begun. It was the battle that would lead me away from a world I knew and to a place that was completely new.

Sally opened her eyes to find herself shackled in a dark dungeon. She did not know where she was. After she was kidnapped, she had been given a strange drug. She was sure it was a potion that had knocked her out. Potion or drug, they were synonyms to Sally. She felt a deep pain in her head. A throb pulsed behind her eyes.

With what vision she had, she examined the room. It was a dungeon for sure. Cobblestone surrounded her from head to toe. There was a large iron door, the grates of an unused fireplace, and Reno, who was still unconscious and shackled as well. In Reno's condition, Sally thought she would have been better off in the crate.

Cobwebs clung to the ceiling. Sally heard rats squeaking and scurrying across the room next to the wall. Terrified at the rats' presence, Sally tried to move, but to no avail. The shackles on her wrists held her in place.

She sat down, waiting for the worst when the iron door swung open. Monty appeared in his human form, the Master Scepter in his hands. A suspended lantern flickered in the room behind him. "Welcome to my home, Ms. Serene," said the sorcerer. "This was the basement of an old monastery, which was abandoned about a hundred years ago. I've gotten some good use out of it for the last year. I'm not one who lets things go to waste when they're still useable. Yes, I know it's a touch creepy, but you'll manage."

"What do you want, Monty?" said Sally. "Why are you doing this?"

"Oh, you want to know why I'm after Jacob and Clipper, do you? Well, I see no reason to hide the truth at this point.

"My father was a wizard on the Second Earth. He practiced untainted magic. He insisted that I find 'peace' and 'hope'. Years passed and he died prematurely. A premature death! If I deserved peace and happiness, why did I have to lose my father?" He did not make eye contact with Sally for a moment. "I-I loved him! Well, I eventually stumbled across a mountain on a desolate isle. There, I discovered a dark being, a king who will someday get what he deserves. He gave me real happiness: the happiness I don't have to wait for! That king gave me the power to become the Keeper of the Three Worlds. He named me Triathra. I was told to travel to this Earth and find the two dragons disguised as humans. While I was young, I had to wait for them. I had to find them and prevent them from traveling back to our home. I used my first name, Monty and invented my last name, Victor. I suppose you were not expecting to be taken hostage by a sorcerer that first time, were you?"

Sally struggled in her shackles. "I don't even know what you're talking about. What is this Second Earth? But sorcerer or not, scepter or not, you will never win. You need to sacrifice short term, superficial pleasures to gain true happiness. Wickedness is not the way! It's not *true* happiness! It never was!"

Monty sniffed. "Convincing idea, though I'm not buying it. I left the Guarded Forest after you tied me up there. I traveled to New York, thinking that you were going there after you were cursed into a different era. While you were under the curse, I cast a spell on the scepter to make it disappear. It came to rest in the lands that lie to the west, where Jacob and Clipper fought my people. I can now go through with my plan."

He took a short breath.

"I returned to the Guarded Forest when I learned that Jacob and Clipper had finally transformed themselves back into dragons. Yes, I knew that would happen eventually. As I've said, as a sorcerer, I am the Keeper of the Three Worlds. I serve one who is the true leader. I'm simply in charge of this world, which is dry of man's views of magic. I have the dwarves at my disposal."

Sally was puzzled. "What do you mean transform *back* into dragons?"

Monty jeered. The lantern outside the door dimmed and burned green. "No matter. I have the Master Scepter. I am not a dwarf myself, but I'm among them. I am the sorcerer. On this Earth I'm Monty Victor. I'm Triathra everywhere else. I'm the leader of the Monolegion tribe! When your dragon friends fall, this world will enter an age of sorcery. Every nation will bow to one king. One step to hold power on the Three Worlds!"

Sally had heard enough. She could not bear the eerie dungeon any longer. She decided to ask the question she had uppermost in her mind, "Why did you choose this, going from good to bad? What's your real motive?"

"*My real motive?*" Monty snarled. "You mentioned small sacrifices. Why? Why must we suffer for others? We should be able to live our lives the way we want to. All this 'good' and 'joy' is not freedom! I tried being good once, I lost my father in that mindset." Tears ran down Monty's face. "He was going to teach me to be a wizard. We had plans. All my good deeds… and what was my reward? Death! I was only twelve. Not only did my father die, but so did a dear friend after I had pledged allegiance to the king. We were the best of friends. After weeks of education on how to become certified sorcerers, we started questioning if evil was necessary or not. One day, we found two young goblins beating a baby dragon that was even younger than this one. My friend decided to cover up the dragon's body because it was crying and badly hurt. Unfortunately, that turned out to be a fatal mistake for my friend. He… he was beaten to death by the goblins, along with the dragon!" Another set of tears found their way to the corner of his eye. "He was 'good' and he died in an instant! That was the last straw for me. I could be good and pay, or I could give in and have anything I wanted at any time."

"That's not true," Sally argued. "If we make sacrifices here or there, it could not only make us happy in the end, it can make others happy. We can rise together. We don't need mindless power. We need agency so we can know right from wrong."

"False!" Monty barked. "There is no guarantee that it will happen!"

Sally looked at the ground in despair. There was no reasoning with Monty. She knew that her words stung him. Those words were still true in Sally's mind. Agency and humility brought true happiness. "There's no more that I can do," she said. "Kill me now and get it over with, but please spare Reno. Her life is just beginning."

"I'm not going to kill you, Sally. I want you to join me." Monty tapped the jewel on the scepter with his finger. "Then *you* can find out what true happiness is. Imagine having the world at your fingertips, having what you want when you want it." Monty's voice rose to a fevered pitch with each sentence. His eyes were wild. Finally, he took a deep breath and spoke almost calmly, "You have one hour to make your choice."

Monty said no more. He turned around and left the dungeon. The iron door slammed shut. The black mist dissolved. Sally sat down on the floor. Reno was finally waking up. She limped to Sally and sat on her lap. Sally patted Reno's head, praying for the best.

"A cold, stone dungeon. Fitting for an evil magician. He's just angry at the loss of his friend and father. I wish I could turn that around." She was going to ask about the things Monty spoke of, but she knew that would do no good. She was in the dark about his mention of the Second Earth and this king.

MONTY STEPPED OUT OF THE DUNGEON. RAYMOND WAITED IN THE room above it, under an electric light. Monty climbed to the top of the stairs and closed the trapdoor, then went to a wooden box and opened it. A syringe was inside the box. It was filled with a mysterious yellow substance. He held it in his left hand as he raised the scepter in his right. A thick mist surrounded his left hand for a few seconds. When the mist was gone, Monty opened his hand. The syringe was gone, as if he had completed an elusive magic trick. Not a sound was heard.

"Where did it go?" Raymond asked.

"There is currently a battle against the dragons in Indonesia," said Monty. "Jacob and Clipper attacked one of our bases. I sent the syringe to Greyhair via the scepter. He'll know what to do with it. It'll be easy to defeat them with the new potion I've created. Remember when they had just turned into dragons? They were uncontrollable and caused chaos. This potion will put them in that state again. The small needle can slide between their thick scales with no problem. There is a chance that whoever is affected by the drug will glimpse their home world with no memory. When they come back to this Earth, they'll not know where they went. They'll panic and attack everything they sees with no control over themselves."

Raymond did not like that. He shut his eyes and pressed his palms into his temples. "I can't deal with this!" he said to himself. "I'm leaving."

Monty ignored Raymond as he made his escape, not knowing where his servant was headed. His mind was on what was happening on the other side of the world.

MORE ARROWS THAN BULLETS FLEW OVER OUR HEADS. I ASSUMED the Monolegion's supply of ammunition was running low. The albore lights above us showed no signs of stopping.

"Get back!" I roared to Clipper.

Composite bowmen were lined around the base ahead of us. Clipper and I withdrew to the cover of the jungle. Leaves, sediment, and arrows skipped around my face. Even though the zaps were becoming more tolerable, there was nowhere for us to go. The Monolegions were holding us back. Fire was out of the question because of the flame-retardant mounds and branches.

"There must be some way to enclose them," I said. "Clipper, stay here. I'll circle around from behind."

Clipper agreed. He did not argue about being the arrow fodder. I crawled backwards, away from my spot of cover. My black scales camouflaged with the dark of the night as I circled around. The lightning did not follow me. I saw the enemy army fire at Clipper.

What shocked me even more was the familiar face commanding the Monolegions. It was Greyhair, the dwarf that had been the warden of the prison in France! I saw that he was one of many who had albores. The wand in his hand jumped around as it cast its spells. I leaped forward and tackled him. My claws created countless gashes in his arms and legs. I may have even broken one of his arms in my pounce. I was about to spit venom in his eyes, but numerous sharp pains pricked my back before I could. Several arrows struck me, some stuck in my wings. I fell next to Greyhair.

Clipper saw me on the ground. "Jacob, no!"

The fighting stopped and I stood back up. My back felt like it was strained. I lifted my head up to the glowing sky that signified dawn, but I wanted to close my eyes as soon as I had opened them. Several Monolegions surrounded me under the remainder of the albore lights. One dwarf aimed a blowgun at me. I tried to move, but an invisible force kept me pinned.

To keep my courage up, I taunted my enemies. "So this is the second time I've been captured in Indonesia. This must be a record."

"Silence, dragon!" shouted Greyhair, standing up. He winced in pain, holding his arm to his chest. "You may have won in France, but this time it will be different."

The dwarf with the blowgun was about to fire it. I tried to escape but was unable to move. One of the spells stiffened my muscles. Fighting the force, I stood back up just in time for the dart to hit me in the back of the neck. Almost instantly, I felt a tingle throughout my whole body.

Greyhair grinned. "The serum that is in you is a potion that Monty had created. You'll go into a brief sleep. Then the killing stage will come. The stage that made you out of control after your transformation will return. You'll go on another killing spree. And after that, you'll never regain your memory."

I felt my legs weaken and tremble. My vision began to cloud once more. I saw Greyhair laughing devilishly, claiming his victory. "You've lost, Jacob Draco."

To even the score, I managed to give one last flame out of my mouth. The flame set fire to Greyhair's clothing. In panic, he ran into the building where I had once been held captive. The last bit of light I saw was the building going up in flames, more than likely taking Greyhair's life. My eyes closed and I felt myself fading. I could hear Clipper running towards me. "You'll never take Jacob!" he roared.

It was too late. His roar faded from my mind. Other memories started to flee. The last thought I had was Reno, standing in front of me and smiling. The infant faded in the darkness. She was gone.

Everything was gone.

CHAPTER 30

REQUIEM FOR JAKARTA

Clipper no longer cared about his own safety in the midst of the terrible sight. The idea of losing a friend was something he did not want to experience. He ran into the hornet nest of dwarves, his eyes on me. A great number of lightning balls struck him along the way. There were so many that he lost his balance. His joints started to stiffen from all the electricity. Having to deal with all the hostile magic was simply too much for Clipper. He did not think of casting fire at the dwarves right off. The use of venom came to his mind first, but it proved useless. With little time to do anything else, he decided that fire would be more effective. That did not overcome the albore defense, either. Clipper was stuck and powerless. His blood began to pulse faster through his veins. He, too, was falling into wrath. Clipper thought it was necessary under the current circumstance. With a roar, he planted his claws in the soft, lush grass. He charged forward after casting another wave of fire. It felt like his horns worked for a moment until questionable forces pressed him down again. The green lights taunted him as they flowed around his head. His wrath, as much as it was growing, was not going to save him this time.

"Come one step closer and he's dead," one of the bow-armed rebels sneered.

Another rebel dwarf took control after Greyhair's death. Clipper heard the others call him different names. One of them was Longbeard and he surely lived up to his name.

"The ship is set for Jakarta as planned," Longbeard said to his troops. "As your new officer, I order you to put Jacob in the crate and ship him there. Those poor city inhabitants will not know what hit them."

Several rebels had albores at the ready if Clipper moved. He wanted to fight back, but he knew that was not a good idea. The next best thing was to return to James. Clipper blew an un-aimed flame in Longbeard's direction then quickly flew off to the camp where the sergeant was waiting.

Clipper reached the base before the sun shone over the jungle's canopy. James was concerned to see him arrive alone. The sergeant looked around nervously. "What happened? I saw some strange colors in the sky. Where's Draco?"

Clipper beat his wings a few times to calm himself. "Sergeant, can you stay here and make sure the dwarves stay where they are? They're shipping Jacob to Jakarta. I need to go there right now!" He gave all the information he knew to the sergeant.

James agreed, promising to get to Jakarta himself just as soon as he had things under control on Komodo Island. Clipper immediately took to the air. He was not flying directly to Jakarta for fear of getting lost over the ocean. Instead, he searched along the island's coast for the ship that Longbeard had mentioned. He searched until fatigue overcame him. Not even his sense of smell offered any help at the moment. He landed in the water with a splash and began swimming as fast as he could. Before long, fatigue overcame his legs as it had his wings. He needed to rest, but he knew he had to press on. He surfaced only long enough to take a gulp of air before diving back down, gliding invisibly beneath the surface. There was no sign of the ship.

Luck was with him when he spotted a little fishing boat on the horizon. That meant land was near! Clipper had to do what he had always avoided: he had to talk to a stranger. Staying underwater, he swam up to the boat and once again rose to the surface. The frightened fisherman, stared silently at the dark red dragon climbing into his boat.

Clipper spoke before the old fisherman could react. "*Jangan takut*. It's okay. I'm a friend." He spoke in Indonesian.

"Wh-Who are you?" the fisherman shivered as he replied in his native language. "You look like a… a… sea monster!"

"Have you by any chance seen a cargo ship pass by?" Clipper asked as cordially as possible.

To his fortune, the fisherman trusted Clipper's peaceful nature and answered honestly, "I did. I did not see the crew, I'm sorry to say. There was a big crate that was roped down tight. I wondered what was in it. If I was to guess, I think the ship is going to the harbor that I am going to. I live near there."

Clipper looked around the fishing boat and found a long rope. He tied one end to his four-clawed foot and gave the other end to the fisherman. "I know this sounds crazy, but I need your help," he said. "We need to get into the harbor as fast as we can. I'm able to swim fast. I can pull the boat into the harbor to save time."

The fisherman quickly tied the other end of the rope to the front of his boat. Clipper dove into the water and was off. His strength, greater than any human, towed the boat forward. The fisherman held on tight as the boat sailed. A few hours later, the two arrived at a dock in the harbor. Clipper jumped out of the water, onto the dock to search for the cargo ship. His joints were so sore he could hardly walk.

It was not long before Clipper spotted the familiar vessel. He was surprised to find some sailors on the docked boat making a thorough inspection. While Clipper stayed out of sight, the fisherman stepped up and spoke to one of the sailors. "Where did this boat come from?" he asked.

"We don't know," replied the sailor. "It came here with no crew. It's a ghost ship."

The fisherman was thoughtful for a moment, then decided to introduce Clipper. "Excuse me, sir. I have met someone who is searching for this boat. He says there is very dangerous cargo on board."

"Can I talk to this man?" the sailor asked.

The fisherman stepped to the side. Clipper showed himself to the sailor. "Please don't be afraid, I'm a friend. I'll help you."

The surprised sailor held his ground. "I… I have heard of you. I did not believe you were an actual dragon from the stories. Are there not two of you?"

"Yes, my friend is on this ship," said Clipper. "It's a very long story, but we've got to evacuate this harbor. The other dragon was given something that will make him very dangerous. We need to get everyone to safety and I'll try to talk to him."

The sailor obliged. He left to sound an alarm, but two other sailors were already attempting to remove the crate. They each took out a knife to cut the ropes holding the crate down. Clipper sprinted over to stop them, but it was too late. The moment the crate was free, it shattered. I emerged from the splinters of wood.

Exposing my sharp teeth, I drooled beyond control. In fear, both the sailors jumped into the water, not knowing of my amphibious nature. I followed them without a moment's hesitation. Clipper reached the railing and gazed down into the water. The sailors never surfaced. He was shocked at what had happened. He knew I would never kill any living thing unless I truly had to. This was just too much for him. He made his way to shore and sat down, groaning until I climbed onto land. I growled, feeling threatened at the presence of another dragon.

"Jacob! Snap out of it!" he shouted at me.

All I heard was blabber from his mouth. I did not understand what he was saying. I was surprised that he was chattering like a human. It was not right in my clouded mind. I lowered my horns and charged him. Clipper bent down and waited for my coming. When I struck him, our horns interlocked. Clipper flipped up on his hind legs. I was helplessly tossed through the air and landed on the ground with a thud, causing the entire dock to quake.

I immediately stood back up. It was a time for a real fight. I shot a flame at Clipper, which caused him no harm. The heat was not my intention, though. I intended it to be a distraction. The flames reached the ship, as I had planned. The entire vessel was soon burning, from bow to stern. Clipper did not know what to do. I jumped like a cat in the air and collided into him. He executed simple fighting tactics. My attacks were far more barbarous than he had expected. I clawed and bit him with all my power.

"Jacob! It's me, Clipper! Please stop, this isn't you!" he cried.

His talking only made me angrier. I struck him in his side with the sharp ends of my horns. He slipped off the dock and fell in the water. I cackled, then I decided to attack the rest of the city, any person I could get my paws on. Clipper quickly emerged from the water just as the ship started to sink. He knew he had to stop the fire on the ship from spreading. The blaze eventually went out when the ship sank below the surface. Clipper looked around to see what he had missed. Several people were on the ground, some were dead while others were seriously injured. Clipper felt ashamed that he could not help the victims at the moment. He had to track me down.

"Jacob did not do this," he wept. "He's not himself. I've got to find him before something else happens!"

NUMEROUS BUILDINGS WERE BURNING BY NOON. IT WAS A TRAGIC scene. Some people were seriously hurt. Others were covered in soot and cinders. The city was in despair. At a military base yet to be touched, James spoke to an Indonesian general, explaining what was going on.

"I will prepare my troops to attack," the general replied.

The two shook hands. They both knew this was not an easy task they were up against. Before James left, he explained to the general that Clipper was not the threat.

It was not going to be too difficult to find a dragon. Even in my rabid state I knew that. The frontline guard searched for me. James was astonished at the carnage. Hundreds of buildings were left to burn to the ground. Many people were lying in the streets, wailing in pain. It was a saddening sight to see. James led his small group of soldiers through the scene of destruction. He kept a sharp eye. Clipper found the small army moments later. He dropped gently onto the ground and greeted them.

"Any sign of Draco?" asked James.

"No, but I might be able to find him from his scent trail," Clipper replied.

"He could be anywhere. Just keep your eyes open."

I was actually not too far away. Clipper was about to leap into the air when I found someone wandering on the street, looking for safety. The woman let out a scream when I flew after her.

Clipper jumped on my back before could take the life of my victim. I stood on my hind legs and backed into a wall. When Clipper charged, I butted him back to the wall with a powerful force. Clipper lay on the ground with his four paws over his sickened stomach.

Turning to my next victim, I noticed James ready to fire a high-powered rifle at me. Instinctively, I jumped about ten feet in the air and landed on top of him. I smacked the rifle out of his hands as I pinned him to the ground; my tail wavered back and forth. James tried to wriggle free, but his strength was not enough. I raised one of my arms and stripped him of his body armor. Slowly and painfully, I slid my claws over his bare chest. When I was finished with him, I flew off. Clipper rushed over to James. The sergeant lay with a deep, open wound in his chest and two broken bones where I had stood on him. Clipper could see that James's wounds were critical. If I had clawed any deeper, I would have punctured his lungs or pierced his heart.

"We need to get you some medical attention," said Clipper.

James gasped for air. "Save… Jacob… Save him for me."

Clipper yelled for a medic. Two men arrived and carried James away. When he was gone, Clipper fell to the ground and sobbed. He sobbed for the fallen, and he sobbed for me. "This is not the Jacob I know," he said softly before taking a moment of devastated silence.

After a few deep breaths, he pulled himself together. He vowed revenge on Monty and the Monolegions for the sorcery they had used. Clipper was not an expert in magic. All he knew was that he hated the magic he had to face. If it came to the point where he had to kill me, he would never forgive himself. He decided to make every effort to reach the reasonable part of me. The alternative was too unthinkable.

SALLY LAY ASLEEP ON THE DUNGEON FLOOR. RENO SLEPT ON HER back. Their fitful slumber was interrupted by the arrival of Monty, laughing in his cunning nature. The door swung open with a loud bang.

"It worked!" he said. "The potion worked!"

Sally shivered. "What do you mean?"

"My dwarves have told me that Jacob is terrorizing everything in his path. He's a tornado! The poor citizens of Jakarta never stood a chance. Not even Clipper can get past him! One of my rebel spies said that the two fought, and guess who took the decisive victory?"

Sally was horrified. "I just can't believe you would let something like this happen. You're a monster! You're responsible for the deaths of hundreds of innocent people all for a little hostility on an old foe!"

Monty was untouched by her insults. He took in the joy as he felt the power of the scepter come to him. "Old foe," he scoffed.

Reno got to her feet and glared at Monty. Even at her young age, she knew he was an entity of evil. He was the one who had imprisoned her when she was a hatchling, after all. Making an immature roar, she jumped on Monty's right ankle, biting down hard. She exhaled a small flame that added to the pain. Without a word, Monty grabbed Reno by the neck. He raised her up and hurled her against the stone wall. Reno bounced off it with a loud smack. She fell to the cold floor, bellowing in tears.

Sally bent down to examine Reno. "What did you do? She's hurt! I was right; you are a monster!"

With blood sizzling out of his shin, Monty clutched the scepter. He transformed into the green demon, filling the entire dungeon. "If she does that again, she'll die! Earlier I asked you a question. Have you made a decision?"

Even though Monty was almost three times his normal size, Sally faced him bravely. "I have. I will never join you, even if you torture me. Do your worst, you green slime!"

Monty grabbed Sally's neck with his demon claws "You want torture, do you? I'll give it to you. I'll start slow, I'm patient."

He shrank back into his familiar sorcerer form and moved to the door. "You will stay here with no food or water."

He pointed his scepter to the fireplace. A hissing blaze spontaneously combusted behind the metal grates.

"In the words of the common man, that will heat things up for you." Monty exited the dungeon, slamming the door behind him.

The temperature rose with each passing second. The heat did not bother Reno one bit, but Sally was already sweating. She knew she could not do anything, so she sat down and gently rubbed Reno's injuries. Reno licked the back of Sally's hand in return. The two did not give up hope. Sally believed they would be rescued, but she did not know when.

CHAPTER 31

Helping Jacob

Help reached Jakarta later in the day. The injured were taken away for immediate care. Clipper sat on the side of the road, tears streaming from his eyes. The Indonesian general tried to comfort him. "I'm sorry about this," he said. "We did the best we could to capture your friend. He must be special."

Clipper sighed. "Jacob has been my best friend ever since I left Canada. Not once did I see him this violent. He was always kind and caring. Now he's completely the opposite. I... I wish this could all end!"

"Everything will be fine," said the general. "It was that potion that made Jacob lose his mind. Trust me, he'll be back the way he was when it wears off. I'm sure of it."

Clipper took a deep breath. "He will never be the same again. After this stage passes, he'll forget who he is. He'll lose his memory. Oh, he's even worse now than his first stage after we were turned into dragons. He didn't kill anyone then. I remember going through that first stage myself. I remember hearing a small voice that kept me from killing. But now, all of Jacob's humanity is gone. It's hopeless."

"Don't worry," replied the general, "we've spotted Jacob. He left Jakarta, headed to another island. We'll get him back. How about this? You come with me to that island. You're a dragon, maybe you can reach him when his mind clears."

Clipper silently nodded, blinking away the tears. Deep in his mind, he doubted that he could reason with me. The general led Clipper to a cargo plane. As it took off, Clipper looked down at the recovering city. It was hard to feel any hope with such a terrible sight below.

Night fell as the plane reached the island. The door on the side opened up to the sky. A humid wind rushed past Clipper's face.

"Remember what you should do," the general reminded him. "Try to get him back, but don't let him leave the island."

"I'll do what I must, but I won't hurt him," said Clipper.

He jumped out of the plane and glided to the shore. His paws pressed through the sandy beach as he landed. Searching up and down the coastline, he was unable to find my scent. A feeling of despair washed over him. He then realized how sore he was. All that flying and swimming, and no sleep for several days, was taking its toll. With no scent to track, Clipper dug a little depression in the sand to rest in for a moment. His eyes eventually grew heavy. But before he started dreaming, he heard a voice in his mind,

"Did the Monolegion cry victorious? Did you lose your heart? Feel my comfort. Your friend lies in the woods, battered and weak. If you listen closely, you'll hear him speak."

Clipper opened his eyes, startled at what he had heard. It was the dragon of old. He understood what the spirit was saying. Clipper had lost his passion. He had to bring me back in order to go home. No matter his fatigue and soreness, he could not stop. He started sniffing up and down the coastline again. At last he caught the scent. That alone dissolved all his exhaustion.

"I'm coming Jacob. I'm coming!" he yelled.

He disappeared into the forest. He knew there was no guarantee that I would be my former self. The only way to stop the Monolegions now was to renew our friendship. This was a risk Clipper had to take.

I LOOKED AROUND MY NEW ENVIRONMENT. THE OUTSIDE OF MY head throbbed; the inside was muddled. I pressed my front paws

on my head, trying ease the pain. There was no way I could stop the headache. I was exploring the island when I heard something in the jungle. Not knowing what it was, I took off running in the opposite direction. I reached a clearing and stopped, out of breath.

It felt strange. I had no idea who I was or why I was here. All I remembered was that I was simply a dragon trying to survive. As I looked around, trying to find answers, I heard a voice in the jungle. At first I did not understand what it was saying, but then it came to me.

"Jacob, are you here? It's me, Clipper!"

I was unsure if this stranger was talking to me or not. I did not know who Jacob was at the moment. Clipper, on the other hand, was following close behind me.

"Jacob, I'm here!" the voice called.

From the sound of the voice, I believed it belonged to another dragon like me. This made me curious. I saw Clipper enter the clearing where I was. To camouflage into the night, I bent down in the grass, holding perfectly still.

Everything was confusing. Clipper looked around and sniffed the air. He knew I was nearby, no question about it. He continued to walk towards me. I started to crawl backwards when I stepped on a stick that broke in half. The red dragon followed the noise and found me in the grass. I was very nervous.

"Jacob, it's you! I'm so glad to see you!" he said happily.

I did not buy his kindness. I hissed at him and spoke in fear. "Stay away from me! Leave me alone!"

The strange dragon seemed to know me. He addressed me as Jacob. I cowered back.

"Keep away!"

"Jacob, it's me, Clipper."

"You can't fool me! I don't believe you!"

"I'm your friend, Clipper. Let me help you."

He gave me his paw and helped me to my feet. I stood up, deciding to give him a little trust. Our paws touched together.

Unfortunately, this did not reveal anything about my past. Clipper told me to follow him back to the coast. Reluctantly, I did so. Following him, we flew to a ship that was a few miles out to sea. I was tied up on the ship as she prepared to sail. I whimpered at my desperate situation.

"Don't leave me, Clipper. I don't want to be alone."

Clipper sat down beside me. "I won't leave you, friend. I'm right with you."

"I know I attacked those humans," I said. "I didn't mean to. I didn't know what I was doing! Why are they imprisoning me?"

Clipper turned to one of the sailors onboard. "Untie him, please. He's been through enough."

The sailor did as he was told, leaving when I was free.

"We're on our way back to Komodo Island, Jacob. What do you remember?"

I took a moment to reach into my limited memory. "All I remember is traveling by myself in a peaceful forest. It was a wonderful place. Fairies surrounded me. Everything was fine. The fairies were the only people who took care of me. I was so happy when they told me to travel through Pearl Forest. Then it went dark. When I woke, I was in shock. I didn't know what I was doing. Buildings of rock were everywhere with the people I had never seen before. Against my own will, I attacked!"

Clipper's tail slithered. "That's strange. Where did the fairies come from? You were passed out on a boat the entire time. You didn't wake up until you reached Jakarta. How could you be in two places at once? Oh well, everything's okay now. I'll take care of you."

The ship was on her way back to Jakarta. I still felt fearful and confused about the recent events. Clipper sat next to me, puzzled about my blurry memory. All he wanted to do was to decode what really happened.

"So, Jacob, what exactly happened to you during the past few days? Just tell me all what you experienced."

"All right," I said, "I'll tell you what I remember. It's strange. I remember it, but I don't. It was like a dream. I know it sounds crazy. The earliest thing I can remember is that I was running down a muddy path through a dark and dense forest, not as humid as the island where you found me. I refused to stop, for dark-scaled dragons were not well respected in the region."

CHAPTER 32

THE VISION OF PEARL FOREST

*E*ach breath I took was shorter than the last. The monsters of the night had been tracking me down. I presumed that they were goblins or ogres or something. No matter what they were, I could not let them find me, or else I would face some sort of peril. I did not know why I decided to run and not fight. My legs were sore and I limped on my back legs, but that was not my greatest concern. I was overly fatigued when they poisoned me. I was aware that I had the ability to breathe fire, but I ran like a coward.

When I had gone as far as I could go, I found myself at the edge of a wood. "Enchanted" was the only word to describe it. I stopped in my tracks and sniffed the air. I could smell the magic of the forest. As I continued, I suddenly felt a small, sharp twinge of pain in the back of my neck. Somehow it weakened me even more. I had no idea if it was the goblins doing or not. When I woke again, I found swelling cuts all over my scales, which should have protected me. I wiped a small amount of blood from my mouth. When I did so, my wounds instantly healed. I felt completely rejuvenated.

The next thing I saw made me freeze from the inside out. I found myself surrounded by fairies. Kind, pure, human-sized fairies. Their thin wings fluttered gently in the peaceful breeze; their dresses of many colors reached down to their bare feet and up over their shoulders; their hair of brown, blonde, and black waved softly. The fairies smiled at me. For the first time I could remember, I felt respected. I managed a small smile in return. A warm feeling washed over me. The peaceful air blew past my face, just the feeling I enjoyed. It was as if I had returned home after being gone for many years. A sense of contentment stole over me.

One of the fairies held a roll of parchment in her hands. She said, "Take this map and walk its path. You'll find the greatest gift of life. Its worth is beyond that of the greatest treasure." She handed me parchment.

I unrolled the map to find many drawings. There was a thick black line that represented the path I was to travel. Finding a hanging willow branch, I broke it from the tree and fastened it like a rope tightly around my abdomen. I slid the rolled map between the rope and me. Thanking the helpful fairies, I set out on my journey.

My quest was to learn why I was loved in this world. I felt like I was home. As I began my adventure, I was alone, though I did not mind. The woods were quite peaceful. Once in a while I would hold perfectly still and listen to the birds singing and the nearby forest inhabitants scurrying through the underbrush. But the feeling of joy seemed to dissipate as I covered more ground. A few hours later, the peaceful ambience died away completely. Silence engulfed the forest. I felt apprehensive. I hoped my last encounter with the goblins would be my final fight.

How wrong I was.

Once night fell, I made a small campfire. I used the fire's glow to study the map. My trail started at the Odno Plains. It led to Pearl Forest and into the swamplands. I still had to pass the Skalisk Canyon and other places with funny names. It gave me chills to think about them.

I studied the map for a few minutes before sleep crept into my mind. Before I closed my eyes, I rolled on my back and stared at the night sky. The night sky! I could not look at it without getting tears in my eyes. It was not just a mass of black space. What looked like a violet nebula cloud pirouetted across the sky while several millions of *stars danced above the milky nimbus. The image that melted my heart the most was a ringed planet that stood gallantly in the night. Its blue face comforted me greatly. The heavenly body evoked great emotion within me. It seemed to be bigger than the world where I rested on my back. I still had tears in my eyes when I drifted off to sleep.*

Morning dawned with a promising glow, and I pressed on. The night sky was fresh in my memory. I would never forget the celestial sight as long as I lived. With the wonderful empyrean in my head, I held my nose forward. A nearby river gave me an opportunity to have breakfast, for it had many different kinds of fish. The sun rose higher and higher in the sky. I took an occasional swim in the river to keep myself full of energy. I would not play for long, though. I had to find whatever the fairy had meant by "the greatest gift of life". I did not expect to find anything dazzling or glamorous, but something out of the ordinary at least.

As hour after hour passed, the terrain continued to change. The smooth, rolling hills gave way to another forest; this one was thicker than the last one. All was quiet until the goblins I had long feared ambushed me. I wanted them to leave, but they continued approaching me. Their greenish skin and disheveled gray hair helped them blend in to the surrounding undergrowth. The spears they had did not look dangerous, but I did not know for sure. I had had cuts in my scales last I remembered.

It all happened so fast. The goblins said I was dangerous and that I should die. But before they could do anything, I charged them. The strong charge sent many of them flying off into the thicket. I took care of the rest with venom. Fire would have been too risky in the forest. With the goblins out of the way, I raced down the path and out of sight of the goblins. They might have been very angry if I killed whomever I had charged, which I probably had considering my sharp horns. Sprinting at full speed for about five minutes, I took flight when it was clear to do so. I believed I had lost them after flying for several minutes. As luck would have it, I found a sparkling blue pond on the wooded floor. The color was so intense that I could not see the bottom. I landed at the water's edge to inspect it. The glittering water astounded me. I jumped feet first into the pond in the shallow end so only the refreshing liquid would engulf only my feet. As I lowered my head to get a drink, I saw the reflection of a strange little man standing behind me. I leaped out of the water and back onto land, standing face to face with the overjoyed person. He was very short and he wore rags for clothing. On his head was a red stocking cap that sat above his ear-to-ear smile.

"You have freed the grøls and my family from the horrors of the goblins! Yip! Yip! They have plagued us for years! Thank you, dragon, for saving us! Yip!"

I watched the tike, who was about a quarter of my size, prance around in circles. Others of his kind soon joined him, much to my surprise. Before long, the little people were everywhere. There were fifty or so of them, male and female of all ages. Despite all the noise around me, I was puzzled at what the goblin had told me. I was dangerous and I should die. I tried to think what I had done to anger them, but my memory would not unlock the vault of the past that I needed. All I remembered was that I was a lonesome dragon on the run from the green savages. Why were they after me? Did I really do something bad? I thought the little man who called himself a grøl might know a thing or two.

"Excuse me," I said to the particular family of grøls. "I was wondering if you could tell me where I am."

They all burst out with laughter. "You silly little dragon," the mother grøl said. "This is Pearl Forest, named after the lovely land itself, much like a pearl. It's just a small section of all of Elsov. Yip! Yip! Yip!"

Elsov... Elsov... That name rang so many bells in my head. The word sounded like another language, yet it was so familiar. It was as if I heard it hundreds and hundreds of times before. I pulled out the map and examined my location. I had just entered Pearl Forest. I must have started out at the Odno, or Fairy Plains. That made sense. It looked like I had to follow the path across more wooded lands and around numerous lakes before I would make it north where the so-called "gift" should be. I had no desire for great treasure, but I was curious to know why I had met the fairies and why they felt I should find the gift, whatever it might be.

Brushing aside my thoughts, I focused on the map. The whole land, even the plains, was known as Elsov. At least one of my many questions had been answered.

"I's worried when you arrived," the father grøl told me. "Dragons are known to be villainous, but you've shown that yer a peaceful sort. Black dragons don't come from here. Come, I'll invite you to our first dinner in freedom that we have not 'ad in years. No more sludge from our slavers!"

I calmly accepted. The rest of the grøls continued to prance around with joy. Over the course of the day, the sun slowly set in the west. I found myself inside a circle of more grøls with an open fire in the center. I could see that some of the houses where they lived were inside trees. These trees were much wider than any of the others. They were the perfect size to house a family of grøls, considering how small grøls were.

After several minutes of chattering and laughter under the night sky, the father, who I had met first, stood up and addressed his family and friends, "Ahem! Listen to me, my friends. For many dark years, the vile goblins have enslaved us an' robbed us of our freedoms. All we could do was serve their selfish needs. Occasionally some of us'd band together to try and free ourselves. Still, there were just too many of our enemies. Earlier today, our heroic dragon friend fought 'em and we were rid of 'em in just a matter of seconds. Thank you, dragon. We're greatly in your debt."

The group of small people applauded. I humbly bowed my head. The applause soon died down when an elder of the group stood to speak. "I've heard many stories about dragons with black scales. They come from the lands far across the sea. I've heard that they are prideful, selfish, and wicked. They pillage and plunder everything just because they want their treasure, covered in the blood of the innocent. They're many times worse than goblins ever could be."

The entire tribe gasped. I dropped my jaw at his description. I may have a desire for the treasure I was seeking, but I would never think about killing the innocent or plundering their belongings. That sounded horrible!

"Please understand me," I said to the group of grøls. "I admit that I do have natural temptation to be proud, but I can overcome that. I know what the goblins did was wrong and I'm not going to do the same thing."

The tribe gasped again.

"If that's so, then what have you done in the past few days?" the elder asked me.

"To tell you truth, I don't know," I replied. The group murmured in disbelief as I continued. "All I remember is fighting ruthless goblins, similar to the ones who enslaved you. After they poisoned me, I tried to flee. They were always right behind me. I tried unsuccessfully to fight them off and I was wounded badly. The fairies nursed me back to health. When I was ready to leave, I was given this map that's leading me to a great gift"

The elder stroked his chin. "You don't know yer name or yer native land?"

"No. I have no idea how I came to be on the plains," I answered. "Maybe you're right. I could be someone evil, sent to destroy you. Like I said, I think I'm naturally evil."

I heard more murmuring among the rest of the grøls. I sincerely hoped they trusted me. The father grøl spoke in my defense, "If he was evil, surely he would have done something to us by now. He freed us from those goblins. I believe he's on our side."

The group of grøls stopped murmuring. In the same breath, they cheered. My ears twitched from the celebratory noise.

"Now let us have a festival to our freedom! Yip! Yip!" the father announced.

The grøls led me to the center of their small village, if a village is what they consider it to be when they were slaves. More of those houses in trees were lined together to form a U-shape. Some of the grøls vanished into their houses, only to return with round tables or chairs that were no bigger than me. Some of the grøls placed green or blue cloths on the tables. Others brought wooden spoons or cups that looked like they were coated with bark. When the food was served, everyone sat down. I sat at a considerable distance from the tables so I would not be in the way.

Their vegetarian food did not appeal to me. I asked permission to go fishing in the nearby pond instead. They graciously allowed me to catch my dinner. I walked over to the pond and stepped in. While splashing in the small body of glittering blue water, I gazed back up in the sky. Again, I saw the nebula, the stars, and the beautiful ringed planet. At first, I thought I was in a dream. But it was not a dream, everything was right before my eyes.

I kept an eye on the heavens as I finished eating. The younger grøls left for bed. Only the father grøl and I were awake in the dim, sapphire light. The trees at eventide were gorgeous with the reflecting light coming from the blue planet.

The father noticed where my attention was. "Do you enjoy the sky?" he asked.

"I do very much. I never thought it could be so alluring," I said.

The father pointed to the ringed planet. "You see that up there? That grand body is called Alsov. You can hear the resemblance to the name of our own world, Elsov."

"Yes, I can," I said.

"So, you are searching for this gift of life?" the father asked, spontaneously changing the subject.

"Yes, sir, I am... I think. I would appreciate any help."

The father sadly shook his head. "I'm sorry I cannot do that. It's difficult for grøls to travel. But I do know someone who might give you more help than I can offer."

I paid close attention. "You do?"

The father pointed to my map on one of the tables. "If you continue onward down the path, Pearl Forest can't get any more lovely. At night, the trees sparkle in countless colors while a calm voice can be heard singing through the air. The singing comes from the nymphs. They love to croon in the night. When you reach that spot, try to find a nymph. They're bigger than us grøls. When you find one, ask for Treetop. That's the name of one of the nymphs. She is the most adventurous out of all her colony and she is as beautiful as the forest around her. But be aware, these nymphs are quite prejudiced. They will not tolerate any threat against themselves. Black dragons have a reputation for being just that: a threat. When you find a nymph, keep calm and peaceful. It may take a while until they trust you, but getting yourself a guide, especially Treetop, will prove helpful t'you."

"Very well," I said. "I'll set off on my mission tomorrow morning. Thank you for your help."

"And thank you for freeing us from the goblins. You'll never know how happy we are. You've done us a great service. Again, thank you very much. Now that you've defeated them, they will never bother us again. Never again! Yippity! Yip!"

I only charged into them and ran off, I thought.

He shook my paw with his puny hand, then retired to his home where he spent his first night in freedom. As for me, I simply dug a small burrow near the pond and slept in that. I slept peacefully in the hole throughout the night.

A few hours before dawn, I set off. I strapped the rolled-up map under the vine that was around my abdomen. Once in a while, I pulled out the map to make sure I was traveling in the right direction.

Most of the time I flew. Occasionally I walked to make sure I was not losing my way. It took almost the entire day, but I finally reached the other end of Pearl Forest. There were no nymphs in sight yet, so I decided to rest and wait until evening. I found freshwater lake that was even more beautiful than the one near the land of grøls. I caught some fish and a rabbit for my late lunch. I rested in a thicket near the pond until it was twilight. I decided that I would enjoy traveling at night more. Also, I guessed the nymphs would be emerging nearby soon enough. They had to.

I sat quietly and tried to think of a plan to make peace with the nymphs. When I had an idea, I got into position. Removing the vine from around my abdomen, I tied one end to a weak branch on a dry spruce. Setting the map down beside the path, I held onto the other end of the rope and waited for one of my targets to approach.

It was not long before a nymph wandered in my sight: a young female who whistled a slow tune. She was about a foot taller than a grøl, but not nearly so chubby. She wore a clean outfit that looked like it was made of silk. Sure enough, everything was just as the elder grøl had told me. The father grøl was also right about the trees. Orbs of light blew off the trunks and branches and floated around my head. Despite how lovely they were, I kept my focus on the nymph, who continued her sweet tune. She was enjoying the night as I was. Clutching my end of the rope, I yanked it as hard as I could. The sound of the snapping branch was hard to miss. The nymph jumped up, alert, and looked around.

"Who is there?" she asked.

Not saying a word, I looked down and found a rock that was slightly smaller than my paw. I picked it up and hurled it in the air. It landed in front of the nymph. Shocked and panicked, she took off in the direction she had come, which happened to be in my direction. Clearing a bush, she stopped right in front of me. The moment she saw me, she turned around. With my quick paws, I was able to grab her before she could escape. I tried not to hurt her, but in her struggles she did get a few cuts.

She was at my mercy. She squirmed and attempted to scream, I held tight and tried to calm her down. I had to be extra careful so she would not receive any more cuts.

"Please quiet down," I said gently to her. "I'm a friend. I don't want to hurt you. Just calm down and I'll let you go."

She must have trusted me. If I were any louder, she would have not believed me. She ceased to squirm and began to calm down. Eventually I let her free.

The nymph turned around, looking at me in awe. "Are you going to harm me?" she whimpered.

"I'm not here to hurt anyone. I need the help from one of your people," I said.

The nymph looked at me in a strange way. "Since when did a black dragon wander in these lands and not seek death or destruction? Since I was young, I have heard stories about your kind. Black dragons are often evil, never to be trusted."

I chuckled in an attempt to put her at ease. "I guess I'm different."

The nymph's face did not change expression. She did not seem to know if she should believe me or not. It took her a moment before she accepted my offer. "Very well, I will lead you to my home."

She started to make her way along the shore of the lake. I followed her quietly when she suddenly kicked, planting a foot right into my chin. I yelped as I lost balance and splashed into the water. I emerged to see her reach for a small pouch. She flung a strange powder at my eyes. My tongue and eyes stung. I dipped my face in the lake to wash away the powder. The nymph took off down the road while I was distracted. I gained distance by bounding in the air. I flew a good twenty feet and landed next to her. A good winged jump does provide great distance. She stopped again to avoid running into my claws.

"Listen to me. If I was evil, I would have hurt you already," I said.

At that point, the nymph knew she was powerless against me. If the powder could not slow me down, nothing would. She had to know there was no way out, so she had to trust me once and for all. I let her go again. She cooperated by walking alongside me to the village where she lived. There were no tricks this time.

"What is your name?" the nymph asked.

I sighed at the question. "I'm not sure. I don't really have a clear memory of my past. All I remember is that I was being pursued by goblins. So now you know, I don't know what my name is."

I noticed the nymph smiling at me. "You do not speak like the dragons I have read about in books. Your accent is much clearer, but I still find it different."

JORDAN B. JOLLEY

I had noticed that when I met the grøls; my accent did not sound the same as the inhabitants of the rest of Pearl Forest.

"My name is Alexia," the nymph said.

"Nice to meet you, Alexia," I replied cordially.

We reached the village of the nymphs at the edge of Pearl Forest. It looked much bigger than the grøls' township. Alexia had me wait where I could see the other nymphs without them seeing me.

"You wait here," she politely directed. "I will go and find my parents. Hopefully, they will believe me… and you. Then we can get someone to help you. Stay where you are."

She left me and joined the other nymphs in the village. The village was made up of small houses and other establishments on the ground as well in the trees. Unlike the grøls, the nymphs did not live inside the trees. There were suspension bridges, vines, and ladders hanging everywhere, connecting the elevated houses. Some of the ladders were made of rope while others were carved into tree trunks. With everything I saw that was nymph-made, they appeared to be one with nature. Nymphs moved back and forth in the canopy.

I soon heard the voice of a male adult nymph from one of the grounded houses, "Alexia. My, you are back so soon. I thought you would stay at the lake."

"Father, we need to discuss something privately. Can we go into our home?"

I watched the two enter their house. I sat down on the soft dirt and waited. As I did, I wondered how far I had to go with my potential nymph guide. I had left my map at the lake's shore, so I could not study it. Alexia soon came out of the house with her father. Both came towards me.

"All right, Alexia, let us put his nice attitude to the test," the father said to her.

I knew they were in the middle of a conversation about me. I stepped out onto the path. Alexia's father nearly jumped out of his skin.

"Oh my! You are… you are here," he gulped.

"How about we take this talk somewhere else?" I suggested.

I followed him away from the village, just off an alternate path that connected to the main road. The father was very cautious. He seemed prepared to flee at any act of aggression.

"All right, dragon. What are you doing here? Do you not know that we nymphs dislike hostile beings? I will not be fooled by any false behavior from your kind, I warn you."

"What do you mean 'my kind'?" I questioned. "I understand that black dragons are usually evil, but I'm not."

The nymph folded his arms. "I see. But for a dragon, dark scales are a mark of evil. I do not mean to sound hostile. I am simply cautious."

I was becoming frustrated for an unknown reason. The father had a right to be cautious, but he seemed too concerned over my scales. I wanted to give him a piece of my mind. Despite the anger bottling up inside me, I held my tongue. I knew I had an issue with anger, but I still had control of my own mind; and I did not want to give into rage. I spoke in a softer voice, "You might be right, sir. Perhaps at one time dark scales meant we were evil, but I'm not evil and I don't want to hurt you. I'm not trying to cause trouble. All I'm asking for is your assistance. If you won't help me, then perhaps you're the selfish one. I don't think that you're that kind of person."

It took a moment for the nymph to answer. "You are right. I agree. I will help you. Now, who do you wish to see?"

I answered him as sincerely as I could. "I'm in a bit of a struggle right now. My mind is not clear, yet I'm seeking something. I know that sounds weird. The fairies told me about it, so I guess it's import-ant. They gave me a map, too. I'm looking for someone to guide me. After I freed the grøls, they mentioned an adventurer by the name of Treetop. Do you know a nymph by that name?"

The father held up his hand. "You freed the grøls from the gob-lins?" It appeared as if some spell entranced him. "So, you want Treetop to help you?" He immediately stepped away from the bush where I noticed a crowd of other nymphs who had witnessed the entire exchange. My eyes widened.

One of the nymphs stepped forward and introduced herself. "My name is Treetop. I am the one you seek. And yes, I trust you. I am willing to help you."

I felt relieved that I would get the help I was looking for. The next morning, when Treetop was ready, she joined me at the lake. I found my map and retied the willow branch around my abdomen. Before I rolled up the map, I examined it with my new companion.

"It looks like we have to go due east, into the swamplands," Treetop said. "I would be careful. I have heard vicious and aggressive monsters infest that land. The most infamous are the ogres. They do not bother us because we are just inside Pearl Forest, and rarely do we venture into their land. I have only been in the swamps once in my life."

I rolled up the map and fastened it through the willow branch. "Don't worry, I'll keep us safe."

We started our trek down the eastern road instead of the southern path that lead to the nymph village. Nothing stood in our way. I did not know things were about to change for the worse.

Clouds covered the swamplands. The road was muddy. The low-hanging trees made the area dark. Various insects buzzed around my ears. The smell was foul, even for a dragon. I did not like this swamp in the least. Suddenly, I heard a strange moaning in the distance, as if someone was about to be killed.

"What was that?" I asked.

Treetop scratched her head. "I have traveled long and far. Never before have I heard a sound like that. They could be ogres. Prepare to fight." She pulled out a dagger and hid behind me.

The moaning was heard again, followed by footsteps that eventually became louder until it sounded as if someone was right beside us.

"Show yourself!" I demanded with a sprinkle of courage. "Answer me now!" For some reason, my vision did not seem as sharp as it should be. "Stay with me, Treetop, I'll protect you," I said.

She did not answer. My vision got even worse. I felt as if my internal organs had turned to ice. There was no sound except for the insects until I heard a low and faint voice.

"A promise is a promise. You shall be banished to the outside."

I had heard that voice before. It belonged to the goblin that I had defeated while freeing the grøls. I was about to turn to Treetop when the poor nymph screamed. I blew a ball of fire for light.

"Treetop! Are you okay? I won't let them take you. I won't! Where are you, goblin? Talk to me now!"

I got into a defensive position, then I heard the words "Too late!"

Before I could do anything, the air was filled with an odor alien to me. It felt like my nostrils were frying. I tried to jump forward to save Treetop, but the world around me fell into a spiral, making me very nauseous. Before my vision turned completely black, I envisioned what was yet to come.

Rock-hard buildings burned and the blood of innocents flowed throughout a city. I realized that it was a torn-up city, possibly the place I was about to encounter. Then it happened... I only saw darkness. I was in a small area, like a box. People freed me. I wanted to make peace with them, but I could not control myself. I began attacking the humans, one by one. I even fought with you, Clipper, against my will. I would never attack a human, let alone another dragon who cared for me. After ranged weapons started hurting me, I escaped to an island that was infested with jungle. I thought that that would be a fitting place to be, since it reminded me of the swamp. Somewhere in the back of my mind, I expected to find Treetop. I searched around until I had to admit that Treetop was not to be found. I had a tremendous headache and I could not even walk straight for the moment. When you found me, Clipper, I thought people were still trying to kill me.

Clipper tried to calm me down after I began crying again. "Jacob please, stop."

"I have no idea how you know me," I whimpered. "You treat me like we've known each other for years. I don't even think that my name is Jacob."

"We *have* known each other for years," said Clipper. "Believe me. Your name is Jacob Draco. Your last name suits you well. We're best friends. I'm not lying!"

"But, why don't I know you?" I asked.

"We help people. We're friends with Sergeant Nelson. I'll explain later who he is, but we've been fighting for good. Fighting for good! You must remember, Jacob. We were once humans like him until…"

"We were once human?" I said in disbelief.

"That's the truth!" exclaimed Clipper. "We were turned into dragons by our own formula during a science experiment. Dragons used to roam this world, but they disappeared. We're the ones who will end a dark force, the Monolegions. You are very important!"

I blinked away some of my tears. "It sounds like we've been through a lot. But I still don't want to be here. I want to go back to Pearl Forest."

Clipper looked down at his feet, shaking his head. "Jacob, you have to remember. You *want* to be right, but you're not. You have to tell yourself you're wrong. You taught me that already. I know you want to go back, I understand. But we must do something first. For now, your home is here. Do you remember your roommate Chang, or Sally and Reno? We have been through so much. Trust me, when this is all over, we'll figure this out."

His words meant little to me. What he said sounded believable, except that I had no way to connect it to my past. I wanted to go back to Pearl Forest as soon as possible to save Treetop. Clipper was about to give up when he thought of something else. "Okay, this is a test to see if you've completely lost yourself. What noise do you love to hear?"

Confused, I thought of an answer. It took me a moment before I thought of something. "I love the sound of distant thunder during a light, spring rainfall when the land turns green."

Clipper's ears stood up. "That's good. I always knew you loved the sound of thunder. You told me that before. You love it just as you love basketball. Do you remember playing basketball?"

I swallowed, thinking about what he said. "Fleeting images dance in my head. I don't know, but it sounds like something I'd enjoy."

"You see, you *do* have a slight memory of your former life. You're coming back to your true life here."

I bared my teeth and recoiled. "What you're talking about is not my 'true' life! My true life is in the peaceful Pearl Forest in my world of Elsov."

Clipper sat down in distress. Bringing me back was going to be no easy task. With nothing to say, he thought of my story of Pearl Forest. I could see in his eyes that he pictured the night sky, the grøls, the nymphs, and the different lands and terrain I had mentioned on the map.

"You said Pearl Forest is on Elsov. I think the old man in Georgia mentioned that place."

I did not know what he meant by the old man in Georgia. "He mentioned Elsov?"

"I'm pretty sure he did," said Clipper. "The dreams I've had… Elsov…" He paused for a moment. "I'm sure we'll find out."

Throughout the voyage, Clipper kept on repeating the word "Elsov". I was not sure what was going on in his head. It seemed like he was sorting out a big, complex puzzle. Whatever he was doing, it clearly bothered him a lot. Later in the day, the boat landed on the coast of Komodo Island.

"What are we doing here?" I asked him when we disembarked.

"This is where we left off," Clipper said. "You lost your memory on this island during a battle against the Indonesian rebels, a part of the Monolegion army. This was only a few nights ago. They're still here, so be prepared for a surprise attack."

My head hurt as I tried to comprehend his words. "Indonesian rebels? Monolegion army? What does this all mean? You said a few nights ago. My memory of Elsov lasted several days."

Clipper sighed with frustration. "All this means is that there are dwarves, evil ones. Just watch out for any attacks. You can handle it."

"I know what dwarves are. I can't explain why," I said. "The only ones here are evil? That's sad."

I followed Clipper inland. He appeared alert for anything. He glanced from side to side as if someone was hunting us. If he was right about these dwarves, then we *were* being hunted. After traveling down a rugged road, we reached what looked like an empty outpost. Clipper appeared to be confused, yet he said nothing. In the area, lay the remains of a building that had been destroyed by fire. All that was left were some charred outer walls.

"This place looks much different than before," Clipper said, "and you're responsible for that shed's destruction."

I sniffed around the black walls. "I did? Why did I destroy it?"

Clipper was about to explain when he was interrupted by a low, rumbling noise. I saw Clipper fold in his legs into crouch. "Get down," he warned.

I copied his action, assuming that he was protecting himself from whatever created the noise. A sorry looking vehicle rumbled into view, following the road around the island. Several short men in mythical Viking dress were seated inside. I was both boggled and amazed at their way of transportation.

"They didn't spot us. Good," Clipper said when the vehicle left. "Jacob, come with me. We need to find out where that Jeep came from. Just follow me and you won't get lost."

I was about to question him again, but I realized that he trusted me to be his ally. As we flew into the sky to follow the Jeep, I had thoughts ran through my mind. I had been a little stubborn with Clipper. After my story, he still thought I was his long-time friend. He trusted me. He also seemed concerned about Elsov. There was some connection between our two worlds. I knew it. He knew it.

"I assume those were dwarves in that Jeep?" I asked.

Clipper flew closer to me so he did not have to yell. "They were Monolegions, yes. Dwarves."

"I think I understand that part."

The Jeep moved quickly, but slow enough that we had to circle behind it. We stayed close to the ground and behind it to prevent being seen. The Jeep pulled into a clearing at the center of the island.

"So that's where their other base is," said Clipper when we landed. "Stay with me, Jacob. We don't want to get caught."

Following his lead, I kept a low profile. I did not let Clipper out of my sight. Getting lost or captured was something I did not want to deal with. There was already too much confusion. I struggled through the jungle floor, which was covered in thick trees and creepers. Staying behind Clipper was not too hard until a sharp pain entered my head. It was not a physical pain.

Clipper stopped when he saw me. "Are you all right?"

"I'll be fine," I said, blinking.

"Okay, you stay here and I'll infiltrate the area," said Clipper. "It'll be better if only one of us goes in. You're going to get your memory back, I promise."

I sat down and waited for Clipper to leave. When he was out of sight, a feeling of loneliness crept in. If only I knew Treetop was safe, I would feel much better. I fervently wished that I were back on Elsov so I could rescue her. She was in trouble because of me. But if Clipper was right, was Elsov even real? But if it wasn't, why was Clipper so bothered by Elsov?

CLIPPER TRIED THE BEST HE COULD TO AVOID THE GUARDS. He came across a number of ancient biplanes and military vehicles. *How had the Monolegions had acquired them?* he wondered. He chose not to dwell on it for long, for he knew he had a mission to complete. Eventually he came upon a large building made of bamboo in the middle of the base. Clipper slipped through the open doorway and down the hall.

At the end of the hallway, he came to a dark laboratory that was overgrown with vegetation. Curiosity struck Clipper when he found a small chest on one of the tables. It almost looked like a miniature treasure chest. Clipper glanced at both ends of the hallway to make sure he was alone, then he sank his teeth in the soft, wooden door-frame. He entered the laboratory after scraping off pieces of wood that had stuck onto his sabered fangs. He opened the chest and examined several different capsules. He inspected each one when he heard a nearby door opening. Clipper rushed to one of the far corners. Two dwarves walked in, one of them using an albore to produce light. They missed the rip in the doorway since there was no actual door to begin with. One dwarf was the Monolegion that Clipper knew was the new leader of the base: Longbeard. The other Monolegion wore a white overcoat and was speaking to Longbeard. "Here's my proof," said the dwarf in the overcoat. "Enough of Tri-athra's potion to be used on the sabered dragon."

"For being a sorcerer and not a potion-maker, he did an excellent work," said Longbeard. "To think that not long ago our central power was confined to the Guarded Forest. Now here we are, making this a part of our dominion. Our magic is a useful tool. With this potion, we will be unstoppable. Those dragons will regret running our families out of their homes."

"It gets better," said Longbeard's companion. "In case one of our own kin gets infected by a similar substance that affected the black dragon, I have been working on an antidote. We should always be ready for an incident, despite the slim chance. It's sort of an anti-potion in a thick, liquid form. I only have one vial for now. It's in the chest. More of the antidote will be created soon."

The word "antidote" thoroughly excited Clipper. As the two dwarves walked out of the room, Clipper crawled over to the chest and opened the lid. He found a glass vile labeled: ANTIDOTE. The substance inside was thick and gooey, almost like the potion that had turned him into a dragon. Only this potion did not change color, remaining yellow.

This is perfect, Clipper thought. He grabbed the vile gently between his teeth and retreated back to the jungle.

CLIPPER RAN TOWARDS ME WITH THE DELICATE VILE IN HIS MOUTH, snickering with delight. He sat down next to me and dropped the container into his paw. Using his claws, he sliced off the lid. Inside was the thick, yellow liquid.

"Here," he said. "Drink this potion."

He gave the vile to me. I could see the disgusting slime inside. I looked at Clipper and grimaced. "Will I remember Elsov? Will I remember that I need to save Treetop?"

"Yes. We'll go back there together. Now just drink it," he said politely.

I lifted the vile over my mouth. The substance slithered down my throat. I cringed from the awful taste, waiting for a change. Nothing happened. I blinked. Everything remained the same. There was nothing new in my limited memory.

"Jacob, do you remember Reno?" Clipper asked in certainty.

I thought long and hard, but nothing came; not a speck of memory. I shook my head. "I don't know. Maybe I am right. I still believe my home is Elsov." I bowed my head and started to feel the stinging guilt for the loss of Treetop again.

Clipper clawed the side of a tree beside him, growling in anger. "This is an antidote! It was supposed to work! Why isn't it?"

"Maybe they didn't make it properly," I said. "Or maybe I'm right after all."

Clipper was going to say something, but no words came out of his mouth.

"Are you okay?" I asked.

"Jacob, I know you want to go home," he said softly. "I've had dreams of a place like Elsov. You're not the only one who wants to go there. I know why you want to return. I dreamt of everything you've spoken of in your vision. I saw the nebula and even Alsov in the night sky. But, I didn't know what it all meant until now. I didn't know what Elsov meant until now."

"If this is true, and I'm sure it is, how does this fit with my other past that you talk about?" I said.

Clipper sounded like he was choking on his words. "I don't know. I think even Chang mentioned Elsov… Now I know! The old man! He said that we came to this world to stop a dark force. He mentioned Elsov… Yes he did! Maybe, maybe Elsov is our true home. Don't worry, Jacob, when the Monolegions are a thing of the past, we'll learn more about this."

I now understood how close of friends Clipper and I were. "I'm starting to think you're right. Maybe I did lose my memory. Everything you say is blurry, but that doesn't mean you're wrong."

Clipper blew a small puff of smoke. "We'll go back there together when we can. But first, let's live here: our other home. Let's hurry and get our job done."

CHAPTER 33

A SLIVER OF HOPE

I knew the dwarves would come searching for us once they discovered the antidote was gone. Clipper told me that the officer Longbeard would be looking for us. Sooner than we expected, we heard shouting from among the base. The dwarves spotted us and formed three lines around us. Luckily, there were only seventeen in the entire base.

First arrows whizzed towards us, then the gunshots. The sound of the rifles rang in my ears. It was almost unbearable. One bite of a bullet told me there was nowhere to go until the area was clear. Finally, came the albores' spells, summoned by two dwarves. Green balls of light burst above me, followed by the balls of lightning. My current situation made me frantic for relief. Lightning kept zapping me. If I moved, arrows or bullets would strike me. I had to act fast to escape the enemy fire.

As I climbed over a dirt mound, I let out a breath of fire over my enemies. Several more Monolegions appeared to replace their fallen comrades. I blew another large flame in their direction that sent them diving for cover. Clipper rushed in and claimed the area, taking out the two with the albores. The fighting was fierce, but short. The Monolegion soldiers knew there was no way out due to the fire and surrendered.

Longbeard did not realize he was the only one left. He exited the nearby building, only to be cut off by us. He tried to sound brave. "Go ahead and kill me," he said. "It will just be one more casualty.

You may have conquered this island, but you will never beat us in the end. Triathra will stop you."

"My red-scaled friend told me that we conquered another one of your bases on this island," I said. "This is the last base. Not even your magic can save you."

Longbeard did not give up. He aimed a loaded revolver at me. The sight of his weapon infuriated me. With a deep snarl, I did something I never thought I would do: I jumped forward and bit down on his shoulder. My acicular teeth sank deep in his flesh. I flung my head sideways and he tumbled off to the side. Longbeard wailed, yelling various curses at me. He scrambled up, holding his bleeding shoulder. I spat venom into his eyes. He fell next to the sad carnage of his small army.

Clipper was speechless. I licked the top row of my teeth in dread. "I'm sorry. I never thought I would bite him. I felt anger coursing through me. I couldn't help it."

"Well, that's how I remember you," said Clipper. "You've always had trouble holding back your anger. At least it did some good this time." He suddenly stopped speaking to me and raised his ears.

Before I could ask what he was hearing, a voice came into my head.

"*Victory is nearly yours! This island is in your control. You only need to defeat the sorcerer now. Travel to New York immediately.*"

"Did you hear that?" Clipper asked.

"I *felt* it," I said. "I don't know what that voice was. It wasn't a physical sound."

"It's the spirit," said Clipper. "The dragon of old. He used to live on this Earth. Now he's speaking to us. He wants us to go back to New York. Monty must be there."

I was pleased to hear that, but there was something else bothering me. "That Longbeard one mentioned a name: Triathra. You said Monty."

"Right. Triathra and Monty are the same person. He's still a threat." Clipper's ears drooped when he mentioned the two names, but he was exactly right. The war was not over yet. Our greatest obstacle lay ahead. We still had to defeat the sorcerer of the Monolegions, the one with the Master Scepter: Monty Victor. At the time he mentioned him, I did not recognize the name.

"How powerful is this Triathra or Monty?" I asked.

"Very powerful. He's the one behind all of this," Clipper answered grimly. "And he's the one responsible for your aggression earlier. Just follow me. I know what I'm doing."

"I'm quite aware of that. If not, we would have been killed. I'm happy you're with me, Clipper. I understand why we're good friends."

Clipper felt honored. "For being two friends that made it this far, I'd say we're very loyal to each other."

ROHESIA RETURNED TO THE ROOM WHERE CHANG WAS WAITING. The two had sought safety at a bed and breakfast in Preston. They were not sure if there were more dwarves about, so they avoided hotels in and around Logan. Fatigue was written on Rohesia's face when Chang saw her.

"Looks like you've had a long day," Chang said. "You were gone an awfully long time. What took you so long?"

"I stayed at the library for hours. I believe that educating myself about this era may help our effort to defeat the Nibelungs," said Rohesia.

Chang smiled. "That's a good idea. Well, your day can only get better. I just heard that Jacob and Clipper were successful on Komodo Island. The dwarves aren't all gone, but they're cut off from outside help. Their power will soon be strangled to death. Jacob and Clipper are coming home."

Rohesia took a deep breath. "Victory for us. I feel silly being deceived by the dwarves in my father's kingdom. I never thought they would want to conquer us."

"Good thing that one dwarf cursed us to your castle. If it weren't for that mistake, we would have lost the war before it even started. We were the ones that sent them into Norway just by sending one attacker with a message to his village."

As the two discussed the outcome of the war, the telephone in the room rang. Chang answered it.

"The person who called had a message from Clipper," Chang said when he hung up. "He's telling us to get to New York right away. Clipper says Monty is there, but something happened to Jacob. Clipper said he went crazy and lost his memory. But he's still with us."

Rohesia shook her head. "What's wrong with Jacob? Is he ill?"

"I don't know. He's still our friend, no matter what. We should leave right away. If we do, maybe we can find out where Sally and Reno are. I sure hope they're okay."

Rohesia agreed. Despite her best efforts to calm herself, she was deeply worried about Sally and Reno's fate. If the Monolegion power were being strangled, the sorcerer would become desperate. She feared that something bad would happen to her friends.

CLIPPER AND I TOOK A HELICOPTER TO HONOLULU, FOLLOWED BY a ride in a transport plane all the way to New York. After the airplane had landed and the passenger door opened, the two of us hopped out. I took a deep breath, wincing at the unfamiliar Atlantic smell.

"Where are the friends you mentioned? Shouldn't we be...?" My question trailed off. *Why couldn't I speak?* I wondered. My mind clouded and my vision blackened, despite the bright sun hanging in the sky.

Clipper's voice echoed in my head. "Jacob? Are you all right? Answer me, please!"

As I lay immobilized, I had a glimpse Elsov again. The beautiful fairy who gave me the map appeared before me. A voice spoke to me that was not the fairy's. It was a voice I remembered.

"To find your answers, you must live in the first and second worlds. You must destroy the dark force once and for all. I will give you your memories. They will flow back inside you."

I slowly awoke. I was back in front of Clipper. A ring of yellow fog encircled me. Terror rendered me speechless for a second. A bright flash appeared. I could see Elsov *and* New York at the same time! Then I finally got it. The First Earth was the world where I currently lay my feet. The Second Earth, where I thought was home, was Elsov. All I needed to discover now was the Third Earth.

I also knew who spoke to me. It was the dragon of old! I remembered him. All my previous memories flooded back into my head. I stared at Clipper, my life-long friend. I was back. I remembered!

"It came back to me!" I roared happily. "I'm Jacob Draco! We just beat the Monolegions. Clipper, I remember!"

Clipper's jaws opened into a gigantic grin. Skipping up and down, he gave me a playful smack on my side with his horns. For about a minute, we celebrated and danced. The odd, Atlantic smell was now familiar. I never thought I would appreciate it this much.

But deep inside, I still did not feel at home. I felt the tug on my heartstrings telling me that my true home was Elsov. With my memory back, my vision of Elsov did not feel any less real. Treetop was still in the swamp, still in trouble.

"I'm sorry, Clipper," I said. "Something's not right. I remember everything and I'm glad I'm back, but I know Elsov is real. I still feel like I *need* to go back. I must find Treetop. And not just that, there is something I need to find. This was no dream. I felt the presence. I can still picture Alsov clearly in the sky. It still feels like my real home."

Clipper did not seem at all upset. He blew a cloud of smoke in the air. "Don't worry, Jacob. A promise is a promise. We'll go there once Monty is out of the way."

Fighting back a tear, I nodded.

"When the general told me about the conversation with Chang, he told me that they would be in your old dormitory room," said Clipper.

"Okay, time for a little skyscraper hopping," I said.

Clipper smiled at my comment as we took off into the sky. I was beginning to sound like my old self, apparently.

Hundreds of feet from the ground, the majestic city stretched as far as they eye could see. We flew over various boroughs of New York City, to our college dormitory rooms. We landed on the rooftop and glided down to the grass. This time, several college students noticed us. Most were frozen in shock, others ran away, screaming in fright. We were not bothered by our exposure. There was no time for that.

Chang and Rohesia were in my room to greet us. Rohesia expressed her joy with a pet between my horns. "Oh, how I missed you, my friends!" she said.

I looked around my room, but I did not smile. "Sally's not here. Monty still has her and Reno. How could I forget little Reno? If only she was with me in her true home. Then she would… Sorry, long flight home. You can find some answers while I get some air. I'm feeling a little queasy." I stepped out to the foyer.

"What was wrong with him? Is it a symptom of that potion you told me about?" I heard Chang ask.

Clipper tried to explain. "Well, after his rampage across Jakarta, he was very depressed. He talked about another world where fairies, nymphs, and other creatures live. I know it sounds crazy, but he insists that it's real. I have the same feeling. It feels like our true home and we want to return. It's a world called Elsov."

I thought Chang would not believe Clipper. Surprisingly, he sounded like he did. "I understand. Monty mentioned another place where others like you live when they had me alone in the Guarded Forest. Elsov… yes. I don't think you're crazy at all."

"Elsov," Rohesia said thoughtfully.

"You sound like you've heard the name before," said Clipper.

"When I was but a young girl, my father told me stories about an enchanted place where fairies, elves, nymphs, and even dragons lived. I have always been told that most dragons, save a few, were evil. After Jacob convinced me that he was peaceful, I began thinking about Elsov. In my young age, I no longer believed in the magical land. Now Jacob has shown me otherwise."

I was about to leave the building, but I stayed in the hallway to listen to the conversation.

"For the past few days, I've been having dreams about this place," said Clipper. "At first, I thought that it was just my subconscious telling me a story. Now as I look back, it felt like more than a dream, except it wasn't a vision or 'visit' like Jacob said we went through.

"But since then in my dreams, I've been told by a fairy that I have been a dragon my whole life in your form on this world. It wasn't until I reached the age of eighteen that I would return to my true form. I think that before Jacob and I lived on this Earth, we lived as dragons in Elsov. I think it's true; Elsov is our true home."

"So you and Jacob, my old roommate, hatched from eggs?" Chang began to chuckle. "You weren't a human like us in the first place! You were just in the form. I've got to say... that's kind of funny."

With Clipper's knowledge, he ran out the door of the dormitory room to inform me of his conclusions.

"Jacob, you won't believe it!" he said.

I lifted a paw in the air. "I heard. You think we were born as dragons, on Elsov."

"That's right."

I thought back my dream while in the French prison. "The dragon of old said that we would come to our true home. The old man said it was Elsov. We *will* return once this is all over. It does connect!"

"Like you said, once this is all over. There's business that we need to focus on other than dwarves. I sense that Monty is somewhere in this city, with the scepter in his hands."

"That's a scary thought," I said. "But we can't shrink back in surrender. We've got to give Monty all we have. I sure hope Sally and Reno are okay."

The reminder agitated Clipper. "Me, too."

I made my way to the main door. "Tell Chang and Princess Rohesia we're leaving. Let this battle against Triathra the Sorcerer begin."

Clipper reared on his hind feet in agreement, his wings spread from wall to wall. We both knew the final battle with Monty was nigh at hand. One side would stand, one side would fall.

CHAPTER 34

BATTLE OF MANHATTAN

The layout of Monty's complex remained the same as it was the last time we were there. Clipper followed me to the entrance of the complex. The main room was large and dark. It was an eerie place to be; the only sound was the echo of dripping water. It was the perfect environment for an old nemesis to stalk you. I could not smell Monty, but I watched for him in the shadows anyway.

"We should find the dark tunnel," said Clipper.

"If I know Monty, Sally and Reno will be in the basement where I found the samples," I said. "I really hope so."

It did not take long to find the dark tunnel. Crossing through it was no hassle, but the early evening provided a spooky environment for us. We were in an old, dark building at the approach of night, with the sensation of someone or something watching us. I found Monty's old office, but Monty was nowhere to be seen.

"This is creepy," Clipper moaned.

I ignored his remark. I went to the room with the secret stairway. There was no need to use the hidden handle; it took no effort to break down the door. In the basement, the walls were bare and an unlit bulb hung from the ceiling. Sally was nowhere to be seen.

I hissed with frustration. "I thought they'd be here. Where are they? I hope they're not hurt."

Clipper looked harder and found a well-concealed trapdoor. "This place isn't the basement. There's a bit more than meets the eye."

After opening the enormous trap door, we descended even further. The dusty basement turned into a place that resembled a grim corridor of Saint Cassius Castle. The carpet became cobblestone under our claws. It felt like I was in a time warp when I caught sight of iron maidens, thumbscrews, and cells with skeletons of unknown souls trapped inside. A wooden tub, a noose, and other brutal devices that I dare not describe were littered the area. My hopes of finding my friends alive staggered. My heart ached for them.

We continued searching the dungeon until we reached an iron door. There was no handle and it was shut tight. That did not stop me. Lowering my horns, I charged through the door. I was met with a burning furnace. I found Sally and Reno shackled to the adjacent wall. I could tell they were suffering from heat and hunger. Sally was soaked in sweat. They both looked up at me and smiled weakly.

"Sally! Reno! You're alive!" I cried. I no longer felt the pain of loss.

"You've… You've come to rescue us," Sally said in a weak voice, who was just as happy.

"How's Reno?" Clipper asked.

Sally explained what had happened and that she and Reno had not eaten in days. I tried to unshackle them, but couldn't without the key. I had to get them out of the dungeon as soon as possible. My only solution was the one I loved the best. I placed Reno's chain in my mouth and bit down as hard as I could. With a flame spouting from of my mouth, the chain glowed white until it melted into a liquid state. Clipper used the same technique on Sally's chains, except he did not use fire. Sally hugged the two of us when she was free. Reno slowly crawled onto my back, chattering emotionally.

"Oh, Jacob!" Sally wept. "What happened? Monty told me what he'd done. I was afraid the potion was going to change you.!"

My smile fell. "It did, but it's a long story. As much as I like to tell you all about it, I'll do it later. We need to get you out of here first."

Knowing that Monty was nowhere nearby, we left the complex. Sally purchased some food near a dock. After eating her fill of fish, Reno played in the water. I sat next to Sally on the shore while Clipper kept watch in the air.

"I just knew you'd rescue me," Sally said to me, fiddling with the loose shackles on her wrists. "You always show up when I need you the most."

I quietly smiled while Sally finished her chicken sandwich. I had no need to purchase my food. I had eaten my fair share of fish with Reno.

"I only wish we could've come sooner," I said.

"You weren't too late. You came at the right time. Thanks for saving me, Jacob."

Sally ran her fingers along the side of my nose. My insides felt like they were going to shatter. I was pleased that I could save her. Unfortunately, Clipper interrupted us. He flapped his wings in agitation. "You might want to see this," he said nervously. "I saw something at the top of Rockefeller Center. It could be Monty."

"Sally, you keep Reno. Clipper and I will check it out," I said.

Sally gave each of us a hug. "Good luck. I know you'll beat him." She started crying again as we flew off.

RENO RETURNED TO SALLY'S SIDE SOON AFTER WE LEFT. THE TWO of us disappeared into the city. Reno watched us leave once again. All she wanted was be with her own kind. Sulking, she begged for the rest of Sally's sandwich after smelling the grilled chicken.

"It's okay," said Sally, giving her a piece, "they'll be back soon."

Reno was not convinced. She wanted to help her two friends. After swallowing the piece of the sandwich. She spread her wings and took flight after us. Sally tried to catch her, but was too late.

"Reno, get back here! You'll hurt yourself."

Reno ignored Sally. She searched everywhere for us. She flew over numerous office buildings until she found a peculiar green glow atop one of the towers. *Perhaps that was the thing Clipper was talking about,* she thought. Reno hovered in midair to keep the strange tower in sight. Squinting her eyes, she spotted us climbing the tower's side. She immediately flew to the observation deck of Rockefeller Center. That was where she saw Monty, holding the scepter in his two hands. The Master Scepter emitted the green glow. Reno realized that Monty was expecting us to reach the top of the building. It was an ambush! He had used the light to attract us. Reno had warned us before we got to the top and met our doom. She tried to remember the words to use. Understanding a few of them, all she needed to do was say something simple. Thinking hard, she remembered what Monty was holding.

"Sss… Sssscepter! Wook out!" she called.

CLIPPER AND I HEARD THE RENO'S CRY AND STOPPED CLIMBING. I prepared to jump off when the wall that we hung from began to quake. We immediately let go and flapped to the roof of another building.

"Who shouted about the scepter?" asked Clipper.

"I don't know," I replied.

I turned to face the Rockefeller Center again. Monty glared at us and starting waving his scepter in a circular motion. Thinking quickly, I jumped in the air just as the roof below me shook violently. Monty attempted shot after shot of lighting, but could not seem to hit Clipper or me.

Enraged, he searched for the one who had alerted us. If not for the warning, Monty may have truly had us. In fury, he cast the spell upon himself to become a demon once again, with the scepter on his back. This time he sprouted wings that were longer than my own. I saw Reno look up in horror. Clipper and I stared in awe. It was a sight I could not bear.

"We've got to get her out of there," said Clipper.

"Where do we go?" I asked.

We both jumped off the edge of the building just as a whirl-wind formed over the spot where we had been. The high wind, following us, nearly blew us off course. Our wings brought us safely to the ground when the whirlwind dissolved. When I looked back up, Monty turned back to the Rockefeller Center and saw Reno flying towards him. Just as she got close enough, Monty raised a giant fist and smacked her out of the air. She fell, unable to use her wings in her position. I took to the air and intercepted Reno's fall. I descended safely to the ground. Reno smiled innocently.

"Thhhh... thane... thank you, Ja... Jacob," she managed to say.

I could not believe my ears. Reno had spoken to me! I lowered my head and rubbed her nose with my own. "Reno, you saved my life. I'm in your debt," I said gratefully.

Our joyful moment was cut short. Monty descended to the ground and charged me. As he was about to grab me with his enor-mous green claws, I dropped into a prone position. Crawling for-ward, I wriggled under his legs and jumped on his back. Wrapping my front paws around his throat, I used my foot claws to dig into his back in an effort to loosen the Master Scepter. Monty, screeching in annoyance, fell backwards on the ground, crushing me. He stood up and kicked me in the ribs. He then picked me back up and threw me into the street where countless pedestrians and motorists ran for their lives, all screaming in terror at the unearthly sight.

"Come and get me!" roared Monty. He jumped high into the air, beat his wings and broke through the side of a window.

Clipper was not looking up to the fight. I could read it on his face as he rushed over to aid me.

"I know you don't want to do this, Clipper, but we have to," I said. "He's blocking our way back to Elsov."

As I spoke, one simple fact burned into my mind. I knew it, Clipper knew it, and Monty had to know it, too.

This was the final battle that would judge the victor between Good and Evil.

I spread my wings and chased after the sorcerer. That proved to be a bad decision. Monty knew I was coming. He pounced on me, dragged me down the side of the building. I stuck my claws into the wall to slow my fall. Losing his grip, Monty slipped away and plunged downwards, but used his new wings to return to the fight. Before I could do anything, he collided with me and we both shattered through the wall, into a deserted office room. Monty was the first back on his feet. He pinned me to the floor. My paws were sprawled while my wings lay flat.

"You may have wiped out most of my Nibelung tribe, but not all of it!" he yelled. His demon voice was far too loud for an enclosed room. "I'll win this fight of ours and restart the tribe. The human race will never know what hit them. First, I have to wipe out the dragons that still exist, starting with you. The rise of the dragon has come to an end!"

He pushed me out of the window where I landed back on the street. Pieces of pavement cracked and jumped from my impact. Monty leapt out and landed next to me.

"This is going to be your bitter end!" he growled.

I tried not to express the pain in my back from the fall. "You're wrong," I said. "The rise of the dragon is just beginning."

The scepter on his back caused a rattle in the ground. The sky turned from bright blue to a clouded, mucky green. The sight made me shudder a little. Using the Master Scepter once again, Monty summoned a deadly looking blade. It looked like it was made of blue ice, but there was some sort of moving liquid inside it that looked thick and viscous, like the potion and antidote I had taken before. Monty pressed the point to my chest, and I knew he was ready to run me through with the cursed weapon.

"A rare thing that can pierce a dragon's hide," Monty laughed. "I've spent all this time trying to get you out of my way. I hate to say this, Jacob, but I now find it necessary to kill you."

Just as he got a good hold on the emerald-green handle, Clipper jumped in the way and attacked Monty with his horns. Both friend and foe fell beside me. Unaware of the sword's nature, Clipper jumped on Monty once again. I tried to stop Clipper, but I was too late. Monty swung his sword. The blade slid across Clipper's chest. Clipper collapsed bleeding profusely. Forgetting about the world around me, I rushed over to help my friend.

Clipper gasped for air. "It hurts so bad! I can hardly move." He tried to say more, but he closed his eyes and lay silent. I shook him. He did not wake.

A river of tears left my eyes. "Clipper, wake up. No!"

I held a paw over his mouth. He was breathing, though I did not know how long he would last. My grief was unbearable. He wanted to go to Pearl Forest with me. That was his promise.

Loathing the sorcerer for what he had done to Clipper, I stood up and searched for Monty. Going to Clipper would have made me vulnerable. There was no sign of Monty, however. I turned back to my wounded friend. "Don't worry, Clipper. I'll stop Monty. You'll make it, I'm sure. I'll find Monty... I'll find Triathra."

I continued to search but I could not find him. I was starting to get angry when I heard a familiar voice in my head. It was the dragon of old.

"Clipper is not dead, he is elsewhere for now. He will only return if you complete this task. Have you not noticed: there is no sign of life anywhere near you?"

I slowly spun in a complete circle around the street. The dragon's spirit was right. I was still in the heart of the city, but there was no sign of any living thing. All the trees and plant life on the sidewalks were wilted. Not even Reno was present.

"Where did everyone go?" I asked Monty, knowing he was the only one nearby.

"You're the only living thing up to my challenge, Jacob. You are alone. Not even Clipper is here," Monty answered, still nowhere to be seen. His voice echoed across the dead city.

I heard a noise so disturbing that it made my stomach twist inside me. Many skeletal figures approach me, each armed with an iron sword that flashed dark violet. The sight looked like something straight out of Greek mythology. And they were attacking me! How was Monty able to summon them? I never imagined that Monty had the power to do that.

"Have fun getting past them!" Monty gloated. "They are the souls from the underworld. I've brought them up to get rid of you. This was the nicest way to show you the third world, in my opinion. You will be defeated, and then you'll join them!"

This could not be happening, but it was. I was not ready for these skeletons to scare me into surrender. That was what Monty wanted. My blood raced through my veins. A strong surge of anger stirred in my chest. This was again the wrath that was difficult to tame. I did not bother to try this time. With a roar, I jumped on one of the skeletons and tore its ribs to shards of bone and marrow. I then incinerated several with a good breath of fire, which was my most effective weapon. Burning the army of what Monty had said was from the third and final world was quite easy!

My thoughts turned the other way when a skeleton behind me took a slash at my back leg. I yelped from the sting, releasing a flame that turned the soulless monster into ashes. The slash on the leg could not have been that bad, could it? It was just a sword after all. What damage could it do? As I examined the wound, I realized that it was much worse than I anticipated. There was a big, bloody gash in my leg. I could even see my bone! Moving my leg was pure torture. I almost fainted from the disgusting sight. What kind of blade had the ability to deal this much damage? It was just as dangerous as Monty's icy sword.

I kept an eye on the sword wielded by one of the skeletons that was ready to attack me. The flashing purple color replaced the gray steel.

Keeping humor was one way to distract myself from fear and most especially the pain. I incorporated it into my wrath. "How can you kill me?" I hissed. "You're just rotting pieces of a human body! What makes you so powerful?"

There was no reaction from them. They were intent on striking fear in me. Unaffected by my insults, they advanced. I felt a tingling in my wounded leg and the pain began to subside. No doubt the spirit was helping me.

"Thank you, dragon of old," I called out. "You are here, I know it!"

I was ready to charge back with all my legs healthy. I aimed my horns directly at the skeletons. It was a shame for them; they did not have any reflexes at all. I missed some, yet I sent many undead soldiers flying. Ribs, femurs, and skulls were tossed into the air like plastic toys and clattered on the street.

I raised my head again to cast a flame at the skeletons. I laughed with enjoyment that hid my angst. That was until a blade slammed down beside me. Before my enemy could raise it again, I swiped its skull with my claws like a grizzly bear. Its head flew clean off. The remains of the skeleton stood back up. I used a single snap of my teeth; the arms fell dead and were no longer mobile, but the skeleton still tried to attack me. I dropped the arms and reached for its legs. I bit down on its right femur, crushing it into powder. I ripped off the other leg as well. Only the backbone and pelvis remained, twisting helplessly on the ground. After the damage I had dealt, it was no longer a threat to me. Taking out a few more skeletons with fire and my horns, I realized this was quite fun. Not even my leg gave me problems, thanks to the spirit. I added more and more bones to my pile. As I continued in battle, the sky started to clear a little. A small spot of blue smiled at me. Taking out another skeleton, I tore off the arm and lifted it in air and roared in triumph. I threw it aside then searched for more skeletons.

I felt like I was winning. All was well when my triumph was suddenly interrupted. Monty showed his demon face, standing in front of me. "So, you want more, eh? You will never see your friends again, I'm afraid. They'll end up like your human father... dead!"

His statement got to me. "That storm may have taken my human father's life and everything I loved. It destroyed my childhood, but you won't destroy me as a dragon. I was always a dragon. I have always been a dragon, and you can't change that in any way!"

He should have known I had a short fuse. He laughed an emotionless laugh. "You'll never live in the first world again. You will now face the depths of the prison for spirits. I respectfully call it Purgatory, a part of the third world."

I was about to send a flame to him when I felt a slimy rope wrap around my hind legs. I tripped and fell on my front, being dragged away from my mortal enemy.

"Farewell, Jacob," the sorcerer said. "With you out of the way, I'll have the Monolegion army rise again under my power. The human race here has no dominance over this Earth. They will serve my king."

I always wondered who this king was that he constantly mentioned, but there was no time to think about it. Watching Monty walk away from me, I turned on my back and sat up like the human I once had been. My tail slid in front of me. The black slimy rope dragged me to a pit with hundreds of other ropes ready to pull me down into what Monty called Purgatory. I tried to bite them, but they were too rubbery to break. Fire did not help, either. A small gap emerged from the piles and piles of ropes. I heard the screaming of helpless souls in dire torment.

I had learned about Purgatory from literature classes, and I did not want to endure it. I was being dragged along the paved street, closer to the pit. I panicked.

"Triathra! Clipper! Sally! Reno! Father! Help! Nooooooo!"

It was hopeless. I was heading for endless misery. I had lost the war. The First Earth would be taken over. I shut my eyes, ready to meet my doom when out of nowhere came the voice.

"*Save yourself!*" it called. "*You need to win against evil. It's for every living thing there ever was. Dragons may be evil, but you don't have to be!*"

THE TALES OF DRACO

The voice belonged to the spirit. I remembered the last time he said the last words to me. It was the spirit of truth and good. I knew it.

I heard a different voice. *"Listen to the spirit, Jacob. You are good, now conquer Monty!"*

That was Clipper's voice! He was reaching out to me. I had to win, and to do so, I had to *kill* Monty! I have said this many times already: I would never intentionally take a life. But against something evil and wicked, I had to do it! I raised my elbow blade and ran it across the rope. It snapped. I took too long, unfortunately. More ropes started wrapping around me. One was over my neck, choking me.

I instantly cut that one, plus another, and another. More ropes grabbed me, replacing the ones I cut. It seemed hopeless. I would die just trying to slice myself free! I struggled and squirmed; that did not help. The screaming out of the hellish world was louder than before. One rope crossed my eyes, blinding me. I was having trouble breathing, now I had trouble seeing. All hope was lost, lost in the mist of defeat. I took one final breath before I passed out.

When I exhaled, I also gave whatever flame I had left. I felt about half the ropes melt away. Strange, they had not melted before. I could breath again, but I still could not see. I starting cutting more ropes and let out another flame. Even more ropes gave way. Maybe, just maybe, I stood a chance. Maybe I could make my way out of this. I continued cutting, flaming, over and over. The rope over my eyes vanished, and I could see once more. The sky above started to turn blue again. With just four ropes left, I cut one and flamed the other three. I was free! The open hole to Purgatory began to close and the screaming silenced. I jumped out of the pit just as it shrank to nothing. The world was getting brighter now, but not all the way. The sky was getting bluer, but still had tinges of green. I still had Monty to finish off. I searched and searched until I found him standing in a corner of an abandoned street.

"You just won't give up, will you?" he said.

"When it comes to the freedom and rights of the living, you're right. I refuse to give up. You thought you could drag me to that other world. You failed."

Monty was filled with anger. He must have thought the Master Scepter had given him the power to kill me. He decided to start a fight that was a lot more physical. He raised his fist to strike a blow to my back, but I jumped forward with my horns aimed up. I charged, hitting him in the stomach and he fell onto the ground. As he stood up in pain, I turned around and used my front feet as the pivot point. My hind feet sent him back to the ground.

"Seize him!" Monty yelled to his remaining skeletal army.

Only five bony bodies remained. *This'll take no time at all*, I thought. Spreading my wings, I took to the air. Diving like a peregrine falcon, I halted in midair and flapped my wings, causing a giant wind to blow the skeletons off their feet.

The wind was much stronger than I had expected. It caused my enemies to tumble away.

With the skeletons getting back to their feet, I used another breath of fire. Two of them dropped their swords and burned. I grabbed one of the swords and hurled it like a javelin in the surviving skeleton's direction. The rest of the skeletons fell apart, lifeless.

"Killing *three* birds with one stone," I said, attempting to regain my sense of humor.

Seconds after my final strike to the skeletons, a large, bright flash from the sky caused me to shield my eyes. When I opened them, I saw the sky in its former blue color. The trees were alive with their cheerful green leaves, just as it should be for being late spring. I still could see no people. They all fled; at least life was bright and alive. I was winning the war! I raised a claw of approval to the world around me. It had not been long, but I missed the blue sky.

Finally, I saw Clipper on the ground, slowly waking. Monty was nowhere in sight.

"Clipper!" I roared with excitement.

Clipper groaned from his wound. "What happened? Did I miss anything? Where am I? Am I back in the city? All I remember was that I met these fairies…"

I clawed the street below me, remembering my lost memory with the vision of Pearl Forest. "Not again! I know this place seems strange, but don't worry. I've seen Pearl Forest, too. You may not believe me, but your name is…"

Clipper held up a claw. "Jacob, I know. Don't worry, I didn't lose my memory."

"You haven't? That's a relief."

Clipper scratched the back of his neck with his set of four claws. "Something weird is happening. Like you, I just had a vision of a strange, magical place. Right before I fell asleep, I found a vial sitting next to me. A small, glass vial like the one that had the antidote. I don't know how it appeared there. I picked it up, only to have it shatter. Some of it fell into my wound. Before I knew it, I was somewhere else. I was in a different place, I think it was Elsov."

I paid close attention as he continued.

"Like you said, it was more than a dream. I was actually there! I saw the grøls you mentioned too. I told them about you. They understood! Jacob, my life's been changed. Reborn. They actually remembered you. A fairy told me that someone from their home sent me the liquid in the vile. That's why I found it in the street. She said that it was the same potion used to heal you. The fairy also warned me that you were in danger. I used a special power I never knew was possible. I think I spoke to you."

I fell silent, thinking about Clipper's voice when I was trapped in the pit of slimy ropes, dragging me down to Monty's version of Purgatory, a realm in the third world. My pondering halted when I saw another familiar figure fly around the corner of an office building.

"Reno!" I called. "I'm so glad to see you!" I shed tears of relief as I saw her approaching.

Reno spotted us and landed, letting out a small flame. I placed a paw on her back. After reuniting and touching noses, she clung to Clipper as well. She acted as if she had not seen us for days, and I understood; after my encounter with Monty, I really wanted to see her again. There was no time for a full reunion, though. I knew Monty was somewhere close by. I did not want Reno to get hurt. If she spoke to me, I believed that she could understand what I wanted her to do.

"Okay Reno. Clipper and I have to do something big. I want you to find Sally. Lead her to Chang and the princess. I want you to protect them."

Though a little rusty with words, Reno understood what I had said. She nodded and took off to find the others.

"Triathra is ours," said Clipper. "We can beat him."

CHAPTER 35

ONE FINAL EFFORT

Sally returned to the college where Chang and Rohesia were waiting. Both were glad she was safe. They brought each other up to date about the recent occurrences, but they could not bear waiting for the conflict to conclude.

"When will this end?" Sally groaned.

"We must be patient, they will make it. I know they will," said Rohesia.

Sally tried to think of something else, but failed. "Why doesn't the military do anything about this?" she asked. "Why don't they fight alongside Jacob and Clipper?"

"Dragon's business," said Chang. "That's the term they use. It means that it's something only *they* can take care of, considering what's involved."

"Your soldiers must really trust them, as if they know Jacob and Clipper are going to win the battle," said Rohesia. "Their faith is as strong as mine."

"Faith is what we all should have," Chang said.

Reno interrupted them by swooping through the open window, tumbling harmlessly on the floor. Sally picked her up and hugged her. "Reno, you're not hurt! Thank goodness!"

Reno chattered, imitating other animals. She used the sounds to communicate, everything from a hissing gecko to a moaning baby polar bear.

Sally set her on Chang's bed.

"I believe Reno is trying to speak," said Rohesia.

Reno finally spat out a few sloppy yet pellucid words, "Jagob… and Quibber bofe okay."

Sally's eyes lit up. "She said something! Listen to that, 'Jacob and Clipper are both okay.' Maybe leaving me wasn't so bad after all."

The three laughed. Reno's report allayed their worries about the conflict downtown.

CLIPPER STRUGGLED TO HIS FEET. HE WAS STILL WEARY FROM HIS encounter with Monty's ice blade. We looked everywhere for the sorcerer but found no trace of him, except for the gloomy environment. A few remaining green clouds dotted the sky and nobody else was around. I assumed the military blocked off the area to the public.

"I don't get it," Clipper said, rubbing his wound rather than his fangs. "Why doesn't Monty show himself? He wants us out of the way after all."

I decided to take to the air and scan the skyline. Clipper followed, refusing to look down.

"Do you see anything?" he asked.

I did not answer. I looked left and right, searching for Monty. Soon enough, I found something off in the distance.

"I see him!" I called, pointing. "He's east of us!"

We landed back on the ground. I could see the enervated look on Clipper's face. I could tell he only had a portion of his energy since his injury. Despite his wound, he wanted to help.

"How about you fly up to him?" Clipper suggested. "That way he can see a target. I'll reach the top of the building from the inside. I'll make my way up there while you distract Monty. I think I can handle that."

I did not mind that plan at all. I was up in the air once again, spiraling up the building.

CLIPPER CHARGED THROUGH THE FRONT DOORS, HALTING IN THE lobby. *Which is faster, the stairs or the elevator?* he wondered.

Thinking fast, he picked the elevator so he would not get tired from the stairs. He pressed the button to go up. It took only seconds before the doors opened. Clipper casually walked in when he felt something holding him back: his wings.

"Ugh! I thought even a big person could go anywhere he wants. Why can't I? All I have is just a few extra claws, a tail, and my wings. I guess that's too much now that I say it."

Folding his wings as tightly as possible, he squeezed inside the cabin. He was unable to move after the doors closed. His hindquarters pressed against the far side. Only his forepaws touched the floor. It was a relief when the door opened on the top floor.

I WAS ALMOST AT THE ROOF WHEN MONTY SPOTTED ME. HE USED the scepter on his back to grant his wishes and a bow materialized in his hands with arrows piled next to him. The arrowheads contained the familiar blue fluid, showing that these arrows could kill me if they struck me in the right spot. Monty nocked his first arrow and aimed.

"Why don't you attack me like a real demon?" I taunted.

"I can kill you without moving from this spot," Monty replied. "And I'm about to show you."

Watching as Monty prepared to shoot the arrow gave me just enough time to dodge it. Monty nocked another arrow and fired. He missed again.

"Why can't I hit you?" he muttered.

Clipper eventually reached the top floor and bashed open a window. Sticking his head out over the city, he looked down in terror. He closed his eyes, took a deep breath, then crawled out the window and up the wall. I noticed that his plan was working. Monty was well occupied with me. Clipper waited for Monty to pick up another arrow.

"You'll never beat me, Jacob!" Monty thundered. He summoned another ice blade. Clipper saw what was happening and rushed to the rescue. Reaching Monty just in time, he spat venom and then fire.

As before, the demon was not immune to the dragon's breath. Monty yelled from the pain of the heat. He used the scepter's magic to form an ice shield around himself; real ice this time. I noticed that the scepter on his back trembled when the deep freeze overcame him. It almost slid off when Monty let the shield dissolve. Had the scepter slid off, it would have made Monty powerless!

An idea came to me. If there was a way to give Monty an arctic blast, the Master Scepter might just fall off!

I had to first make a quick getaway if I wanted to get the tools I needed. I leapt in the air and landed on top of Monty's shoulders. Just to make sure, I tried to claw the scepter off his back. That did not work. The scepter seemed to be practically a part of his body.

Monty jumped to the side and prepared to plunge the ice blade at my throat. As he did so, Clipper jumped in the way. The blade reopened his previous wound. He fell onto his side, the damage even deeper than before. Blood spread across the tarpaper roof where it joined the water from Monty's melted ice shield.

"Clipper! Not again!" I cried.

"That fool of a dragon made a fatal mistake," Monty jeered. "Now you and that infant of yours will be at my mercy. You will not win."

As he spoke, I began to form fire in my lungs. I blasted my flame at Monty's face before jumping up and clawing him. Monty fell, giving me time to finish my plan.

But I had to help Clipper. I examined the wound in his chest. His eyes, like last time, were closed. He did not even twitch, yet he was gasping for air.

"Wake up, Clipper. Come on. You can make it."

Clipper's eyes opened halfway. "Jacob, I'm hurt badly... Defeat Monty for me..."

"I *will* defeat him," I said. "That's a promise. Just *hold on*."

"If I die, you can go back to Pearl Forest with peace."

I wished he had not said that. "Forget it. You're not going to die. We will make it out of here. We'll be free and find Elsov together. We've got to save the world we're in right now. I've got an idea that may work, but I can't do it without your help. You have to find something cold. Whatever it takes: Freon gas, liquid nitrogen, ice, you know. Can you help me?"

Clipper groaned. "I'll try my best. But doesn't the cold make things stick together? I don't want the Master Scepter to do that more than it should."

"I don't know why, but the Master Scepter trembles in the cold," I said. "I'll go to the armory. It's time I make more powder bombs. Meet me there at the armory."

I flew off. When Monty regained his senses, he was after me. Clipper slowly rose to his feet, his weak legs trembling. He was still bleeding from his chest. He had just enough time climb down the wall and find a cold solution, so to speak.

WHEN HE MADE IT BACK, CLIPPER SEARCHED FOR ANYTHING HE could use, despite his groggy and weakened state. His search eventually brought him to the front of the main campus at the Atlantic College of Biology. He charged through the door and entered a laboratory that he recognized.

He searched around for anything useful. There were two tanks of liquid nitrogen in the far corner. He placed the tanks into a cart and wheeled it out of the room with his horns. Once outside, he kept an eye out for Monty and searched for a source of transportation. He found the perfect solution: a large truck with the picture of an ice cream cone on its side that was parked at the curb. Clipper remembered that Freon gas was used to refrigerate the tasty treats inside. All the better.

Clipper quickly stored his equipment in the truck. Moving to the cab, he used all his might to tear off both doors. He was happy to see a key already in the ignition. Climbing inside was nearly impossible, so instead he clung to the outside of the doorway. Only the right side of his body was in the truck. When the engine roared to life, Clipper placed his foot paw on the gas pedal. His front claws gripped the steering wheel. He kept his wings close together as the truck moved forward. The agony from his wound did not give him much confidence. A bad gash in his chest, wind-resistant wings that were hard to fold while moving, and the uneven weight on the truck were all working against him.

He kept his right paw over the pedal. The childish tune from the speaker above tormented him greatly. He pressed his foot on the brake then climbed to the top, crushing the speaker with his jaws. But the roof could not hold his weight. The sheet metal tore away and he fell back inside the cab. His wings kept hold on the broken windshield and the rear side of the cab. The force yanked at the joints in his wings. Clipper cried out. He fought back tears of pain. He crawled out and returned to his side-hugging stance. This time there was no roof. He was covered in tiny cuts and shards of glass were embedded in his bleeding wings. *When will this end?* he thought.

CLIPPER HEADED FOR THE ARMORY TO RENDEZVOUS WITH ME ONCE he got his bearings. Things were working out on my side as well. I reached the armory and found the ingredients for the powder bombs. I loved the fact that no one knew how to construct the bombs except for me.

They piled up one by one in my knapsack that I had picked up at the dormitory rooms. My friends had been quite happy to see me, even briefly. I took my bombs outside the armory and waited for Clipper. While I waited, I heard a loud roar above me. That was Monty.

He swooped down to attack. Tossing the knapsack aside, I ran back inside the armory. Monty bashed through the glass doors after me. The main foyer divided into two hallways. I was at the wall while Monty strode towards me, his demon face as ugly as could be. I was glad he paid no attention to the knapsack I deserted.

"So, you decided to hold your ground rather than flee. Are you surrendering to my sorcery? I won't offer any mercy."

He prepared to produce another ice blade when a sudden crash off to my side caused us both to jump. Monty and I turned. An armored truck crashed through the wall, destroying it. A lone figure jumped out of the cab and ran away.

When Monty turned around to battle against the metal monster, I used the opportunity to breath flame on his back. Monty turned back to me. He lifted me into the air and tossed me down one end of the hallway. With me out of the way, he smashed the fender of the truck with one strong blow.

Puffed up with pride, Monty left the foyer and jumped onto the roof. He was greeted by a surprise. It was a surprise to me, too. Reno swooped out of nowhere, showing off her capability to breath fire as she sailed past her target. The tenacious little dragon had joined the fight. She must have followed me when I left the dormitories.

"I had her imprisoned once. I'll get her back," yelled Monty.

"You won't get her ever again," I hissed grimly. I doubted he even heard me.

Emitting a loud roar, Monty summoned a brownish vapor. I did not even ponder if it was another curse or not. I jumped out of the hole in the wall. The spell seemed to have a mind of its own. It followed me wherever I went. I was doing the best I could to avoid it when I heard another truck's engine. I found Clipper holding onto the side of the ice cream truck as he fought for control of the steering wheel. The truck lurched to a halt after hitting the curb in front of the armory. I turned around to return to the battle, but Monty was gone again. I explained the rest of my plan to Clipper with the extra time we had.

"I'm still bleeding from my chest and my joints hurt from that ride!" Clipper exclaimed. "I'm done with it." His anger faded. Lethargy came over him. "Jacob, I don't know if I'll make it."

I started panting in anxiety when he said that. "Clipper, don't worry. You'll be okay."

Clipper kept his eyes on the armory. He coughed out a hot cinder and continued speaking in a groggy voice. "Like I said before, when I got hurt that first time, I had a vision of Elsov. I remember the fairies telling me that you were there with no memory. I also remember the grøls, nymphs, and even the goblins. Everything you described there I saw, plus more. Inside Pearl Forest, I heard the singing. Those little specks of light were hypnotizing. I saw Alsov in the night sky."

I closed my eyes at his description. The vision came back to me.

"The only thing that was different from your adventure was that I had my memory," Clipper continued. "I still remembered my name and where I came from, though I had the same feelings you had, Jacob. I believe we were dragons the whole time, just in human form. I wish I was in Pearl Forest, on the Second Earth."

His words moved me. I had the same desires. I, too, wanted to live in Elsov. "You're not going to die," I said. "Let's get Monty and then we'll go there. You promised we'll find a way back to Pearl Forest. We both promised we would."

Clipper smiled. Some of his energy slowly came back. "Great. What do we need to do now?"

"I know you don't feel up to it, but you have to get our equipment up to the roof of the next building."

"That'll take multiple trips," said Clipper. "How can I do that without Monty noticing me? I'll die for sure!"

"Clipper, listen to me," I said with a firm growl. "I know you're hurt. I know you're bleeding, but I know you're up to this. I know you'll survive. You're a dragon, remember? You have the power, Clipper. You can do it."

Clipper said nothing else. I took flight. Listening closely, I heard Monty in the distance. The sky had changed once again. The setting sun disappeared into a starless night sky. A cloud, violet, not green this time, started to swirl in a supercell-like fashion around Liberty Island. It was impregnated with deadly spells. Whatever Monty was doing, it did not look good.

"So, that's where you are," I mumbled.

"Not quite," said a low voice. "I come and go so I can get my spell in order."

Monty appeared from behind me and grabbed my neck with his long, monstrous claws. Hissing, I barked out a flame just in time. Clipper, watching from the ground, struggled to his feet. He started unloading the Freon and liquid nitrogen from the truck. Monty noticed him and prepared to attack.

I continued with my plan of action. I had to distract Monty from Clipper. Diving down to the sorcerer, I made several deadly swipes at Monty with my claws. I fought differently this time. I never thought I would fight with such aggression since my insanity at Jakarta. I fought like a true dragon. I bit, scratched, and fought, dare I say, dirty.

CLIPPER PAID NO ATTENTION TO THE FIGHT. HE WAS BUSY TAKING the first canister of gas to the top of the office building. He held the canister with the claws on his rear feet. After reaching the top, he lay on the roof from nausea.

"As big as Monty is now, I don't even know if the Freon will do anything. The nitrogen should." He dropped the canister and swallowed hard. "Whatever blade he used, it sure did something."

With his wound, he did not feel ready to take the two tanks of liquid nitrogen. Making sure the coast was clear, he fluttered back down to the truck. His back claws hooked to the knobs on the tanks and he started flying back up.

As I saw Clipper making his way up, I fought even more aggressively than before. I was determined to not let victory slip from our grasp. We only had one shot or the long war would result in a catastrophic defeat. Fighting the dwarves, even the ones with albores, was nothing compared to Monty.

While my eyes were on Clipper, Monty got a hold of me and threw me onto the concrete. The impact hurt, but it could have been worse. That gave me another idea. I pretended to have been seriously wounded. I was on my back, wailing in false pain.

"What's the matter? Getting too tired?" Monty goaded. "It looks like you're not prepared for what's next. My Nibelung army will rise again." He bent down to meet my eyes. "This little uprising of yours will haunt you for the rest of your life. Vesuvius will bring death to you."

When he leaned closer to me, I latched my claws onto the back of his demon head. Monty tried as hard as he could to free himself, but I did not let go.

"I'm just getting started," I said.

My surge of adrenaline gave me power that was stronger than any magic the Master Scepter could muster. Monty whispered to the scepter to get rid of me. The muscle in the back of his neck soon gave away. Monty fell facedown into the street. Looking beyond, I caught a glimpse of two police cars blocking off the street.

"Make sure no one enters this area!" I called to the officers. "This is a very dangerous situation!"

They responded by alerting other officers to keep a strict guard around the perimeter of the battle zone. Police cars and other personnel blocked the street. It was a good idea, if I may say. I wondered what the average person would think of a dragon versus sorcerer battle.

When Monty tried to get back up, I jumped on his back and pinned him down with my four paws. I knew I could not physically remove the scepter from his back. Except from the user's command, or something cold, it would not remove itself. I needed the icy air and fast!

Keeping Monty helplessly squirming on the ground, I checked on Clipper's progress. My hope drained when I saw his condition. It was not good.

CLIPPER WAS EXHAUSTED FROM THE VERTICAL FLIGHT. ABOUT three quarters of the way up, he could bear no more. His wings failed him. Clipper grabbed the sill of a window just in time. He dangled on the wall with his foot paws still holding onto the two containers. The roof appeared to be so far away.

"Augh! I can't make it. I'll fail Jacob. But I can't. I can't let Monty win!"

He tried to climb, only to find no other places to hold. His claws were slipping. "I've been afraid of heights my whole life. Now I'm going to die from it!"

Clipper started panting. He was in a bad situation. Just as he was about to let go, a mental picture reached his mind: Elsov. He remembered Elsov and how he longed for a visit. Along with the picture of Elsov, a voice rang in his head, "*Apply. You are a dragon now. Dragons are evil, but you are not. Don't let your outer evil win.*"

Clipper bared his teeth. "Spirit, I know you're here." Knowing the dragon's spirit was with him, he gained courage. He set his eyes on the roof above. This time it seemed closer.

"I can do it," he huffed. "I can do it. I won't let Monty win."

Knowing that the only way up was one step at a time, he dug his right set of claws on a ledge. He did the same with the left set. One after the other, he moved to the top. The tanks he was holding with his bottom claws gave him no trouble.

"I can do it," he said again. "I'm going to."

Clipper was no longer thinking about death. He was thinking about the life ahead of him. He continued climbing until he found himself on the roof. There he dropped the tanks and stretched his back legs. He took a deep, fiery breath and examined the wound on his chest. The gash was still there, but the bleeding had stopped. This gave him even more hope.

MONTY LET OUT A GROWL AND SET HIS SIGHTS ON CLIPPER. I FOL-lowed him to the top as I had intended. I was very relieved to see that Clipper had made it. To keep Monty down for a few more seconds while I joined Clipper, I decided to use one of my powder bombs to distract him, followed by a flame. But I had left the powder bombs back in the armory! Roaring with anger, I only used fire instead.

Monty jumped back down to escape the heat. I pumped my wings hard to make my vertical climb, desperate to beat Monty to the top. Reaching the roof, I landed alongside Clipper. Monty flew up after me.

"Get ready," I warned. "We've only got one shot at this."

I grabbed the four tanks of nitrogen while Clipper handled the Freon gas. With one tank in my paw, I walked on my hind feet to the edge of the roof. This was nerve-racking. We only had one chance.

"Steady," I said. "Get ready."

Seconds later, Monty appeared from below. Before we could take action, however, he took off, rocking in the air like a vulture.

"Catch me if you can!" he shouted. "Did you really think I would fall for your cold trap? The statue out in the water is going to give me strength that will make you two cry like hatchlings!"

I hissed. The perfect shot and we missed the chance! Monty flew far out until he was a mere speck. I caught sight of him landing on Lady Liberty's torch. How absurd! He was using the symbol of freedom as his spawn-point for evil!

I looked at the sky above the statue and felt sick. The clouds were circling and churning around the torch. If I wasted any more time, the world as I knew it would end. As I jumped off the roof, an electric shock from the sky met me. A bolt of lightning reached down and zapped me. This lightning was much more potent than the little lightning balls created by the dwarves. I crash-landed in a painful roll.

The sky was turning a purplish, greenish color. Monty must really love those colors. The thunder sounded like a growl similar to mine. A sound I often enjoyed hearing, the thunder, was the sound that was stopping me.

"He's using his dark magic to strike me down. It's not too late. I won't let him win," I vowed.

Standing back up, I found myself near a sporting goods store that was completely abandoned due to the fight. I asked myself, what would happen if I launched myself into the air? Would that work? Probably not, but if I did not try, Monty may have won the battle and possibly the war! If he won, his dark force would spread throughout the world. I could not let that happen.

Bashing through the glass of the sporting goods store, I looked for one particular thing: bungee cords. Grabbing two of the long, elastic ropes, I climbed to the top of a tall construction crane that looked directly at the Statue of Liberty. Latching one end of the bungee cord to the braces on the boom, I looked to my left. Another crane was in the exact same position. Strapping the other bungee cord on the other boom, I tied both ends together. I now had a slingshot; and I was going to be the missile.

Leaning back on the center of the two cords while keeping anchored on a flat roof, I stood on two feet and stepped backwards until the line was stretched to the limit. I glared straight ahead at the statue's torch. Monty was there, and I was sure he was ready to revive his skeletal army, or dwarves, or something just as deadly.

"Here I go," I said. "This is for freedom! *This is for Elsov!*"

I launched myself forward. The wind roared past me as if I was on a roller coaster. The bungee tactic worked! Lightning bolts reached after me. I soared through the air, my wings angled straight back. Nothing could stop me, or so I thought. I was going a little too fast, headed down. Just as my plan was about to be foiled, my body swerved sideways and crashed into an open window. I stopped in front of an office desk, sighing with anger.

"I was nowhere *near* the harbor!" I huffed.

Without a second thought, I jumped back out the window and took flight, only to realize what the consequence would be. I could get struck down at any second! I shut my eyes, expecting the excruciating shock.

No charge zapped me. Opening my eyes again, I looked around. Bolts were touching down in several places, but nowhere near me. I knew the lightning was under Monty's power. It was not headed for something conductive so it must be after a certain target. Why was it not striking me? Looking around the buildings, I spotted Reno clinging to the side of a skyscraper. She was creating a diversion to protect me. Monty could not hit her when she was up against the wall.

Without hesitating, I flapped my wings as I came nearer and nearer to Monty's location. The lighting suddenly ceased reaching for Reno as Monty a turned his attention back to me. I had to make the first move as I reached the torch. I clawed, spat venom, and coughed out a blaze, but nothing seemed to work this time. I veered off course and started falling back down to Earth. I used my wings to regain control.

"You won't win this one!" Monty called.

Just then, he caught a glimpse of something behind me. I spun around in mid-flight to see where he was looking. Clipper had joined the fight. Monty smiled, exposing his monstrous teeth. A fight with Clipper would be too easy. Clipper was injured, giving Monty the upper hand. As he flapped his way to Clipper, back to the city, I exhaled the scorching radiation in Monty's direction. Roaring in anger, he landed on top of a lesser office building near the harbor. First fire, now ice, I thought. Clipper was attempting to lure him back to our trap. Monty must have realized that. He was after both Clipper and me.

"You won't win this one!" he yelled again. "Even if you kill me, the Wrath of Vesuvius will come down on you!"

As he approached Clipper, he was right where I wanted him to be. I landed on the roof next to the tanks.

"Fire!" I roared.

Ironically, the phrase "fire" created an intense blast of frozen air when I released the tank of liquid nitrogen. Startled, Monty fell to the rooftop in front of us. At that exact moment, Clipper sprayed the nitrogen all around Monty's back. The Master Scepter quivered then rolled off. Monty began to shrink to his former size. The sorcerer attempted to do one last bit of damage as a demon. He saw the scepter next to him and was about to retrieve it. Reno swiftly snatched it away as she flew by.

All was lost for Monty. He helplessly morphed back into his normal self. Writhing around on the rooftop, he unintentionally rolled off the edge of the building. I heard Monty screaming as he fell. The scream got to me. As much as I loathed Monty, I could not let him fall to his death. I dove off the edge as well. I intercepted his fall and he landed on my back. Gliding out of control, I crashed into the side of a building just five feet above the ground. Monty hit the ground. He was bleeding from where he had met my spikes. It looked like his arm was broken as well. Cradling his arm, he made a cowardly dash away from me.

Now the war had truly turned! I was after *him*, not even running at half my top speed. I gained on him, but his head start gave him just enough time to enter the closest building. Sadly, he ran into the wrong one. He had run into the burning armory in what appeared to be sheer panic, though I did not know for sure.

As Monty dashed through the flames, his foot caught the strap of the knapsack filled with powder bombs. He tripped and fell to the floor next to the boiler room door. He sat back up, filled with fury. Viciously pulling the strap of the knapsack from his ankle, he fell into the burning boiler room.

By the time I reached the armory, it was too late. The fire caused the powder bombs to explode, taking the boiler room with it. That particular section of the armory burst in fire and sparks. I ducked to avoid the flying debris. I looked back up when all I heard was the roar of the massive fire. Clipper joined me in front of the burning armory, followed by Reno.

Immediately after the explosion, the swirl of clouds over Liberty Island blew away in the evening breeze. I felt the breeze I love sooth the many wounds of battle that covered my body.

"Triathra is dead," I said to Clipper.

"Now the Monolegion tribe no longer threatens this world. We did it." Clipper limped wearily beside me.

"I'm sorry that we had to kill them in order to defeat him. I just wish there were other ways," I said with regret. "Sometimes my wrath…"

"We did what we had to do," said Clipper before turning to our third companion. "And thank you, Reno, for helping us out. Without you, I don't think we would have made it."

Reno smiled. She managed to say another sentence, "You're welcome."

And that was that. The three of us walked away from the wreckage.

"*My soul has spoken truth,*" the spirit said to me. "*You have destroyed the enemy and restored peace. Thank you, Jacob, for your bravery and good.*"

I felt grateful. All my worries since the day I learned of the Monolegions were gone. We had finished our quest on the First Earth.

CHAPTER 36

NOT THE END

It was a little crowded back in the dormitories. I sat in the center of my old room with the tips of my wings touching both walls. The Master Scepter was in our possession, no longer in the hands of evil.

"So that's that," said Chang. "The Monolegions have fallen."

Princess Rohesia took another look around the room. "I still cannot believe how this new adventure came upon me. At first, life seemed so simple. It still surprises me how a normal life can be changed in an instant."

"The unknown scares all of us," I stated.

"I'm ready to return to my home at Saint Cassius," the princess said in a tone that sounded almost sorrowful. "I want to reunite with my love, Prince Roger. I know my parents miss me as well."

Clipper nudged me with his horns. "Speaking of home."

My eyes lit up. "Right, Elsov. Maybe we can use the scepter to help us return there. I still need to rescue poor Treetop. Chang, Sally, if this works, we'll come back and say goodbye."

Sally came over and hugged me. "Go find your world. I'll miss you two, and Reno."

Picking up the Master Scepter, Clipper held it between us. He closed his eyes, his brow furrowed in concentration. Nothing happened. "I don't know what's going on," he said.

I felt crushed. I thought we had the power, yet we did not. "There must be a way to return," I said in disappointment.

The hopes of leaving for Elsov vanished before me. I wanted to return so badly. Why was the scepter, the *Master Scepter*, not performing Clipper's command? I knew it was possible. I traveled to Elsov when I was poisoned on Komodo Island. Clipper had traveled there when he was injured. So why were we not going back now?

"This can't be," said Clipper. "I wasn't sure about all this before your vision, but I've been there myself. I met the grøls and the nymphs. The fairies guided me down the right path until I came back here."

His frustration did not help. Engulfed in sadness, he let the scepter clank on the floor. He sat down and tried to fight away a tear. I knew he was serious. I wanted to go back as well. His own visit to the second world may have affected him differently, but I knew he wanted to return as I did. Sorrow filled everyone's hearts, except for Reno's. She stepped up to Clipper and sat down next to him. She rubbed her head on his leg, just beside his elbow blade. The sight of the young dragon seemed to light something inside Clipper. With moist eyes, he gently placed a paw on her head. That moment not only gave Clipper hope, it gave me hope.

"Maybe scepters only work for sorcerers," I guessed, "or, more than likely, Monty just knew much more magic than we do. But don't worry, Clipper. The three of us will return someday. In the meantime, this world is our home. We became who we are in the first place to restore peace here. Trust me, when we can, we'll be on Elsov. I'll be sad to leave our friends, but we can visit them if we want."

Chang did not know how to react. I knew from his expression that he believed what I was saying, but he did not like the fact that we could not leave.

Clipper's ears suddenly rose in the air. "Wait a minute. I remember a fairy told me that in order to return there, we had to complete an important task."

"We defeated an evil force, so we should be getting close," I said. "Ever since I had that vision, I've had the urge to go back. It's going to be hard to wait, but I will."

"I love my friends here and I'll miss this place," said Clipper. "I loved my life as a human. But I know there's a way back to Elsov. It's where we're from, Jacob." He turned to Sally and Chang. "I know this must sound confusing to you."

"It's not so confusing," said Sally. "I understand. If dragons and other magical things exist here, they must exist somewhere else as well. It doesn't surprise me to know your home is somewhere else. But stay with us before you go. However, Princess Rohesia wants to go home. Maybe we can give her the Master Scepter when she uses the albore to return. Letting the princess return home is possible. When she returns to her castle, she can hide the Master Scepter somewhere. It'll be safe from doing any more harm."

"Like you said, Princess, you can return to the moment you left. That way your father won't miss you at all," Clipper added.

"I believe that is possible," said Rohesia. "And I promise that I will never reveal this era openly. To my father, mother, or Roger, I may. But I will say little."

Sally picked up the Master Scepter and held it out. Rohesia was ready to use the albore to travel to her own time.

"Keep the scepter with you," Sally directed. "The dwarf tribe will still be in existence when you get back. Hide it as quickly as you can. Thank you, Princess Rohesia. You took part in this great effort to take down Monty."

"And my thanks to you," Rohesia said. The two young women, who had become close friends, fondly embraced.

After one last farewell, Princess Rohesia vanished back to her former time. It was a guarantee that she would hug her father when she returned.

"Wouldn't our time travel change history?" Clipper asked.

I thought about what he had said. "It's already been changed. We're the reason why the Earth is what it is right now. What I'm saying is that it's impossible to change history because it's already changed, and therefore it's not changed. It's strange when you think about it."

Clipper understood what I was saying. He wanted to continue the conversation, but a familiar figure showed up at the open door. He had bandages over his body and he was in a wheelchair. It was Sergeant Nelson.

The moment I saw him, I was overwhelmed with guilt. "Oh, Sergeant Nelson! I'm so sorry for what I did to you. I didn't mean to. You have to know that!"

James looked steadily at me. "Of course you didn't, Draco. Listen, you two dragons have wiped out an entire army of sorcery all alone, so I've been told. And we barely helped at all. You may not be officially recruited, but we will still be willing to help you in the future. If you need some assistance, I can help. If you need to travel anywhere or need a hand, we'll be there. I must warn you, we don't have much experience with magic."

Clipper and I turned to Chang. "We could use someone who can pilot us anywhere at any time," I said.

Chang gave a shy smile. "You remember my interest in aviation, Jacob? I can go into special training. I think I'll still major in zoology, though."

"…especially when there's more out there than you think. Thanks for helping us," I finished.

The three of us formed our own special force. Chang would provide helpful transportation by becoming a pilot while Clipper and I could do the rest. Chang was told that he would start training in the upcoming summer.

When all was finished, James said we would eventually be living in a rural area near Los Angeles, California. James said it would take time finding the right home, for it had to be perfect. We were going to live in a designated land for the summer until the home was ready. At first I thought it was outlandish, moving to another city. James searched extensively to find a home for us that was somewhat isolated, but the sergeant would be nearby in case we needed his assistance. I guess that was a good idea. Besides, I would only live there until I could find a way back to Elsov.

As the day before our departure drew to a close, Chang returned from the college to the dormitory rooms where the rest of us were beginning to move out. Chang noticed a bowl of water that Reno was drinking from. "Wouldn't drinking water affect the fire breath?" he asked.

"Water goes to the stomach," I explained. "The fire is formed by chemicals in the lungs. Clipper mentioned that before the experiment that started all this."

Reno finished drinking and stood right beside me as we decided to lie down for the night. Chang slept in his bed while I lay on the floor next to my young friend.

The next morning, we stood at the door of our empty room. Chang noticed me staring blankly forward. "Jacob, are you all right?" he asked me.

"Something just dawned on me," I said. "We just discovered that there is more to life than meets the eye. Dragons *have* lived on this Earth before, but they've gone to another place. When the dwarves started taking over, we put a stop to them and ran them up north. I have a feeling we haven't seen the last of all this. There's going to be much more, no doubt about it. We've just scratched the surface of whatever's out there. I believe that someday we'll find a way back to Elsov. And you heard Clipper, he feels the same way."

"Are you saying that...?" Chang began.

"I'm saying that this isn't the end," I continued. "We're going to travel on another journey; we'll write a new story. In the meantime, we should be prepared." I looked down at Reno. "Like I said, this isn't the end, we're just starting. Right before we removed the Master Scepter from his grasp, Monty threatened that the Wrath of Vesuvius would come down on me. I have no idea what that meant, but we've got to be ready for a bigger and maybe a costlier battle."

I did not know what was yet to come or what this "Vesuvius" concern was, but I could sense that a new adventure was yet to come. Someway, somehow, I would return to Elsov. I knew that the second world was real. It was not just a dream. Treetop was in trouble. I had to help her and discover what the Wrath of Vesuvius was.

Overwhelmed by those thoughts, I decided to go outside and clear my mind. I found a quiet and lonesome patch of grass. Lying down, my thoughts went to the Pearl Forest in Elsov again. I could not get it out of my mind. I felt like I was about to erupt with my burning thoughts about the magic forest. To ease the feeling, I blew a harmless puff of smoke.

I heard the spirit's voice again:

"Jacob, I know you miss your real home. Don't worry. You can return there if you make the right choices. I'm pleased that you have removed the Monolegions from your world, but you and your friends will have a much bigger challenge. If you want to return to Pearl Forest, you must find the path on your own. Trust me, if you work your hardest, you will return to your home. Because you are now the being you truly are, I will leave you until you need my help again. I am not one to tarry in another's heart."

Hearing his voice gave me a fresh breath of excitement. A new adventure! This could mean that I would travel back to Elsov! But still, there was a major obstacle in the way. Was this Wrath of Vesuvius something to be truly concerned about? The chance was likely or else Monty would not have said that. But I was far from scared. Despite my questions about the Wrath of Vesuvius, I smiled.

"Someday I'll return," I said with confidence. "Someday I will."

EPILOGUE

M onths passed. It was mid-summer. Clipper and I were at a place where we could just spread our wings and fly in peace. While Sergeant Nelson searched for a suitable home for us on the Pacific shore, we had permission to stay in the Pennsylvania countryside. We did not stay in a particular spot, though. We made the decision to live the way we wanted to in a green hollow in the northwestern region of a national forest, near the border of New York. I loved being there. It was certainly a place where a dragon should be.

After a short flight ,we landed on a soft patch of grass.

"I wish we could stay here until we find out how to get back to Elsov," said Clipper. "It's amazing."

"Sergeant Nelson said we should be with Chang once he's been trained," I said. "Your old roommate Joshua will be with us, too. They'll transfer him to the university along with Chang. You know, I wonder how the Atlantic College is taking all this. Sally told me that most of our peers think we've been transferred along with Chang and Joshua. I'm glad they don't know what really happened to us."

Clipper tapped his fangs. "It's hard to think that not too long ago we were normal people, gathering the blood of various animals. I never thought I would be here as a dragon, waiting to go home. One shot of the potion and we become who are now. No substance we created could do something like that. Of course, we now have the abilities of many other animals, but there's more to make an actual dragon like you or me."

"This is no coincidence," I said, stretching. "I don't think we were born here. Wait! If this is all true, our parents may be, just may be, still alive!"

Clipper's ears lifted. "You think so? Our true parents? Wow. I don't know how to take this in! Our parents alive…"

We were both breathing heavily. We still missed our human parents, no question about that. We would love them forever. But our parents by blood, dragons for that matter, could be waiting for us to return. We were sure to return; we had done it before. But we did not know how at the moment.

"There must be some way to get back to Elsov," said Clipper. "After our fight with Monty, Sally mentioned how he came to be our enemy. He started out as a sorcerer on our world. He knew that we would become dragons, and that was why he tried to stop us even years prior. That proves our point."

"I would sure love to see my true parents," I sighed. "They must know we left. They wouldn't forget us. If they remember us as infants, they'll possibly recognize us today. Hhh… this is such a strong feeling! We've got to find this thing the fairies wanted to give me, find our parents, and most importantly, rescue Treetop."

"Of course. We have to do it ourselves. Remember Jacob, we must work as a team. Two heads are better than one. If we work together, we can make miracles. We'll return to Elsov someday."

I believed everything he had said. He stood back up as we prepared for another flight. We spread our wings, lifted from the ground, and flew toward the setting sun.

The Tales of Draco: Appendix

This section is about various places, objects, and creatures that have been mentioned so far in the *Tales of Draco* series. Not everything will be revealed in this current appendix.

The Three Worlds: There is a triangle of three worlds. Each world has its own unique qualities, opportunities, and dangers.

First Earth (The Human World): The First Earth is large and diverse. Most of this world is explored, making travel fairly easy. It has a diverse kingdom of animals, including humans. Dwarves and other human-like races also inhabit this Earth. There are several ways to travel here (via portals, potions, etc.).

Second Earth (Elsov): Many places on this world are unexplored due to the different uses, not necessarily the lack of, science and magic. Many spells, curses, and potions originate here. Some humans from the First Earth have limited knowledge of this world. During the day, the sky looks very similar to the First Earth. It is blue with clouds and a yellow sun providing light. But at night, the differences between the two worlds become more noticeable. At the right location, it is possible to hear the nymphs or other creatures sing. The night sky presents a violet nebula and bright stars. Unlike the First Earth, more than a moon made from rock that can be seen. There is a second planet that is close enough to act like a moon. With a much bigger mass, this ringed planet is farther from Elsov than the Moon is from the First Earth. Also like the Moon, it has different phases of visibility. This planet is named Alsov.

Third Earth (Spirit World): This is the world for the spirits who have completed their mortal life. The living are not certain what this world is like. Triathra referred to a realm of this world as 'Purgatory'.

These three worlds are watched over by a single wizard or sorcerer. He or she is known as the Keeper of the Three Worlds and is the only living being who can access the Third Earth.

Objects and Relics of the Three Worlds: There are many relics and potions of magic in existence. Some on this list may be used to create more complex creations (this will be explained later).

Albores (pronounced in singular, all-boar): It comes as no surprise that these special wands have a lot to do with magic. But what you may not know is what it takes to make an albore. It does not matter what type of wood an albore is made of. An oak albore is just the same as a birch or spruce albore. It is the handle from which its power is drawn. The handle is made of gold and has an engraved rune. This rune has the look of Chinese writing, though it is not known, save by wizards and sorcerers, what it reads. Only a wizard or sorcerer can care the rune. If carved by anyone else, the albore will be powerless. Though albores are useful tools, their abilities are determined by the user's experience. It takes more than an albore alone to create a portal to the other worlds.

Master Scepters: These are much more powerful than albores. Like albores, they can only be created by well-trained wizards or sorcerers. They are usually about five feet in length. Most of a Master Scepter's power is utilized by the wizard or sorcerer, but others can control a sliver of its magic. Their power can temporarily weaken in frozen conditions.

Note: If an albore or Master Scepter is to be destroyed, it must be done so properly. If not, the magic within them could be released and may cause danger to those nearby. The process of destroying one of these is a difficult process and will be explained later.

Potions: There are many types of potions and they are used for different reasons. Each potion has a unique name, but they will be mentioned later. Some of these potions are meant to be swallowed, others absorbed, and some just require simple touch.

The first potion that was mentioned in this story causes the subject to shapeshift. If a person or creature takes the potion a second time, the subject will transform back into his or her original form.

The other potion, created by Triathra, is one of few ways to transport a being from one world to another. This potion is to be ingested like the first potion. If ingested, the one who takes it will pass out briefly. Their body travels to the Second Earth but only for a short amount of time. When the time expires, the body returns to its original location. There is a good chance for the taker of the potion to keep his or her memory. If the memory is lost, it takes an outside force to restore it.

There are many other potions with a variety of side effects. Some are temporary, some are permanent.

Creatures of the Three Worlds: A few types of people and creatures will be mentioned from the first two worlds. Not every type of person or creature will be mentioned in this appendix.

Dwarves: Dwarves are a type of human race. The Nibelungs were the dwarves of the First Earth. The word Nibelung is German, and the name is used in Germanic folklore, as explained in Chapter 12. The Nibelungs in this story, who belonged to the Monolegion tribe, were under the influence of sorcery for thousands of years. Dwarves, Nibelung and Elsovian alike, are very quick and agile. The average dwarf is only about half a foot shorter than the average human. And like other humans, it is up to the dwarf whether if he or she wants to be good or evil.

Grøls: A grøl's appearance may be compared to that of a garden gnome. Found all over the Second Earth, grøls are usually friendly, but also very shy. They often hide when larger creatures pass by. They are known to live by ponds in special homes; these homes are inside large trees. You can tell if a grøl lives in a tree if you can see a small door at the base and windows farther up. They love to feast and are well known for their "Yip!" when they get excited. Sadly, many of them are enslaved by goblins or ogres and are forced to serve the higher power. Occasionally they may unite and rebel against their enemies, but they are rarely victorious.

Nymphs: Nymphs are slightly shorter than dwarves. Like those in Greek mythology, Elsovian nymphs are very judgmental and despise those whom they believe are against them. But unlike their Greek counterparts, Elsovian nymphs can be both male and female. They live in enchanted forests and enjoy singing. Normally dressing in clothes made from silk or even leaves, they choose to live simple lives. They are aggressive when it comes to warfare and are excellent in stealth. Over the years, they have been in many informal wars against the goblins and ogres.

Humans: There is not much to talk about because chances are you are a human yourself. They are found on both worlds. They are quite tall and very curious. Most humans use a unique type of magic and like to focus on scientific technology. They are often kind-hearted, but that can vary.

Wizards and Sorcerers: Wizards and sorcerers, or enchantresses and sorceresses in the case of women, are humans who possess strong magic. They are most powerful when in possession of a Master Scepter. Wizards practice light magic. Sorcerers practice dark magic, or sorcery. The two terms can be used interchangeably based on the wizard's choices. Both wizards and sorcerers live in the first two worlds. One wizard/sorcerer is selected as Keeper of the Three Worlds.

Goblins and Ogres: These two types of creatures inhabit Elsov. Ogres are commonly found in or near wet swamps. Goblins like to live in dark environments, but can be found anywhere. They are about the same size as humans with a greenish skin tone. Goblins have dull-pointed ears and similar body shapes to humans. In battle, they wear thick, leather armor. Ogres are naturally armored with a layer of blubber and are much bigger than goblins. Many goblins and ogres enslave grøls.

Fairies: You may be able to see the strong magic a fairy possesses in just a single glance. Because they almost never touch the ground unless at rest, they wear no footwear. When they hover in the air, their wings flow softly and gracefully. If you ever come across a fairy, you should not be puffed up with pride. They will not help you if you are. Do not even try capturing one, for they can disappear in the blink of an eye. If you find a fairy, remember that it is trying to help you. Trust them and do what they say. If you abuse their help, you will be cursed with bad luck.

Dragons: Dragons are mostly on Elsov, but they are known to occasionally wander to the First Earth. They like to live in caves or pits and can be any size (Jacob and Clipper are about the size of grizzly bears, though not as bulky). Dragons have long snouts and are covered in armored scales. Dragons are also excellent swimmers and can hold their breath for a long time. They are omnivorous, but they mostly eat meat, often seafood and land mammals. They breathe fire and can spit hallucinogenic venom. When filled with adrenaline, they can push very heavy objects by using their horns. These smooth horns are made of keratin. They are long and straight with pointed tips. Dragons tend to charge enemies larger than they are. Despite the presence of long and sharp claws, dragons have fingers that can lift a variety of objects. Each dragon has his or her unique color of scales and other personal qualities. This gives limited opportunity to know the identity of a dragon if you see one.

(Note: There are many other creatures and people out there: elves, kangrui, unitaurs, krakens, sea serpents, lilinges, ice dragons, and beyond. You will learn more about them later.)

Dear Reader,

I'm glad you devoted time to read this novel. I hope you found it entertaining and interesting. I may be young for an author, but my spark has been lit.

If you enjoyed this, there is a sequel. Jacob, Clipper, and the others are ready to find a way to Elsov in *The Tales of Draco: The Six Pieces*. A new adventure is underway and many questions about dragons and beyond are yet to be answered.

Until then, I hope you loved the start of the *Tales of Draco* series!

Sincerely,
Jordan B. Jolley

References Concerning Folklore & the Nibelungs

Ashliman, D. L. (2018, April 8). The Nibelungenlied: A Summary in English Prose. Retrieved from Return to D. L. Ashliman's folk-texts, a library of folktales, folklore, fairy tales, and mythology.: https://www.pitt.edu/~dash/nibelungenlied.html

Chinese Folktales. (n.d.). Retrieved from World of Tales: https://www.worldoftales.com/Chinese_folktales.html

Compton's by Britannica. (2007). In Compton's by Britannica vol. 8 (pp. 12; 259-270). Encyclopædia Britannica, Inc.

Nibelung (2018, July 24). Retrieved from Wikipedia: https://en.wikipedia.org/wiki/Nibelung

Nibelungenlied. (2018, July 24). Retrieved from Wikipedia: https://en.wikipedia.org/wiki/Nibelungenlied

Nibelungenlied. (ca. A.D. 1200). The Song of the Nibelung. Germany.

World Book Encyclopedia. (1976). In World Book Encyclopedia vol. F (pp. 12-13; 282-283). Chicago, Frankfurt, London, Paris, Rome, Sydney, Tokyo, Toronto: Field Enterprises Educational Corp.

For more information about
The Tales of Draco: Rise of the Dragon
and other works by Jordan B. Jolley, be sure to visit
www.thetalesofdraco.wordpress.com

CPSIA information can be obtained
at www.ICGtesting.com
Printed in the USA
BVHW071054190519
548432BV00001B/3/P

9 781643 880549